"As I intend to be here through the night, I decided to get comfortable."

The slow unknotting and unwinding of his neck cloth was next. Then he began rolling up the sleeves of his shirt. She'd seen him naked. Why was it the baring of only his forearms was so much more provocative?

Loosening the top two buttons of his shirt, he returned to the bed, sat on its edge, and reached for the tray, picking up a cloth she hadn't noticed.

"You're not going to wash me."

He arched a brow at her. "Do you really want to engage in a battle you can't possibly win?"

"You shouldn't assume just because I'm a woman that I would lose."

"I'm not assuming that at all," he said, his voice low and raspy, sending warm tingles along her spine even as she recognized the threat of a challenge when it was being delivered. He leaned in until she could almost see her reflection in his dark eyes. "But I am assuming, as much as you pretend otherwise, that there is a measure of feminine vanity in you and you will be in want of a clean face when I kiss you."

By Lorraine Heath

WHEN A DUKE LOVES A WOMAN
BEYOND SCANDAL AND DESIRE
GENTLEMEN PREFER HEIRESSES (novella)
AN AFFAIR WITH A NOTORIOUS HEIRESS
WHEN THE MARQUESS FALLS (novella)
THE VISCOUNT AND THE VIXEN • THE EARL TAKES ALL
FALLING INTO BED WITH A DUKE
THE DUKE AND THE LADY IN RED
THE LAST WICKED SCOUNDREL (novella)
ONCE MORE, MY DARLING ROGUE
WHEN THE DUKE WAS WICKED
LORD OF WICKED INTENTIONS
DECK THE HALLS WITH LOVE (novella)
LORD OF TEMPTATION • SHE TEMPTS THE DUKE
WAKING UP WITH THE DUKE
PLEASURES OF A NOTORIOUS GENTLEMAN
PASSIONS OF A WICKED EARL
MIDNIGHT PLEASURES WITH A SCOUNDREL
SURRENDER TO THE DEVIL
BETWEEN THE DEVIL AND DESIRE
IN BED WITH THE DEVIL • JUST WICKED ENOUGH
A DUKE OF HER OWN • PROMISE ME FOREVER
A MATTER OF TEMPTATION • AS AN EARL DESIRES
AN INVITATION TO SEDUCTION
LOVE WITH A SCANDALOUS LORD
TO MARRY AN HEIRESS • THE OUTLAW AND THE LADY
NEVER MARRY A COWBOY • NEVER LOVE A COWBOY
A ROGUE IN TEXAS • TEXAS SPLENDOR
TEXAS GLORY • TEXAS DESTINY

LORRAINE HEATH

WHEN A
Duke
LOVES A
Woman

A SINS FOR ALL SEASONS NOVEL

AVONBOOKS

An Imprint of HarperCollinsPublishers

WHEN A DUKE LOVES A WOMAN. Copyright © 2018 by Jan Nowasky. All rights reserved. Printed in the United States of America. No part of this book may be used or reproduced in any manner whatsoever without written permission except in the case of brief quotations embodied in critical articles and reviews. For information, address HarperCollins Publishers, 195 Broadway, New York, NY 10007.

First Avon Books mass market printing: September 2018
First Avon Books hardcover printing: August 2018

Print Edition ISBN: 978-0-06-267602-3
Digital Edition ISBN: 978-0-06-267604-7

Cover illustration by Victor Gadino
Cover photography by Image 1st LLC

Avon, Avon & logo, and Avon Books & logo are registered trademarks of HarperCollins Publishers in the United States of America and other countries.

HarperCollins is a registered trademark of HarperCollins Publishers in the United States of America and other countries.

FIRST EDITION

18 19 20 21 22 QGM 10 9 8 7 6 5 4 3 2 1

For Mary D. and Emily G.
For keeping me sane during insane times
To forever friendships

WHEN A
Duke
LOVES A
Woman

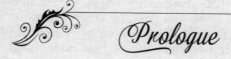

Prologue

*E*ttie Trewlove was accustomed to the echo of babies wailing. After all, she had four, but these haunting cries came from beyond her thin wooden door. Waiting for the harsh knock that would call her forth, she looked at her darling boys, lined up in their tiny bed, asleep, and wondered how she would manage if she took on another. The few meager coins placed in her palm wouldn't be enough to feed and clothe the newest one for long. It never was.

"No more," she whispered. "No more."

She had to be strong and turn this one away, no matter that it broke her heart doing so, no matter that she was possibly condemning the child to a worse fate.

But the knock never sounded, yet the keening continued ringing in her ears. Slowly, ever so slowly, she approached the door—the frigid whistling wind slipping past its edges—released the latch, opened it, and gazed out. Big fat snowflakes floated down from the heavens, coating everything in pristine white that would soon turn black, including the wicker basket on her doorstep and the red-faced child within it, whose bare arms flailed ineffectually at the cold, the injustice, the harshness of life.

Stepping out, Ettie glanced up and down the dismal

street, not even a streetlamp to aid in her quest, only faint light feathering out from a window here and there. Not a soul to be seen, no one scurrying away. Whoever had deposited this bairn on her stoop had made a hasty retreat, but then humiliation seldom had anyone lingering in her presence.

"Not even decent enough to leave a few pennies behind," she grumbled as she bent down, lifted the basket into her arms, and carried it, along with its precious bundle, into the protective shelter that waited inside. She set it on the table and studied the little one, who continued to bellow indignantly.

The covering was too thin to provide any sort of protection. Moving it aside, she saw that she'd been brought a girl. The child wore no clothing, no nappy. By the looks of her, she was only a few hours old. Life in the rookeries was neither kind nor safe for a lass.

Cradling the babe as though she were delicate porcelain, Ettie Trewlove eased into the rocker before the hearth where a few lumps of coal released heat insufficient to warm most of the room. When she'd become a widow a little over three years ago, she'd needed some means to provide for herself. A woman she knew had boasted about the lucrative practice of caring for the well-to-do's by-blows. Foundling homes wouldn't take those conceived in sin, born of shame. Neither would workhouses. What was to be done with them when their very presence was a mark of disgrace?

But she could no longer bring herself to cast aside the innocents as many did, which was the reason she had four boys dependent on her. And now this little one.

She might not have much in the way of creature comforts to offer the child, but she did have love. She prayed it would be enough.

Chapter 1

*H*e died because of a damned timepiece.

Antony Coventry, the ninth Duke of Thornley, took what comfort he could from knowing word of his idiocy would go to the grave with him.

Although at that particular moment, any sort of comfort was difficult to come by. The ruffians were indeed rough, two of them tugging off his boots, another his jacket, while the fourth struggled to unhook the watch chain from his waistcoat button. Odd thing that the thief was now taking such care when only moments before he'd landed a blow to the side of Thorne's head that had left him temporarily senseless.

Which might have resulted in his decision to stand his ground over the watch.

Without much of a fuss he'd handed over his purse and signet ring. He wasn't a fool. Four to one odds weren't good. Money and rings could be replaced. The punch to his temple had come about because he hadn't surrendered the items quickly enough for the ringleader's satisfaction.

"We want the timepiece faster," the lout had stated with a sneer.

The timepiece. It had been handed down through

four generations. The engraved crest on the cover had been worn thin from one duke after another rubbing and worrying his thumb over it when faced with a difficult decision. He'd been ten and five when his father, on his deathbed, in a moment of rare lucidity, had placed it against his palm and folded his fingers over it. "Your legacy. Guard it well. Make me proud."

So to the oafs surrounding him in the dark mews with the fog swirling about, he'd announced, "I fear, gentlemen, I've handed over all I intend. The watch stays with me."

He might have answered differently had he seen the knives earlier. No, he bloody well would not have. They'd gotten him in the thigh, the side, the shoulder, the arm. The blows from hard knuckles and booted feet that had followed when he dropped to his knees had taken him down completely, left him lying there in the dirt and grime, feeling his warm blood soaking through what remained of his clothing and turning cold. The edges of his vision had long been darkening until all he could see were the grubby hands closing around the treasured watch.

"Got it!" the bastard cried.

"No!" screamed through the pulsing thrum rushing between his ears. Must have screamed through his mouth as well because the thief widened his eyes just as Thorne's tightly balled fist, backed by whatever lingering strength remained to him, landed a solid punch to the miscreant's jaw. The satisfying crunch of bone cracking echoed through the night just before another knife slid through skin and meat and muscle—

"Oi! What the devil are you lot up to?"

The men froze as the demanding shout reverberated around them, bouncing off the walls of the surrounding buildings.

"Christ, it's Gil. Let's get the bloody 'ell outta 'ere," the leader muttered as though his jaw was no longer properly hinged.

He heard their thundering feet fading away in the distance as they raced off. Another sound followed, softer footsteps but more hurried. He became vaguely aware of a presence, someone kneeling beside him, gentle hands touching him with care.

"Ah, hell, you're a bloody mess."

An angel's voice. He didn't think she was swearing, but making a truthful statement regarding his blood-soaked clothes. Where had she come from? A companion to the fellow named Gil? Had he gone after the footpads? He wished he could see her more clearly but the darkness was closing in on him. "My . . . watch."

She leaned nearer and brought with her the scent of . . . beer? "Pardon?"

"Watch." The blackguard had dropped it. He'd heard it fall. In desperation, he patted the ground at his side. He needed to find it.

Then she took his hand, cradled it within hers, long slender fingers closing around him. "There's no time-piece, pet. Nothing here."

There had to be. He was supposed to pass it on to his son someday. But there would be no son now. No heir. No spare. No wife.

Only death. In a rotten-smelling, mucked-up alley-way that had suddenly turned frigid, causing ice to form in his veins, to leak through to his bones. The only warmth offered was where she touched him.

He tightened his hold, hoping her heat would spread through him, would give him strength. He couldn't die, not like this, not without a fight.

He couldn't give up. Not until he found Lavinia.

Gillian Trewlove worked her arm around the man's shoulders, tried to leverage him up, and swore softly. "You're bloody heavy."

Stretched out as he was, it was difficult to tell precisely, but she'd place him at a couple of inches taller than she was, which put him on the higher side of six feet. She patted his bristly cheek until he stirred from the depths of oblivion into which he'd fallen. "Come on now, pet. Up with you."

He nodded, struggled to push himself up to a sitting position, while she did what she could to assist him, tugging here, pushing there, and ignoring his groans of pain. The coppery stench of blood scented the air. His clothes were wet, and it wasn't from the dampness of the heavy fog settling in and wrapping around them like a wispy shroud.

"Look, I can't carry you on my own. I know the darkness is calling to you, and she's a tempting mistress, but you have to resist. You've got to fight her and help me here."

Another nod. A grunt. Labored breathing. She slid in against him, slipped beneath his arm, giving him her shoulder to use as a crutch while she snaked her arm around his back, closed her hand against his side—he released another groan muffled by clenched teeth—and felt the liquid warmth pour over her fingers. Not good. Not good at all.

Leaning on her, using the brick wall for support, he

pushed, she pulled, until he was on his feet. Ah, yes, well over six feet.

"All right now. My place is just up here. Not far." As usual she'd closed up her tavern at midnight, her employees had all headed home after setting the place to rights, and she'd worked on her books for a while. She'd finished up at half past one and had been taking out the rubbish when she heard the commotion, not at all pleased to find nefarious deeds occurring behind her establishment. She didn't allow for shenanigans inside; she certainly wasn't going to allow them to occur on the other side of her walls. Her tolerance for misdeeds was a low threshold that went even lower when it came to causing injury to people.

Their pace was slow, his breathing harsh and uneven, and more than once he stumbled, staggered, righted himself. Cooing gently, she encouraged him with words of praise for each step taken when he didn't falter or fall. She considered hauling him into the tavern, but it would be bad luck if he died there. Better option was her flat, although the stairs would be a challenge. Finally they reached them. "Grab the banister, pull yourself up. Lift your feet a little bit higher."

"Right." The word came out low but determined.

"You're going to make it."

"Better. Have some scores to settle."

A man with a purpose could survive a hell of a lot. Her brothers had taught her that. "Save your breath and your strength for the climb."

It was long and arduous, but she had to give him credit for never faltering, even though he'd begun to shiver, and that concerned her. It was a cool night, but not so much that one needed much of a wrap, and their efforts were keeping her far too warm. But then she had a great deal more blood rushing through her, while his was leaking out, leaving a trail marking his progress. He dropped to his knees three steps shy of the landing, and she nearly tumbled on top of him. Catching her balance, she knelt beside him. "Almost there."

Crawling, he laboriously took one step, then another. She hopped to her feet, located her key, unlocked the door, and swung it open. "When you get inside, you can collapse on the floor."

He did just that.

She rushed out, down the stairs, and back into the tavern. "Robin!"

The little urchin who slept on a small bed near the fireplace, in spite of her best efforts to move him into a proper home—he simply wouldn't have it—sat up and rubbed his eyes. "Aye?"

"Fetch Dr. Graves to my flat immediately." She slapped some coins into his hand. "Take a hansom if you can find one. You need to be quick. Tell him there's a man dying on my floor."

"Did ye try to kill 'im, Gillie?"

"*Him,*" she repeated automatically, emphasizing the *h*, always striving to improve his pronunciation of words because she'd learned early on that speech affected people's perceptions of a person. "If it'd been me, there wouldn't have been a *try*, now would there? He'd be dead."

"Wot 'appened then?"

Another *h* lost, but she didn't have time to correct him again. "Later. Fetch Dr. Graves. Be quick about it."

The lad shoved his feet into his shoes and took off at a gallop. Hurrying back to her lodgings, she was discouraged to find the man hadn't moved a muscle during the time she was gone. Placing her fingers above his upper lip, she felt his faint breath whisper over her skin. Relief washed through her. Leaning near his ear, she commanded, "Don't you dare die on me."

HER VOICE CAME to him through the fog, soft but slightly raspy, urging him on, keeping him tethered to this world when his aching body and wounded soul wanted to sink into a vast oblivion where peace hovered. She draped a thick woolen blanket over him, but his shivering continued unheeded, his clenched teeth doing little to prevent their clattering. She pressed a hand to the worst of the gashes. Hurt like the very devil, but a distant part of him that could still process thought understood she needed to stanch the flow of blood if he were to have any hope at all of surviving.

"Stay with me now," she urged. "Dr. Graves will be here soon."

Graves? One of the physicians to the queen? How did she, living in the squalor of Whitechapel, know such an illustrious man?

"What's your name?" she asked.

The other thoughts flittered away as he worked to concentrate on responding to such a simple question. "Thorne."

"I'm Gillie."

Was she the Gil the ruffians had run from? He'd thought it short for Gilbert. Squinting, he fought to bring the hovering person into sharper focus, but his vision had never been particularly clear when it came to viewing things that were near. He made a reach for his spectacles housed in his jacket pocket before remembering the ruffians had taken it. So he concentrated on what he could determine about the individual who'd come to his aid.

Short hair, cropped just below the ears. A dark shade. He couldn't discern specifics in the dim lighting. Blouse . . . not a blouse. Shirt. Similar to his. A kilt? No, no tartan. It was plain. A skirt? It made no sense. Why would the ruffians run from a woman?

"I own the tavern downstairs."

A man obviously, a man with the voice of an angel. He didn't care. Bloke was keeping him from leaving this realm behind. That was all that mattered.

Then the angel began reciting the process for brewing beer. Definitely a man. A woman would have described the various stitches in a sampler. His mind was a muddled mess. Of course it was a man. A woman's presence wouldn't have chased off four ruffians, hauled him upstairs, entertained him with an accounting of the differences between various liquors.

He didn't know why he was disappointed with the truth. He knew only that the fingers combing softly through his hair were the gentlest he'd ever known.

$\mathcal{S}$he lost him. Somewhere during her explanation regarding the difference between brandy and cognac, he'd drifted away. Realizing it had been a punch to her gut. She didn't want to lose him, had wrapped a strip of cloth tightly around his thigh, stuffed linen into the other wounds—in spite of his crying out— and pressed her hand against the worst, the one at his shoulder, which seemed to be the deepest gash. Beneath her fingers, the stream of blood had slowed to a trickle, seemed to have stopped in other spots if the lack of liquid creeping up to turn white linen crimson was any indication, but he was so deuced pale as though very little life-affirming fluid remained to give him color.

The pounding of rushing footsteps hitting wooden planks echoed up the stairs, vibrating off her door. Thank God! The resounding knock was brisk.

"Hurry," she yelled, hating the few seconds of delay, wishing she hadn't closed the door but she'd wanted to trap as much warmth as she could inside in hopes of keeping the stranger from shivering to death.

William Graves was through the portal and kneeling beside her before she could take much notice of his disheveled appearance. She supposed Robin had woken him, and he'd been quick to dress, probably using only his fingers to tame his riot of pale curls. Stubble marked his jaw.

"Caw! Blimey! 'E's a bloody mess!" Robin declared as he followed the physician in and, with big round eyes, stared at the man lying prone on the floor. "I ain't swearin', Gillie. I promise. I'm talkin' about all the blood."

"I know, Robin. You did a good job. Off to bed with you now. You don't need to be seeing this."

"But—"

She gave him a glare that had him backing up two steps. "To bed. And don't tell anyone else about him."

"Why?"

"Because I said."

He treated her to a disgruntled look, obviously not satisfied with her reasoning, before turning on his heel and shuffling his feet as he went out the door. Honestly, the male of the species sulked more than any female she'd ever met. Life was full of disappointments. Best to learn from them before tossing them aside like so much rubbish and moving on.

"What happened?" Graves asked, bringing her attention back to him. He'd moved aside the blood-tinged blanket.

She wondered how his voice could sound so calm. "He was set upon by thieves in the alleyway. He goes by Thorne. First or last, I don't know."

"Could be his title."

"What would a lord be doing in this decrepit part of Whitechapel?"

"What is a woman of means doing here?" he asked distractedly, as his hands moved swiftly over the man, locating each wound, giving it a quick peek before moving on to the next.

She hadn't had the means when she'd begun. Her oldest brother had set her up, and she was still working hard to make something of herself. "Providing drink to those who want it, employment to those who need it."

He slid his pale blue gaze over to her. "I was making a point, Gillie. Don't assume you know what you don't." He jerked his head toward the small kitchen area. "Now, can you take his feet, while I lift him by the shoulders, and help me haul him onto the table?"

It was a struggle, but she had height on her side to give them the leverage needed to get the man off the floor and stretched out onto her wooden table. He was a tall tankard of ale, his legs below the knees dangling off the oak. He had some heft to him. She could see that, splayed out as he was. Broad shoulders, a working man's shoulders. The lean torso of a chap who didn't spend the better part of his days or nights engaged in gluttony. Activity ruled him. She very much doubted he was a toff. But based on the fine threads of the clothes that remained to him and how perfectly they were cut to fit him, he, too, had means.

"Warm water," Graves said absently, snapping her attention away from a perusal she had no business making. Time was of the essence if this man was to be saved, and the physician, rightfully so, expected her to see to his bidding, to assist with his endeavors.

She shoved some wood into the stove, got a fire going, filled a pot with water, put it on to warm, then stared at it, suddenly uncomfortable that she had not one but two men in her flat. She didn't bring men here, didn't entertain visitors, not even her brothers. These rooms served as her sanctuary, the place where she could escape from the harsh realities of life and find a measure of peace that made it easier to go out in the world. Her tendency had always been to withdraw because the hustle and bustle of a great number of people tended to sap her of energy. In order to survive, she'd taught herself not to retreat, but she still required a haven where she could restore her calm in order to better face the world.

Testing the water, she decided it was warm enough, poured it into a large bowl used for mixing pastry, turned around, and very nearly dropped the porcelain dish. Graves had removed the man's clothing, every stitch, and was examining the wound in his thigh—the one near his cock, flaccid but still impressively thick and long.

As a child, she'd seen her brothers' personal areas when they got their weekly baths, but they'd been boys, and this gent was certainly no boy. From head to toe, he was quite the imposing specimen, with well-defined muscles. The hair on his chest was dark and curly, arrowed down to his pelvis, down to that part of his person that should not have made it difficult to breathe. She set the bowl on the table near his head, scampered over to the linen cupboard, and yanked out a sheet.

"Good," Graves said. "We'll need some strips."

She swung around. "I was thinking of covering him, for his modesty's sake."

Understanding crossed over the physician's face as he held out his hand. "Sorry, Gillie. I wasn't thinking." She realized he was very much aware that it was her modesty at stake.

Taking the sheet from her, he spread it over his patient, leaving the wounded thigh bared along with most of his torso. The draped sheet molded itself to the man's contours, did very little to stop her from envisioning what was beneath the white linen. She feared she was blushing like a modest chit, not an experienced tavern owner. "Is he going to live?"

"Hope so. Shoulder and thigh are the worst, but nothing major hit. He has a deep gash in his backside. Got lucky with the stab to his side and the one on his arm as it appears both were just glancing slashes, not deep enough to have nicked anything important. But he's still lost a lot of blood." Looking up, he held her gaze. "He's fortunate you found him when you did."

"Tell me what I can do to help."

"I need to thoroughly clean out these wounds, which will be an incredibly unpleasant process for him, and then close them up. I don't want him waking and fighting me, so I'm going to use chloroform. Once I have him in a good sleep, I'll need you to keep him that way until I'm finished with my work. I think you're sharp enough to follow my instructions, if willing."

She nodded jerkily. "Whatever you need."

"You won't swoon on me?"

"Don't be daft."

Although her stomach did get a bit queasy if she watched him work, so she concentrated on studying the patient, searching for any signs he might be stirring from his slumber. His face was marred with bruises, one on his jaw, one on his cheek. His eyelid was swelling. Three punches then. Not to mention the dark discolorations on various areas of his arms and torso. He'd fought. Hard.

She didn't understand people not just handing over their valuables. Objects weren't as dear as life. But then, going by looks alone, this man seemed the uncompromising sort.

He had a strong jaw, shadowed by dark stubble. He'd not taken a razor to his face recently, so she didn't think he'd been wandering the area in search of a woman. Most fellows tidied themselves up a bit, even if they were paying for the loving they were going to receive.

Before Graves had begun his work, she'd poured warm water into another bowl. Now she dipped a cloth into it and gently began wiping away the dried blood on the stranger's face, not much liking what she was revealing. Even with the cuts and bruises, he was the most beautiful man she'd ever seen. He did funny things to her insides, made them feel all tingly and fluttery, a new sensation for her. Men didn't usually cause any reaction in her at all, except for a watchfulness. She'd learned early on that when it came to her person, she couldn't trust men to behave, so she was always ready to put them in their place and ensure they knew they'd get nothing from her that she wasn't willing to give. Until that moment, she hadn't even gifted any bloke with the press of her lips to his.

Her mum had worried about her safety in the rookeries, and as a result of her apprehensions had dressed her in her brothers' discarded clothing, cropped her hair, and bound her breasts when they'd begun to appear. She was nearly grown before she'd donned a skirt. She was comfortable not garnering attention, preferred it. Even at the tavern, she favored staying behind the bar, seldom going out among the customers, unless trouble was brewing.

Her presence intimidated. Her height made her impossible to overlook, her glare promised retribution. Not from her fists, necessarily, although she did have a rather decent punch. But she had four brothers with mightier fists who were always at the ready to defend her, and everyone knew it.

No doubt that was the reason the ruffians had run off when she'd called out to them, which meant they were from the area. That sickened her, the thought someone she might have served would do this to a man, a man as gorgeous as this one, a man it was a pleasure to touch, even if linen separated her skin from his. When all the dirt was removed from his face, she wanted to lean in and kiss away the scrapes and bruises, wanted to heal what she had no power to mend.

She'd never been very motherly, the reality of her youth shoving aside those instincts. Whenever her brothers had been roughed up, she'd seen to their injuries with a dispassionate air, always mindful of protecting her heart. It hurt too much to care. She knew her limits, knew her path. It didn't involve marriage, children, or love.

The injured man made her wish she was softer than she was, that she could wrap herself around him and give him all the comfort she'd hoarded for years.

"There," Graves said, breaking the ridiculous spell under which she'd fallen, staring at a man as though he would awaken and be pleased to find himself within her arms. "That should do him for now."

She rather regretted she wouldn't get to clean the rest of him, was almost envious of the lucky person who would. Setting the cloth into the bowl, she carried both to the sink, knowing they needed to be out of the way for what was to come next.

"If you'll give me a hand, we'll move him to the bed," Graves said.

Her heart hammering, she swung around. The bed?

It wasn't supposed to come next. The physician's carriage was. "You're not leaving him here."

Graves closed up his medical satchel, straightened. "I don't see that we have a choice."

"We put his clothes back on—"

"Afraid I cut and tore them to get them off."

"Well, that was a silly thing to do."

"However, it was the most expeditious. Besides, they were ruined."

But that left the man with nothing to wear, she wanted to shout in frustration as an odd emotion that resembled fear—when she'd never been afraid of anything in her life, except once—welled up inside her. He couldn't stay here. What in God's name would she do with a man in her bed?

"Then we wrap him in clean linen, a blanket, and cart him down to your carriage." She was pleased her no-nonsense tone revealed none of her misgivings, her trepidation, her teetering toward terror.

"Bumping along in a conveyance is likely to reopen the wounds. He's lost a lot of blood. I don't think he'll survive losing much more. It's better if he remains here for the time being."

"It won't be a jarring ride if you travel slowly."

"Gillie." He gave her a pointed look that made her feel like an unreasonable child asked to sit still in a pew. "If you are willing to risk his dying after I've gone to the bother of stitching him up, why send for me at all?"

"I didn't think he'd have to stay with me."

"He's going to be too weak to take advantage of you or the situation."

She scoffed loudly and in a most unladylike manner. "As though that's my worry. I have cast-iron skillets about that I can wield with determination, and I have a decent aim. One good whack and he'd be done for."

"Then what's your objection?"

A man in her bedchamber, in her *bed*. Nearly thirty years old, she'd never had a male in either. No good ever came from having a bloke in a woman's bed. Her mum hadn't found herself saddled with six by-blows because men were such saints.

"I have a business to run," she stated succinctly, defensively.

"You have several hours before you open. Perhaps he'll be recovered enough to move later in the day."

Meanwhile, she'd have to keep watch over him, finish cleaning him. Although earlier she'd been regretting relegating that task to someone else, when faced with the reality of having a man between her sheets for hours, she was embarrassingly unsettled, which only served to irritate her more. She took a deep breath to calm herself, to set her trepidations aside, determined to overcome this concern. "Can you send a nurse over?"

"You want me to wake someone this time of night?"

Yes, absolutely. What a daft question. "No. But perhaps first thing in the morning."

He gave a brisk nod. "I'll see what I can do. Meanwhile . . ." He moved to the man's shoulders and arched a blond brow. If he hadn't once saved one of her brothers, she'd yank that brow right off his face.

She charged into her bedchamber and tossed aside the covers before joining the physician at the table. With care, she moved the sheet past the man's knees, determined to keep the most male part of him covered, although every part of him was distinctly masculine. He had long legs, strong legs, muscular hairy calves, large feet. What she'd heard about men's feet in relation to their endowments was apparently true.

The chaps who frequented her establishment often became ribald after too much drink and would say things a lady's ears shouldn't hear, but then she was no lady.

She slid her arms beneath his knees, lifted and, like a crab she'd once seen in a fishmonger's stall, scuttled back. He was a sturdy load, and it occurred to her that if the odds had been slightly more even, he'd have triumphed. Thankfully the sheet stayed in place as they lowered their burden to the bed. Sprawled over it as he was, he dwarfed it, made it look like something in which a child would sleep.

"In some cultures," Graves said quietly, "you're responsible for someone after you've rescued them."

"He's not my responsibility." She wasn't very pleased that her words lacked conviction. Gently, she pulled the covers over him.

"I'll leave laudanum for his discomfort and some salve to help with the healing, prevent infection. Bandages should be changed a couple of times a day. Send word if he becomes fevered and delirious. Try to get water and broth into him if you can."

Her long drawn-out sigh echoed her displeasure. "He's going to be a lot of bother."

Chuckling low, he said, "The women I know would tell you most men are. But maybe he'll be worth it."

She very much doubted that. "How much do I owe you?"

"I'll settle up with him once he's recovered." He

grabbed his things, stared at her. "Don't forget to send word if I'm needed."

Giving a brisk nod, she saw him to the door, closed it, and leaned against the oak, more exhausted than she'd ever been in her life. She glanced around, the usual peacefulness of her place missing. It was almost as though it had been violated. Brutality and violence—or at least the results of it—had been allowed in. She had a strong urge to scrub it all down with boiling water.

Instead, she settled for scrubbing down the table, as well as the pots and bowls that had been used. She gathered up the stranger's tattered clothes. They could be mended. For all she knew, they were the only possessions left to him. He might have fancy garments, but that didn't mean he hadn't fallen on hard times. Otherwise, why was he here? She'd wash them later.

Only then did she notice her own clothes were stained with blood, his blood. She had to get out of them as quickly as she could, before he awoke, before she needed to tend to him again.

HE BECAME AWARE of the intense agony first, throbbing through various parts of his body. He tried to recall what had happened. The footpads, the struggle, the theft of his belongings, the man with the angelic voice who had saved him.

With a Herculean effort, he opened his eyes. The room was dark save for a single lamp on the table near the bed and the low fire burning in the hearth, the glow of which outlined someone standing near the fireplace, dragging a shirt over his head, the short strands of his hair falling quickly back into place as

the shirt was tossed aside. He watched in rapt fascination as the person began to unravel linen from about
his chest until firelight danced over a magnificent pair
of breasts. "You *are* a woman."

A shriek rent the air. Her movements were so quick
he couldn't decipher them with his addled brain, but
when the excruciatingly sharp pain tore through his
left shoulder, he realized she'd hurled something at
him. His anguished groan filled in the space left by her
screech coming to an end. Instinctually, he grabbed
his shoulder, rolled over, and made matters ten times
worse as pain ripped through other parts of his body,
mercilessly reminding him that the villains had used
knives on him earlier—blast their deranged hearts.
He was bloody well going to die because of an innocent comment. How many times could a man face
death in a single night and come out the winner?

He issued another low groan as the bed shifted.
Suddenly cool hands were guiding him onto his back.
As much as he wanted to fight them off, they felt so
marvelous, soft, and tender that he surrendered to their
urgings.

"I'm sorry," she said, "but you startled me."

He no longer cared about the agony. Suddenly the
prospect of dying didn't seem so dire, not when a man
was leaving this world with a lovely bosom swaying
in his face, near enough to kiss. He might have made
the effort to do just that if he didn't fear she'd smack
him hard enough to send him flying off the bed.

"Damnation, you're bleeding again."

She pressed the heel of her hand in to the curve of
his shoulder. He very nearly howled at the jolt of pain,
except his pride kept him silent, gnashing his back
teeth together, tightening his jaw, determined not to

embarrass himself any further than he already had. Stars clouded his vision, darkness began to creep in at the edges, but he fought to stay focused on her because he didn't want to slip back into oblivion, didn't want to again become lost. He didn't want to leave this woman who had saved him, who was his tether to life, who even now shoved her own modesty aside to stanch the flow of his blood.

Sometime later she stated matter-of-factly, "Bleeding's appeared to have stopped." Most women he knew swooned at the mere mention of blood, much less the sight of it.

Straightening, she eased off the bed. He caught sight of something cradled in her hand, couldn't determine what it was. Turning her back on him, she said, "I'll get some linens, change that bandage."

She set the object on the mantel from where she'd originally swiped it, marched over to the wardrobe, grabbed some clothes, and headed for the door. Stopping just shy of it, she held the bundle to her chest, leaving her throat and upper shoulders bared, and he imagined the pleasure a man could take from trailing his mouth slowly over them. He had to be fevered to be in such discomfort and have his mind drifting to places it shouldn't.

"Don't leave the bed," she ordered like a general addressing an army, as though she was accustomed to giving commands and having them obeyed without question. Then she was gone, the door closing in her wake, leaving him alone to count the minutes until her return.

Chapter 3

$\mathcal{S}$he was trembling with such force that it was a challenge to dress herself. Her nipples were hard little pebbles, aching and painful. Never before had a man's fevered breath wafted over her skin. The sensation created had been at once alarming and welcome, welcome in ways she'd never anticipated or considered. And certainly never desired.

Using one arm, she'd braced herself above him when she'd dearly wanted to sink down until her lower ribs met his, to feel the pleasure of warm smooth skin against heated flesh.

With her bloodied clothes in a heap on the floor and a clean shirt and skirt finally properly secured on her person, she trudged over to the kitchen, poured cold water into a bowl, and repeatedly splashed it on her face in an attempt to cool her cheeks. She didn't have to look in a mirror to know they were burning bright red, were fairly scalding. She was surprised they didn't steam.

Shaking off the lingering water droplets from her hands, she grabbed a towel and patted her face dry, feeling more in control, ready to see to the stranger, although he hardly seemed one any longer, not after the unintended intimate position she'd found herself in with him.

She needed to get some broth into him. Then finish cleaning him, in spite of the intimacy of the act. Never in her life had she blushed in front of a man. She certainly wasn't going to start now.

But when she returned to the room, his eyes were closed, his breathing shallow and even. She wasn't particularly happy with the relief or the disappointment that swept through her. Curiosity about him had her wanting to pepper him with questions. Embarrassment that she had marveled at his breath blowing over her flesh had her wanting to avoid him.

He could eat later. For now, she needed to remove the last of the dirt and blood from him. Scrubbing her home or tavern had always been her least favorite chore. Odd then that now she was quite looking forward to the task awaiting her.

CONSCIOUSNESS SLOWLY CAME to him. He hurt. He hurt all over, but the pain came in varying degrees. His left shoulder, his right thigh, his right buttock provided the brunt of the agony. He wasn't certain he'd ever move them again.

Before he could groan, growl, or cry out in protest, he became aware of the nearby presence, the gentle touch of a warm, damp cloth, so he concentrated on that, shoving aside the aches, relegating them to the farthest corners of his mind, where he shoved all unpleasantness rather than dealing with it. The linen moved slowly over his chest, and he imagined the holder of said linen counting each rib as the cloth journeyed down, until there were no more, only the flat of his stomach, his hip.

Struggling to open his eyes, he managed to create only very narrow slits through which to peer. His rescuer sat on the edge of the bed, a little farther away, still blurry, but not as much, and he wondered why he'd ever doubted her gender. Her hair and clothing were confusing, but her face, limned by lamplight, was a delicate, refined silhouette. A small button of a nose, a rounded chin, a long slender neck. However, it was her eyes that drew him. He couldn't determine the color, the lighting was too poor for that, but her compassion, her concern, was evident in the way she studied what the cloth had brushed over. She was gentle with the bruises, not so much with the dirt.

It was a bit of a shock to realize he wore no clothing; only a mere sheet draped loosely over his hips provided a modicum of privacy. When he'd awakened before, he'd noticed very little beyond her. She'd captured all his attention, keeping him spellbound. He'd wanted to stay awake until her return, but obviously he'd not managed that feat, which might have left him disappointed if he weren't certain she'd have not taken such liberties with him had he been awake.

Now she seemed to take great care in working around the flimsy covering, moving it aside as needed to reach his thigh, his calf, his foot, but ensuring his cock was always hidden away—as though it might take a chill if exposed to the air. But that seemed hardly likely considering the warmth in the room, no doubt a result of a fire dancing on the hearth if the undulating shadows were any indication of what was happening beyond his vision.

Not that he cared about any of that. He cared only about her and the gentleness with which she touched him, as though he were something to be treasured, protected, appreciated. Not a man from whom women ran.

Her ministrations with his lower body completed, she brought the sheet up over his waist, dropped her head back, rolled it from side to side and released a low groan that would have had him growing hard under different circumstances. He wanted to reach out, rub her back, ease her aches as she'd eased his. "Thank you," he croaked.

She came up off the mattress fast enough to jar the bed, and the pain that had taken up residence in his body protested by increasing, causing him to moan low.

"I'm sorry." She reached for him, then withdrew her hand, stepped farther back as though not quite certain what to do with him—or herself, for that matter. "You startled me yet again."

"It seems to be my way."

"I didn't realize you were awake."

The dimness from the nearby lamp allowed him to see her more clearly, but the faint lighting prevented him from gaining a complete picture of her. She was tall, possibly the tallest woman he'd ever seen, a couple of inches shorter than he was. Slender, but not in a sickly way. There was meat on her, strength in her.

"Are you thirsty?" she asked.

It was an effort, but he nodded.

"I'll get you some water." She wiped her hands on her skirt, before leaving the room, and he wished he'd kept his need to himself, but his throat was so dry he could barely swallow. The urge to drift back off to sleep was strong, but he fought it because he didn't want her going to such trouble for nothing, so he focused on his surroundings. Or what he could see of them. A rocker by the fire and a thickly padded chair nearby. Mermaid and unicorn figurines on the mantel. He thought it was the mermaid she'd thrown earlier, when he'd first startled her. Was he doomed to always startle her? She didn't strike him as a nervous sort; she'd braved the ruffians to save him. Yet he seemed to cause her to be wary. But then what did she really know of him or him of her?

She was courageous, no doubt. She possessed inner and outer strength that had forced him to reach deep into his own well of determination in order to get himself up the stairs, which might have possibly saved his life. She was kind, gentle, not quite comfortable with his presence. Was she married? Were there children? How did she manage?

Speculating about her sapped what little energy remained to him so he returned to his perusal. A dresser. A wardrobe. Not much else. Nothing particularly fancy or decorative. She had simple tastes, this woman who had been out and about when decent folk were abed. Was she a harlot? If so, she didn't dress provocatively enough to sell her wares profitably. In addition, her enunciation was too refined for the streets, not quite cultured, but she'd definitely received some sort of education. She could have had a position in a noble house, or perhaps one of her parents had. In rebellion, she'd run off and now she was here. What did it matter? Yet, somehow it did. He didn't like the notion of men pawing at her when she had risked herself to save him. What if the footpads hadn't dashed off? What if they'd decided to take advantage of her? And yet they'd run off because *she* was the one calling out. Who the devil was she?

Hearing footsteps, he turned his attention to the

door. She moved too quickly to be seen as clearly as he'd have liked, but he did note her clothing gave the appearance she had no curves to speak of—although he knew that to be a falsehood—but her shirt, hugging her nowhere, billowed out when she walked, like a sail striving to catch the wind. She didn't want her feminine attributes to be noticed. He wondered at the reason.

She set a tray on the bedside table, grabbed the glass, sat on the edge of the mattress, slid a hand—cool and comforting—beneath his head, and lifted it gently. "Easy now."

He didn't know if anything had ever tasted as good as the water trickling into his mouth, along his throat, quenching his thirst with a sweetness that was almost painful.

"Just a bit," she cautioned, taking the glass away and setting it back on the tray. "We don't want you to make yourself ill."

As though he could feel any worse than he did at that moment. She began fiddling with something on the tray. A bowl, with steam rising from it. She dipped in a spoon, stirred, seemed to concentrate on her actions as though her very existence depended on doing it correctly.

"You didn't think I was a woman," she said quietly.

It took him a moment to realize she was referring to the statement he'd uttered upon his first awakening, when she'd thrown the figurine at him. The blow to his head must have rattled his senses. He did hope it wasn't permanent, because he suspected carrying on a lucid conversation with this woman would be an unforgettable pleasure. "I couldn't see you clearly. The bastards took my spectacles."

"Bastards," she repeated softly, giving her attention

back to stirring the bowl. "That word is tossed about so carelessly."

"Apologies. I meant no offense. I'm not quite myself."

He could see the corners of her mouth curling up slightly, and suddenly the loss of his watch paled in comparison with the theft of his spectacles. He'd have liked to bring her into sharper focus, to make out the concise edges of her nose, her chin, her jaw. He wanted to make note of any freckles or blemishes, flaws and perfections.

"You have had a bit of a rough night."

"I owe you my thanks."

"You're not out of the woods yet. Dr. Graves says you can't travel for a while, because of all your wounds. They'd reopen and you'd die." She didn't sound at all happy with him. "I've kept some broth simmering in case you should awaken again." He wasn't heartened by her tone, which implied she'd had doubts regarding the likelihood of his avoiding an eternal sleep. "Shall we see if we can get a spoonful or two into you? You've got to keep up your strength."

Whatever strength he might have had seemed to have abandoned him completely. Still, she was correct. He needed to recover quickly, and nutrition was the path to rapid healing. But when he tried to lever himself, his body didn't want to cooperate.

"Don't move," she commanded, once again giving the impression she was accustomed to being obeyed. Most of the younger women with whom he associated wouldn't dream of telling a man what to do, ordering him about, expecting him to fall into line with her wishes. Yet, considering how rotten he felt, it was nice to have someone else in charge.

Standing, she came nearer, sliding an arm beneath

his shoulders, lifting him slightly, adjusting the pillows behind him so he was partially sitting. She was a strong one, but then he'd known that, recalling how she'd borne his weight when he'd been so weak, sapped of strength, encircled in a vortex of agony. He was rather embarrassed that even now he still required her assistance, that she should see him in such an enfeebled state. But with her nearness, she brought a conglomeration of smells: oak and yeast, dark and rich, yet underneath it all was a fainter, more feminine fragrance, the scent of a woman. He would blame his injuries for his earlier idiocy in ever doubting her gender.

With him sinking back into the pillows, she settled on the edge of the bed and raised the bowl, again stirred the contents, then lifted out the spoon and carried it to her mouth, her upper lip touching the edge of the liquid, then her tongue darting out to touch her lip as well. In spite of the pain radiating throughout his body and extremities, the lethargy that wanted to drag him back into oblivion, he was mesmerized by her actions, felt his mannerless cock twitch in response to her sensual—but he was rather certain innocent—gesture. She wasn't trying to lure him into her arms; she was striving to get him out of her bed.

He nearly laughed aloud. That was a first. Women were never in a rush for him to leave their beds. Lady Lavinia would have discovered that fact tonight had she not left him standing at the altar that morning.

SHE WATCHED AS emotions rolled over his face like storm clouds chasing the sun, so quickly she might have missed them if she hadn't been scrutinizing him so closely. Initially, he'd appeared to have a spark of yearning, which was ridiculous because there was nothing about her for which a man as magnificent as he would yearn—well, maybe her ability to grant him a speedy recovery. Then there had been a flash of anger, followed rapidly by what seemed to be mortification. He'd averted his gaze as though embarrassed. On the other hand, he was lying in a stranger's bed without a stitch of clothing. He had to be feeling rather helpless and vulnerable.

"Here we go," she said as flatly as she could, having no desire to bruise his pride any further. There were far more men than women in her world, and she'd replaced enough glassware to know what idiots those of the male gender could be when their vanity was at stake—as though throwing a glass or a punch at an offender would suddenly proclaim the tosser as courageous and strong. Carrying the spoon to his mouth, she wondered why he had to possess such gorgeous lips that made her imagine the wicked things he might do with them. Her stomach tightened as he sipped the broth, then licked his lips and closed his eyes as though he'd never tasted anything so sublime.

"How long?" he rasped.

"Pardon?"

"How long have I been here?"

"A few hours. Sun'll be rising soon." She'd indulged herself and taken a good deal of time and great care while removing the blood and dirt from his person. She scooped up more broth, tested its temperature—

"Stop doing that," he commanded with a forcefulness she'd have not expected in his weakened state.

Startled, and a bit angered by his tone, she said succinctly, "I don't want you to burn your mouth."

"I'll take the risk."

She fought not to be offended, lost the battle. "My mouth is clean."

"I need to get out of here," he grumbled, made a move to get up, groaned, dropped back down.

"Did I not remark on Dr. Graves saying you can't leave for a spell? Not to mention he cut off your clothes. I'll have to mend them before they're serviceable. I'm not any happier about this than you are."

"Your husband will be even less so."

"I have no husband."

He narrowed his eyes. "With whom do you live?"

"No one."

"You're a woman living alone?"

"Don't get any naughty ideas. I could lay you flat if I had to." She set the bowl back on the tray. "You should probably try to get more rest. The sooner you regain your strength, the sooner you're out of here."

"Who knows I'm here?"

What the devil difference did it make? "Me, Graves, Robin."

"Who's Robin?"

"The lad I sent to fetch Graves. I'm really not enjoying this inquisi—"

"No one can know I'm here."

Again, another spark of anger. "Worried about your reputation?"

"Worried about yours."

Taken aback by his words, she felt her anger dissipate. She owned a tavern. Her reputation had long ago gone to hell. "My reputation is hardly your concern, and it's not likely to take a beating."

"You're a spinster with a man in your bed. I won't be able to marry you."

"I bloody well wouldn't want you to, you arrogant

arse." Coming up off the bed, she picked up the tray. "Get some sleep before I decide to ignore Graves's warnings that you could bleed to death and kick you out into the street."

Storming from the room, she couldn't help but think that men were the most irritating creatures God had created.

GOOD LORD! HE'D never had a woman yell at him. He found it rather invigorating. If he weren't in so much pain and so embarrassingly weak, he might have reached out, grabbed her, and brought her down to the bed so he could taste that tart mouth of hers. But he *was* weak and in pain and so bloody tired.

Her reputation wasn't the only reason he didn't want to have to explain his presence here—not so much in her bed, but in this part of London. What did it say about him that his bride would choose to run off to Whitechapel rather than exchange vows with him?

When the time for the bride's appearance had passed, Thorne had begun to have a bad feeling about things. Then her brother, the Earl of Collinsworth, had walked down the aisle to the front of the church without the bride on his arm and whispered to him that Lavinia had asked the coachman to deliver her to Whitechapel. The man, loyal to the earl, had refused, and so she'd gone off in search of a hansom. Thorne had announced to those in attendance, "It appears Lady Lavinia has taken ill. As I wish our wedding day to be one of fond memories for her, the nuptials will be postponed until she is feeling more herself." Then with humiliation mingled with fury coursing through him, he'd stormed out to go in search of his bride, determined to locate her at all costs and discover why she had decided to make a fool of him in such an incredibly public manner.

In hindsight, he'd been an idiot to strive to find her on his own, under the misperception that if he just wandered the streets, eventually their paths would cross. As he'd gone deeper into the night, his stubbornness had asserted itself and he'd continued with his quest, even knowing it wouldn't bear fruit. He'd had his carriage bring him to this area of London, and then sent his driver on his way, fully intending to hire a hack when he was ready to return to his residence. Obviously he'd not been ready soon enough. And it had cost him.

As oblivion beckoned, he answered the call and began sinking down into the welcoming fog, distantly wondering how what should have been the most important day in his life could have gone so horribly wrong.

SHE DIDN'T DARE return to the room, not until she heard the snore. It was a soft hum, more the purring of a cat than the snorting she'd heard from drunkards who fell asleep in the corner of her establishment. Rousing them so they could stagger home was never any great enjoyment. If the chap was a regular customer, someone she liked well enough, she'd give him leave to sleep it off where he'd landed. Besides, it made Robin feel important when tasked with the chore of keeping an eye on the inebriated blokes for her, as though he were guarding her place from miscreants.

She'd considered rousing Robin, having him keep watch over the man known as Thorne, but doing that would force her to admit to her own cowardice. He troubled her in ways she'd never been bothered before, which was the reason that once she heard the snore, she quietly slipped into the room, stood beside the bed, crossed her arms over her chest, and studied him.

He was so incredibly lovely to look upon, every aspect of him—except for the injuries and bruises—a pleasure to behold. Never before had she simply wanted to stare at a man, and she certainly couldn't allow him to see her gawking when he was awake. She wouldn't marry him—or anyone, for that matter—because upon marriage her tavern would become his, and she wasn't going to hand it over to a man who wouldn't appreciate it or care for it as she did. Nor did she have any desire to become chattel. She'd been independent as long as she could remember, running through the mews with her brothers—all merely a year older than she was—and getting into scrapes alongside them. They'd never treated her like a girl, not like the way they treated their sister Fancy.

Gillie had been heading toward her thirteenth birthday when Fancy was born. At fourteen, her brothers were already strong, strapping lads. By the time Fancy was old enough to be playing outside without being under their mum's watchful eye, no one wanted to run afoul of the Trewlove brothers. As a result, Ettie Trewlove had never felt a need to disguise the gender of the daughter to whom she'd given birth. With five of her children adding their earnings to the family coffers, she'd even been able to purchase proper frocks for her youngest. Everyone tried to protect her, perhaps because she was so much younger than they were. Or more delicate, more feminine. By the time Gillie had seen a dozen years, she was as tall as she was now, slender as a reed, but there was a firmness to her muscles that came from the hard work in which she'd engaged as a child, a firmness that had only intensified when she'd reached adulthood and begun hauling casks from the cellar and slovenly drunkards into the streets.

But for the tiniest of moments, when the stranger had expressed concern about her reputation, she'd thought how welcoming it might be to be cherished and protected by a man. Not that her brothers wouldn't protect her if needed, but that hardly counted, as they were family and that's what family did. None of them were related by blood, but their mum had raised them to understand some bonds were stronger than blood.

Like the bond that existed between a man and a woman, the connection that caused a woman to want to marry him, lie with him, and bear his children. Or lie with him without the benefit of marriage. It was the reason she and her siblings existed. By-blows who'd come into the world because some man had enticed a woman into his bed and then refused to do right by her. She wondered if this Thorne fellow was prone to that sort of abhorrent behavior. But if he were, would he worry about her reputation?

She didn't like the way her insides had fluttered and her skin had warmed as she'd given him a sip of water and a spoonful of broth. She didn't relish at all that she rather enjoyed caring for him, had experienced a sense of satisfaction when he'd seemed so pleased with the simple broth that hadn't taken her any trouble at all to prepare.

Suddenly he moved, flailed about. With her heart hammering at his quick movements, she stepped briskly to the bed and pressed her palm to his forehead, grateful to find only tepid warmth. "Shh. Shh. It's all right. It's all right."

His brow furrowed, but he stilled, his breathing shallow and rapid, and she wondered if he was reliving the attack, if the nightmare of it was visiting his slumber. "You're safe," she whispered. "I won't let anyone harm you."

Beneath her fingers, his brow relaxed. "That's it. Let your worries go. They don't exist here. Go to a peaceful place and let your body heal."

His breathing slowed, went deeper. She had no reason to keep touching him, yet she seemed incapable of removing her hand. His dark forelock had fallen over her fingers, and it was as though the silken strands had captured her as effectively as the coarsest of ropes.

Before him, she'd never touched a man. Oh, she'd slapped her brothers on the shoulder, hugged them, even come into contact with their skin when she tended to the numerous wounds they'd received in their youth during a time when their actions were guided more by anger at their circumstance than common sense. But she'd grown up with them; they were familiar. She'd certainly never looked at one of them and thought, "I'd jolly well like to skim my fingers over him, test the cords of his muscles, the silkiness of his flesh."

She found it difficult to swallow with the realization she could touch every inch of the fellow, in secret, him unaware of her actions. All she had to do was move aside the sheet, and he would be presented to her like a gift. Naturally, however, if a man took those liberties with her, she'd bloody well kill him—slowly and most painfully. If she even suspected those thoughts had entered his head . . .

The riotous musings invading her mind were unconscionable. Still, she seemed unable to prevent her hand from slowly trailing down his cheek and lightly brushing over his shadowed jaw. She rather liked his unkempt state, which made him appear dangerous, strong, a man to be reckoned with—even if the four thugs had managed to drop him to his knees. She hadn't seen the entire encounter, but she'd seen enough to know he hadn't gone down easily.

Of their own accord, her fingers traced his lips. His warm breath fanned over her knuckles, causing an unsettling sensation in the pit of her stomach, lower still to an area between her thighs. Once, when she was no more than seven, she'd nicked an apple from a vendor's cart. She'd run off feeling both satisfied and ashamed. In the end, she hadn't eaten her bounty, but had passed it off to a dirtier urchin. It hadn't lessened her guilt. She hadn't stolen anything since.

But this felt like stealing, these precious moments of caressing a man. How many nights had she gone to sleep, aching to be held, to have her limbs entwined with another's, to touch and be touched? While she'd always telegraphed that she had no interest in men, wouldn't take kindly to their advances, her actions didn't lessen her loneliness, didn't make her yearn any less for what she knew could take place between a man and a woman.

She wanted to run her hand over his shoulders, his chest. Instead, she balled it up tightly and placed it in her lap, only then realizing she was holding his other hand there. He wouldn't do right by her. He'd stated as much. Not that she'd want him to. She didn't need a man. Well—looking over her shoulder, she shifted her gaze to his hips—she needed a portion of him.

She nearly laughed aloud. Whatever was wrong with her to entertain such lascivious thoughts? Her mum would be appalled. *She* was appalled.

Perhaps if he didn't smell so good. Beneath the blood, sweat, and dirt she'd washed away was a woodsy scent that reminded her of the freshly turned earth in her mum's garden. And with it mingled the essence of him, sharp and tangy.

With care, she turned his hand, clasping it palm up, within hers. So smooth. Not a scar or callus to be found. But not weak. There was strength in those long, slender fingers. She imagined them slowly caressing, stroking, squeezing. Touching a woman, loving her.

Trailing the fingers of her other hand over his, she could feel the potency housed there. If she pressed the heel of her palm against his fingertips and flattened her hand over his, she could almost reach his wrist. All parts of her had always been long and lanky, but the width of his hand compared to the slenderness of hers made her feel almost delicate, almost—

He shifted, closing his fingers around hers, drawing their joined hands up to nestle in the center of his chest as he started to roll slightly, groaned, and halted. His eyes fluttered, then settled into stillness. She barely breathed, waiting for him to awaken, to fling her hand aside when he realized he was cradling it as though it were an injured dormouse. She had one as a pet when she was a girl, and at that particular moment, she wondered if it had felt as trapped when she'd first held it as she felt now. Trapped and comforted in the same instance, as though this injured person would protect her. She'd never taken much physical comfort from men, viewing them as being more trouble than they were worth, but she had an odd urge to wiggle her way up beneath his arm and snuggle against him.

These strange musings were only because it had been a long, stressful night, and she should be abed by now. Only he was in her bed, holding her hand against his chest as though he treasured it. Faintly, she could feel the beating of his heart, reaching between his ribs to thrum against her fingers where they furled against his skin.

She should shove herself off the bed and settle onto the sofa in the other room, but never before had a chap held her hand. Even though this one did so lost in the realm of dreams, unaware of whose hand he actually held, she couldn't quite bring herself to break free of him. It was lovely really, to have the warmth of another human being—of a man—seeping through skin and muscle and bone to heat her throughout. Oddly she felt as though he held all of her. Perhaps that was the reason she seemed unable to move.

Lost in slumber, he appeared younger, more innocent, more approachable. Leaning forward, with her free hand, she combed back the silken strands of dark hair from his brow. "What the devil were you doing in this area, alone, so late at night? What was so important you couldn't wait for a more reasonable time of day?"

In response, he released a soft snore. She imagined how comforting it would be to hear that snuffle occasionally through the night, to know another person was about to share the sheets, the dreams, the troubles. What fanciful thoughts. She had her mum, her brothers, and on occasion her sister. She certainly didn't need a stranger who caused her to wonder about the delights that might not be in her life. If not happiness, at least contentment filled her days and nights. She wanted for nothing more.

But as her gaze drifted over to those lush, full lips, she couldn't help but feel a yearning in the center of her chest for all the things she'd not experienced: sweet words whispered in the dark, a heated mouth doing deliciously wicked things, a gaze smoldering with pleasure at the sight of her. A ridiculous thought as she'd never intentionally bared herself to a man and had no idea if what she possessed beneath her clothing would be pleasing to a bloke. She took great pains to give no hint at all regarding her true shape. No sense in giving the gents who visited her tavern any ideas or temptation. Or to discover she appealed not in the least.

She was still indulging in the luxury of combing her fingers through his hair when the brisk knock at the door had her jerking her gaze to the window, where the first rays of morning sunlight filtered into the room through a part in the yellow curtains. When had daylight arrived and how long had she been sitting there lost in her musings about this man?

Careful not to wake him, she gently twisted her hand free of his hold and hurried to the entrance, as the knock again echoed through her lodgings. With care, she opened the door only slightly and peered out. A small woman, slender and petite, one who more closely resembled the size of a normal female, smiled brightly with perfect teeth and sparkling blue eyes. "Hello. I'm Alice Turner. Dr. Graves sent me, said you were in want of a nurse."

"No."

The smile dwindled. Alice Turner blinked. "I thought

there was a man here in need of looking after. Knife wounds and such."

"He got better and left of his own accord."

That smile again, blindingly bright. Too bright. "Oh. Well. That's good news I suppose."

"I'm sorry you came all the way out here for no good reason. Hold on. I'll get a few quid for you."

"That's not necess—"

Closing the door in the woman's face, she rushed over to the kitchen area and reached into a crock on a high shelf where she kept her emergency funds. After counting out five quid, she made a hasty return, opened the door, grabbed Alice Turner's hand, and shoved the money into it, closing her fingers securely around it. "Have a good day."

She didn't wait for a response before once again leaving the nurse on the other side of the threshold. With a sigh, she leaned against the oak that barred her from the rest of the world. For the life of her, she couldn't figure out why she'd just spouted lies to a stranger. Deception was one of the things she didn't tolerate in herself or others, but she'd done it to protect him. Hadn't he stated he didn't want anyone to know he was here? Perhaps he was in trouble, had come to this portion of London to hide out. He wouldn't be the first.

Or perhaps the truth was that she'd done it simply because she hadn't wanted another woman seeing to the needs of the man in her bed.

Chapter 4

"*I* need you to manage things for the full day and night, until closing."

Jolly Roger—no one believed that was his real name, but in this area of London one changed names as easily and sometimes as often as one changed stockings—narrowed his eyes and pursed his lips as though he couldn't believe the words she'd just announced, words that had seemed foreign rolling off her tongue as she stood by the polished counter near the back of the public taproom of her tavern. Never before had she missed an entire day of work or put him in complete charge. Not that she didn't trust him to do the job—she did. Occasionally she took some time to herself in the afternoon, and he'd handled matters while she was away, but her absence never lasted longer than a couple of hours because she'd never had anything better to do or anything she cared about more than her tavern.

Seeing to the needs of the man upstairs wasn't going to be more to her liking than managing her tavern, but she felt an obligation to ensure he survived and had decided she was the best one to guarantee his survival—especially after she'd been daft enough, due to lack of sleep no doubt, to send the tiny nurse on her merry way.

"Are you not well?" he asked in a voice as robust as he was, with his barrel chest and stocky legs that served him well when he hauled casks up from the cellar. His red hair and bushy beard softened the hardness of him.

"I'm a bit under the weather." She hated lying but couldn't tell him the truth. While she trusted him implicitly with her tavern, she didn't trust him not to give his opinion on the wisdom of having a man—even if he was too weak to cause any harm—in her lodgings.

"That's not like you."

"We all have a bad day now and then."

He nodded. "Women and their monthly ills." And walked away to begin lifting chairs down from the tables where they placed them each night at closing to make it easier to sweep and mop up.

"It has nothing at all—" She cut off her tirade, not liking one bit what he was thinking, that she was having her courses and succumbing to the pain of the monthly hell. Damn Eve and her bite into the apple that had cursed women for all eternity. But she wasn't going to argue with Jolly Roger or set him straight, because that would only lead to more questions she wouldn't answer and word would reach her brothers—and then the man who didn't want to marry her would find he didn't have a choice.

She strode through the kitchen and the door that opened onto the alleyway and very nearly tripped over Robin, who was setting out a saucer of milk on the stoop. In charge of keeping the stray cats in the area happy so they kept the rats unhappy, he twisted his kneeling body around to squint up at her. "Did 'e die, Gillie?" he asked conspiratorially, as though that had been the sought-after outcome.

"*He*," she repeated.

He rolled his eyes at the correction. "Did *he* die?"

"No." Bending down until her gaze met his, she reiterated, "Remember, you're to tell no one about him."

He shook his head forcefully. "I like 'aving— *having*—secrets."

"This one you keep forever."

"Right-o."

Satisfied by his response, she stalked up the outer stairs, irrationally irritated because she was changing her routine for a stranger. She shouldn't have turned the nurse away but would look like a cabbage head now if she sent word to Graves to send Alice Turner back. Shoving open her door, she strode over the threshold and was in the process of slamming the sturdy wood shut when she stopped, considered. He hadn't asked for her help, had done nothing to deserve her wrath. By the morrow, he should be well enough to leave. She'd borrow her brother Mick's fancy well-sprung coach, as it would provide a comfortable ride without much bouncing around, smooth enough that it could rock a newborn babe to sleep. So the gent required only a few more hours of her time, and then he'd be on his way and her life would return to normal.

She closed the door with a quiet *snick*. Strange how different her apartment felt, as though the stranger's presence had seeped into every aspect of it, every corner. It made her uneasy, mostly because she realized how absent of company and comfort her life was. She'd been so hell-bent on making a success of her tavern she hadn't made room for much else. Even time spent with her family had dwindled in recent years. She saw her brothers when they stopped by for a pint.

Every couple of weeks she checked in on her mum. She'd usually see her sister, Fancy, then—if she was about. If she wasn't, she didn't go out of her way to try to find her. Fancy was only seven and ten. Not only did the years separate them, but so did the fact that they were very different people, destined for different lives. Mick—determined Fancy would marry well, an aristocrat if he had his way—had paid her tuition to a posh school where she'd learned refinement and the art of being a genteel lady and managing a household. While no one expected Gillie to marry, even if she'd been willing to hand over her tavern. No gent was going to marry a woman who refused to be viewed as property, not that any man had ever eyed her as though he might be considering making her his help-mate. She appealed to men as little as they appealed to her. If she were to have a man in her life at all, she had to accept the relationship would lead only to a tumble, nothing as respectable as marriage.

With some surprise, she realized while all these thoughts were swirling through her mind, she'd made her way to her bedroom. The man was asleep, the sheets a tangled mess around his hips and legs as though he'd wrestled with them a bit. One long arm rested along the side of his face, crooked over his head, the other hand curled near his groin. It was an exceedingly masculine pose, and if she weren't so certain he was beyond reasoning, she'd think he'd set himself up like that on purpose, just to set her womanly instincts on edge. She'd worked so hard not to be attracted to men, and in the space of a single day, she was discovering all her efforts had been for naught. She could become unraveled by the sight of a lovely chest covered lightly in hair that arrowed down and disappeared beneath the coverings where something even more masculine resided.

With a groan and a quick flick of her wrists, she snapped the sheets back over him. She considered waking him for a bit of broth, but he appeared to be in a deep sleep, and his body probably—in order to properly heal—needed that more than what she was going to offer. Best just to leave him be. Still she pulled the sheet up to his neck in order to hide that distracting chest and brushed her fingers lightly over his jaw. His stubble was thicker, darker. If he went much longer without using a razor, he'd have a beard like Mick. It would be a shame to hide that strong, chiseled chin with an abundance of facial hair.

And there she was, once again, spending too much time pondering him, when she needed to get a bit of sleep herself. He took up most of her bed, not that she'd entertain the notion of lying beside him. He caused her womanly parts to riot enough as it was. If their proximity to him were any closer, they'd keep her awake with a longing she'd managed to keep in hibernation for a good portion of her life. However now that it had been disturbed, it seemed starving for sustenance. A good rest should send it back into submission.

She considered the sofa in her front room, but settled for the large plush chair beside the fire in this chamber, so she'd be certain to hear him if he called out in distress. Besides, she'd fallen asleep there many a night while reading. Over the years, it had begun to retain her shape, and when she sank into it and it molded around her, it was like coming home. In no time at all she was lost to slumber.

AWAKENING WITH A start from a deep sleep, she stared groggily at the man flailing about in her bed, kicking at the sheets as though they were irons dragging him down. Disoriented, she couldn't quite figure out what he was doing there, why she would have a man so near—

Then everything came rushing back. Shooting out of the chair, she glanced toward the window. Darkness had fallen. She'd slept the day away, obviously more tired than she'd realized. With the speed of a racehorse, she arrived at the bed, focusing on the stranger's face rather than the fact he'd successfully rid himself of any covering, leaving everything of importance exposed. She placed her palms on either side of his face, surprised by the heat that greeted her, a heat that could easily singe a babe's bum. "Shh, pet. It's all right. Calm down now."

He opened his eyes; there was a fever to them, a wildness, a desperation in them. "Have to find her."

She didn't like the kick to her gut, the phantom pain, she felt with the knowledge a lady, clearly one extremely important to him, resided in his life, that she might have unwittingly acquired the answer to her question regarding why he'd been in a dangerous area of London at an even more perilous time of night. "You will find her, but first you must heal, regain your strength."

"Step . . . aside." He tried to shove her away, made a move to roll out of the bed, but she stood her ground, clamping her hands over his shoulders, digging her fingers into firm muscle, striving to avoid causing the wound in his shoulder to bleed again.

"You're no good to her dead, and you will be if you don't mend."

He continued to struggle against her hold, endeavoring fruitlessly to push her away, but getting into tussles with four brothers had taught her how to cling, how to leverage her weight to put herself at an advantage. Mustering all her strength, she gave him a hard shake. "Thorne!"

She'd not addressed him by his name before. It somehow seemed intimate, made him more to her than he was. "Don't fight me or I'll be done with you." Her tone, the one she used when ousting drunkards from her establishment, was designed to break through the thick fog of confusion that sometimes addled men's brains when they were viewing the world through a haze of alcohol.

He went still, so still, his breathing labored, his eyes the shade of Guinness boring into her. For a heartbeat, he seemed suddenly aware, his expression intense. "Don't let me die."

Then his eyes closed and he sank back into the softness of the mattress, once again lost to the world, lost to her. She brushed the hair back from his fevered brow. "You won't die, pet. Not if I have a say in it."

Since he was in her bed, she had a good deal to say about it. Reaching down, she brought the sheet back over him. He reacted not at all, lost in a deep sleep, possibly unconscious. She rather hoped for the latter as it would make tending to him easier, would prevent him from experiencing what was bound to be more than a bit of discomfort.

She began by redressing his wounds, adding a tart-smelling salve Graves had given her to ward off infection. The areas were red, but she couldn't see any signs of putrification. One of her brothers had nearly died from a wound becoming poisoned, so she knew what to look for. She also knew what had to be done to clean it out. She preferred to avoid that unpleasant task, assumed her patient would welcome not having the procedure visited upon him.

Her patient. What a fool she'd been to send the nurse away. Not that she regretted it, not really. She enjoyed tending to this man's needs, wiping a cool cloth over his brow once she was finished tending to each of his wounds. He was fevered, that couldn't be denied, but he didn't seem delirious or out of his mind. She'd take what little victories she could.

She could hear some of the revelry from belowstairs. Strange how it didn't call to her, how she was able to ignore it. She trusted Jolly Roger to take care of it, but it was more than that. For the first time in her life, something seemed more important than pouring ale. Even without conversation, he was more interesting than the chaps who ambled up to her bar and stammered a few words of greeting. Perhaps it was because he was a mystery. A well-heeled gent in this part of London that time of night, concerned with her reputation—

"Who are you?"

The question asked in a low, raspy voice mirrored the one she'd been asking herself about him. Slowly she lifted her gaze from his neck, where she'd been wiping away the dew, to his eyes. She'd told him before, but perhaps he'd been in too much pain to pay attention or to remember. "Gillie."

His head moved slightly from side to side as though the answer were inadequate or made no sense. "More. Tell me more about you."

No gent had ever cared to learn more about her. Perhaps he just needed a distraction from his discomfort or some noise to tether him to this world. "Broth first."

With a strength to his fingers she'd not expected, he wrapped them around her wrist, stilling her attempt to leave the bed. "Won't be able to keep it down."

"You should at least try."

Again, that slight movement of his head. "Talk to me."

She gave a nod, and he released his hold on her wrist, trusting her not to go back on her word, an action that caused something inside of her to swell with longing, the way it had when she'd been a small girl and seen a doll, dressed more finely than she, in a shop window at Christmas. Every day she'd returned to the shop to see it, had wept the day she discovered it no longer there. As though she would weep to find him no longer in her bed. She dipped the cloth into the bowl, wrung it out, and patted the dampness from his neck where it flowed into his chest. "I own the tavern downstairs."

"Name?"

"The Mermaid and Unicorn."

A corner of that beautiful mouth of his hitched up. If he weren't so weak, she suspected he'd have given her a blinding smile. "You threw the mermaid at me."

Her own lips twitched. "I've always favored the unicorn a tad more."

"Why?"

She shrugged, embarrassed to have shared that, not wanting to share more, but how could she not if it would keep him distracted from his pain? "It always seemed more mythical, yet also more believable. I couldn't quite bring myself to accept a woman could be half a fish, but it seemed plausible that at one time, somewhere in the world, a horse might have a horn. Don't you think?"

He merely stared at her, no doubt because she had spouted such utter nonsense. "I know it seems silly—" she began.

"Not silly. Endearing."

"You will have me blushing, if you're not careful with your flattery. So, there, now you know everything about me."

"I doubt that."

She dipped the cloth in the bowl, squeezed out the excess water, and gently dragged the linen just below his collarbone from shoulder to shoulder, carefully avoiding the wound. "What were you doing out in the streets at such an ungodly hour of night, alone, a target for footpads?"

He averted his gaze, turning his head toward the fire. The golden light danced over his features, in a macabre display of shifting shadows he almost seemed to welcome hiding within. "Chasing a dream."

Disappointment, sorrow, and the beginnings of defeat wove their way through his quietly spoken words. What sort of a dream would a man search for within these wretched environs? She nearly laughed aloud at the absurdity of her question. Her own dreams were anchored here, although there were times of late when she found herself yearning for more. She wouldn't pester him with probing inquiries, as she doubted he would answer anyway, but she couldn't allow him to give up. "Instead you found a bit of a nightmare, didn't you?"

He released a solitary huff of breath that might have served as a laugh if he had more strength in him. She longed to see him well and robust, imagined how bold and daring he might appear under other circumstances. "A bit."

Turning his head back in her direction, he seemed to be struggling to keep his eyes open. "They knew you, called you by name."

"Did they now? I thought as much, that they might know me, since they ran off with little more than a shout chasing after them. I don't suppose you got a good look at them."

The shake of his head was barely noticeable. Now was not the time for an inquisition. But she'd keep an eye out, take notice if someone suddenly appeared flush from fencing off some items stolen from a gent. "You should try to get some sleep."

"Might not awaken."

"You've a fever, but I've checked your wounds. They're not festering. Still your body has to fight, and rest will serve it well."

"Keep talking."

"About what?"

"You."

It was wrong to lose patience with a man who was suffering. "I've told you everything there is to say about me. I'm not very interesting."

"Tell me about the mermaid . . . and unicorn."

She didn't think he was asking about her tavern but rather why she took a fancy to those creatures, why she'd chosen them. Once more she wrung out the cloth. Hoping to cool him, she set it across his brow. After dampening another piece of linen, she wiped it across his chest, careful to avoid his brown nipples, and thus something that seemed far too intimate. Then she dragged it along his sternum where more sweat gathered. "They can never be together. I have a soft spot for things that can never be together . . . I think because of my family. We're the result of people who couldn't be together." Except for her brother Mick. They'd recently learned his story was a bit more complicated, but it wasn't one she'd share with this stranger—even if he were no longer a stranger. It was Mick's story to tell, not hers. "We're all by-blows, you see."

His eyes nearly shut, he didn't react. Perhaps her voice was lulling him into slumber or he was lost to the fever, beyond comprehending what she was saying. That thought emboldened her a bit. She wasn't much for talking, but if the noise would keep him beyond death's reach and it wasn't really making much sense, then what did it matter what she said? "The mermaid lives in the sea. The unicorn can't go there, now can he? The mermaid can come to land, but not for very long. So they can have a friendship, but nothing more than that. Silly name for a tavern where mostly blokes visit. I should have named it the Black Boar or something that would make men feel strong when drinking there. But I wanted something a bit softer. There wasn't a lot of softness in my life when I was growing up. Not a lot now, either, really, but now it's by choice. I work hard because I want to work hard. And now I'm rambling like a bloody idiot."

His lips twitched, which caused a strange tightness in her chest. He was listening. Made her wish she'd kept her tongue still, although if she were honest with herself, she also liked that, in spite of his pain, discomfort, and fever, he was paying attention to her words. She wished only that she had more interesting stories to share with him.

After a few moments of silence, he mumbled, "More."

More. He might be near death's door, but she thought it unlikely he'd step over the threshold. There was a command in his tone. He was obviously accustomed to giving orders, probably didn't take kindly to her bossing him about, wouldn't heed Death's orders either. But then few people had a choice in the matter. If her voice would keep him from answering the knock, so be it.

"I said my life was hard, but it wasn't awful. When I was very little, I'd help my mum make matchboxes. My tiny fingers were suited to the task. We should have known then I'd be tall, because they were so long. But the chore required tedious hours of sitting, and I grew bored rather quickly. I wanted to follow my brothers on their adventures. They were always off doing one thing or another, finding the odd job here and there, but I reasoned whatever they were doing had to be more fun than my labors. When I was eight, I began working as a step-girl." Although based on the clothing she wore at the time—trousers, shirt, jacket, and cap—they'd all thought they were hiring a boy.

He gave no reaction except for the fluttering of his eyelashes, as though the lids were too heavy to lift. She replaced the linen on his forehead, placed another damp one at his throat, then went about outlining each of his ribs with a cool cloth. "You strike me as the sort who doesn't pay any attention to how his house is kept tidy. It takes more than sweeping to keep the outside steps clean. Takes scrubbing to get it done. I'd start at one end of the street, yelling, 'Steps cleaned! Three-pence! Three-pence to clean your steps.'" She released a caustic laugh. "Three-pence per house, not per step. But I liked the independence of it. I could go off for a wee sleep when I got tired. Sometimes if the cook was kind, I'd get a jolly good meal or maybe a bit of pastry or a biscuit. I seldom went home hungry, which left my mum with more to feed the boys. Caw, you'd think they were starving every time they sat at the table." She dipped the cloth into the bowl, lifted it out, began to wring it and, for the first time in ages, truly noticed her hands. Marred with tiny scars, callused. "I'll never be mistaken for being a lady," she muttered.

Her patient was breathing a little more heavily. "Do you want some laudanum, pet?"

"Words." It came out soft, strained as though he'd pushed it out from the depths of his soul.

She searched her memory, trying to find something of interest, latched onto it and laughed. "Ah. There was this one time, I was cleaning the front stoop and the toff's son shows up on his horse, rides it right up the steps, past me, and into the house. And wouldn't you know it? The horse left me a damned present, right there, before he went over the threshold. Which made it my business to clean up. They didn't give me any more coins. Only my three-pence. Never took a fancy to horses after that. Well, except for the mythical kind, of course."

"Take you . . . riding. Change your mind . . . about them."

Her heart slammed against her ribs so hard she was fairly certain one cracked. He was delirious with fever, of course. He didn't mean the words. Men spouted all sorts of nonsense when they were in pain, fevered. When he was recovered, he'd look at her and laugh to think he'd ever suggested the two of them going together on an outing. Ridiculous. Not unless hell had frozen over. She wanted to make light of it, to tease him, but a small corner of her soul, a traitorous part, longed for him to be coherent, to have uttered the words with true purpose, wanted to find herself in his company when he was healed and well again.

What a silly chit she was to wish for things that could never be. Even though she knew little about him, she recognized they were worlds apart, that she had chosen an occupation and a life no man would welcome in a mate.

"WHERE'S GILLIE?" AIDEN Trewlove asked as he drew back a chair and dropped into it, joining his brother Beast at a corner table in the tavern. It was an odd thing to walk into the Mermaid and Unicorn and not see his sister standing behind the bar, nodding at him, and turning around to pour him a drink.

"Jolly Roger says she told him she wouldn't be coming in today or tonight."

"What? She's not working at all?"

Beast shrugged a brawny shoulder that always came in handy when a brawl was needed. He was also a man of few words, which made him the ideal drinking partner for Aiden, who always preferred listening to his own voice.

"Gillie always works," he reminded his brother.

"Not today."

"Why?"

"She didn't say. Gave no reasons apparently."

"Is she in her rooms?"

"Supposedly."

"You didn't go check on her?" Shoving back his chair, he started to rise.

"She might not want checking on."

Aiden froze, glanced back at his brother. "Why ever not?"

Beast looked at his tankard of ale as though he feared it might sprout legs and run off. He cleared his throat. "Jolly Roger thinks it might be a womanly thing."

"Like what?"

His brother gave him an impatient glare.

Ah, her monthly. "It's never stopped her before."

"Then I don't know. Maybe she's just feeling under the weather or has a cough or something."

He dropped back down. "Someone should look in on her."

Beast grimaced, shifted in his chair as though it had suddenly become spiked. "What if it is a womanly thing? I don't want to have to talk about that. It's only a day. Maybe she's reading a good book and didn't want to put it aside."

"She's not you. Doing anything that requires sitting for any length of time makes her want to clamber up a wall. Something must be wrong."

"Aren't you the optimist?"

He scowled. "It's odd is all. I'm worried about her."

"You're worried about who is going to bring you your beer."

Aiden grinned. "There is that. If she was here, I'd have it by now." He signaled to a lass walking by. "I'll give her today, but if she's not back tomorrow, I'll know the reason why."

Chapter 5

*H*is last memory was of her clearing horse dung off doorsteps because some oaf was idiotic enough to ride his horse into a residence. The lout could have been any one of a dozen swells he'd known in his youth when he'd gone through a recalcitrant period of which he wasn't particularly proud, rebelling against the strict restraints that had been placed on him at such an early age. He'd also been vying for attention, striving to elicit some emotion, other than dispassionate non-caring, from his mother. He'd welcomed the heat of her anger over her cold frost. This woman's story made him even more ashamed of his rebellious past, grateful he'd been too exhausted, was too exhausted still, to reveal much about himself.

He opened his eyes to a room of shadows. She sat nearby, a lone lamp providing the light by which she worked a needle through material, her head bent over the task, her profile to him. He thought her hair, cropped short as it was, should have provided her with a masculine bent. Instead it gave her an elfin appearance, faerie-like. His grandmother had told him tales of faeries. Tiny delicate creatures who lived in the gardens. He wouldn't describe this woman as delicate, but she was definitely feminine in her own unique way.

And she had ministered to him for hours. It had been years since anyone had paid him so much attention or seemed to care whether he lived. His mother was a demonstrably cold woman. His father had been warmer, but his expectations regarding proper behavior were such that the warmth was often lost in his rigid disciplinarian attitude, leaving Thorne to long for a closeness that had never truly existed. Odd to realize all that now. The possibility of death seemed to bring certain aspects of life into sharper focus. But he needed his damn spectacles to bring the woman sitting nearby into the precise clarity he yearned for. "What—"

Her head came up so quickly, he might have heard her neck pop.

"—have you there?"

She lifted what appeared to be a bundle of rags from her lap. "Your fever broke near dawn, after which you slept the day away. I was hopeful you might soon be in need of your clothing." She seemed embarrassed to have been caught mending what remained of his attire. "Could you do with a bit of shepherd's pie?"

"Probably more than a bit." He'd never been so hungry.

She gave him a bright glorious smile that would have rocked him back on his heels had he been standing. "I'll get it for you." While coming to her feet, she set her bundle in the chair, a smooth graceful movement, made even more so by her willowy height.

Instead of immediately heading for the door, she stepped forward and placed her cool palm against his forehead. If he were more recovered, stronger, he might have placed his hand over hers and brought it to his lips to demonstrate his gratitude. A chaste kiss against her knuckles or palm.

Her hand lingered longer than he'd expected, then she curved it around to cup his cheek. "You're in need of a shave," she said wistfully before pulling her hand back as though his fever had returned and burned her. "But I haven't a razor. I shan't be long."

She spun on her heel and quit the room, leaving him to wonder why he wasn't ecstatic with the knowledge he would soon return to his world and his quest to find Lavinia, why it was he wished he could remain in this small, cramped space longer.

It wasn't a need to escape his responsibilities. Nor was it that he didn't appreciate the privilege into which he'd been born. Yet for some time now, a dissatisfaction had been harping at him, and he'd been unable to identify its exact cause. He'd thought it was his advancing age and lack of an heir. At thirty-six, he was past the time when he should have a wife and a son. But if he were honest with himself, which was becoming increasingly difficult of late, he'd been rather relieved to have been spared the exchange of vows when his bride never appeared.

His pride had been rather mortified. Hence his foray into the darker realms of London, where much to his surprise he'd discovered a ray of light.

Now his thoughts were turning pathetically poetic. He'd very nearly died.

Shifting his body, striving to push himself into a sitting position, reminded him quite forcefully of that fact as his wounds protested those particular portions of his anatomy being put back into use. With a great deal of effort that caused him to break out in a cold sweat, he finally managed to be upright, his back pressed against a mound of pillows.

It was only then he realized his exertions had not been accompanied by the unpleasant odor of illness, but rather the scent of her. A faint waft of vanilla. She'd bathed him, no doubt after his fever broke, when he was lost in a deep sleep. She'd also managed to change the bedding without disturbing him. Casting aside the crisp and fresh sheet, he noted the bandages protecting his thigh and side were pristine. He rather regretted he'd slept through her ministrations. He wondered if she'd blushed, if she did indeed blush. The room was more shadow than light, and he suddenly longed for the roof to crumble away and sunlight to stream in, longed to be in possession of his damned spectacles.

When she walked into the room, he almost asked her to wait at the threshold, to give him a moment to study her, to appreciate her features in sharper focus, but she'd no doubt believe the fever had addled his brain. Besides, his interest in her was probably a result of the close quarters, the intimacy of his being in her bed with only a sheet and blanket separating his skin from the air, and the attention with which she'd cared for him. Once he walked out of here, he was unlikely to give her any further thought. He had more important matters requiring his attention, matters directly affecting his holdings and his status and duties.

"I'm glad to see you found the strength to sit up," she said as she set the tray on his lap. "Because you should give feeding yourself a try."

Taking up the bundle of clothes, she sat in the chair and watched him, encouragement and hope reflected in her eyes. From this distance, within these shadows, they appeared brown. Strange how he had no desire to disappoint them.

Using the spoon, he gathered up some lamb, carrots, peas, and potatoes. His hand shook slightly, from weakness he supposed, as he carried the utensil to his mouth, acutely aware of her easing up in the chair, ready to assist if necessary. He'd rather die than continue to exhibit weakness in front of her. It was bad enough she'd had to tend to him, bathe him, keep him alive. But all his unhappy thoughts dissolved as the food hit his mouth. Never in his life had he tasted anything so good. His stomach fairly leaped up in an effort to get to it sooner, and he nearly groaned with pleasure. "You're an excellent cook."

"I'm a lousy cook." Settling back in the chair, she smoothed out the trousers in her lap. "I retrieved it from the kitchen below. I have an excellent cook who works for me."

"I've never known a woman to own a business."

"I'm not the first." She began sewing. "It took a bit of help from my brother, though."

Her tone was telling. "You weren't pleased about that."

Her chin came up, her shoulders stiffened, her gaze never left the needle, which was suddenly moving with greater speed. "I'd have preferred to do it on my own, but I couldn't get a loan from the bank."

"How many brothers have you?"

"Four. And a sister." She did look up then. "You?"

"None now. Illness took my brother and sister. And my father. All those deaths have made a wreck of my mother."

"Had to be hard on you as well."

"It made me appreciate that Death could visit at any time. I thought he was breathing down my neck the other night, swore I could see him hovering in the corner. But you wouldn't let him have me."

Her lips turned up ever so slightly and there was a twinkle in her eyes. "I'm stubborn that way."

"How fortunate I am then that it was you who came to my rescue."

She nodded toward the bowl. "Would you care for more?"

Only then did he realize it was nearly gone. He'd been talking between bites, paying more attention to her than the food, regardless of how delicious it was. She was much more appetizing and interesting.

"Perhaps later. I don't want to overdo it." Besides, the effort had sapped nearly all his energy. He didn't want her to have to spoon the pie into his mouth as though he were a babe.

Getting up, she took the bowl from him, set it aside, and returned to her chair. "Do you think you might feel up to traveling? Have you a home to go to?"

Her question took him by surprise, although on further thought he realized, living in this part of London, she probably knew a great number of people who didn't have a shelter. "I have."

"Your mother must be worried."

"I doubt it. I was never her favorite."

"I find that difficult to believe. Every child is a mother's favorite."

"Not in our family, I'm afraid."

"I'm certain you're wrong on that score. Sometimes—"

The knock on the door came loud and quick, followed by a shout. "Gillie!"

A man's voice, an irritated man if he judged correctly. "I didn't think you had a husband."

"I don't, but I do have a brother." She was already on her feet and heading for the door. "Keep very quiet," she tossed over her shoulder before leaving the room and closing the door behind her.

Tossing back the covers, he gingerly moved his legs off the bed. Breathing far too heavily, he cursed the footpads who had left him in such a weakened state. He needed to at least get to the door, listen, and ensure he wasn't needed to come to her aid. Although he couldn't quite envision the most remarkable woman he'd ever met being in need of rescue.

MICK TREWLOVE DIDN'T wait to be invited in. As soon as she opened the door, her oldest brother strode boldly over the threshold as though expecting to find something amiss or some nefarious soul about who might try to stop him. Coming to a halt in the middle of the room, he glanced slowly around before finally turning to look at her. "I've heard you haven't been working for a few days now. Are you unwell?"

"No. I simply wanted some time to myself."

His eyes narrowing, he shifted his attention to the closed door that led in to her bedchamber. It took everything within her not to leap in front of him and bar his view, as though he had the power to look through wood to see what was being harbored on the other side. "I've been working since I was a wee girl. I didn't think my absence would put everyone in an uproar."

His gaze returned to her, but she could see suspicion lurking in the blue of his eyes. "I'm not in an uproar, but the others had concerns."

"So they sent for you." Because he was considered

the oldest, even though none of them knew the exact date they were born—only the day they were delivered to Ettie Trewlove's door. Interfering brothers, the lot of them. "That must have pleased your wife immensely, to be abandoned—"

"I'll make it up to her when I return home, much to her delight I'm sure." His gaze darted back over to the door. "Jolly Roger said you pop down every now and then to check on things—"

"Yes, everything's running smoothly. He knows what he's doing."

"Do you?" he asked sharply, his eyes once again homing in on her, as though he were well aware she was harboring secrets.

But if he found out there was a man in her bed, it wouldn't matter that the gent was injured or too weak to create a fuss or take advantage. Mick would see her married. Her brother cared far too much about respectability, which was one of the reasons that, two weeks before, he'd married an earl's daughter. The other, and more pressing motive, being that he'd fallen madly in love with her. "Don't you ever get weary of working all the time?"

He crossed his arms over his chest. "What aren't you telling me, Gillie?"

"Nothing. I'll return to work tomorrow." She heaved an impatient sigh. "I'll return this very minute if you're so bothered—"

He held up his hand. "Don't be rash."

"I'm not the one who burst in accusing—"

"I wasn't accusing you of anything. I was concerned. It's not like you to disappear for days on end—"

"It was a couple of days and I didn't *disappear*."

"You retreated."

"I didn't retreat. Damn it, Mick! I just wanted some time to myself."

The flare of her temper seemed to satisfy him as her words hadn't. He gave a brusque nod. "All right then." He glanced around once more, his gaze lingering on the blasted bedroom door. "I'll leave you to whatever you were doing."

He headed for the front portal. His abrupt departure irritated her almost as much as his arrival had. What if she wasn't finished speaking with him? "Did you arrive in your carriage?"

Stopping, he faced her. "I did."

She could go in search of a hansom, but his carriage would provide a more comfortable ride. "After your driver takes you home, could he return here? I have a use for a carriage this evening."

Those irritating, penetrating eyes of his narrowed once more. "I'll escort you wherever you need to go."

"I don't need you to escort me." She threw up her hands in frustration. "Never mind. I'll get a hansom."

"Don't be daft. My carriage is safer. My driver will protect you if need be."

"I don't need protecting. I simply want to take a drive through London at night. I'm always working in the evening, and I am curious regarding what the city looks like for those who have leisure after darkness falls." What rubbish! That she could say all that with a straight face astounded her, but as long as she didn't make him suspicious regarding why she needed the carriage, perhaps he wouldn't question his driver on the morrow. And if he did, well, by then the man would be out of her life and she could stand up on her own to Mick's scrutiny. The key was to ensure he didn't confront Thorne now, didn't learn of his presence.

"I'll have my carriage return for you then."

"Give me your word you won't ask your driver where he goes tonight."

"Gillie—"

"It's nothing nefarious, I promise. But if you can't give me your word on that, I'll hire a hansom."

He studied her for a long moment before finally sighing in defeat. "You have my word. I simply hope you know what you're doing."

"I do. Have your driver bring the carriage around to the mews. Although it may be a few hours before I'm ready to go out, so he's welcome to have a pint while he waits in the tavern." She'd also offer him a small stipend to discourage him from volunteering any information to her brother.

"He'll appreciate that." He turned for the door.

"Mick?"

Once more he stopped, looked back at her.

"Thank you for stopping by to ensure all was well."

"We know you're a strong woman, Gillie, perfectly capable of taking care of yourself, but you're our sister and we do worry about you being all alone here."

"I know you do. I'd tell you if something was amiss."

"See that you do." And with that he was gone.

She released a huge sigh of relief that she'd gotten away with him not learning the truth regarding her absence. Now she had a way to send her guest on his way. Odd then that she wasn't happier about it.

She returned to her bedchamber to find Thorne sitting on the edge of the bed, studying the floor as though it contained some code to be deciphered, the sheet draped across his hips, sweat beading his face and neck, his breathing labored.

"And just what do you think you're about?" she

asked, standing in the doorway, arms crossed, legs akimbo.

He lifted his gaze to her. "It was my intent to be ready in case you required assistance."

Men were the most stubborn of creatures. "If you'd fallen flat on your face I'd have had to pick you up. Back into bed with you."

"No. I'm weary of lying about. I need to sit up for a while, gather my bearings."

He probably had the right of that. When she was under the weather, she worked through it, fearing if she showed any weakness at all, she'd succumb to the demands of the illness. "Would you care for a cuppa tea? Or whisky?"

He grinned. She did wish he wouldn't do that. It caused her insides to riot. "Tea with a splash of whisky."

"I shan't be long." As she headed for her kitchen, she rather regretted that before dawn, she'd be sending him home.

SHE DRAPED A blanket over his shoulders before handing him the cup of tea with whisky. Surely it was only his imagination that caused him to feel revitalized by the brew. Or perhaps it was the woman sitting nearby working fastidiously to mend his clothing. She'd finished with his trousers and was now busily weaving needle and thread through the fabric of his shirt. As the white linen wasn't stained with his blood, she'd obviously washed it at some point. He wondered what else she might have done of which he was unaware.

"I'm sorry I don't have any boots for you to wear," she said quietly. "I thought mine might do but I fear your feet are much larger."

"A curse that affects the men in my family." He couldn't be certain but she appeared to be blushing. Interesting.

"I thought about asking one of my brothers to lend me a pair but then I'd have to explain . . ." Her voice trailed off as she lifted a delicate shoulder. Hard to believe now that shoulder had provided him with such solid support the first night, when she'd never waivered in her determination to get him up the stairs so she could tend to him.

"That wouldn't do."

"I'm afraid not. I know you're not fully recovered, but I think you've healed enough that you won't bleed to death in the carriage."

"That's jolly good news."

She lifted her gaze to him. "My brother has a fine carriage. I'll instruct the driver to go slowly."

The time had come, the minutes left to them were slipping away, and there was still so much about her that he didn't know, that he wanted to know. "I can't imagine a merchant or trader would have allowed his daughter to work as a step-girl."

"I should hope not." Her focus returned to her needle-work, and he found himself envious of his clothing because it garnered her attention.

"I'm striving to be delicate here, but you don't speak as though you come from the streets. And if you own a tavern, you must have had a basic education."

"A ragged school opened near where we lived and my mum made certain we went. She struggled to read and cipher, and always felt her lack of learning had limited her options for finding work when she became a widow. She wanted us to have better lives."

He was familiar with ragged schools, so named because most of the children were destitute and came to school dressed in rags. The Earl of Shaftesbury was legendary for his commitment to establishing the free schools in the poorest sections of Britain, a good many of them here in London. Thorne didn't like having the confirmation that she'd grown up in poverty. She'd obviously risen above it. His present surroundings were Spartan, but he recognized well-crafted furniture when he saw it. "You seem more educated than that."

"I've picked up a few things here and about." She lifted the garment until she was able to bite off the thread. "There. That should do it." She tossed the shirt onto his lap and stood. "Do you think you can dress without my assistance?"

Apparently, he wasn't going to learn anything else about her and rather regretted that. "I'll do my best."

"I'm going to let the driver know he needs to finish his pint as we'll be needing him soon. I'll return shortly, and we'll see about getting you on your way."

She headed out of the room, closing the door in her wake. He couldn't seem to find the wherewithal to function, to put on his shirt and trousers. He should be happy, ecstatic, about leaving. He needed to return to his life, his quest, and his responsibilities. But he wasn't happy—at all.

NEAR THE HOUR when she'd first discovered him, with one arm securely wrapped about his waist, she ushered him out her door and began the slow, arduous trek down the stairs. From her box of items abandoned by customers, she'd managed to find a walking stick. Not a fancy one, but it would help support him so he could keep the bulk of his weight off his bad leg.

The tavern was closed up for the night. The streets were mostly inhabited by rodents, scurrying about. Mick's carriage was not too far off.

"Good God, what's this then?" the driver suddenly blurted, charging up the stairs, his heavy footsteps causing them to shake and rattle. He eased her aside, taking over her role.

She hated relinquishing her claim on Thorne, but it was pointless to argue with the coachman. Besides, the stranger who no longer seemed like a stranger didn't belong to her, not really. She'd never see him again after tonight. Perhaps she should have given him another day to heal. Silly chit. She had a business to run and he had a life to get back to, chasing whatever dream had brought him here in the first place, a dream that no doubt involved the woman for whom he was looking, the one he'd mentioned during one of his less lucid states.

When they reached the carriage, he resisted being shoved inside. Instead, grabbing the door opening with one hand, he turned to her and ever so gently cradled her face with the other. "I don't know how to properly thank you."

"Capture that dream you were chasing, but do it with a bit more care."

His grin was small, but a grin all the same. "And at a more reasonable hour, I daresay. Thank you, Gillie."

She felt an odd stinging in her eyes. If she were the sort of woman who wept, she might have thought the discomfort was caused by tears. "You take care of yourself now."

"I shall. You be happy."

"I always am." Or she had always been. Why wasn't

she overjoyed by the prospect of him being on his merry way so she could return to a life she'd always cherished?

With the driver's assistance, he managed to get into the carriage. She heard their low voices, no doubt as they discussed where he was to be taken. She was grateful that she couldn't make out the words, couldn't be tempted to stroll through his neighborhood and past his residence in the hopes of running into him. The coachman slammed the door shut, doffed his hat at her, and climbed up onto his seat. With a flick of his wrist, a slap of the reins, he urged the horses into a steady clip that had the conveyance disappearing quickly into the fog, leaving her with an unsettling sensation that it was taking a part of her with it.

"So who was that?"

With a low groan, she swung around and glared at Mick. "You were supposed to go home hours ago."

"Did you think I couldn't tell you were hiding something, Gil? I couldn't see him clearly, but he looked to be a beggar. How did he come to be with you?"

She wanted to tell him it was none of his business, but her brother wasn't one to give up easily. "He was attacked a few nights ago. Injured. I ran the ruffians off. I was only caring for him until he was strong enough to be on his way."

"And you felt a need to keep that from me?"

Sighing, she rolled her eyes. "A man in my quarters. I thought you might force me to marry him. He feared you might."

"He should be so lucky."

Stepping nearer, he placed his arm around her shoulders, drew her in close. She was only an inch or so shorter than he, which made it easy to press his head to hers. "Gil, you never have to keep secrets from me. There is nothing you can do, nothing you can say that I would judge harshly. And I would certainly never insist, under any circumstances, you marry a bloke you had no wish to marry."

Deep inside, she'd known that, of course. "I'm sorry I made you worry."

"Any idea who he is?"

She shook her head. "He goes by Thorne. That's all I know. You're not to ask your driver where he delivered him and you most certainly are not to pay him a visit."

"I gave you my word earlier I wouldn't make inquiries of my driver. I'm not a man who goes back on his word."

"I know, but I can tell you're tempted."

"I am, but I won't. Do you know where he's going?"

"I don't want to know. He seemed pleasant enough. Spoke like a toff. But it really doesn't matter. I'm certain I'll never see him again."

Chapter 6

*H*e was grateful to have arrived in the dead of night. The only person about was a young footman who'd no doubt been charged with being on hand to assist him when he returned from his adventures and, based upon the rubbing of his eyes, had seen fit to fall asleep in a chair in the foyer.

When fully awake, the man dropped his jaw and widened his eyes, obviously unprepared for the sight of his master's disheveled appearance and lack of footwear. "Your Grace." He sounded positively appalled.

"Alert my valet I'm need of his assistance, then fetch my physician. Be quick and quiet. Awaken only those needed to see to your task. There is no reason to alarm the entire household."

"Yes, sir." He bolted down a hallway that would eventually lead him to the servants' quarters.

Thorne began the slow, arduous climb up the grand sweeping stairs, using the banister to pull himself up one step at a time, recalling another night when he'd done the same, only a woman had been tucked beneath his arm, providing him with support and words of encouragement. He found himself running those same words through his mind now. The pain was not as great, but the discomfort was still there. He was far more weakened than he would have liked, but he was regaining his strength. A few more days and he'd be as good as new.

At the top of the stairs, he turned down a corridor that took him away from the bedchamber and suite of rooms designated as belonging to the duke and duchess. He had yet to be able to bring himself to claim those rooms as his since it would mean casting his mother from hers and he had no desire to sleep in a bedchamber next to hers. As long as she resided in his residence, those rooms remained her domain.

By the time he arrived at his bedchamber, he was breathing heavily and sweating profusely. His stubborn nature had refused to allow him to rest until he'd reached his destination—the same stubbornness he'd employed the night he met Gillie, who had demonstrated an equal stubbornness. Gingerly he lowered himself into a plush brown chair near the fireplace. It was an odd thing to sit there wishing his rescuer had witnessed his accomplishment.

"Your Grace."

He wasn't surprised he hadn't heard his valet enter. The man had the good manners to walk about without making a sound. However, he did hear the concern etched in his voice. "Speight. It seems I got into a spot of bother. Help me undress. The physician should be here soon."

"Your absence had us most worried." His valet went to work.

"I was not in a position to send word."

"So it would appear," Speight said slowly once he'd removed the shirt and encountered the bandages. "The duchess will be most distressed."

He very much doubted that. "We're not going to tell the duchess. I'm on the mend."

With assistance from his valet, he discarded his trousers.

"Whatever happened, sir?" As a rule, Speight never pried, but then never before had Thorne shown up in such a state.

"I was set upon by thugs." He made his way to his bed and crawled beneath the covers. "Bring the physician here as soon as he arrives."

"Yes, sir." Speight gathered up Thorne's clothes and headed for the door.

"Where are you taking those?"

"To the rubbish heap."

Which was where they belonged. They were no longer serviceable. Still, he couldn't help but think that his rescuer's stitching deserved a better end. "Place them in the wardrobe for now as a reminder of my stupidity."

"As you wish." He'd taken two steps before stopping and looking back at Thorne. "We were supremely disheartened to hear the marriage did not occur."

He suspected they were more discouraged there was not yet a new duchess of Coventry House.

"We are all praying for Lady Lavinia's hasty recovery from whatever illness befell her."

Thorne slammed his eyes closed. Ah, yes, everyone believed she was ill. He had to find her, discover why she had felt a need to run, and determine if they could still make a go of it, lest he be made to look a fool. Although that result might have already occurred. "Send in the physician when he arrives," he repeated, not feeling a need to confide in his valet.

He must have drifted off to sleep, because the next thing he knew someone was gently nudging his shoulder. When he opened his eyes, he was disappointed to find himself staring into the bearded face of his physician and not the perfect oval of the woman who'd cared for him. "Anderson."

"Your Grace. I understand you're in need of my services."

He gave a brief accounting of his injuries, avoiding the specifics of what had led to him being attacked. Then he endured the discomfort of the doctor examining each wound.

"Graves is quite skilled, Your Grace. You're fortunate he was called for. I see no sign of putrefaction or infection. I daresay he cleaned each wound thoroughly before stitching it up as they all seem to be healing quite nicely. How do you feel overall?"

"Tired. Weak. Frustrated by my limitations."

"You no doubt lost a considerable amount of blood. I'd stay abed a few days if I were you. You're on the mend, but you don't want to push it."

After Anderson left, Thorne told Speight, "When the duchess makes an appearance, inform her I have returned but am not quite myself, and will see her when I am. Send a missive to the Earl of Collinsworth and alert him I shall call on him Sunday afternoon." The wedding was to have taken place on Wednesday. Lavinia had chosen that particular day because according to an old wives' tale, it was the luckiest of all days. Perhaps that was the reason he was still alive. Another day might have brought him death.

No, he was alive because of a tavern owner's determination to make it so.

By the time Sunday morning rolled around—after hours of sleeping or sitting in a chair staring at a fire and wondering how things had gone so horribly wrong—he was still experiencing considerable discomfort and weariness, but was determined to get on with his life and set matters to rights. Following a bath and a shave, dressed in proper attire for the day, he felt more himself, even if it was a slightly ghostly version of himself, the bruises on his face fading but still visible.

Slower than he would have liked, he made his way to the breakfast dining room. From her place at the table, his mother sniffed, her nose in the air. "It is unseemly for you to go off on benders and get into brawls as though you were a commoner with no pride about you at all."

Unlike most married women who took their breakfast in bed, she had always come down for hers as though she felt a need to serve up an argument with the meal. Her husband had accommodated her. Thorne was not so inclined. "My health is much improved. Thank you for asking."

He had a footman assist him with his plate before joining her at the table.

"That girl made laughingstocks of us," she said tartly. "I don't care how ill she was—"

"She wasn't ill, Mother. She ran off."

Staring at him, she slowly blinked. "Then why in God's name did you announce she was ill?"

"To save my pride." He shoved his plate aside. "To give myself a chance to determine how best to handle this situation."

"You handle the matter by finding the girl and marrying her. Otherwise, we shall be made to look even greater fools."

He very much doubted he could look any more foolish, but he did need to find Lavinia. Whether he could go through with the marriage was another matter entirely. Although he'd promised *his* father on his deathbed that he'd honor the contract made with *her* father. Her dowry included a large estate, Wood's End—an estate every Duke of Thornley before him had coveted—that edged up against the Thornley ancestral estate, land that would expand Thornley Castle from four thousand acres to six. But the previous earls had proved somewhat lacking when it came to producing girls. Until Lavinia. Their fathers had signed the contract. Her fate and his had been sealed. Perhaps when faced with the moment of exchanging vows, she'd realized she needed more. In hindsight, he couldn't claim to be unhappy that he was not yet wed. "I don't know that marriage to her is the answer."

"Make it the answer."

With a sigh, he shoved back his chair and stood. "I shall handle the matter as I see fit. This afternoon, I shall meet with Collinsworth."

"You have a duty—"

"I am well aware of my responsibilities." Heading out of the room, he made his way to his office, one of the smaller libraries in the residence. Books adorned the shelves, windows looked out on the gardens. At fifteen, sitting behind the desk with the full weight of his rank bearing down on him, he'd been terrified of making a mistake. Now he took his place in the leather chair with the full confidence of a man who was comfortable in his position.

His butler had laid out the letters from each day's post with a note before each stack identifying the day of their arrival. The two letters from Thursday were from his estate managers. Friday's stack was a bit higher. Taking the top letter, he tore the envelope and took out the parchment.

Dear Duke,
Your kindness to your bride, putting her
happiness above your own pride, will long be
remembered. You touched the hearts of ladies
everywhere.

Yours sincerely,
The Countess of Yawn

The next was no better.

Dear Duke,
I fear all ladies will now feign illness at the
church to test our devotion at the altar. You did
us other chaps no favors.
We pray you will delay your next wedding
date until after the regatta.

Not as sincerely as you might like,
The Duke of Castleberry

The next three letters ran in a similar vein. The ladies
commended him, the lords wished he'd made his bride
get on with things. He was on the verge of tossing the
whole lot of unopened letters in the rubbish bin when
he realized the next one gave no indication on the
envelope where it was from. The wax that held the
envelope closed was merely a blob, no distinguishing
seal. With care he opened it, and read the letter.

Dear Thorne:
I hope you will accept my sincerest apology for
having left you at the altar, but I did not see that
I had a choice. Upon my birth, your father and
mine signed a contract sealing our fate without any
consideration for what we might want. I thought

I could be a good daughter and carry through on my father's promises and wishes, but being a good daughter has never been my strong suit.

I regret now that I did not speak with you but as my brother assured me nothing I said would change the outcome, I feared our marriage would be off to an awkward start if you knew I had misgivings. I was taught to see to my duty, but as I stood in the vestry, I could not bring myself to condemn us both to a life of unhappiness.

If you are honest with yourself, I suspect you will find you were quite relieved by my failure to show. While you never treated me unkindly, I cannot help but feel that the only thing to bind us was a piece of property, and you deserve more. For whatever embarrassment I might have brought you, I am sincerely sorry, and I hope eventually you will find it within your heart to forgive me, although I suspect I shall never forgive myself for my cowardice. There are a good many things for which I cannot forgive myself, and in the end, they would have made me an exceedingly bad wife indeed.

I wish you only the very best. If you have any kind feelings for me at all, know I am well, safe, and sheltered.

With my warmest regards,
Lavinia

"GOOD GOD, OLD boy! What the devil happened to you?" Collinsworth exclaimed, getting up from behind his desk as Thorne limped into the earl's library in late afternoon.

He knew he looked a fright, with a bruise about his

eye, a scrape on his chin, his left arm in a sling to keep the pressure off his shoulder, and an old walking stick—with thorny vines carved in the wood and a golden lion's head at the tip—that had once been used by his grandfather providing support for his healing leg. The cane Gillie had given him had been serviceable, but hardly dapper.

"I got into a bit of bother a few nights back in White-chapel, looking for your sister."

"And had no luck finding her, I'd wager." Collins-worth wandered over to the sideboard and poured whisky into two glasses. "Make yourself comfortable."

Thorne lowered himself into a rather plush chair near the window, welcoming the warmth of sunlight. Setting his walking stick aside, he took the glass the earl offered him and savored the flavor.

"I don't suppose she's returned." Based on her letter, he thought it unlikely, but there was always hope.

"No, although to be honest, I expected her back by now. I thought perhaps it was simply a lark or she'd gotten cold feet."

Collinsworth took a nearby chair, cupped his glass in both hands, and leaned forward, his elbows on his thighs. "I didn't know precisely how to explain things on the day you were to marry and I don't know what to say now. She'd asked for a few minutes in the necessary room. I couldn't very well deny her the opportunity to relieve herself. I didn't expect her to sneak out the window. I don't even know how she managed it. I've searched for her myself and have hired two men to find her."

Her actions spoke of a desperation that worried Thorne. "I've had a letter from her, letting me know she is all right."

"Yes, she sent us a rather terse note informing us she was safe and not to come looking for her," Collinsworth said.

Thorne had a feeling there was a good deal Lavinia had not included in her letter. "Yet, you've hired men to find her."

"She has an obligation. Our fathers signed a contract. You and I came to terms. She will be found and she will see to her duty."

"I'm not going to force the girl into marriage." He could envision nothing worse than taking to his bed a woman who had no wish to be there. "She told you she had misgivings."

"Did she tell you that in her letter? Silly chit. She was going to become a duchess. Any misgivings she had were trite when compared with all she would gain."

"I'm surprised she didn't run off the night before."

Collinsworth shifted uncomfortably in his chair. "She may have been locked in her bedchamber," he said quietly.

Thorne was beginning to question his friendship with Collinsworth. "You imprisoned her?"

"Mother saw to that. I'd have not approved had I known, but she mentioned it only after Lavinia ran off."

"She spoke to your mother about her doubts?"

"I suppose. There is power, prestige, position that comes with marriage to you. She is five and twenty. On the shelf. The truth is the two of you should have married years ago, before she became accustomed to being unwed and doing as she pleased." He leaned forward earnestly. "Mother wants this match as much as Father did and is insistent she will marry you."

"And if I no longer wish to marry her?" Lavinia had the right of it. Knowing she had doubts regarding him made it incredibly difficult to see a path toward an amicable marriage.

The earl downed his whisky, settled back, and studied Thorne. "I'll add the estate of Foxglove to her dowry for the inconvenience her theatrics have caused if you'll see your way clear to still marrying her once she is found. It will be less mortifying for all concerned if the marriage goes forward. You announced she was ill. Do you really want to now announce to the world that your bride abandoned you?"

"I'm thinking it might be preferable to marrying a woman who abandoned me."

"Let's not be rash. She had no reason not to marry you. She has a tendency to be flighty and overdramatic."

He'd never noticed either of those particular traits in her. As a matter of fact, he'd always found her to be levelheaded, and had thought she'd manage his household with a great deal of aplomb.

"Besides, it could just be that she had doubts because your courting of her was lacking."

He hated to admit that Collinsworth might have the right of it. He'd shown her attention, but in retrospect he'd been rather lazy in his pursuit of her because pursuit had not been required. The marriage had been arranged, and aware of her age, he'd realized he might be bringing her mortification by not taking her to wife as soon as he might have. He needed to speak with her, to understand fully what had sent her fleeing. "Why Whitechapel?"

"I haven't a clue," Collinsworth said.

"Who does she know there?"

The earl appeared completely flummoxed. "As far as I know, she's never visited that area of London. It's not as though there are any shops worth her while there." He bent forward. "Look, old chap, I will see her found. I will see she understands her duty. She's a spinster, well on her way to becoming an old maid. She should be groveling at your feet."

Only Thorne didn't want a woman who groveled, and an image of a woman who would never grovel flashed through his mind. "Let's see what she has to say for herself once we find her. Since I announced only that the marriage was postponed, perhaps both our prides can be salvaged."

"I promised Father I would see her well married. She's gone and made a mess of things."

And he'd promised *his* father he would see Wood's End annexed onto the Thornley Castle estate, bring only honor and no scandal to his title, and marry an upstanding noblewoman to carry on the untainted bloodline. He'd promised to make him proud. It was quite possible that promises made would prove to be the ruin of them all.

Chapter 7

$\mathcal{S}$he knew the moment Thorne strode through the door and into the tavern. It was as though every particle of air had become charged with his power, his confidence.

Mortified to admit it, since the carriage had carried him away two nights earlier, she'd imagined this moment, wished for it, yearned for his return. She'd missed him, which was bloody ridiculous. He was nothing to her. More importantly, she was nothing to him.

Now that he was here, she rather wished he wasn't. The entire establishment had gone deathly quiet, as though each person knew someone significant had entered, something momentous was on the verge of taking place. Perhaps it was the way his gaze had latched onto hers, held her captive. Or the way he stood there, just waiting for God knew what, decked out in well-tailored clothing that fit him to perfection. A flawlessly knotted white cravat, a muted gray brocade waistcoat, a dark blue coat, tanned trousers, brown gloves. He'd removed his hat to reveal hair tamed into a style she doubted would allow the strands to wrap around her fingers. Very recently, he'd taken a razor to his jaw. And he carried a walking stick, much nicer than the one she'd given him.

He was so incredibly beautiful that it fairly hurt her eyes to gaze on him.

Even if she wanted, she'd have not been able to look away. Instead, she feasted on the sight of him as though he were a gift from the gods or a god himself. In spite of all her wishing for his return, she hadn't truly expected he would.

Then he began striding across the tavern, a slight limp not distracting from his bearing in the least, working his way between the tables and drunkards with such confidence and purpose some men simply leaped out of his way as though afraid he'd mow them down. Although it was impossible, it seemed the place got even quieter, the customers even more still.

Her brother Finn, leaning negligently against the bar waiting for her to hand over the pint she'd poured for him, was alert, and out of the corner of her eye, she could see the tension radiating off him as though he sensed trouble might be afoot. Any other night, any other moment, she would have reassured him, told him to relax, but she couldn't find the wherewithal to speak. She was mesmerized like some silly chit who had dreams of being romanced, courted, loved, and who believed the only man capable of fulfilling those fantasies had entered her life.

Then he was standing before her, and for all her imaginings of this moment—all the times in her mind that she'd been calm, witty, and oh so very clever—the actual reality hit her as a bit disappointing when she heard herself ask, "What are you doing here?"

Both corners of that glorious mouth that had haunted her sleep hitched up. Slowly, ever so slowly he reached into a pocket inside his jacket, withdrew gold-rimmed spectacles, and perched them on that sharp aquiline nose of his. How could he suddenly appear even more masculine than before? "I wanted a better look at you."

That look no doubt included a swath of red racing up her neck, over her cheeks, and into her hairline. She wasn't one for blushing, but if the heat swarming through her was any indication, she was doing so now with unerring success.

"Why the bloody hell would you want that and when did you get a not-so-good look at her before?" Finn asked, with stony calm. Anyone who knew him recognized that tone usually preceded the swing of a fist.

Thorne merely arched a brow, and gave him a once-over as though her brother were nothing, of no more consequence than a fly. "What's it to you?"

Oh, yes, if four men hadn't jumped him, he'd have not been taken down. One or two, possibly three, would have met their match. The fourth had sealed his fate.

Breaking free of the unconscionable spell under which she'd fallen, she set the pewter tankard on the bar. "He's my brother. It's all right, Finn. Our paths crossed a few nights ago. Head off to enjoy your brew."

"Not until I know who this bloke is."

"Finn—"

"Antony Coventry, Duke of Thornley."

Bloody hell. The curse slipped out low, under her breath, but still he heard it. Those Guinness eyes narrowed. Of course he was a duke. And all those ridiculous thoughts she'd had of him sweeping her off her feet were even more ludicrous. She knew all about the nobility, their ranks, how they were to be addressed, because Mick had been involved with a duke's widow in his youth, and in exchange for his "services" she taught him a good deal about how the upper class set themselves apart from the riffraff, and Mick had shared his knowledge with her and their brothers. They'd always all been in it together—bettering themselves and doing what was needed to rise above their station—sharing anything they learned with each other. So she was well aware that a nobleman wasn't going to fall for the likes of her, a tavern owner raised in the streets who used one knife, one fork, and one spoon when she ate. He was here merely to express his appreciation. If he offered her money, she was going to punch him in his uninjured shoulder.

Finn seemed unimpressed, but then he had no love for the nobility and wasn't above displaying his disdain.

"Off with you, Finn," she ordered.

"Does he have anything to do with you not working for a few days?"

She slapped his upper arm, always surprised by the firm muscle that greeted her. He was no slouch, her brother. "None of your business." Then she looked past him to the gaping horde. "You lot! Quit your staring and get back to your drinking before I toss you all out on your ears." She returned her glare to her brother. "Same applies to you. Get on. Beast is over there waiting on you."

With deliberate calm, he picked up his tankard and lifted it toward the duke. "I'll be watching."

He strode off to join Beast at a back table. She wasn't surprised her other brother had stayed put. He wasn't one to interfere without an invite to do so, unless he determined the situation was such that an invitation *couldn't* be issued. As a rule, he was more thoughtful, slower to respond than the others, but when he did react, he poured every bit of himself into his actions.

"Pleasant fellow."

She gave her attention back to Thorne. Thinking of him as such seemed too informal now that she knew Graves had been correct and this man's moniker was a shortened version of his title. "He has his moments. I hadn't expected to see you again."

"I owe you, although I wasn't quite sure how much." He reached into his inside jacket pocket. "I was thinking—"

"You don't pay a good Samaritan."

"I want to show my appreciation."

"Then give it to a foundling home."

He studied her for a long moment that seemed to stretch into next week. "I've insulted you."

"Yes."

"That was not my intent."

"Then when you remove your hand from your pocket, be sure it's empty."

He gave a slight nod. "You're a stubborn wench."

"With a fairly powerful right-handed punch when I need one."

Grinning, he removed his gloved hand from inside his jacket. She was glad he'd heeded her warning, as she'd have not enjoyed pummeling him. "What can I pour you?"

"Whisky."

Not bothering to ask if he wanted the expensive stuff, she simply poured it and set it before him. "On the house."

"Join me."

She did wish those two little words didn't make her heart go all aflutter as though he were implying something more personal, something that might result in her losing her spot in heaven. "I have a policy of not drinking with customers. No good ever comes from blurring the lines." She did hope he understood that lines between them couldn't be blurred, that she was a mermaid and he was a blasted unicorn.

"If it's on the house, I'm not paying for it, so I'm not a customer. I'd like to have a word. Perhaps at that corner table where there aren't so many people jostling about."

She was fairly certain he wasn't accustomed to being denied anything he'd like to have—even a conversation. If she were smart, she'd continue to deny him what he wanted, make her position clear: they were not and never would be friends. She might have embraced a bit of whimsy when naming her tavern, but she understood the realities of the world, that there were those born into privilege while the majority of people were simply born and had to shape their own world. If she did deem to join him, she'd have to ensure she didn't make a fool of herself. She signaled to Jolly Roger that she was taking a break, poured herself only a bit of whisky, and led the bloody duke to the table he'd indicated, taking a chair before he had time to pull one out for her—if he even would have. Once he was seated, she lifted her glass. "To your good health."

She took a sip, watched him do the same, fought not to squirm as he studied her over the rim of his glass, the spectacles making his gaze seem more intense, his features more distinguished. Why did he have to be so frightfully gorgeous? She'd spent her entire life avoiding being drawn to men, and this one was melting her resistance without even trying. He was dangerous because all these unwelcomed feelings he stirred within her had her comprehending why women would lift their skirts. "You wanted a word," she finally said impatiently, anxious to get back to the bar where there was a wooden barrier between them.

"You're not happy I'm a duke."

So much for her ability to keep her feelings from being on display. "Makes no difference to me."

Leaning back, he tapped a finger on the table. "You have me at a disadvantage, as I don't know your full name."

"I don't see that it matters."

"I can make inquiries. Could probably ask that gent two tables over."

She sighed, because the less they knew about each other, the easier it would be to keep her distance. "Gillian Trewlove."

"Trewlove." He repeated the name as though it were a tasty morsel. "You're not related to Mick Trewlove, are you?"

"He's my brother."

He squinted, seemed to be racking his brain. "I don't recall seeing you at his wedding. Did you not attend?"

She laughed lightly. "As though you'd have noticed me if I had."

"Oh, I'd have noticed you."

ALTHOUGH THE INSIDE of the tavern was more shadowy than he'd have liked, with his spectacles firmly in place, he could see her more clearly, more sharply than ever. Her hair reminded him of the burnished autumn leaves at Thornley Castle. He'd always fancied walking or riding through the forest when the cooler air arrived and the trees brought forth their fall colors.

He imagined the pleasure of sinking his hands into the luxurious tresses cascading about her shoulders—no, he'd only be able to indulge his fingers by burying them in the thick short strands. He'd take great satisfaction from that, however.

As much pleasure as he took from simply gazing on her. She'd had freckles as a child. They'd left behind faint markings that made her features all the more interesting, gave them character. She wasn't polished alabaster. She was life, adventure, daring. He doubted she'd ever worn a hat, but preferred to let the sun have its way with her.

Would she let him have his way with her? Staring into her eyes that seemed to be a mix of green and brown, he very much doubted it. They were from different worlds: a mermaid and a unicorn. He very nearly laughed aloud at that whimsical thought. Still it was the fact that their worlds were different, that she was so comfortable in this one that had brought him here. Well, that and the fact he'd desperately wanted to see her again.

Since he'd been bundled into the carriage, not an hour had passed that he hadn't thought of her, wondered what she was doing, who might be calling on her, who might be enjoying her laughter within these walls, who might be the recipient of her rare smiles.

His thoughts should focus around Lavinia. Yet this woman before him occupied his musings in a way no other ever had. It was an odd thing to find himself inexplicably drawn to a tavern owner. She intrigued him. It was more than her height, the unusual way she wore her hair, her lack of feminine artifice, her unflattering clothing. It was her strength, her kindness. She'd taken him in, not knowing who he was, and had worked like the devil to ensure he survived, expecting nothing in return. All his life, anyone who assisted him, expected something in return. Even the women before Lavinia had required constant doting and numerous baubles in order to ensure their devotion. But a woman who required nothing—how did one ensure her devotion?

Not that he would ask or expect it of her. She was not for his world. His mother would have an apoplectic fit were he to introduce her. Not only because she was a tavern owner, but because she had no pedigree. She'd admitted as much while caring for him. "I daresay many were surprised the Duke of Hedley granted leave for his ward to marry your brother."

Crossing her arms over her chest, she settled back in the chair and gave him a steady glare. "He has more wealth than God."

"But he's not . . ." He cleared his throat. Merely blinking slowly, she wasn't going to make this easy on him. He shouldn't have started down this path, but he wanted to know every small detail about her. "His family is not known as I understand it." As he clearly knew. Mick Trewlove was a bastard, plain and simple. He wore the label like a badge. Or at least he had before he'd married an earl's daughter.

"I'm his family. Or at least part of it."

"When you were caring for me, you were offended when I used the term bastard."

"Not offended. Disappointed."

Her words were a hard kick to the gut. He didn't know why he had no desire to disappoint this woman or why he was intent on impressing her to such a degree that he'd removed the sling supporting his arm before exiting his coach so she wouldn't view him as a complete invalid. He'd been brought up to recognize that he had an exalted place in Society simply because of the circumstances surrounding his birth. "People are judged by their entry into the world."

"Unfortunately. It's not right for opinions regarding us to be based on something over which we have no control."

He gave her a slightly mocking grin. "You swore when you learned I was a duke. Practicing what you are now preaching against?"

Uncrossing her arms, she ran her finger along the edge of her glass. "It wasn't because I was judging you poorly. It was . . ." Her voice trailing off, she glanced around her establishment, then released a quick harsh burst of laughter before bringing her gaze back to his. "We can't really be friends, can we? Different places in Society, and all that. I suppose, when you walked through the door, I'd hoped we might be."

He'd rather hoped so as well, but she had the right of it. Every person he considered a friend could trace his or her lineage back generations. Their blood was untainted. They were purebreds. "Do you know who your parents are?"

Taking a small sip of her whisky, she shook her head. "I know nothing at all about my parents or where they came from. I was left in a basket on Ettie Trewlove's doorstep."

She spoke as though it hadn't been devastating to be abandoned in such a manner, but how could it have not been? "Aren't you curious?"

"Not even a smidge. She's my mum. She, along with my brothers and sister, are my family. I'll be honest with you, Your Grace, I don't give a bloody damn that I'm illegitimate, was born out of wedlock. The circumstances of my birth don't affect me now. I've got my family, my friends, my tavern, my home. That's all that matters to me. And I'm happy. I don't go hungry or cold. What more could I ask for?"

Love came to mind, which was an odd thing when he hadn't even considered it a necessary requirement for marriage. Love was an emotion other people were allowed to experience but a man in his position couldn't indulge in such frivolity. "A husband and children of your own?"

She smiled, her eyes twinkling. "You offering?"

Her bluntness nearly had him reeling back in his chair, as did the realization he wasn't as opposed to the idea as he should have been. She was wrong for him on many levels and he was wrong for her on many more. Yet he couldn't help but think she'd bring a warmth to his life that had always been absent. Still there was no hope for them, and she was teasing anyway. "Afraid not."

"Then it's not really your business, is it?"

"I suppose you have a point."

She scooted back her chair. "It was good to see you're recovering, Your Grace, but I've customers to see to."

"I'm not done here."

Halfway out of her chair, she gave him a look that no doubt would send many a man scurrying for the door. "I'm not one of your servants to be ordered about."

He assumed the scraping of a distant chair was her brother coming to his feet. "I apologize for the blunt wording, but I came here for a purpose and I've not yet seen to it. Please sit."

Looking past him, no doubt to her brother, she gave

a quick shake of her head before dropping back into her chair. "Get on with it then."

"I need your help finding someone."

"The footpads who made off with your watch?"

"No. My bride."

Chapter 8

*H*is pronouncement shouldn't have twisted her heart, crushed her chest. She was a silly goose to have entertained for even a few seconds he might have been making an offer when he'd mentioned husband and children. Of course they'd never marry. He was a bloody duke and she a tavern owner. But still, the knowledge that he wanted her to help him find a bride was ludicrous. Perhaps he'd taken a blow to the head that had turned him into a simpleton. "You want me to serve as a matchmaker?"

His lips twisted into an ironic grin. "Hardly. I was in this area of London the night we met searching for the woman who had left me standing at the altar earlier in the day."

"Don't take this wrong, but if she left you"—she couldn't imagine any woman being daft enough to do such a thing—"mayhap you'd be better off letting her go."

"No doubt. But that is presently not an option. It's imperative I find her."

He had to love her desperately to be so intent on locating her. "What makes you think she's in this area?"

"She'd discussed her destination with one of the staff after making her retreat from the church."

"On the day you were to wed?"

"Yes."

"That must have been a shock for you. And mortifying as hell."

"I've had more pleasant days. So where would a lady go if she wished not to be found?"

"She's nobility then?"

"The daughter of an earl."

"Her name?"

"I don't see that knowing it would assist in our search."

So he was striving to protect the woman's reputation even if she didn't seem to give a bloody damn about his. She didn't particularly like how his calling it *our search* had pleased her. She wanted to be irritated at his assumption she'd help him, but that too pleased her, that he wanted her assistance, was banking on it, felt as though he could rely on her. "I at least need to know what she looks like."

"Then you'll help?"

"I'll make some inquiries." Leaning forward, she placed her forearms on the table. "Why would you think she'd be roaming the streets during the dead of night?"

"I was out of my mind with worry, driven by anger, and well into my cups, having stopped for numerous pints during my quest—for fortification, of course. I'd been searching for her ever since we'd discovered she'd left."

"What did you do to make her want to cry off?"

"That is an excellent question and I very much look forward to learning the answer."

"Could she be with child?"

"Don't be ridiculous. She's a genteel woman of good breeding. I've never touched her."

While his confession came as a relief to her, she also found it difficult to believe. "You never *touched* her. Ever?"

"When we danced, of course. I offered my arm when we went on a stroll about the gardens. I kissed her hand when she accepted my offer of marriage."

She stared at him. "You've never done more than kiss her hand?"

"I am a gentleman."

"Are you a virgin?"

"Good God!" He seemed absolutely appalled. "A lady doesn't ask such impertinent questions."

"But I'm not a lady. So, are you?"

"What has that to do with anything?"

"Are you?" she insisted.

"Of course not."

"Did you not desire her?"

He studied the little bit of whisky that remained in his glass. "I do not see how the specifics regarding our relationship are going to help us find her."

He was correct, of course, but some little devil inside her was envious of a woman she'd never met, because she'd garnered his affection. Still, she could not help but wonder what about him had caused a woman to run off. While searching for the elusive bride, it might behoove her to make inquiries about him as well. Maybe he wasn't the sort to whom she'd want to return the girl, but even as she had that thought it seemed incongruous with what she knew about him thus far. "Description?" she asked, changing the path of her inquiry as he had the right of it and her previous question had been rude and truly none of her business. Nor would the answers assist them in their search.

He lifted his gaze to hers. "Short of stature. I barely have to raise my arms when we waltz."

That was certainly something he wouldn't be able to say if they waltzed. Not that they ever would, not that she suddenly wished they would. Nor did she wish to envision another woman in his arms. "Hair?"

"She's fair. Blond."

"Light blond? Dark blond?"

His brow furrowed. "Blond."

"You're certainly a man for detail. Eye color?"

He looked lost, as though she'd asked if his betrothed possessed a tail. "Surely she won't be identified by her eyes."

"Does she have freckles? Is there anything that stands out about her?"

"She's quite fetching."

She fought not to laugh. "That will make her easy to spot."

He scowled. "I have a miniature of her that I could bring to you."

"That could prove helpful." And ensured she'd see him again. Reaching across, she placed her hand over his clenched fist that rested beside his glass. "You've set an impossible task for yourself. If she doesn't wish to be found, you won't find her. This area is crowded with immigrants and the impoverished. There are warrens of slums. Two, three, four families are crowded into dwellings."

"I'm well aware of that. Still I need to try."

"Why don't you return here tomorrow afternoon? We'll have a look 'round some lodging houses and shelters."

He gave a brisk nod. "I appreciate your willingness to help."

"Her absence could mean nothing at all. Maybe she simply got nervous about getting married. Now she's afraid to return home, fearful you and her family will be angry."

"Or maybe, as you've implied, she had a rather good reason for not walking down the aisle. I won't rest until I know what it is."

IT WAS AN odd thing that the whisky was not as tasty as what he'd had earlier. He'd always favored Dewar's, but as he sat on his terrace, staring out into the darkened gardens, he wondered if his absence of enjoyment had more to do with the company he was keeping—his own.

He'd felt rather inadequate responding to questions regarding Lavinia, his answers falling well short of the mark. He tried to recall her more clearly.

Her eyes. Closing his, he dropped his head back and envisioned them. They were the color of moss mixed with the shade of freshly turned earth. A narrow black ring circled her iris. When she became passionate her eyes darkened with her intensity. When she laughed they lightened with her joy. He could see them in exquisite detail. The eyes of a tavern owner.

But for the life of him he couldn't recall Lavinia's.

From the moment Gillie had called out in the alleyway that fateful night, he could recount every word she'd spoken. Try as he might, he couldn't evoke a single conversation he'd had with Lavinia. Other than his proposal to her, which, in retrospect, had been quite bland.

"Will you honor me by becoming my wife?"

"I'd be delighted."

It had been lacking in passion, but then passion

wasn't needed for marriage. Of course, a commoner wouldn't know that. Commoners were ruled by baser instincts. It was the reason they gave birth to children out of wedlock.

He couldn't imagine the sort of person who would leave a babe on a doorstep. What if the woman hadn't taken her in? What if she hadn't been discovered until the elements had their way with her, snuffed out her life?

The rage that burst through him with the thought caused his hand to tremble. No doubt his reaction was the lingering result of a dying man grateful to the woman who had saved him. That his heart had sped up at the sight of her when he'd first entered the tavern, that he was anticipating seeing her on the morrow was merely coincidence, the consequence of not yet shaking off how close he'd come to death and how she had pulled him from its gaping maw.

Chapter 9

Standing in front of the mirror, Gillie studied her reflection, disgusted with herself because she wore one of her finer dark blue skirts and a white blouse, both usually reserved for when she paid a visit to her mum. She'd added a short dark blue buttonless jacket with tiny red hollies embroidered on it, which she generally wore at Christmas. That particular occasion was months away, but there she was dressing to impress a duke.

She blew out a great gust of air. She'd change into her normal working clothes but little time remained before the tavern would be opening at ten, and she was running behind. This morning she'd bathed and washed her hair. Naturally today the short strands had decided to mutiny once they were dry and had been sticking up like the quills of a hedgehog. So she'd had to wash it again and brush it continually to keep the locks from rebelling as they dried. Then she'd debated her attire as though he wasn't accustomed to seeing ladies dressed in the finest of silks. She'd decided to add the jacket at the last minute because, although it was August, it was possible it might be cool out.

With another put-upon sigh, she spun on her heel and headed out. She should not have agreed to help him. Yes, she knew these streets but he'd set an impossible task for himself. "A needle in a haystack," she muttered as she entered the tavern through the back door that led into the kitchen.

"Caw, Gillie, is it Christmas already?" Robin asked from his place at the large wooden table where those who worked for her took their meals.

"No, lad, but I have an errand to run later and thought it might be cool out."

"Going to see Father Christmas?"

"No! It's not yet time for Christmas."

"I think you look lovely," Hannah said as she stirred a large cauldron on the stove. There was no doubt her cook enjoyed the meals she prepared. She'd been a skeleton of a widow when Gillie had hired her, but now was plump curves that provided a comforting cushion for her children, even if they were nearly grown.

Gillie felt the heat warm her face at the compliment. "I dressed for the weather."

"Of course you did. Jolly Roger told me you had a gentleman caller last night."

"Don't be daft. He was merely a customer."

"You don't sit with customers."

"It's difficult to explain."

Her cook grinned slyly. "He said he was a handsome fella."

Rolling her eyes, she released a quick burst of air. It was going to be a day for sighing. "Is that soup going to be ready when we open?"

"It's ready now. Would you care for some?"

"No, thank you." Her stomach was stupidly knotted up. She doubted she could eat anything at the moment. "I simply wanted to make sure everything is ready."

She marched through to the taproom, the main part of the tavern. Standing behind the counter with two rows of casks lined up at his back, Jolly Roger was setting up the till. "You are the biggest gossip this side of the Thames."

He glanced over his shoulder, his gaze lifting slightly to meet hers. For all of his breadth, he didn't match her in height. "What'd I do?"

"You don't need to be telling people my business."

He shrugged offhandedly. "Not every day a toff walks in here. And you've never sat with a bloke before."

"I sit with my brothers."

He laughed, returned to counting out the money. "Not the same, Gil. Not the same."

She should dismiss him for talking to her with such disrespect, let him struggle to find work elsewhere. Pity she liked him as much as she did, and he was a good worker. "When things slow down this afternoon, I'll be stepping out for a bit."

"With your gent?"

"He's not my gent."

He closed the till, turned, leaned against the counter, and crossed his beefy arms over his broad chest. "You need to be sure he knows that. I seen the way he looked at you."

"He's spoken for."

"He married then?"

"Not yet."

"Many a man changes his mind before he gets to the altar."

This one obviously wasn't. He'd been to the altar, been stood up, and still wanted to find the woman. Clearly he saw her as his future. She sighed once more. "He can change his mind all he likes. I have no interest in finding myself saddled with a man. Open the door. Let's get to serving."

"Takes only one, Gillie." He started lumbering toward the entrance.

"I beg your pardon?"

"Takes only one, if he's the right one, to make you change your mind."

"I'll be thirty come December."

"And I just turned forty-three, but here I am as smitten as a schoolboy."

"With whom?"

He grinned broadly. "Figure it out."

He opened the door and the throng rushed in, giving her no time to figure anything out, least of all the reason she'd really said yes to assisting a duke.

"So what is she like?"

Thorne glanced over at the woman striding beside him along the crowded street, her level gaze as questioning as her voice. He'd never before spoken to a woman without having to lower his eyes. He liked that he could look directly into hers. He also liked that he didn't have to shorten his stride to accommodate her gait. Her long legs easily kept pace with his, or they would if his steps weren't hampered by a slight limp. Even with the walking stick, his thigh and backside periodically protested his movements.

The hat she wore bore no frills whatsoever. No ribbons, no flowers, no bows. It reminded him of something a farmer might wear as he plowed his fields. He supposed she didn't have enough hair to hold a hatpin, so keeping a more fashionable lady's hat in place would be a challenge since she strode briskly more than ambled. Men doffed their hats to her. Women smiled at her, greeted her by name as they passed. Children ran up to her, hugged her legs, received a wooden token from her in return for the gesture, and darted away.

It amused him to observe her, comfortable and relaxed in these environs that made him expect to have his pockets fleeced at any moment. "I told you. Short of stature, fair."

She scowled at him. "No. What is *she* like? Not, what does she look like. What does she enjoy doing? What are her hobbies? When she wants time to herself, what does she do? How does she fill her day?"

He was embarrassed to admit he hadn't a clue. "She makes morning calls naturally." All ladies did. "Goes to the dressmaker. Shops. Engages in charitable works."

"Such as?"

"What difference does that make?"

She easily sidestepped a rotund man who didn't seem willing to give up his share of the path. Her bared hand skimmed across his gloved one, and he cursed the supple leather that formed a barrier between their skins.

"If she works with orphans, we could visit orphanages or foundling homes. If she does what she can for beggars, we could make inquiries at a shelter or mission. Perhaps someone there saw her."

How was it that he'd known Lavinia for years and yet knew so little about her? She was a proper lady with a sterling pedigree. He had a vague understanding of how ladies spent their day, but knew none of the details when it came to the woman he'd intended to marry. They spoke of books and gardens and weather. Had he truly intended to spend the remainder of his life talking books, gardens, and weather?

"We often took a carriage ride through the park, but other than that, I'm ashamed to admit I'm not familiar with the specifics regarding how she spent her day." He couldn't tell if she was disappointed or disgusted by his lack of knowledge.

"Then we have a challenge before us," she said lightly as though the matter was of no consequence, but he suspected she'd have not inquired if that were the case. "Do you know if she had any funds on her?"

"Her brother would have given her an allowance. If she saved it perhaps." He hoped she had an abundance of money. He didn't want to think of her sitting against a wall or curled on a stoop, with vacant eyes staring out at nothing, like numerous people they'd passed. He didn't want to consider her being hungry or cold or frightened, not knowing what awaited her. He shook his head to throw off the morose thoughts. "I don't know if she'd been planning to run away all along or if it was a spur-of-the-moment decision."

She had been increasingly quiet of late. Had she begun to have doubts regarding marriage to him? Lady Aslyn had been betrothed to the Earl of Kipwick before she'd tossed him aside in favor of Mick Trewlove. Lavinia had been unusually silent and reserved at Lady Aslyn's wedding, almost melancholy. Had Lady Aslyn's change of heart planted seeds of doubt for Lavinia?

"Spur-of-the-moment," Gillie suddenly announced.

He nearly laughed. "How can you sound so certain?"

"You seem the reasonable sort. Why wouldn't she simply tell you she had reservations, had changed her mind?"

"Perhaps she feared I'd attempt to convince her otherwise."

"Would you have not let her go?"

"To be honest, I don't know. I'd made a vow . . ." And a deathbed vow was not to be taken lightly. Besides Lavinia was not a flighty debutante. She was of an age when she should have known her own mind, should have understood the solemnity of accepting his offer.

"I suppose there's some comfort in knowing you're a man who stands by his vows. But sometimes even the most well-intended oaths are best not kept."

He wondered if she'd ever made any she'd not kept.

Stopping beside a small lad sitting against a lamppost, she bent down and held out one of her wooden disks. The boy simply stared at it. She said something Thorne couldn't hear. Then with a wide grin, the imp snatched it from her fingers and tore off down the street. When she straightened, he asked, "What are those?"

Seemingly embarrassed by his question, she slipped her hand into the pocket of her skirt, causing the clatter of other tokens, and carried on. "They can be swapped for a bowl of soup at the back door of the tavern."

She'd handed them out to men, women, and children. "How do you know who is in need?"

She shrugged. "It's the eyes. The eyes tell you when someone is hungry."

So caught up in his own worries, he hadn't been paying attention, while this woman was incredibly aware of her surroundings, seemed to notice everything. "Did you go hungry as a child?"

"More times than I could count."

He couldn't imagine it. His belly had always been

full, more than full actually. "How do you know people aren't taking advantage of your generosity?"

Stopping, she met his gaze head-on. "If you weren't in need, would you take charity?"

He gave a long slow nod of understanding. It had bothered him when she'd refused to take payment for tending to him after he'd been attacked. He didn't much like being in debt. He owed her for her assistance today as well. It would no doubt take a bit of creativity to ensure he repaid her properly, a payment that might provide him with an excuse to spend more time with her. "No, I suppose not."

"There you are then," she stated briskly. "Let's inquire here."

Without waiting for him, she marched up a path, climbed three steps—steps she might have scrubbed as a child—and knocked smartly. She was without a doubt the most independent woman he'd ever known. She didn't require his arm for support or his permission for action.

The door opened, and a hunched-over woman gave him an excruciatingly slow perusal before turning her attention to Gillie.

"Hello, Mrs. Bard."

"Gillie."

Did the tavern owner know everyone? Did they all know her?

"Any new lodgers of late?"

"Me rooms have been filled for a couple of months now. No one new."

"And in your common room?"

The old woman shifted her feet as though she'd been caught in a lie. "They comes 'n' goes. 'Specially them what sleeps on the ropes."

He was still trying to process what she was referring to when Gillie turned to him. "Did you bring the miniature?"

"Ah, yes." Reaching into his pocket, he removed the tiny portrait of Lavinia that she'd given him a few weeks after their betrothal. He'd assumed she'd been marking her commitment to him.

His search partner took it and gave it a passing glance, before holding it near Mrs. Bard's nose. "Has she slept here?"

Narrowing her eyes, the older woman leaned nearer and shook her head. "Ain't seen 'er."

"Are you certain?" he asked.

One eye narrowing even further, she glared at him. "Ye questioning me eyes or me tongue?"

"Neither," Gillie said quickly as she handed the portrait back to him. "He's simply striving to find her."

"Run off from ye, did she? Ye beat 'er?"

"What? No! Of course not. Don't be ludicrous."

"Oh, a man of big fancy words. 'E ain't your sort, Gillie. Too much of the posh in 'im."

"Will you let me know if you see her?" Gillie asked.

"I might."

"There's a crown in it for you, and your first pint at the Mermaid is on me."

She gave a sly smile and a quick nod. "Ye've got me devotion now."

"And . . ." Gillie handed her several of the wooden tokens. "For those sleeping on the ropes tonight."

She tucked them into the pocket on her stained apron. "If there was more like ye in this world, Gillie, it'd be a better world."

"There are plenty like me, Mrs. Bard. You have a

good day." She turned on her heel and headed back toward the street.

He made a move to follow.

"Ye 'urt 'er, people 'round 'ere will kill ye."

He glanced back at Mrs. Bard. "I've no plans to hurt her."

"Just cuz ye don't plan it don't mean it won't 'appen." She shut the door, leaving him feeling the worst sort of scoundrel because he did enjoy Gillie's company, but now worried he was taking advantage of Lavinia's disappearance to use it as an excuse so he had a viable reason for limping along beside Gillie as she knocked on one lodging house door after another. He had to admire the manner in which she could speak to people without offending them. It seemed if he opened his mouth, they took an immediate dislike to him. He didn't know some of the terms she used. He certainly didn't know these people by name.

They'd just left their sixth house when she made an abrupt turn down an alleyway and unerringly approached what looked to be a makeshift shelter, some sort of tarp or cloth supported by thin sticks. Debris littered the ground, and he worked to avoid stepping in anything that might require he burn his boots. She crouched in front of what appeared to be an opening. In spite of his leg protesting, he joined her and nearly recoiled from the foul stench of human waste and rotting carcass cast off by the bearded, wild-haired, nearly toothless shriveled man huddled within the enclosure.

"Hello, Petey." She greeted him as though he were a favorite relation. "I was wondering if you've taken in any timepieces of late."

He was eyeing Thorne, taking his measure, rather than looking at her. "I might 'ave. Wot's it to ye?"

Thorne's heart jumped within his chest. He was searching for Lavinia, but if he could also regain his timepiece—

"Five quid if you still have the one I'm looking for."

The scruffy man reached beneath his backside, pulled out a pouch, and dumped three watches onto the dirty rags in front of him and then waved his hand over them as though presenting a gift. Thorne didn't have to examine them to know the silver pieces were not the gold one for which he was searching. "Do you have a gold one?"

He shook his head, but looked guilty doing it.

"Have you had a gold one?" Gillie asked.

"Not recently."

Twisting around on the balls of her feet, she turned to Thorne. "Did it have anything unusual on it?"

"A crest that had a vine of roses circling a lion with a thorn in its paw."

Her grin made him want to reach out, cup her chin, and stroke his thumb over those lips. "A thorny vine, I suppose, and a thorn in the paw for Thornley."

"I fear my ancestors were not the most imaginative."

She gave her attention back to the old man. "Anything like that, Petey?"

"Nah. I don't git brung the good stuff."

"If you hear of it making the rounds, let me know. I'll see it worth your while." Then she took hold of that grimy hand—willingly placed her hand on it—turned it up, put two wooden tokens into it, and folded his fingers around her gift. "You take care now."

"You too, Gil."

Straightening, she began walking away. He joined her. "I take it he's a fence."

She glanced over at him. "He is."

"Not a very successful one to live like that."

"He lived much better before his wife and son died a few years back. Cholera. Now he's simply sad."

He remembered how he'd wanted to close himself off from the world after his siblings perished and then later when his father passed, but in both instances his responsibilities prevented his withdrawal.

"You're in pain," she said sympathetically. "I hadn't given much thought to the fact you're still recovering."

He didn't like admitting that his leg was fairly killing him. "I'm fine."

"Your limp has worsened. I could do with a bit of a rest myself. There's a coffee house around the corner."

"I say we push on."

"You can push on if you like. I'm going to have some coffee."

"You are well aware I haven't a clue regarding who I should approach."

That smile again, only this time there was a hint of triumph in it. "Then I suppose you'd best join me."

SHE WAS ONE of the few ladies in attendance, not that she seemed bothered by it. A couple of the women, standing about, were giving him the eye and every now and then a sultry smile. He watched as one led a gent up the stairs. It was not uncommon for a coffee house to also serve as a brothel, letting rooms by the hour. He wondered if Gillie was aware of that. He suspected she was. She seemed to be intimately familiar with all aspects of this area of London.

He wondered if she'd ever taken a man—other than a wounded one—to her rooms. He doubted it. She wasn't the flirtatious sort, and yet something about her was decidedly coquettish. Perhaps because she didn't appear to be aware of her appeal. Even downplaying it with her plain garb and her short hair couldn't diminish it. She was like the sun, hiding behind clouds, but the brilliance of her still shone through.

Lifting the heavy mug, she placed it just below her slender nose and inhaled the aroma. Her eyes closed and her expression of bliss had his lower body tightening painfully. He'd like to be the one responsible for causing the soft sigh that escaped through her slightly parted lips just before she took a sip of the dark brew.

With an easy smile, she opened her eyes. "I love coffee."

"I'd have not guessed." Which was a lie, as it was obvious she enjoyed the flavor. "What did you mean when you asked Mrs. Bard about the people sleeping on the ropes?"

She seemed surprised by his question. "Not everyone has the luxury of a bed. She has a room where she has lined up pallets. If people haven't the means to afford one, they can sleep on a bench for fewer coins. There's a rope strung the length of it about chest high so they can put their arms over it in order to not tumble off the bench once they fall asleep."

He was rather appalled by the notion. Many lords and ladies were involved in charitable works, and while he had made numerous donations to their causes he was unfamiliar with this practice. "Sounds terribly uncomfortable."

"Oh, it is."

His gut tightened at the thought of her hanging over a rope. "Have you slept in such a manner?"

"When I was fifteen, and only as a lark to see what it was like. My mum always provided me with a bed before I could afford one of my own."

"Your voice always softens when you mention her."

Lifting a shoulder, she took another sip of coffee, looking at him over the rim of her cup. It was an odd thing that he couldn't remember Lavinia ever studying him and had no memory of ever scrutinizing her either. But then he'd known her for ages, because their fathers had ensured they met and understood they were destined to wed. "I have to admit to being surprised you know the area and people, so well."

Blinking, she set down her mug. "I thought that was the reason you asked for my help."

"Well, yes, but still I underestimated your knowledge. I assume you grew up here."

"Not in Whitechapel specifically, but nearby. I've been here since I was nineteen, ever since I opened my tavern."

"What's that then? A half dozen years?"

She laughed, a sound that caused gents to turn their heads, and he suspected he was the envy of some, to be sitting at a table by the window with her. "A little over a decade."

Which made her a mature woman, not an innocent, untried lass. Surely a woman who'd had lovers. Or at least at some time a husband. Perhaps she was a widow. He didn't like the thought of her with another man, sipping coffee, sharing whisky. Something akin to jealousy rushed through him at the thought of another man lying in her bed, opening his eyes to find her tending to him. "Have you never married?"

"Nary once."

Most women would be a bit embarrassed by the fact but she seemed to view it as a badge of honor. "Why ever not?"

"I'm not the sort men love, and I won't marry with out love. I'm content with what I have."

He furrowed his brow. "Why do you think that?"

"I'm not small and delicate, the sort who makes a man feel all the more manly, the kind he'd like to pu on a shelf and look at, take down now and then to play with. Nor am I docile. Men are threatened by women who stand up for themselves. Then the gents get ugly Makes them difficult to love. I've no one to tell me what I can and can't do. Maybe that's the reason you bride ran off."

"Are you implying I'd have ordered her about?"

She gave him a pointed look.

"I assure you that I would not have. One of the reasons I asked her to marry me was because she was a paragon of proper behavior and would no have required my instructing her." Which was also one of the reasons he hadn't hesitated to reassur his father as he was dying he would adhere to th terms of the contract.

"A paragon? Oooh. She must have liked it when yo whispered that in her ear."

She was teasing him again, but he didn't much lik the implication. "I never whispered in her ear."

"Why ever not?"

He stared at her. "I beg your pardon?"

"Didn't you do things with her you ought not?"

"Absolutely not. I respected her too much for that."

Leaning back, she crossed her arms over her ches

and gave him a steady look. "How much did you love her?"

Shifting in his chair, he glanced around. This woman's audacity was not to be tolerated. Yet he couldn't seem to withhold the truth from her. He brought his attention back to her. "I loved her not at all."

THE BLOODY NOBILITY. She knew they had their fancy houses and their posh clothes, their pristine lives that were constantly scrubbed clean, but it appeared they didn't dirty any aspect of their existence with something as mundane as emotion.

"Then why marry her?" She closed her eyes, knowing the answer before he spoke. "Because she's a *paragon* and you're a duke. And you needed a proper wife." A woman with pure bloodlines who could trace her ancestors back generations. Something she would never be able to do. She opened her eyes. "And your pride won't let her go."

"My pride might have been driving me that first night, might have resulted in my idiocy that led me into your care. I'm not sure what I would have done had I found her. Express my disappointment. Demand answers. Haul her back to the church." He shook his head. "Her brother and my mother are insistent we still marry, but I will not force her, and I don't want her living in fear that she has no recourse except to hide. I feel something is amiss and I must make it right." He glanced around. "Why would she come to this area?"

He seemed sincere in his quest to reassure and help the girl. "It's easy to lose oneself, to blend in, within these streets because there are so many people about—or to start over. Change a name. No one asks you to prove that's the name you were given when you were born. Or perhaps she knew someone here."

He went remarkably still. "Like whom?"

"Well, I don't know. I don't know her." She held out her hand. "May I see the miniature?" She'd only caught glimpses of it when she'd handed it over to one person after another. Now she studied the delicate features. The woman looked familiar but she couldn't recall where she might have seen her. Had she come into the Mermaid? Had their paths crossed on the street? "She's very pretty."

"The wrong sort could take advantage of that."

He sounded truly worried, and perhaps a bit guilty, as though he had led this woman here. And he spoke true. An improper sort could use her to fill his pockets with coins. "Why her? Why did you ask her to marry you? I'm sure there are an abundance of paragons among the aristocracy."

He gave her a sad sort of smile. "There is a stretch of land that borders my ducal estate. It was set aside to serve as a dowry for the daughter of a particular earl, and every duke before me planned for his son to marry that earl's daughter in order to gain that land, only no earl ever produced a daughter until she came along. The day after she was born, her father and mine got together and worked out the arrangements, signed a contract that she and I would marry. I was eleven at the time. My opinion on the matter was neither sought nor wanted. When I was fifteen, as my father lay dying, I promised him I would honor the terms of the contract and the land that meant so much to every duke before me would become ours. Therefore, it was always expected we'd marry, but neither of us was in any hurry. Her brother is a friend and had begun pushing of late, because she was quite on the shelf. So we decided it was time. She and I have always gotten along famously." He shrugged. "I didn't think marriage to her would be a hardship. Although I am rather upset with myself as I'm coming to realize I might have in fact done her a disservice. I was willing to take her to wife when my feelings for her weren't stronger. When she didn't intrigue me . . . as you do."

Her heart fairly galloping, she wished she was drinking whisky instead of coffee. "You like a bit of the rough, do you?"

"You're anything but rough. You possess the gentlest touch I've ever known. You're generous, giving out your wooden tokens to anyone you think might be in need. You take a moment to offer a kind word here and there. It's obvious people think highly of you."

She wasn't accustomed to praises, didn't like having them showered on her. "They don't want me to stop serving them."

"You're modest as well."

"I need to get back to the Mermaid." She rose to her feet. He got up a bit more slowly and she suspected he wasn't nearly as healed as he claimed. "Today gave you a taste of what you're up against. You won't find her if she doesn't want to be found, but we can keep looking tomorrow if you like."

"I do."

"Right." She wished he'd given another answer, even as she'd hoped he'd give the one he had. Silly goose that she was, she wanted to spend more time in his company, because the truth was that he intrigued her as well.

Chapter 10

That evening, Thorne's gaze rammed into Gillie's the moment he strode into the tavern. It was more crowded tonight, yet she didn't look at all harried. Rather she appeared remarkably happy as she glanced briefly away, smiled at some gent while handing him a pint of beer, before returning her attention to Thorne. She was in her element, comfortable and at ease, very much as the ladies he knew who flittered around ballrooms, delighted to be dancing and visiting for a few hours. It had never occurred to him a woman would find satisfaction in work.

Perusing the establishment, he noted two gents leaving a table near a window and headed for it. A pretty blonde barmaid got to it before him, gathered up the empty tankards, wiped the table, and flicked her rag at a man who reached for one of the chairs, effectively chasing him off. Then, jutting out a hip, she gave Thorne a saucy smile. "Hello, Handsome. Looking for a place to sit?"

"I am, as a matter of fact."

She patted the table. "Make yourself at home." Sidling a little closer, she batted her eyelashes at him. "What's your pleasure?"

"I have it, Polly," Gillie said.

The girl—who he was relatively certain was of an age that if she'd been born into the aristocracy, would have been debuted this Season—swung around, all flirtatious manner evaporating. "I can see to him, Gillie."

"I know, pet. But he's here to have a word with me, and I think all your attention directed his way is likely to leave other fellows without any."

"But I'm thinking he'd give a girl something extra to make it worth her while."

"You'll get the something extra. Go on now and see to the others."

With a pout, Polly flounced away. He had to bite back his laughter. "I didn't expect to create such a stir."

Gillie set a tumbler of whisky in front of him. "Polly is always on the lookout for a gent to marry her."

"I suppose I should tell her I'm spoken for."

She angled her head thoughtfully. "Are you? Your bride's actions would indicate you're not."

"Quite right." Even if Lavinia were still willing, and with her brother's sweetening of the dowry, he wasn't certain he could marry her knowing she had misgivings, knowing he would no longer be content with a marriage lacking in any regard. He wanted to find her, speak with her, reassure her, but taking her to wife was unlikely, in spite of the promise he'd made his father.

"I wasn't expecting to see you until tomorrow afternoon," she said.

"I've been doing some thinking." He pulled out a chair, extended his hand toward it. "Will you join me?"

With a brusque nod, she scraped back the chair opposite the one he'd indicated and dropped into it. He wasn't certain if she wasn't accustomed to the courtesy of a gent dragging out a chair for her or if she was striving to make the point that she wouldn't be swayed by his charms. He took his seat. She moved the glass she'd set on the table closer to him—always the tavern keeper seeing to the comfort of her customers. "You won't join me?"

She shook her head. "I have a good part of the night still ahead of me. I don't want to get into a bad habit of nipping before the doors are locked."

Some considered drinking a sin; she invited people to indulge in it, yet worried about bad habits. He didn't know why that delighted him, but so much about her did.

"Have you decided to give up your search?" she asked.

"No, but it occurred to me that no matter how much allowance she'd saved, she would need to replenish it." He didn't want to think of her sleeping on the ropes or holding out her hand in hopes of a wooden token that would give her a bowl of hot soup. "This afternoon I came to realize my knowledge regarding her was quite lacking. However, I can't see her doing needlework or teaching or"—he glanced around—"serving a gent his beer. But I do recall a recital earlier in the summer where she performed on the pianoforte and sang. She was rather talented, so it struck me, she might, quite literally, sing for her supper."

"We don't have a lot of opera houses in Whitechapel."

"But there are other places where people are entertained."

Her eyes widening, she leaned toward him. "You think she'd perform in a penny gaff?"

It had been years, a decade and a half at least, since he and his mates had sought out bawdy entertainments. He wasn't even certain the place they'd frequented still existed or how to find it, as generally he'd been well into his cups. "If she were desperate. And I have to imagine she is since she ran off without a word. I need her to know there will be no repercussions, she can return home and we can sort this hash of a mess out like civilized people."

"I suppose you want to look tonight."

"If you can spare the time."

Her gaze swept over the room. "I don't like shirking my responsibilities."

"I realize I'm asking a lot. I could pay—"

She snapped her head back around to glare at him. "Don't you dare offer to give me money."

"I feel a need to make it up to you some way, as I'm becoming quite the bother."

"You will owe me. We'll figure out exactly what when we find her."

"I don't generally go into a situation without knowing the cost."

Crossing her arms over her chest, she settled back. "Then find her on your own."

The devil of it was that he could probably find Lavinia on his own, but it would take considerably longer as he didn't have Gillie's resources or know all the people she knew. It was also much more enjoyable searching with her at his side. "I'll trust you to be fair with your demands."

She smiled, a victorious, seductive, wily smile that caused heat, desire, and longing to thread their way through his entire body and into the depths of his soul. "Ah, you silly man." She slapped her hands on the table. "I'll let Jolly Roger know I'll be leaving for a bit."

He furrowed his brow. "Jolly Roger?"

"My head barman."

"His name is Jolly Roger?"

She shrugged. "So he says. That's something else you have to consider. She could change her name, move elsewhere. Just because she asked someone to bring her here doesn't mean she stayed. People escape their circumstances in all sorts of ways."

He understood that. But he wanted to locate her before her brother or the men he'd hired did. "Still I won't be able to live with myself if I don't at least try to find her."

"Very well. Give me a few minutes."

He watched as she walked toward the bar. Unlike the women who worked for her, she didn't sway her hips provocatively or offer cheeky grins. Here and there, she offered a word, placed a hand on a shoulder, or picked up an empty glass. Her movements reflected a smoothness, a casualness, a naturalness that indicated she'd done them all a thousand times, more. They adored her, these men and women who came in here for a chance to relax at the end of a hard day.

It was an odd thing to realize he was beginning to adore her as well.

SHE COULDN'T BELIEVE she was going to take more time away from the tavern in order to help a duke, but he'd sounded so sincere in his need to find this woman that how could she not do what she could to assist him in his efforts? When she reached the bar, Jolly Roger was nowhere to be seen. "Davey, have you seen Jolly Roger?" she asked one of the bartenders they'd recently hired.

He jerked a thumb over his shoulder. "Back in the kitchen."

But when she walked into the kitchen, the only person she saw was Robin, sitting at the large oak table, slurping down his soup. "Robin, have you seen Jolly Roger?"

"Yeah. He's down in the cellar with Cook, helpin' her pick out the best sherry fer tomorrow's soup."

She was glad to hear he was finally remembering to put his *h*'s to use, but what he'd said made no sense. She furrowed her brow. "I beg your pardon?"

"They go down there every night 'bout this time. She don't know nuffink about sherry, ye see, so he has to help her find the best one. That's not easy to do. Takes 'em a long time usually."

Customarily Jolly Roger took some time now and then in the evening to go outside to puff on his pipe for a while. She allowed her customers to smoke their pipes inside the taproom, but not her employees. She hadn't known about him helping Hannah select sherry for her soup, hadn't even known sherry was going into the soup. "Thank you, pet."

He gave her a salute before going back to his dinner. She crossed over to the cellar door, surprised to find it closed. Opening it, she stepped inside. They must have only brought in one lamp because no light radiated up. She started down, heard a laugh and a snicker, and stopped in midstride.

"Do you like that?" Hannah asked seductively.

"I'll give you twenty minutes to stop."

Hannah's laugh was filled with joy, humor, and teasing. "Oh, Rog, you'll never last that long."

She heard her cook whisper something else but was unable to distinguish the words.

"Ah, you saucy wench," he growled.

Gillie crept back up the stairs, closed the door,

and leaned against it. Jolly Roger was smitten with Hannah? How had she not seen that? She was grateful Robin was no longer around. No doubt he was making his way through the taproom, hoping to find some odd jobs for tomorrow. He liked running errands for people, and her brothers—although none were visiting tonight—were good about hiring him to deliver messages and such.

Sitting at the table, she drummed her fingers on the wood and waited, finally hearing footsteps on the stairs echoing up from the cellar. Hannah had been correct. He'd lasted only about half of the twenty minutes. When the door opened, they walked through it and both came up short at the sight of her sitting there. She pushed to her feet and arched a brow. "Did you find the sherry you were looking for?"

Jolly Roger turned so red she thought his face was on the verge of exploding. He cleared his throat. "Damn. I forgot the bottle. I'll go down and fetch it." He disappeared back the way he'd come.

Fearful her face might be just as red as his, Gillie took a step forward. She wasn't looking forward to this conversation but it needed to be had. "Hannah, I overheard you two in the cellar."

Hannah's eyes flattened as she reached back to untie her apron. "And now you'll be letting me go."

"No, no." She touched her cook's arm to stay her actions. "I just want to make sure you were down there willingly, that what was happening was what you wanted."

"Ah, you're a sweet lass. Of course it was what I wanted. I know you don't fancy menfolk and have no experience with them intimately, but what Roger can do with his tongue . . ." Leaning in, she whispered conspiratorially, "He can make a woman forget her name."

Why would a woman want that?

Hannah looked over her shoulder. "You can come back in, Rog. Everything's all right." She winked at Gillie. "He gets embarrassed talking about intimate things."

Roger appeared, sherry bottle in hand, and gave it to Hannah. "There you are, darlin'."

"Ta, Rog."

"I didn't know our soup has sherry in it," Gillie said, although she never had taken an interest in preparing food.

"It doesn't. But we had to tell Robin something. The lad is far too curious," Hannah said.

"Robin says you go hunting for sherry every night."

"Why do you think I'm *Jolly* Roger?" her barman asked, apparently quite pleased with himself, puffing his chest out like some rooster.

"Has this been going on for a while then?"

They both shrugged noncommittally. "Not so very long really," Hannah finally offered.

"Maybe you should find someplace else to do the hunting," Gillie suggested.

"Right," Roger said. "Will do."

"It won't be as much fun as sneaking in a bit of loving here and there," Hannah said.

His expression of warmth and adoration caused Gillie's chest to tighten. "I'll make it fun for you, darlin'."

Hannah reached up and patted his cheek affectionately. "I know you will, love. Now you'd best get back to work before Gillie has a change of heart and dismisses you for all your naughty behavior."

With a wink at her, he started walking toward the door that led to the taproom.

"Wait," Gillie called out.

He swung around, a question in his eyes.

"I was looking for you to let you know I'll be leaving for a while."

"With your gent?" Hannah asked.

"He's not my gent," she said, wondering how often she was going to have to tell them that before they believed it. "But, yes, the duke and I need to go somewhere."

"He's a duke? Stick a blade in your boot," Roger said.

She'd forgotten that only Finn had heard Thorne introduce himself.

"Are you going someplace dangerous?" Hannah asked, her voice laced with worry.

"I think he wants me to use it on the duke," Gillie told her. "He will be a perfect gentleman."

Roger appeared skeptical.

"He will be," she insisted, trying not to be disappointed by her words.

Still sitting at the table, Thorne paid a bit more attention to his surroundings. In addition to numerous smaller square tables, there were several long ones with benches where he assumed groups of people found it easier to gather. Some of the men smoked pipes, the smoke filling the room with a heady aroma. Here and there oil paintings depicting a mermaid or a unicorn or both hung on the walls. At the far end of the taproom, an open doorway led into another room, a dining hall. Stairs ascended to a loft with a railing and he could imagine someone standing up there, addressing the crowd below. The place had a much-used feel to it and yet it was also obvious it was very well cared for.

He wasn't surprised. It was clear Gillie poured all that she was into any task set before her, whether it was managing a tavern or caring for an injured man. Or helping that man find the woman he was to marry. Anxious to get back to that last task, he was tapping his walking stick repeatedly on the floor, wondering what was keeping Gillie, when the urchin—who couldn't have been any older than eight—suddenly appeared before him.

"Caw, blimey, wot's that?" The boy's clothes weren't fancy, nor were they a perfect fit, but they and the lad appeared to be clean.

Thorne looked to where he was pointing. "A walking stick."

"I know that." He rolled his eyes. "That. The gold part."

"Ah." Thorne tossed the stick up, caught it midway between either end, and swung it toward the lad so he could see the tip more clearly. "A lion."

"Is it real or like a unicorn?"

He couldn't help but believe that this might be the boy Gillie had sent to fetch the physician. What was his name? He couldn't recall. But he suspected she'd told the lad all about unicorns. "It's real. Have you never been to the zoological gardens?"

"Wot's that?"

"It's a place where they house animals for people to look at."

"Wot? Like dogs 'n' rats?"

"No, like lions and tigers and elephants. Animals from all around the world. And a giraffe. A giraffe is so tall that his head would break through the ceiling here."

The boy's eyes grew round. "Yer lyin'."

"Why would I do that?"

The scamp seemed to ponder that for a bit and then he narrowed his eyes. "Ye owe me, ye know."

Thorne began twirling the stick, over, under, around his hand. "Do I? Why is that?"

"I fetched the doctor. If I hadn't, ye'd be dead. I used the money Gillie gave me for a hansom, like I was supposed to so I'd be quick. I could have just kept it." The boy seemed to be very deliberate in pronouncing the *h* when he spoke a word that began with one. He wondered how much Gillie might be responsible for that particular mannerism.

"What would you have done with it then?"

"I'm saving it, for something for Gillie."

"What precisely?"

"I ain't tellin'. But you owe me," he repeated with a bit more confidence, as though he'd latched onto the idea and favored it now that he'd put it into words.

"How much?" Thorne asked.

The imp scrunched up his face, then blurted, "A shilling?"

"I daresay, I shall hope my life is worth a good deal more than that."

"A half crown?"

Odd to realize what he considered pittance, could be treasure to another. "I should think at least a full crown, surely."

The lad's face split into a wide grin as he held out a hand.

Reaching into his jacket, Thorne pulled out his purse. "Who is it that I'm paying?"

"Robin."

"What is your full name, Robin?"

"Robin, like I said. Ain't no more to it."

An orphan then, or another left on a doorstep. He located a crown and placed it on the waiting palm. The boy's fingers closed around it and he pressed his fist to his chest. "Thanks, guv."

"What's this then?" Gillie asked.

He hadn't heard her approach, but he immediately shoved himself to his feet. She was wearing a plain cloak and he assumed her fetching of it had delayed her return to him. "Master Robin and I were negotiating how much I owed him for saving my life."

He hadn't expected her to look so sad or disappointed. Slowly, she shook her head. "Robin, we don't take money for good deeds."

"He's a toff. He can afford it."

"Doesn't matter. Give it back."

The lad unfurled his fingers and looked longingly at the coin.

"Surely—" Thorne began, but her sharp look cast in his direction abruptly stopped him from attempting to convince her to let the boy keep it.

"It's only a crown," Robin muttered as he slowly set it on the table.

"Now, don't you feel better?" Gillie asked.

He lowered his brows, pushed up his lower lip. "No."

"Some day you will. Go ask Hannah to dish you up some pudding."

He dashed off.

"The lad wanted the money to purchase you a gift," Thorne said quietly, picking up the coin and slipping it back into his pocket.

"Better he learn to be generous in helping others than learn to take advantage of others' generosity. Shall we be off?"

"Indeed. My carriage awaits in the mews." Leaning on his walking stick, he picked up his hat and offered her his arm.

"It'll give the wrong impression," she whispered before heading for the door.

He followed. Once they were outside, he said, "That I'm a gentleman?"

"That there's something between us." She glanced over at him. "We should probably wait until tomorrow night. Give your leg time to recover from our earlier outing."

"It needs the exercise. Do you go to penny gaffs often?"

"No, but I hear things. We'll go to one of the more popular ones. If she's not there, perhaps someone knows something."

Once they were in his carriage, on opposite squabs, she said, "I hope you don't think I found fault with you paying Robin. I know you meant well—"

"Is he your son?" He couldn't believe he'd had the audacity to ask. With his dark hair and dark eyes, the boy resembled her not in the least, and yet there was this possessive streak running through Thorne that made him want to search out every secret she might harbor, to have confirmation she'd never been intimate with another man.

"Do you think I'm the sort who wouldn't acknowledge my own child?"

She left no doubt she had found fault with his question. He rather regretted asking it but there was not a single thread of her life he didn't want to weave into a tapestry that gave him the whole picture of her being. "No, no, I don't. I simply don't understand your relationship, why you seem to be mothering him and yet not."

She glanced out the window. "I'd given a group of lads some tokens. He was one of the boys. After that first bowl of soup, he came back every day whether or not he had a token, and naturally we gave him a bowl of soup either way. We never turn away anyone who is hungry. One morning I went down to open up and he was asleep on the stoop. I took him to a home for orphans that my brothers and I have set up and the next morning, I found him once again asleep on my stoop. The boys with whom he'd been running about taught him how to pick pockets. I taught him how to wash dishes."

They were traveling without the indoor lamp being lit, but the lantern on the outside of the coach swayed, causing light and shadows to ebb and flow over her face. Her gaze was back on him. "I tried to convince him to live with my mum, but he wouldn't have it. We talked about him moving into my apartment, but he prefers sleeping in the kitchen. I don't know why. Perhaps because when it's locked up for the night, it's all his. He's a good lad."

"So I gathered." He studied her, sitting across from him, taking up hardly any room at all. When he had traveled with Lavinia, her voluminous skirts and petticoats had taken up most of the seat and all of the space between her legs and his. If this woman wore any petticoats at all, it was only one. "It took you so long to return to me that I thought perhaps you were changing your attire."

"I'd rather have been doing that. Instead I discovered my head barman and cook in the cellar stores. Roger had told me that he was smitten. I just hadn't realized it was with Hannah. They sounded as though they were having a jolly good time, and I couldn't bring myself to disturb them. It was rather awkward when they finally emerged from their tryst."

"Getting caught usually is."

"So you've been caught before?"

"In my youth when I was bit more . . . randy and a lot more reckless."

"Do you have any by-blows?"

"No. I was never careless in that regard."

"I'm glad."

So was he. While he'd taken precautions because he hadn't wanted the responsibility of children born out of wedlock, he couldn't help but feel now that his actions had raised his esteem in her eyes. Strange how he didn't want her to find him lacking, but how could she not when he hadn't been able to hold onto his bride?

Chapter 11

She'd ridden in her brother's coach on several occasions, but it was very different when traveling with a gent to whom she was not related. His legs were a bit longer than Mick's and he'd spread them slightly so her booted feet rested between his, the way a man's body might nestle between a woman's. She might have never experienced that sort of coupling, but she wasn't so naïve as to not know how procreation worked. Her mum had taught her early about what went on between men and women so she would know if a fellow was striving to get her into a position where she might find herself in danger of getting with child. Ettie Trewlove was of the belief that many girls found themselves in the family way simply because they'd been too ignorant regarding the act that led to the condition.

"If girls were educated about fornication instead of stitchery, people like me might not be needed," she'd lamented.

Not that Gillie ever regretted being taken to the baby farmer's door. Her life had not turned out so poorly. She'd learned her letters and numbers at the ragged school, attended the full four years that were permitted. It had been with a bit of sadness that she'd celebrated her eleventh year, knowing it would be her last at the school. Her mum had explained the need that they continue learning, so she and her brothers had pooled their earnings until they had a guinea to pay yearly to a lending library. Through the books they'd borrowed, they'd discovered a lot about the world and people. And they'd learned so many marvelous words, even though sometimes they had a time of it finding someone who could tell them what the word meant. But someone at the lending library usually knew. Most of the people with whom she communicated each day didn't use big, fancy words, but because she at least knew a host of them, she didn't feel out of her element speaking with Thorne. Even if her enunciation didn't carry a haughty accent, she could hold her own in a conversation with him. Which had led her to a unique opportunity. Not every woman was given the chance to travel in a coach with a duke. Especially one who smelled so lovely.

No odor of blood mingled with his tart scent as it wafted around her, teasing her nostrils. With the rocking of the vehicle, the shadows moved over him. Whenever they gave way to light, she would catch a glimpse of him watching her. She'd fetched her cloak because she'd expected the evening to be chilly, but he seemed to generate warmth that made her feel a tad too hot. When they spoke, no matter the words, a sense of intimacy was created within the dark confines, as though they were sharing not only secrets but the inner core of their very existence.

"I'm surprised a lady of quality would know about a penny gaff," she said quietly.

"I very much doubt she knows the specifics. If they're

advertising for entertainments, she might believe it will be like a recital."

"You think someone might take advantage of her."

"Yes. I want to be on hand to lessen the damage. And, yes, I am very much aware the odds are against us finding her or finding the specific place where she might be performing, but I feel this overwhelming need to do *something*, not to be completely useless."

"I'm beginning to think she might have been a fool to run off."

"She never struck me as a fool. She must have had a good reason. But to come here? That baffles me beyond reasoning."

"Had she gone someplace you expected, you might have been able to find her more easily."

"As I said, not a fool."

"So you went to her recital. What other things did you do with her?" She didn't think his answer would aid in their search, but she was curious about his relationship with the lady, perhaps a tad jealous as well. This woman seemed not to appreciate what she'd possessed.

"The usual. Balls, dinners, theater, pleasure gardens, parks. We strolled about, we rode, but I am embarrassed to admit I believe I have conversed with you more in the time I have known you than I did with my fiancée during the entire time we were betrothed. We are taught only certain subjects are to be discussed, and they all seem rather superficial now. You are much more skilled at discourse."

She laughed lightly. "The people with whom I converse are usually three sheets in the wind which tends to lend itself toward revealing more intimate details about oneself and one's life. I'm afraid I'm not accustomed to there being barriers regarding what's appropriate."

He flashed a grin just as light chased away shadow, and then the shadow reasserted itself. "I imagine you've heard a lot of interesting tales."

"I have. Perhaps I'll tell you about them sometime. But not now, as we've arrived." She'd given his coachman directions, and he'd managed to locate it on the first try, which made her wonder if the man might have visited the place before. The vehicle came to a stop; the driver's companion opened the door and handed her down. The duke followed. She was rather glad to be in a position to see him gape.

"A church?" he asked, incredulously.

"More a chapel, once upon a time. Then it was converted into the Devil's Door."

HE HAD TO admit the building lent itself well to a place of entertainment. The pews provided the seating and the spot where the vicar had addressed his congregation, a raised area at the front, now served as the stage. He'd handed over sixpence, three-pence for each of them—the price having gone up since he'd last visited during his youth when he'd paid only a penny—and followed Gillie to a small empty space on a back pew. Only after he'd taken his seat did he realize it provided an intense intimacy, his hip and thigh pressing snuggly up against hers. Their shoulders were fairly smashed together, and he had an understanding of how a mummy might have felt—had the corpse had any awareness about him—stuffed into a sarcophagus.

"Don't be alarmed, but I'm going to shift my arm up." Up and over until it rested along the back of the pew, against her shoulders. He was grateful it was his right and not his left. While it was healing, it still ached, and he wasn't certain he'd have been able to maneuver it to the extent needed to free up a bit of space between them.

Or that was his theory regarding what he purported would happen. What actually occurred was that his action allowed her to not sit as stiffly, which resulted in her being nestled against his side, the softness of her tempting him to curl his hand around her arm and draw her in even closer. He cursed his jacket, waistcoat, and shirt for providing a barrier between them. Her gaze remained fastened on the stage where a fellow, dressed as a woman—with a bosom so large it was a wonder he could remain upright—was engaged with a clownish fellow wearing a coat at least two sizes too big and whose hair looked like straw sticking out from beneath his black bowler hat. The end of his bulbous nose was painted a red that matched his cheeks, supposedly to imply he was well into his cups. Their words were ribald, their actions even more so as they imitated what could only be described as fucking—the woman figure bent partially over screeching, the clownish one behind her, swinging his hips back and forth while snorting and grunting.

He'd forgotten how grotesque these performances could be or perhaps he'd been too drunk to remember. Lavinia would not be here. She could not possibly be here.

Leaning over, catching a whiff of Gillie's vanilla fragrance that had continually assaulted him in the carriage, he whispered near her ear, "I've made a mistake. We can leave."

She held up what he supposed passed for a playbill within these wretched walls. "A nightingale is next."

"I have no interest whatsoever in listening to birds."

She turned her head slightly, and he was struck by the amusement shining in her eyes. The gaslights were dim but their glow provided enough illumination to see her clearly. He'd never seen anyone so serene. She should have been positively appalled that he would bring her to such an establishment. Her lips twitched as though she were fighting not to laugh. "It'll be a woman, singing. You might want to get a look at her before we leave."

"I can't continue to subject you to this disgusting display."

"I've seen worse from drunkards. We're here now and might as well make the most of it."

"Right." It wouldn't be Lavinia, yet he was suddenly no longer in a hurry to make an exit, to lose the intimacy of this moment. He wasn't even aware his hand had moved until it brushed along her chin and danced over the short strands of her hair. He could see why efforts were being made to shut these establishments down. With the improper talk and actions on the stage and the people around them joining in with their own renditions of bawdy words shouted and lewd actions pantomimed, how was a person not to send his mind rushing into the gutter, how was he not to imagine taking the first step on a journey that would end with him thrusting his own hips with a bit more finesse?

She licked her lips, and he couldn't help but believe that tasting them would cause the surrounding din to fade into obscurity. They were so incredibly close, so near, that it wouldn't take much, only another inch or two of leaning in—

Cries, shouts, whoops increased in crescendo, and he tore his gaze from what he wanted and directed it toward what he needed to focus on. They were at this god-awful place for a purpose. He couldn't forget that or the importance of finding Lavinia. While he was still put out with her and disappointed in her, he felt a measure of responsibility for her and wanted to ensure she returned to the place she belonged.

The hideous chaps were gone, replaced by a woman in resplendent red walking provocatively from the wings until she stood in the center where the pulpit had no doubt once been. Then she began belting out a tune—in a raspy, throaty voice—that a drunken seaman recently arrived in port might sing. The words, while not lewd, were certainly suggestive of a man bedding a woman in a coarse and ungentlemanly manner.

"Is that her?" Gillie asked quietly.

"No, thank God. Coming here was a colossal mistake. I'm not quite certain what I was thinking."

"You're desperate to find her. Makes it difficult to think straight." She looked down at the parchment, moving it until enough light hit it that she could read it. "There's an act called the Dancing Angels. Does she dance?"

"Nothing that wouldn't be found in a ballroom."

"These ladies will probably be kicking up their skirts."

He couldn't imagine Lavinia saying that as though it were an everyday occurrence, but then he was beginning to realize that Gillie sat in judgment of very little and was incredibly worldly. He didn't want to consider how she'd come to know the things she knew. His stomach clenched with the thought that her experiences with men might be such that she believed the crudity to be normal. He had a strong urge to show her a man's taking of a woman was nothing at all like what was being portrayed on the stage, whether by action or song. "Then they are hardly ladies, are they?" he asked.

She sighed. "Perhaps we should sit through all the acts. There are only two remaining."

The next act was a gent who used a violin to mutilate music. Thorne assumed his purpose was to bring some class to the place. Then it was the Dancing Angels, who did indeed flash a good bit of leg, none of which was very impressive. He imagined Gillie up there on the stage. With her height, her legs would be longer than any of the others. And no doubt incredibly sleek.

He closed his eyes. It was only because she was there with him that he was envisioning her prancing about, kicking a foot toward the ceiling, her skirt falling down her calf, past her knee, to her thigh. If Lavinia were sitting beside him . . . not once had he ever had a lascivious thought about her. Because she was a lady of the highest caliber. A gentleman did not have impure and improper thoughts about a genteel woman. Gillie on the other hand, a tavern owner— was so much more distracting.

"We should probably leave," she said quietly. "They'll be clearing the place out before the next show, collecting another fee from those who wish to stay."

He could think of better ways to spend sixpence. He didn't offer his arm, but simply took her hand and tucked it within the crook of his elbow. "So we don't get separated in the mad rush."

She didn't say anything, but neither did she pull away. Once they were outside, he said, "I need to walk for a spell, get the stench of the place off me."

Merely nodding, she kept her hand where it was and matched her stride to his. He'd be damned glad when the nuisance of a limp was gone.

"There are other penny gaffs," she said.

He shook his head. "I'd forgotten how ghastly awful they are. She won't have gotten herself mixed up in something like that. If someone tricked her into performing, once she realized what it was about, she'd walk out without hesitation." Or at least he bloody well hoped she would. He kept taking what he knew of Gillie and layering it over his memories of Lavinia like a second skin. How could he have paid so little attention to a woman he was to marry? He was the worst sort of scapegrace. "You said you'd heard things about the penny gaffs, but based upon the absence of any abhorrence on your part, I'd have to say you've been to them."

"Before I opened my tavern, or even acquired the funds with which to purchase the building, my brothers took me to a few shows so I would be well aware that men under the influence could be arses."

"You weren't put off?"

"Penny gaffs are designed to encourage lascivious behavior. My tavern is not. I let it be known straightaway that if a man slaps one of my girls on her bum—or elsewhere—he'll be shown the door. Anyone who acts in a worse manner will discover one of my brothers waiting in an alleyway. Certainly men get drunk and say things they ought not. Sometimes they even try to do things they ought not. I've actually had men, after sleeping off a stupor, come into the Mermaid and inform me they are deserving of a punch and offer their chin up in sacrifice."

"And you forgive them."

"Hell, no. I punch them."

His laughter rang out, filling the street, echoing between the buildings, creating a sense of relief in him that he hadn't felt in a good long while. "You are a remarkable woman, Gillie Trewlove."

"Not really," she said, smiling. "But I keep my promises. If I promise a punch is what you'll get if you misbehave, a punch is what you'll get."

He wondered what she might promise him if he kissed her. But based on what they'd seen indoors a few minutes earlier, why would any woman ever want to be touched by a man? The sting of envy pricked him as he imagined another man being granted the right to touch her intimately. And if she'd never had a gent, he felt a need to reassure her.

"What they were pantomiming in there—it was exaggerated into something crude and unappetizing. What actually transpires between a man and a woman . . ." Dear God, he thought he might be blushing. He cleared his throat. "It can be quite remarkable."

"I'll keep that in mind."

Odd that he had no wish for her to keep it in mind with anyone other than him.

HE SEEMED PREOCCUPIED as they traveled back to the Mermaid in his coach. He'd spoken very little since his laughter had floated on the air and circled about her. She'd liked the sound of it: deep, rich, and full.

She wondered if he'd laughed more before he'd been abandoned at the church, before he'd begun his quest to find this woman who obviously didn't appreciate him. It made no sense that a woman would find him lacking.

Earlier, when he'd touched her cheek and then her hair, the way his gaze had wandered over her face before meeting her eyes and dropping to her lips had led her to believe he might kiss her. She wouldn't have objected, even as she knew it wasn't a proper thing to do when he was searching for the woman he was to marry. But the lady wasn't about, might never be found, so where was the harm in giving in to a whisper of temptation?

She nearly scoffed aloud. How many women had thought the same only to find the whisper turning into a roaring shout and nine months later a crying babe? Best to keep every part of her person tightly locked up.

When the coach came to a halt in the mews, he opened the door and climbed out, not waiting for the other fellow, then reached back in and offered his gloved hand. She put hers in it, quivering slightly when his fingers closed tightly around hers as he handed her down.

"Do you need to go into the tavern?" he asked.

"No. It's closed and I trust Roger to have locked it up properly for the night."

"I thought his name was Jolly Roger."

"I don't think I can call him that any longer now that I know he's so jolly because of the things he's doing with my cook in the cellar."

He chuckled. "Tonight seemed to be a night for discovering a good bit of naughtiness."

"I'm sorry we didn't find her."

"The odds weren't in our favor. Perhaps we'll have more luck tomorrow."

"You're going to keep searching."

"Yes. I know it probably makes me appear the fool, but I have to know she's well, and if at all possible, return her to her brother."

Not a fool, she wanted to say, but quite possibly a man who didn't realize he did indeed love the woman. Or perhaps he was merely a very decent sort.

"I'll see you to your door," he said.

"You don't need to be climbing the stairs with that leg. I can see my way up."

"I'll watch you go, make certain you get safely inside."

She nodded. "Tomorrow then?"

"If that is agreeable to you."

"After midday."

"Good night, Gillie."

She sensed he wasn't merely speaking to her but was communicating something to himself as well. She climbed the stairs to the landing, all the while feeling his gaze on her, wondering how she could be so aware of him. Reaching into her reticule, she pulled out the key, unlocked the door, shoved it open, turned back, and waved at him.

His only movement was to touch his fingers to the brim of his hat. So he wasn't going to leave until he saw that she was truly inside. Stepping over the threshold, she closed the door and leaned her back against it, listening for the rumble of the coach leaving. It was several long minutes before she heard the clatter of wheels and the clip-clop of horses' hooves.

She wondered why he'd been in no rush to leave.

Chapter 12

*I*f she was going to spend so much time in the company of a duke, she was going to have to get some new clothes. The shirt and skirt she wore today weren't as fine as the ones she'd worn yesterday, and tomorrow's would be even less fine than today's. But as she stood behind the counter pouring beer for one customer after another, trying to determine when in her schedule she might be able to arrange a trip to the dressmaker's, she realized she wasn't going to change herself for him. While her coffers were far from empty these days, she didn't need a lot of fancy clothes for work, and once they found his bride—which could be this very afternoon— she'd not be seeing him again, so why spend precious coins on clothing that wouldn't be worn for long when the silver could be put to better use?

Although it was quite possible that his bride had already been found or returned home since he had yet to make an appearance and it was already half an hour later than he'd arrived the day before. Not that she was looking at the clock that stood against one wall and watching the minute hand move with maddening regularity without a duke walking through the door.

"Thought you had plans to go out for a bit this afternoon with your gent," Roger said.

"He's. Not. My. Gent. But, yes, we were going out. However as he's not yet here—"

"He's in the kitchen."

She stared at him. "I beg your pardon?"

"I saw him a while ago when I popped my head in to give Hannah a wink."

"How in the world did I miss all this flirtation the two of you do?"

"No idea, Gil."

Not that it mattered, but it was a bit irritating when she'd always considered herself to be so alert, but most of her attention had been on troublesome customers, not bothersome employees. "All right then. I'm off. You're in charge."

"Have fun."

She almost explained that it wasn't an excursion designed to be fun, but even so she was looking forward to it. She pushed open the door that led into the kitchen, walked through—

And could not have come up short so quickly, so unexpectedly, if she'd been hit by a team of oxen.

Wearing his spectacles, Thorne was sitting at the oak table, pointing to something in a book that was open in front of Robin. The sight made her heart do all sorts of funny flips inside her chest, and not just because his clothes, his spectacles, his freshly shaven face, his hair without a strand out of place created a portrait of a devastatingly handsome man, but because he was giving time and attention to Robin.

The lad looked up, his eyes bright, his smile one of the largest he'd ever given her. "Gillie, look! He brung me a book with pictures drawn in it. Of animals. All sorts of animals. Not just dogs and rats and horses. And he said it's mine to keep! And not 'cuz I saved him. Just 'cuz. No reason at all."

"Did he?" She didn't know why the words came out sounding as though she'd been struggling to find them or why two little words should sound so breathless.

Robin bobbed his head so fast and hard that his dark locks flapped his forehead. Then he shoved on Thorne's arm. "Show her the graft."

"Giraffe." He carefully flipped back a few pages, showing utmost respect for the book. Then he stopped, lifted his gaze—that dark liquid gaze, the darkest stout—to her and every speck of air seemed to have been sucked from the room, sucked from her lungs, leaving her feeling light-headed and warm and confused.

"Look, Gillie. It's the tallest animal ever! It's taller even than this building!"

"I don't think it's quite that tall," Thorne said, humor laced through his voice.

Taking a deep breath, regaining her equilibrium, she eased up until she could see the odd creature. "Quite extraordinary." Then she looked at Thorne, wondering why all those confusing sensations hit her again, why he was such a feast for the eyes. "I didn't know you were here. You didn't come in through the front."

"I could tell from the crowd gathered outside you were busy. I didn't want to disturb you, so I came in through the back. And I wanted to give Master Robin the book."

"Can I keep it, Gillie?" the boy asked.

"Yes, of course."

Very, very slowly Robin turned a page. "You have

to be ever so careful so you don't tear the paper," he explained.

"You keep looking at it. The duke and I have to run some errands."

Lost in the drawings, Robin merely nodded.

Removing his glasses and slipping them into his jacket pocket, Thorne stood and reached for his walking stick and hat.

Once they were outside, she said, "That is an extremely nice book." She'd noted the leather binding, and all her forays into the lending library had taught her the value of books. She still paid the yearly fee to have unlimited access to thousands of tomes, although now she would occasionally purchase one if it caught her fancy. "It was very kind of you to go to the trouble to get it for him."

"It was in my library. I noticed it this morning when I was looking for something else, so I simply plucked it off the shelf. No trouble at all."

"But now your library is short a book."

"I've always felt books were meant to be read—or in the case of the one I gave Robin, looked at. If they are simply sitting on a shelf, in danger of not being perused anytime soon, perhaps they'd find joy elsewhere."

"Well, you made him very happy."

"Which made you happy."

She couldn't deny her pleasure that he'd taken time from his quest to give some attention to a lad who very much appreciated it. "It might have lightened my attitude so I'm not quite so put out at having to spend time wandering around on an errand that is unlikely to ever meet with success."

"I'd not pictured you as such a pessimist."

"Look around us, Thorne, truly look around us. You're searching for a needle in a haystack."

"I'm well aware, but I couldn't live with myself if I didn't keep trying. If you'd rather not offer your assistance—"

"I simply don't want you to be disappointed."

"I was left high and dry, standing at the altar with no explanation. I'm already disappointed."

"Yes, I can see that." She sighed, hating that he'd been humiliated in front of his peers.

"So where are we off to today?" he asked. "Inquiring at more lodgings?"

"Maybe later, but it occurred to me that if she ran from the church, she was quite possibly decked out in her wedding finery."

He nodded. "That would be a logical guess. I hadn't seen her, of course, as that's not allowed before we actually meet to exchange vows on that day, but I have attended other weddings where the bride was naught but a froth of silk, satin, and lace."

"Which means, she'd have not been dressed for blending in to these environs, so her first order of business, no doubt, would have been to find something less noticeable to wear."

"Then we should make inquiries at shops or a dressmaker's."

"I was thinking more along the lines of a mission, where they might be offering clothes, shelter, and food."

STANDING INSIDE THE small wooden building, watching as people sorted through piles of rags searching for something serviceable to wear, Thorne hoped to God that Lavinia had enough money on her to go to a proper shop. "She'd have not taken anything from here."

"Beggars can't always be choosers."

But Lavinia was not a beggar. She was the daughter of an earl, the sister of an earl, the fiancée of a duke. He abhorred the thought of her scrounging through these items, which very likely were infested with fleas and the like.

"While I doubt anyone would have use for her gown as it was," Gillie said quietly, "I'm rather certain she could have made a pretty penny off the silk and lace that no doubt comprised it."

She was striving to ease his worries. Perhaps she could sense his consternation because his brow was furrowed so deeply his skull and everything inside it was beginning to ache. He nodded, then shook his head. "She'd have not included this place in her plans."

"So now you're convinced she had it all thought out?"

"Dear God, I hope so."

"Which leaves you with an even bigger question, I think. What was she running from? You? Why not just tell you she wanted out?"

She made things sound so reasonable, as though he came from a reasonable world. "There was the contract between our fathers. Then along with our solicitors, her brother and I hammered out the settlement and signed additional contracts. It's not as easy as saying, 'I've changed my mind.' People are taken to court over broken betrothals. Perhaps she thought to protect her family. I don't know and I won't know until I find her. But I should confess I've had a letter from her stating she had misgivings and begging my forgiveness. It was waiting for me when I initially returned home after you cared for me."

"Why didn't you mention it sooner?"

"Pride, I suppose, or perhaps I feared you wouldn't help me if you thought I was at fault, that she was indeed running from me specifically. Her letter gave no details regarding her misgivings, only that they existed. I need to know specifically why she ran, if it had to do with me in particular, something I did or said. Perhaps there is a chance we can reconcile her concerns."

"You'd still marry her?"

The thought of doing so brought him absolutely no joy. Could he honor the vow he'd made to his father when it meant unhappiness for all concerned? "I don't know. People in my position do not marry for love. We marry for greater gains, out of obligation, for duty."

"I think your lot has the wrong of it. Love is the greatest gain of all."

He offered her a small smile. "So I've heard. If I can't see my way clear to marry her, at the very least, she should be able to return to the bosom of her family, knowing there will be no retribution from me. I need to find her to tell her that."

"Right then. Let's show her portrait around, shall we?"

Another effort in futility, as one person after another merely shrugged and stated, "I've never seen her."

He refrained from asking if they were certain, because they'd surely remember a lady walking in outfitted in an elaborate wedding ensemble.

"Don't look so discouraged," Gillie said. "There are other missions."

But at each they met with a similar lack of success.

After their fourth try, when they were back on the street, he said, "You're being a jolly good sport about all this. I appreciate it."

"Do you appreciate it enough to purchase me a sweet?" She indicated a nearby sweetshop.

He suspected she never asked anyone for anything, that she was striving to cheer him. "Absolutely."

He couldn't recall the last time he'd popped into a sweetshop but the aromas of chocolate and vanilla and cinnamon brought a calming to his soul, as he remembered the many times he'd snuck into the kitchen when at the family estate simply to hear the cook laugh, because there was so little joy expressed by his own parents abovestairs.

A gentleman in a brown jacket was perusing the offerings as was a lady with a little lass in tow. He wasn't surprised Gillie was the sort of woman who knew immediately what she wanted.

"A peppermint ball, Matthew," she announced.

Nor was he surprised she knew the man behind the counter by name. "Make it a dozen," Thorne said.

She swung her head around, her brow furrowed. "I don't need that many."

"It's not a matter of what you need, but what you deserve."

He could see she was on the verge of arguing, but instead gave a nod and acquiesced. "I can share them with others."

Of course she could, and he had little doubt she would. He settled for a dozen toffees, intending to eat only one and handing the remainder over to her to dispense as she pleased. She seemed to enjoy giving out little treats.

After Matthew gave them two brown bags filled with their sweets, and Thorne paid for them, she said, "Let me see the portrait."

He removed it from his pocket and gave it to her. She set it on the glass countertop. "Matthew, have you seen this woman about?"

The sweetshop man squinted, studied it. "No, can't say as I have."

"I've seen her."

With a startled jerk, Thorne looked past Gillie to where the man in the brown jacket on the other side of her was peering over her shoulder. "Where?" he demanded.

The man looked taken aback. "Can't remember exactly. Gave her a ride in my cab."

He was a hansom driver then, could have picked her up outside the church. "When was this? A week or so ago?"

He seemed surprised. "Nah, it was years ago."

Years ago? That made no sense whatsoever.

"Are you certain?" Gillie asked.

He nodded, pointed to the portrait still resting on the counter. "She's a bit older there, but I remember the eyes, sad eyes. I can't remember where I picked her up, but will never forget the posh house where I delivered her. Not often I get asked to go to Mayfair."

"Well, if you happen to see her again," Gillie said, "let me know. I'm Gillie Trewlove. You'll find me at the Mermaid and Unicorn. And you might also tell her, if the occasion allows, I'd like to have a word. There's a free pint in it for you."

He grinned. "I've been meaning to make it to the Mermaid, but my woman considers liquor a sin."

"Then come for a bowl of soup."

"I might do that."

She picked the portrait off the counter and held it out to Thorne. He merely shook his head. "Perhaps you should keep it. You seem to have more luck showing it around."

"At least we know she's been in the area before."

"The question is: For what purpose?"

Chapter 13

$\mathcal{T}$horne assumed if Collinsworth or the men he'd hired had located Lavinia that the earl would send word. He needed to speak with the man who was to have become his brother-by-marriage, but all the activity from yesterday and that afternoon had his thigh and shoulder rebelling at the abuse, so he'd instructed his coachman to return to Coventry House. While he could push through the discomfort, he saw no need at the moment and thought a bit of rest would do him some good. The earl had already admitted he hadn't a clue regarding why his sister had gone to Whitechapel, so it was unlikely he'd have any idea regarding why she might have visited some years before. Besides, her visit then might have nothing at all to do with her going there now. Perhaps she'd simply fancied that area of London, although he couldn't imagine why she would.

Not true. He could see the appeal. While the poverty visiting on that district didn't attract him, a certain tavern owner most certainly did. He appreciated her frankness, which in turn caused him to be equally forthright with her. Never before had he realized he often said what was expected instead of what was actually felt. He was less guarded with her, which he found to be quite liberating.

The coach came to a halt in front of his residence and he disembarked, his leg protesting more than he'd have liked but not as much as it had three days ago. His injuries were improving; just not fast enough to suit him. Patience was not his strong suit.

Once inside, he strode to his office, grateful he didn't pass his mother on the way as he wasn't in the mood for her harping. He poured himself a whisky and started to head for a chair by the window when his gaze fell on the stack of correspondence on his desk. The afternoon postal delivery. He recognized the handwriting on the top envelope. Changing course, he took the chair behind his desk, set down his glass, grabbed the gold paper knife, and slit open the envelope. After taking a sip of whisky, he proceeded to take out the sheet of thin parchment nestled inside.

Dear Thorne,

I beg you to cease searching for me. I should have been more forthright in my earlier correspondence. There is another, you see, who holds my heart.

I know contracts were agreed to and signed. I know what my duty entails, but carrying it out will crush my soul. I care for you too much to burden you with a wife who would view marriage to you as a chore rather than a delight. You deserve better than I can give.

I tried to explain this to my brother, but he would not hear it. Nor would my mother who was quite insistent I carry through with my duties. I had hoped my earlier letter would

*dissuade you from trying to find me but I
misjudged your resolve.*

*Please let me go. Find happiness with
someone deserving of you.*

*Sincerest Regards,
Lavinia*

Considering her words, he leaned back in his chair.
She loved another. He should have felt jealousy or disappointment or betrayal. Instead he felt relief. She'd
told him before she was safe, but that hadn't been
enough to dissuade him from trying to find her. He'd
needed an explanation and now he had it. He was
actually glad for her, glad she had someone she loved,
glad she hadn't married him when her heart had called
to another. When his heart had not belonged to her.
He wasn't certain he was even capable of loving someone, that he even grasped the fundamentals of how
one came to love. His parents had never shown him
any affection, and as a boy, he'd been rather frightened
of them, their sternness, their inability to be pleased
by anything he did.

So when his father had asked him to honor the
contract he'd made with the previous Earl of Collinsworth, to acquire the land that generations of dukes
had yearned to possess, he'd gladly given a vow, thinking he'd please his father at last, that finally he might
gain his love.

In his experience, marriages among the nobility
were frigid affairs. While he'd given Lavinia baubles,
he'd given her nothing of himself. That knowledge
now left him feeling rather disgusted with himself.
Little wonder she had not confided her doubts to him.
They had not been close. They'd both been seeing

to their duty, as outlined by their fathers. He'd always admired those who upheld their responsibilities, but his respect for Lavinia had gone up a notch with her rebelliousness. He rather regretted not making the effort to know her better.

Then another thought struck him. She knew he was looking for her. How had she learned of his quest to find her? Had she observed him yesterday, searching for her? Had he seen her and not recognized her, overlooked her? Had he spoken with someone who had relayed the information to her? Perhaps she had numerous friends in the area, numerous friends along with a love. She was a woman of unfathomable mysteries—but it was no longer his place to solve them.

"I'VE HAD FURTHER word from your sister," Thorne said moments after he entered the earl's library, the butler closed the door on his way out, and Collinsworth came to his feet behind his desk. "Were you aware there is someone else for whom she holds affection?"

With a heavy sigh and a shake of his head, Collinsworth began pouring whisky into two tumblers. "There was a boy in her youth. Father saw to him. I thought we were done with him." He handed Thorne a glass, took a sip. "I suppose there could be someone else."

"Does he reside in Whitechapel?"

"To be honest, I thought he'd been shipped off to Australia."

"Not the good sort then."

The earl dropped into a nearby chair. "No."

Thorne took the one opposite him. He couldn't imagine Lavinia with a possible criminal, but as he'd recently acknowledged, he knew so very little about her. "Her previous letter indicating she is safe seems to bear out."

"As though she has the good sense to judge her well-being properly. I think the fact she left you standing at the altar is a testament to her bad judgment. Unfortunately, the two men I hired have failed to find her or any hint of where she might be hiding out."

"I've been continuing with my search as well." Although based on her latest correspondence he wondered if he should give up his quest. But giving up the hunt meant giving up time with Gillie. "Why didn't you tell me she had a history with someone?"

"I didn't think it would make any difference. It was years ago, and he was entirely inappropriate. A commoner or worse, from what I was given to understand. I didn't know much about him, except that she fancied herself in love. Father put an end to it."

Thorne took a sip of the whisky. It was good quality, but again he didn't enjoy it as much as that served by Gillie. "I won't marry her now, even if she returns here."

"Then she is destined to be an old maid."

Was that such a bad thing when the alternative was to spend the remainder of her life with one man while longing for another? He wasn't quite certain he could claim his decision was based solely on her not wanting him. He was no longer convinced he could be happy, or even content, with Lavinia, not when he, too, would find himself thinking of another. "She could already be wed."

"Dear God, I hope not. Father will be rolling over in his grave if she's with that fellow from before."

And his father would be rolling over in his grave because Wood's End would not be coming into his hands, but suddenly that all seemed unimportant when compared with a woman's happiness. "The missive she sent me came without an address. Can you have these blokes you've hired spread the word that she is free of me?"

Collinsworth nodded. "I shall see it done. I was looking forward to having you as a relation."

"But Lavinia wasn't. Shortly before the wedding, she'd grown remarkably solemn, distant even, whenever we'd have an outing to the park. I assumed it was nerves regarding the approaching nuptials. I didn't question her. My lack of concern leaves me to believe she was quite right not to go through with the ceremony. I wish only that our relationship had been such that she'd been able to confide in me before a church filled with people witnessed my humiliation."

Now he needed to let Gillie know that his need for her had come to an end. Strange, though, how he feared his need for her was only just beginning.

SHE WAS AN idiot, continuing to help him search for the woman he would marry, willingly spending additional time with him when nothing could come of it. She didn't like that he intrigued her or that she thought about him so much. But her interest in him was no doubt simply because she'd nursed him back to health. That sort of thing created a bond.

Just as tending to all these folks who visited her tavern night after night created a bond. She'd come to know them well, could tell when life was treating them kindly and when it wasn't. She knew when Jerome was taking refuge here because his wife was in a foul mood, when Pickens had no luck finding an odd job for the day, when Spud had lost at the gaming tables. She recognized when Canary sauntered in with a full belly and when he was hoping she might set a bowl of soup in front of him and forget to collect for it. She knew when babes were born, children took ill, and misdeeds were done for good causes—to put bread in tiny bellies. She'd poured them drinks, cleaned up after them when they overindulged, and listened to their worries. They were as familiar as the back of her hand.

So standing behind the bar now, while darkness shrouded the streets, she recognized when something was amiss with one of her regular patrons. "Roger?"

Polishing a tankard, her barman wandered over. "Aye?"

"How long has Charlie McFarley had that swollen jaw?"

He narrowed his eyes, puckered his mouth as though those actions made it easier to recall memories. "A while now. Ever since he came in flush. Might have been that first night you were indisposed with the female curse."

Rolling her eyes, she almost snapped that he had the wrong of it, but it wasn't worth the breath needed for an argument. Besides, something else had caught her attention. "Flush?"

"Aye. Came into some money. Told me where he got it but I couldn't understand his mumbling. He paid off what he owed so I poured him a drink. He's been back a couple of times since, but always has coin, so I serve him."

"Right. Keep an eye on him. If he starts to leave, stop him. I want to have a word with him." Turning, she headed into the kitchen. Hannah was done for the night, everything put away except for the myriad of glasses Robin was washing at the sink. "Robin, I need you to fetch a constable."

The boy swung around, his eyes wide. "I ain't done nuffink."

She ruffled his hair. "I know that, lad. But I think someone else has. Tell him to come into the tavern and find me. And be quick about it."

While common sense told her to wait for the constable's arrival, memories of the malice done behind her establishment had her charging across the taproom toward the corner table where Charlie sat with three of his mates. Four chums, all looking a bit weathered, with fading yellowing bruises marring their faces here and there. Charlie had obviously gotten the worse of it, but then she recalled a crack echoing through the alleyway had first garnered her attention to the misdeeds being carried out. It was quite possible that swollen-looking jaw was going to be a permanent addition to his face. "Hello, lads, everything all right here?"

There were some mumbled ayes, but Charlie merely studied his tankard as though he might be required to create a duplicate on the morrow. "Your jaw looks painful, Charlie. What happened there?"

"Mam intu a dure."

"I beg your pardon?"

"'E ran into a door," one of his cohorts said.

"I see. When was this?"

They all shrugged, suddenly taking intense interest

in a thumbnail, a frayed cuff, a knothole in the wood grain of the table, an ear that was apparently itching.

"A few nights ago, I'd wager."

Charlie glared at her. The fact he couldn't move his mouth into a threatening sneer made his glower ineffectual, although she was angry enough she wouldn't have paid it any heed anyway. "Where's the pocket watch?"

"Dunno wot yer talkin' 'bout." Although still mumbled, the words were a bit clearer, as though he felt a need to ensure she understood them.

"I think you do. I checked with Petey. You didn't take it to him, so which fence did you take it to?"

His eyes went a bit wild, a good bit of the white visible. Suddenly he shoved back his chair; his mates scrambled to get out as well. The daft idiots were not getting away.

She launched herself at their leader.

THORNE STRODE INTO the tavern in time to see the melee break out, to watch in horrified fascination as Gillie propelled herself through the air like a mermaid being expelled by a gigantic wave from the sea and landed on some poor bloke, carrying him down to the floor. Suddenly fists were flying, while the thud of flesh hitting flesh, the crash of glassware, the ping of pewter, the clattering of chairs and tables being smashed filled the air. Grunts and yells echoed around him, as he limped hurriedly toward Gillie to offer aid, avoiding one punch after another, shoving one fellow after another aside. He was like a madman in his rush to get to her, as though he alone could save her, as though she was all that mattered.

She was all that mattered. That thought echoed through his mind with an intensity that might have caused him alarm if he wasn't distracted by other forces.

One small fellow was striving to pull her off the larger one she was wrestling, clinging to him as though she were determined to be his jailor. Another was striking her. He saw every shade of red that existed, felt heated fury and then a cold calm settled over him. He dropped his walking stick, picked up a chair, and swung with enough force it took down the one hitting her and sent his mate scurrying back. Without much thought, he grabbed the fallen man by the scruff of his jacket and lifted him up as though he weighed nothing at all and planted his fist in the center of his face. Cartilage and bone caved in, an ear-piercing screech shuddered through the air. He flung the fool aside and turned back to Gillie.

She was lying on the floor motionless, the man who had been beneath her was scrambling away, while another holding the broken remains of a chair was staring at her as though he realized he'd made a grave error in judgment. Perhaps because a slew of fists were headed in his direction and the man he'd sought to rescue was suddenly struggling to escape from a behemoth's grasp.

Dropping to his knees, Thorne withdrew a handkerchief from his pocket and pressed it gently to a gash at the back of Gillie's head. Her short hair made it easy to see the blood, and his stomach roiled at the sight. As carefully as possible, he rolled her over onto his lap, into his arms. Tenderly he patted her cheek. "Gillie?"

It didn't make him feel any better that she didn't so much as bat a lash. He became aware of the arrival of constables, the noise level increasing and then abruptly dimming.

"Did ye kill her?" Robin's nose very nearly touched his.

"Don't be absurd."

A man, who very much resembled the brother he'd met the other night, crouched beside the boy. "Off with you, Robin."

"But—"

"No buts. She'll be all right."

As the lad scampered away, he wondered how the gent could be so sure when he himself had never been more terrified in his life as the thought, "She's not long for this world," skittered along his spine, sending chills through his entire person.

"You the duke?" the man asked, as though there were only one. Maybe he was the only one in her life.

"Thorne."

"Aiden. Her brother. I'll take her to her rooms."

"I'll see to her." He'd used his ducal tone, which gave fair warning he'd brook no arguments.

Arching a brow, Aiden nodded. "All right. But Beast and I will help."

He wondered if her brother could tell that his leg was killing him. Beast turned out to be the behemoth who'd been holding the man she'd leaped onto, a man he realized now as a constable marched him out, seemed to have a broken jaw. Were these the louts who'd jumped him? Now they'd hurt her. He'd see them hanged.

With help from Aiden and Beast, he managed to get to his feet with her cradled in his arms. For such a tall woman, she wasn't particularly heavy or perhaps it was simply that he was built for carrying her.

It felt right to have her curled against his chest as he ascended the stairs to her lodgings, Aiden in the lead while Beast had gone to fetch a doctor.

Using a key, Aiden opened the door. Thorne pushed through and headed into the bedchamber where he gently laid her on the bed.

"You've been in here before."

Thorne twisted around to find Aiden leaning against the doorjamb, arms folded over his chest. "Why would you think that?"

"You didn't look about, didn't hesitate. You knew exactly where to find her bed."

"I was jumped about a week ago. She nursed me back to health."

He slowly nodded. "That explains some things."

Hearing a soft moan, he turned back to Gillie, sat on the edge of the mattress, took one of her hands, and placed the palm of one of his against her cheek. "Easy, sweetheart. Easy."

Her eyes fluttered open; she grimaced. "It was Charlie McFarley and his boys who attacked you. He wouldn't tell me where he fenced your watch."

"That's the reason you jumped him? You idiotic—"

"I wouldn't yell at her if I were you," Aiden said calmly, evenly, but also quite threateningly.

He hadn't been yelling but his voice had been reverberating with displeasure. He reined in his temper; still the thought of this woman coming to any harm had him shaking.

She lifted a hand to her crown, grimaced. "My head—"

Tenderly he took her wrist, pulled her fingers away. "Careful. You've a gash there. A physician is coming."

"I don't need a doctor." She made a move to sit up, dropped back down, groaned. "Head hurts."

"I imagine it does. Someone slammed a chair against it."

A corner of her mouth hitched up. "That wouldn't have stopped me. I'm too hardheaded."

Only it had stopped her. It had knocked her out, left her on the floor where she could have come to more harm. "Let the physician make sure you're all right before you do anything."

She blinked as though trying to sort things out. "What are you doing here?"

"I needed to speak with you."

"About?"

He glanced over his shoulder at her brother. "Must you lurk about like a miscreant?"

He flashed a grin. "I am a miscreant."

"Aiden," she growled, a warning in her voice despite her injured state.

"I'm not leaving him alone with you."

"I've been alone with him before."

"Then he and I will be having a talk outside in a bit. I need to introduce him to my fist."

"Don't be daft. Nothing untoward happened. Besides, I can see to myself. Stop hovering in my doorway."

Unfolding his arms, he straightened. "I'll go prepare you a cup of tea. Door stays open." With that, he stomped away.

"Sorry," she said. "He's a bit overprotective."

"I'm actually glad of it." Thorne cradled her cheek again, stroked it softly, taking unwarranted pleasure from the silkiness of her skin. "What were you thinking to confront them?"

"Having thieves in my tavern is bad for business."

He chuckled low. "So it was all about business?"

"And I wanted to find your watch for you."

"It has been in my family for generations, one of the things most treasured." Leaning down, he pressed a kiss to her forehead. "But it is not of more value than you."

CLOSING HER EYES, she relished the warmth of his lips. The part of her that believed in mermaids and unicorns, that wove fanciful tales where happiness was always nearby, dared to imagine his words meant more than they did. That he wasn't speaking in generalizations about the value of a person but was referring specifically to *her* worth. It made her heart sing, her toes curl.

She couldn't believe how grateful she was to have him once more within her apartment, how he chased away the shadows of loneliness, how his presence brightened the room more than any lamp. When he pulled back, she wanted to wrap her arms around him and hold him near.

She heard a commotion and voices in the adjoining room, realized others had entered, which managed to snap her back to reality. Silly chit, to have all those thoughts. He was merely caring for her as she'd cared for him, probably feeling responsible for her rash decision regarding Charlie. Although she did have little tolerance for those who didn't respect the rights of others, for lawbreakers, she hadn't been able to stop herself from imagining the look of gratitude she'd see on his face when she presented him with his cherished watch. He'd cared about it when he'd been near death. How much more he'd care about it when he was full of life.

Dr. Graves strode in, Beast on his heels, quickly followed by Aiden, not carrying a cup of tea. She'd wager the brat had been skulking near the doorway just out of sight.

"I see you've recovered," Graves said to Thorne.

"Thanks in no small measure to you and this lovely lady here."

She wanted to slip beneath the covers, pull them up over her head. No one ever referred to her as lovely. If her brothers snickered, she was going to leap out of the bed and smack them. Instead they both simply stood at the foot of the bed, arms crossed, as though they were royal guards.

"Let's see what we have here," Graves said as he bent over her and began to examine her head.

Thorne moved to the other side of the bed, as though it was the most natural thing in the world to be sitting beside her in so intimate a setting.

"Stop scowling, Aiden," she ordered.

"I just find it odd—"

Beast elbowed him, which caused him to turn his ire on her other brother. "What was that for?"

"Don't interfere."

"With what?"

"With what's going on here."

"And what exactly is that?"

With a great gust of a sigh, Beast began shoving him out of the room. He was the tallest and broadest of her brothers and when he asserted himself in a physical way, no one could best him.

"Wait. Stop. What do you know that I don't?" Aiden called out just before the front door slammed shut.

She might have laughed if her head didn't hurt so much. Beast was also the most intuitive of her brothers and she wondered what he did know.

"You're going to need a few stitches," Graves said.

As the doctor went to work, Thorne held her hand, didn't object when she squeezed hard. To distract herself from the discomfort of what the physician was doing, she concentrated on Thorne's hand. Although she'd washed it half a dozen times while he'd been under her care, now she was able to experience the strength and power in it as he folded it around hers. She imagined his hands holding the reins, guiding a horse. She imagined them holding a woman as he waltzed her across a ballroom. She imagined him intertwining their fingers as they dashed across a field of daisies.

She wasn't certain when the woman in her imaginings had taken on her characteristics, had become her. She never envisioned herself with men, but she seemed unable to visualize him with anyone other than her.

"All right," Graves finally said when he finished wrapping a strip of linen around the back of her head and forehead. "That should do it. You have a rather large knot there, which leads me to believe it was quite a blow. Probably best not to sleep for a while."

"What's a while?" she asked.

"Dawn. If you haven't lost your senses or consciousness by then, you should be all right."

"I'll see she stays awake," Thorne said.

"You can't stay here through the night," she told him.

"Not to worry. I won't take advantage."

She did wish his words didn't fill her with such disappointment. She made a move to clamber out of the bed and a wave of dizziness assailed her.

"Stay," Thorne ordered, placing a hand on her shoulder and pressing her back down to the mattress.

She wanted to defy him—damn, but the man was dictatorial—except falling flat on her face, which she was likely to do, would hardly serve her purpose of proving she didn't need anyone to see after her. In resignation, she watched as he escorted Graves out of her bedchamber, heard their voices but not their words, soon followed by the quiet closing of a door. Waiting there, she should have been bothered by the occasional clang and bang coming from the other rooms, her kitchen most likely. She wasn't accustomed to having anyone rummaging about her lodgings, and yet she found the sounds rather comforting, soothing enough that every muscle relaxed and her body melted into the mattress.

Surprised her brothers hadn't been waiting for Graves's departure and come barging in, she found herself wondering at Beast's words and what he thought was going on here. Perhaps he had no concerns because he'd seen her speaking with Thorne the other night, was aware she knew him, trusted him. She scoffed. How could Beast know that when she'd only just realized it herself?

As much as Thorne irritated her when he threw about commands—as dukes were wont to do—she did inherently have faith in his underlying character. He wouldn't hurt her, wouldn't take advantage, had no interest in her other than to repay her for the care she'd given him after he'd been attacked. He wasn't staying behind because he *liked* her, was drawn to her, found her fascinating. She wasn't like the delicate flowers who frequented the balls he attended and sat across from him during lavish dinners. But as she heard his footsteps nearing, for the first time in her life she wished she was.

He was carrying a tray that held a bowl and two glasses of amber liquid. He'd no doubt found her whisky. He was also wearing his spectacles now. She didn't like that they caused her to hope he wore them in order to see her more clearly.

As he set the tray on the bedside table, she eyed the bowl, wondering where he might have gotten the soup. "I'm not really hungry. I ate earlier."

"That's good as I haven't prepared you anything to eat. Let's sit you up a bit."

"Oh. I thought perhaps the bowl contained broth or something equally unappealing." She gingerly pushed herself up while he stuffed pillows behind her back, his body so close to hers that she could feel the heat, could inhale his tart fragrance.

"Water."

"I haven't a fever. I'm not in need of wiping down."

Finished with his task, still near, he cradled her chin and used his thumb to stroke the corner of her mouth, making her feel as though she might have suddenly become fevered. "You have a bit of dirt on your face. Scuffling around on the floor with ruffians is not a clean business."

Rubbing at her cheek, she brushed his hand aside in the process, and rather regretted that. "I'm sure it's fine."

His lips formed the barest hint of a smile as he reached for the glasses and handed her one. He lifted his. "To a speedy recovery."

"You're making too much of a fuss. I'm barely injured."

"You shouldn't be injured at all." After taking a sip, he set his glass aside, stood, removed his jacket, and set it neatly on a nearby chair. She watched in fascination as he unbuttoned his waistcoat—how could so simple an action be so spellbinding—shrugged it off, and set it atop the jacket.

"What are you doing?"

"As I intend to be here through the night, I decided to get comfortable."

The slow unknotting and unwinding of his neck cloth was next. Then he began rolling up the sleeves of his shirt. She'd seen him naked. Why was it the baring of only his forearms was so much more provocative?

Loosening the top two buttons of his shirt, he returned to the bed, sat on its edge, and reached for the tray, picking up a cloth she hadn't noticed.

"You're not going to wash me."

He arched a brow at her. "Do you really want to engage in a battle you can't possibly win?"

"You shouldn't assume just because I'm a woman that I would lose."

"I'm not assuming that at all," he said, his voice low and raspy, sending warm tingles along her spine even as she recognized the threat of a challenge when it was being delivered. He leaned in until she could almost see her reflection in his dark eyes. "But I am assuming, as much as you pretend otherwise, that there is a measure of feminine vanity in you and you will be in want of a clean face when I kiss you."

Chapter 14

$\mathscr{T}$aking great delight in the widening of her eyes and the slight parting of her lips, he didn't know what had prompted his words, his dare. He knew only that he had an insatiable urge to spoil this woman, take care of her, kiss her. Ah, yes, he definitely wanted to plunder that bold as brass mouth of hers. He wasn't certain when it had come upon him that he did, but it seemed now that the desire had always been there, just hovering in the shadows, lingering beneath the surface of his desires.

He thought he'd returned to the Mermaid and Unicorn earlier than planned because he needed to alert her regarding the missive he'd received and how it might alter their quest to find his bride, but he realized now he'd come to the tavern simply because he wanted to see her again, because he wanted to speak with her, hear her voice, smell her unique fragrance of vanilla and barley. Lavinia's letter had provided him with an excuse not to see Gillie any longer, and he damned well didn't want to take it.

Moving away from her, he dipped the cloth into the bowl. Out of the corner of his eye, he watched as she downed all the whisky in her glass. Most women he knew would have been sputtering and coughing, but then she wasn't most women. She was uniquely herself. And he adored that about her.

"As though I'd let you," she muttered.

"Care to say that a bit louder with a bit more force?" He wrung out the cloth and shifted his body on the bed in order to face her more squarely. "Don't look so frightened, Gillie. I won't kiss you if you don't want me to."

"I'm not frightened. I don't frighten."

He noted she hadn't said she didn't want him to kiss her. "Aren't you curious regarding what it might be like between us?"

She thrust her glass toward him. "I could do with more whisky."

He couldn't stop his grin, but he did manage to make it look not quite so victorious as he exchanged her glass for his. "Have you ever been kissed?"

"None of your bleedin' business." She took a swallow of the whisky, licked her lips. How was any man to resist such an innocent yet provocative action?

But resist he did as he gently wiped the cloth over her high cheekbone. He couldn't imagine a tavern owner wouldn't have had men in her life. But if she had, why would the thought of a kiss make her nervous? Because of where it could lead? Because of where she wanted it to lead?

She certainly didn't give the impression he repulsed her. Wouldn't she have moved away from him if he did, instead of turning her face toward him like a bud in want of direct sunlight so he had easier access to that side of her face? "Appears you have a slight bruise on this cheek. Does it hurt?"

"No." Her voice was soft, wary.

"Do you often get into skirmishes with your customers?"

"Not usually. Bad for business."

"You think a lot about what's bad for business."

"Without a doubt. I want to have success, make my own way. Not be dependent on anyone."

He moved the cloth down to her chin where another bruise loomed. She thought herself tough but his gut clenched at how easily she could be hurt. "You're to be admired, Gillie."

"I'm not so unlike anyone else trying to survive, except I've been extremely fortunate to be in a family where everyone works together. We help each other out whenever we can. Like right this minute, I suspect my brothers are downstairs, straightening up the mess."

This woman had every right to complain about her life, the harshness of it. Instead she met it head-on and worked hard to make it better for herself. "Is Beast your brother as well?"

"Yes."

"Beast, Aiden, Finn, and Mick. And your sister?"

"Fancy." Suddenly she seemed self-conscious. "She's the only one my mum gave birth to, but even so she was born out of wedlock. She's much younger than the rest of us, and we all strive to protect her."

"Now that you mention her, I believe I recall seeing her at the wedding. Someone pointed her out."

"I wouldn't be surprised if you noticed her. She's very pretty."

"You're pretty as well."

She scoffed, looked at him sadly. "Not like her. She's delicate and refined."

"Beauty comes in all forms, Gillie." A week ago, he'd thought it only came in satin and silk, and now he saw it in coarse muslin and soft linen.

She closed her eyes as he traced the damp cloth along the narrow, delicate bridge of her nose. Her burnished eyelashes, darker at the tips, rested just above her cheeks. Her mouth was a temptation in which he could not yet indulge. He would not take until she was ready and he sensed she was not yet so. Slowly, tenderly, he moved to the other cheek. She opened her eyes, the green and brown rich and inviting.

"Why did you come tonight?" she asked softly.

To see you. Because I couldn't stay away. He almost lied; he almost told her that he wanted to discuss further where they would search for his bride, but he could no more lie to this woman than he could leave her side when she was hurt. "Earlier in the evening, I received another missive from Lavinia. She pleads with me to let her be."

"Lavinia?" A slight pleat appeared between her brows. "A fancy name your bride has."

"Indeed."

"Are you going to stop searching for her?"

"I haven't quite decided. She said there is another. I assume she is with him, yet still I feel a need to ensure all is well."

The crease deepened. "She threw you over for someone else and didn't have the decency to tell you before you were at the church?"

"I suppose she didn't know how to tell me."

"She was a coward. She could have just said, 'I want to marry someone else.' It's not that hard. I'm glad you didn't marry her. You deserve someone stronger, someone with some gumption in them."

Someone like her. Damn it all to hell, he'd planned to wait, to woo, to seduce. Instead she'd wooed and seduced him until all he wanted was her. With a slowness designed not to jar or hurt her, he lowered his mouth to hers.

She tasted of the dark richness of whisky, the sweetness of woman. Her hand came up and gently cradled his jaw, making him grateful he'd taken a razor to it before leaving his residence. Her soft sigh was music to his ears, shimmered through him, over him, around him, wrapping him in a cocoon of desire unlike anything he'd ever known.

He took the kiss deeper.

SHE LOVED THE feel of that lush beautiful mouth against hers. His tongue traced the seam between her lips, almost a tickling, a teasing, and then with a bit more sureness. She no doubt should have admitted she'd never been kissed, had never wanted to be. This fire between them, or whatever it was, was only physical. He was such a gorgeous man, how could she not be drawn to him? Why he fancied her was beyond knowing. Perhaps he was simply tired of the posh in his life.

Then his tongue slid into her mouth, and she no longer was analyzing his reasons. She was simply parting her lips farther and enjoying the full taste and feel of his urgency, his passion, his wildness. She sensed he was holding back, either because he detected her inexperience or was concerned about her blasted injury. The wound ached, her head hurt, and she cursed them both for the unpleasant distraction that hovered at the far edges of her awareness.

She concentrated on him, the thoroughness with which he explored her mouth, his low growl when she returned the favor and slipped her tongue between his lips, tasting him fully and completely, relishing the dark flavor that was uniquely him. Or she thought it was. She had nothing with which to compare but couldn't imagine any other man tasted as flavorful. With one hand cradling his jaw, she skimmed the fingers of the other up into his hair, loving the way the thick dark brown strands welcomed and curled around her. Tightening her grip, she held him, absorbing the warmth of his nearness.

Her limbs tingled, her body grew lethargic. If standing, she'd melt into the floor, and there would be wonder in that as well, falling along the length of his hard, masculine form.

His mouth slid off hers, trailed along her chin, creating a myriad of sensations that heated her to the core. She had this odd need for him to place his mouth elsewhere, on her breasts, her stomach, lower. Dear God, but she felt wanton, yet she seemed incapable of pushing him away as he nibbled along her throat, his tongue lapping at the sensitive skin, before he moved on to the next area. He reached her collarbone and his mouth lingered, suckling gently before journeying back up to her chin and retreating.

His eyes held hers, and she was surprised by how his smoldered with need, need that matched her own. Her earlier statement about never being frightened mocked her now, because she was terrified, terrified this aching hunger within her would never be satisfied, that the fires he'd kindled would never be extinguished, that they would burn until she was consumed by them.

Gently he tucked his finger beneath her chin, stroked his thumb over her lower lip, wet and swollen, still tingling. "We're not done here, you and I. But I won't take advantage of a woman who might not be thinking clearly due to a blow to the head."

Take advantage, her mind screamed, but her tongue had the good sense to remain still.

He rose to his feet. "Have you a book about that I could read to you?"

"A book?"

He began walking around, perusing one thing and then another. "Yes. I need to keep you awake. Reading might accomplish that. Something gruesome with a murder perhaps."

She couldn't help herself. Inwardly she smiled. "Something to take your mind off the kiss?"

Swinging around, he faced her, gave her a wry grin. "I am definitely in need of a distraction."

"You don't need to stay. I'm not going to fall asleep."

"I'm not leaving, Gillie."

She did wish she didn't enjoy so much the way her name sounded on his tongue. Lifting a shoulder, she released a small sigh. "Front room."

He started toward the open doorway, halted in midstride, paused a second longer like so many customers at her bar contemplating which liquor would get them quickest to where they wanted to be. Slowly he turned. "Would you like me to prepare you a bath?"

She stared at him as though he'd spoken to her in a foreign language. Or perhaps the blow to her head had caused her ears to become scrambled in their hearing. "I beg your pardon?"

A corner of that mouth that only a few moments before had been doing wicked things to hers hitched up. "You bathed me when you were caring for me."

"That was different. You were filthy."

"I suspect rolling around on the floor didn't leave you exactly clean. If I were to move your clothing aside, I'm rather certain I'd find dirt elsewhere."

"I'm not going to bathe in front of you."

"I wouldn't dream of asking you to." That enticing hitch went up a little higher. "I would *dream* of it, to be honest, but I wouldn't ask. I am striving to remain a gentleman here."

Don't hovered on the end of her tongue and she nearly bit the tip to keep it from releasing an answer that could send her spiraling into perdition.

"I'll prepare it in here and wait in the other room until you're finished."

"I don't have a lock on that door."

"Gillie." He heaved an impatient sigh. "If I were going to take advantage a lock wouldn't stop me. And I'd have probably done it already."

He had the right of it there. He could have taken advantage when she was with him in the coach the night before or as they'd walked along the street after witnessing the performances at the penny gaff or even inside the venue. No one would have thought anything of it. If they'd noticed, they'd have egged him on. But she couldn't stop herself from pointing out, "You just now kissed me."

"You wanted it as much as I did. Admit it."

She plucked at a loose string on the quilt covering her bed. "I was curious." Then, even though she'd claimed it was none of his bloody business, she admitted, "I've never been kissed before."

Lifting her gaze to his, she was warmed to see the understanding in his expression. "I know."

Panic hit her. She'd always wanted to do everything

correctly. "Did I do it wrong?" Was that the reason he'd stopped? He hadn't enjoyed it as much as she had?

"Hardly. I'd say you're a natural."

Like her mother, no doubt. Her mother had given away her kisses, given away her body—otherwise, Gillie wouldn't exist. The truth was she did feel grimy, soiled. She and Charlie had been locked in an embrace, and based upon the hideous odorous cloud that had engulfed her with his nearness, she could state with clear certainty he was months away from his last yearly dip in a tub. "Yes, a bath would be lovely." She angled her head questioningly. "Although I can't imagine you, being a duke, know how to prepare one."

That grin again. "You would be surprised at what I know how to do."

So how did one go about preparing a bath? Thorne wondered as he stood in the kitchen area. There was a box of wood beside the stove, so he assumed he'd shove some inside and set it alight, fill a huge pot with water, and then another and another.

As he went to work, he admitted to himself that it had been a damned stupid idea to suggest the bath, but he'd been in dire need of some sort of physical exertion to distract himself from thoughts of her enticing lips and how the kiss had undone him. He'd kissed women before, lots of women, all sorts of women, but it had never felt as though any of them had reached deep within him and caressed his soul.

In spite of her innocence and lack of experience, she had poured all that she was into that mating of the mouths and it had shaken him clear down to the soles of his boots. Even as he'd wanted to retreat, he'd felt a stronger urge to rush headlong into an encounter unlike anything in which he'd ever engaged. How was it that this woman caused him to long for things, hunger for things he'd always discounted as the yearnings of fools?

While he waited for the water to heat, he noted the tidiness of the kitchen, then walked into the main room. A comfortable-looking sofa rested before the fireplace, two plush chairs covered in yellow floral fabric on either side of it. Several newspapers were spread out over a short-legged table before the sofa. He couldn't imagine her perusing them for gossip. No, she would read the same articles that gentlemen did, newsworthy pieces that would keep her apprised of the world, industry, Parliament, and matters that might affect the profits of her tavern or provide her with ideas of how to improve it. On the mantelpiece was a small photograph, framed in pewter. They'd gone to a great deal of trouble and expense to hire a photographer to mark the moment, which alerted him that it held significance. He couldn't stop himself from taking it and studying it more closely. In the background was her tavern. She stood before it, with a group of people he recognized as her brothers and sister. Beside her was a smaller woman, dark-haired, neither too slender, nor too round, whom he assumed was her mother. Gillie's arm encircled her shoulders. As a matter of fact, everyone's arms circled the shoulders of the person standing next to them forming a chain of comfort and support, clearly shouting to anyone who passed by that they were all in it together. He had no memory of either of his parents ever embracing him, ever standing so forcefully beside him. Gillie was a bit younger, smiling brightly, hope and joy reflected in her eyes. He couldn't help but believe the photograph had been taken around the time she'd opened the tavern. He wished he'd been there to help her celebrate, to be part of the moment. With a scoff, he set the photograph back on the oak mantel. At the time he hadn't even known she existed.

Turning, he smiled at a painting, wondering why he hadn't noticed it before. A mermaid sat on a rock, her hand resting on a unicorn's muzzle. She did seem to enjoy her mermaids and unicorns. And there was a shelf with numerous books resting on it. Overall, the room wasn't fancy, but it reflected warmth, and he imagined how comforting she found it to return here after work each night.

After checking the water and seeing it was not yet boiling, he returned to her chamber, crouched before the fireplace, and built a low fire in the hearth so she wouldn't catch chill. He could sense her watching him. "Am I doing it correctly?"

"Have you never built a fire before?"

Still on the balls of his feet, he twisted around. "There's a crofter's cottage on the estate. Abandoned. When I was a lad I'd sometimes sneak off to spend a rainy afternoon there. I had one of the servants teach me to build a fire. For some reason, it always irritated me when my father would call for the butler to light or stir the fire and the butler would call for a footman. We're a lazy lot, the nobility."

"But if you saw to your own needs, you wouldn't need servants. Then how would they survive?"

Planting his elbow on his thigh, he studied her. "I hadn't considered that our idleness serves a greater purpose."

She gave him a shy smile. "You're teasing me."

"I am rather." He glanced around, wishing it didn't matter, yet knowing that somehow it did. "Have you ever had a man in these rooms before me?"

"No. Not even my brothers—well, not after they helped me get all the furniture up the stairs. It's always been my refuge."

A knot in his chest that he hadn't even realized was there loosened. She could have met a man elsewhere, but based on the kiss, on bits of conversation they'd had, on her admittance now, he thought it very unlikely she'd ever been intimate with a man—and it pleased him no end to know he would be her first. That thought nearly rocked him back on his heels, but he desired her as he'd never desired anything else in his life. Not that he could tell her that just yet. "It's quaint and cozy. Warm. My residences all feel cold and it has nothing to do with the chill in the air."

"Perhaps they simply need a woman's touch."

"They have my mother's touch. That probably accounts for it. She's a dragon of a woman and quite icy." He came to his feet, walked over to the corner where a copper tub stood at the ready, and shoved it across the floor until it was situated in front of the fire.

"I'm really not sure this is a good idea," she said.

"I welcome the challenge of it."

She laughed. "Of pouring water into a tub?"

"No, of resisting the urge to touch you, to prove I am made of stern stuff."

"You are aware if you do anything untoward I will kill you."

"I can think of nothing I'd like more than to gaze into your eyes before I die."

"I'm serious. I'll not be trifled with."

"I'm serious as well." Incredibly so. Naturally, on

occasion, he'd flattered women with trite words because such was expected, but she was the sort of woman who called for honesty at all times. He crossed the room, leaned against the bedpost, and folded his arms over his chest. "I can't quite decide the color of your eyes. Sometimes they appear green, other times brown. When I look into them I see both colors."

"My mum says they're hazel."

"They intrigue me. I hope you don't mind my staring into them."

There was barely enough light for him to see her cheeks turn pink. "Yours remind me of a dark stout."

Damn, but she did delight him. "I'm not certain I've ever known a woman who described colors in terms of liquor."

"It's what I know."

"Why a tavern? Why not a hat shop or—"

"Because men always find money for a pint. Ladies around here can't always afford a new hat."

Practicality had never seemed so alluring. "Why here? There are better, safer places in London."

"People here need work. People here need a pint now and then to lessen their burdens. I thought in my own small way I could improve a few lives and make a tidy profit in the process."

Practical and generous.

"How did you go from being a step-girl to owning a tavern? They each seem to require an entirely different set of skills."

A corner of her mouth curled up provocatively. "You'll find I have the cleanest steps in all of Whitechapel, in all of London for that matter."

"I've no doubt, but still there is a good deal one

must learn in order to effectively manage a business, any business, but this one in particular seems rather challenging."

Interlacing her fingers, she rested her folded hands on her lap. "I couldn't be a step-girl forever. The pay is pitiful, the work hard. When I was ten and four, I went to work in a tavern."

His gut clenched at the thought of boorish men slapping her bum. "As a serving girl?"

"No. I spent most of my youth wearing my brothers' castoffs. My mum kept my hair cut short, so the tavern keeper thought I was a lad. I started out washing dishes, cleaning tables, working in the taproom. By the time he figured out I was a girl, I'd proven myself to be a good worker, and it tickled him for some reason to know I was going about fooling people regarding my gender. So he took me under his wing and taught me what he knew. His wife, the daughter of a vicar, was a dear soul who believed pronouncing words properly was necessary for bettering oneself. So she gave me lessons in enunciation and grammar, which I shared with my brothers." She lifted a shoulder. "She also believed I needed to be wearing skirts, needed to be all proper. I soon discovered even in a skirt, men barely noticed me. All my mum's worrying that a bloke would take advantage was for naught."

He very much doubted that, suspected the gents had come to like her for who she was, rather than what she was. Besides, she had four brothers with large hands that made powerful fists. "I think the lads all respected you too much by then."

"I think the water is boiling," she said quietly.

He could hear it now, gurgling in the distance.

"Right." Still his gaze lingered on her for a moment. "You're not accustomed to talking about yourself, are you?"

She shrugged. "I'm not so interesting."

He shoved himself away from the bed and headed for the door. She certainly had the wrong of that. He'd never known a more interesting woman.

Chapter 15

$\mathcal{I}$t was a mistake for him to be here. She could get accustomed to having someone to talk with. Having someone to wait on her wasn't a hardship either, although she understood it was the circumstances that had him doing the menial chores he'd normally leave to a servant.

Still it was nice hearing the heavy thud of footsteps, watching as he labored, the way the muscles in his back, beneath his shirt, bunched and flexed whenever he lifted a bucket and poured the water in the tub. He moved with such ease, a man comfortable in his own skin. He knew who he was, *what* he was, which made him incredibly appealing.

"There," he finally proclaimed. "That should do it."

She still wasn't certain bathing with him about was wise, but she did trust him, which was also probably not wise. Obviously the blow had knocked all good sense out of her head.

He stopped at the threshold. "I'll close the door to give you some privacy, but call out once you're situated so I can open it."

"I think it should stay closed."

He studied her for all a heartbeat. "As you wish."

Why was she suddenly hit with disappointment?

"But call out if you need me, and let me know when you're done. If you're not finished in a half hour, say, I shall open the door to ensure nothing is amiss—that you're not sleeping."

"I'm not going to sleep."

Words easier said than carried out once she sank into the heavenly abyss of warm water. Every muscle in her body ached and the heat seeping through to her bones made everything seem so much better. Charlie, blast him, had delivered a few hard blows, strategically delivered to the softest parts of her. Or maybe it hadn't been strategic at all. Merely luck. He'd never struck her as much of a thinker. If he had the ability to reason at all, he'd have deduced that attacking anyone near her establishment would not go well for him, especially when he was idiotic enough to return to the tavern. If he were smart, he'd have gone elsewhere, but he was more a creature of habit and usually stopped in every now and then for a pint.

"Is everything all right?" was bellowed from beyond the wall.

"I'm fine!"

"Are you in the tub?"

"Yes."

"Very good."

Then he began to read in a deep, loud voice that penetrated through the thin walls of her apartment. If her brothers were still clearing up the mess, they were going to hear him. Unless Beast was able to convince him otherwise, Aiden would head up, and she didn't need him to see her soaking in the tub, naked, with a strange man in her flat. "Open the door!" she called out.

He didn't question her or hesitate. Suddenly the

door sprang open. She only caught sight of his arm shoving it. Then he began reading again.

Lowering herself into the water as much as she was able, she hunched over and wrapped her arms around her legs. "Come in."

Again, no hesitation. It took everything within her not to smile at his innocent expression.

"Are you not enjoying the story?" he asked, holding up *The Moonstone*.

"I'm not enjoying your bellowing. You may sit in here, in the rocker, but turn it so your back is to me."

"Very good." He moved the chair into place, keeping his eyes averted. When he was situated, he asked, "Shall I continue?"

"Yes, please." Placing her cheek on her upraised knees, she watched the motion of his rocking, forward and back, forward and back, listened to the mesmerizing cadence of his voice as the narrator explained the origins of a diamond that would play a major role in the story. She'd already read it, but he was bringing the tale to life in a way that simply reading it to herself hadn't. He was carrying her into a mysterious world, not so much woven by the author, but woven by Thorne. He poured energy into his reading. It wasn't just words repeated. His voice wove around her, through her. The light from the flames on the hearth danced over his dark hair, over his shoulders, across his back.

With very little effort, he was luring her, luring her, luring her . . .

Without making so much as a splash, she brought herself to her feet, the water sluicing down her body, glistening her skin in the process. Quietly, she stepped out of the tub and slowly ambled toward him. He barely did more than lift his gaze to her when she took the book from his hands and tossed it aside. His nostrils flared, his eyes smoldered, his lips parted. Desire, want, need shimmered off him.

She settled onto his lap, not at all surprised to find herself dry. She wound a bare arm around his neck, cradled his strong jaw with her other hand. "It should be a sin for a man to be as beautiful as you."

"I prefer handsome."

She skimmed her fingers up his face, into his hair. "You make me want to do wicked things."

Closing her eyes, she lowered her mouth—

"Gillie."

—to his, gave her tongue the freedom to roam—

"Gillie."

—to taste, to explore, to know every nook and cranny—

"Sweetheart, you need to wake up."

No. No. No. She wouldn't leave this fantasy behind until it came to its satisfying conclusion.

"Gillie, wake up for me now."

The concern and worry, the edge of panic woven through his voice broke through the gossamer images. Her eyes fluttered open. He was there, his hands cradling her face. He bestowed upon her a gorgeous smile she would carry to her deathbed.

"You gave me quite the scare there for a minute."

She couldn't imagine him being afraid of anything. "I fell asleep," she said stupidly, unnecessarily. How disappointing to realize it had all been an enticing dream.

"I'm sure my reading is quite boring."

"No, it was lovely." Then she realized she was still hunched in the bathwater, with him so near, but at least he was looking into her eyes, not that she thought he could see much if he did glance down. She should have been self-conscious and perhaps she would have been if not for that ridiculous dream.

He skimmed his finger along the back of her arm. "He bruised you."

"It doesn't hurt."

"That's not the point. He never should have touched you."

"I didn't give him much of a choice."

"I noticed. I walked through the door just as you leaped on him. You have a fetching calf, by the way."

"How do you know?"

"Your skirt hiked up and I was not gallant enough to look away."

She was growing so warm, she was no doubt re-heating the water.

"You're not accustomed to compliments," he said quietly.

"I don't pay them any mind. They're designed to turn a woman's head and I don't want my head turned." Although he did have the right of it. Gentlemen, other than her brothers, never gave her any. But then she never sought them out or gave any indication she'd welcome them.

"How many bruises have you that I can't see?" he asked.

Shaking her head, she lifted her shoulder. "A couple here and there. They're nothing."

"I know women who take to bed because a bit of parchment nicks their finger."

She laughed lightly. "No, you don't. That's ridiculous." And their conversation was becoming ludicrous. Not that she minded. She couldn't recall a gentleman ever making her laugh or feel young, innocent, or silly. Her mum had always told her she'd been born an adult, too responsible for her own good, that she needed to have some fun. Work brought her enjoyment. What more did she need than that? "If you'll return to your chair and your reading, I'll scrub up so we can be done with this."

"How about if I wash your back?"

Her stomach nearly dropped to the bottom of the tub. "That's too intimate."

"You washed my arms, my legs, my chest. I daresay every inch."

"Not every inch." A good many inches had gone untouched and the thought of them had heat scalding her face. She looked to the fire, seeking to regain her senses, then returned her attention to him. "I knew this was a bad idea. Move away."

He did so quickly, scooting back until he was sitting several feet away on the floor, his eyes never leaving her. The speed with which he'd responded made it easier to breathe.

"Only your back," he said quietly.

And she again lost the ability to breathe. "It's improper."

"Gillie, there hasn't been a proper thing between us since we met. I was in your bed, naked as the day I was born. You cared for me, nursed me, and didn't take advantage. I want only to return the favor, give you a bit of the care you gave me. Have you ever had anyone wash your back?"

"My mum. She washed me until I was eight. Then I was old enough to do it myself. Odd thing was, the last time she did it, I didn't know it was the last time. We don't always know when something is the last time."

"No, we don't. The last time my father spoke to me, though, I suspected it was the final time. I was all of fifteen when he placed the watch in my palm and handed it down to me. Although I surmised what his action portended, it still came as a bit of shock when my fears were confirmed."

"We'll make Charlie tell us where he fenced it. I know a good many of the thiefs' pawns around here. Once we know who he sold it to, we'll be able to get it back or find out where the fence might have pawned it."

"Right-o, then. We'll have a chat with him. Meanwhile, your bath, your back?"

She shook her head. If she let him wash her back, she feared she might want him to wash everything. "I can't."

He spun around on his backside and shoved himself to his feet. "I'll be in the other room while you finish up here. Call if you need me."

Watching him walk out, she knew she should have felt relieved. Instead she cursed herself for being a coward, for not trusting completely—not him specifically, but all men. Some man she didn't know who'd done wrong by her mother; the man who had done wrong by her mum and planted a babe in her belly, a babe who was now her younger sister, Fancy; the men who might have taken advantage of her if she hadn't spent the better part of her life going about disguised as a boy. She remembered how odd she felt the first time she put on a skirt, when no seams touched her intimately. She'd opened a tavern because within its walls she wouldn't have to impress anyone. She could keep her hair short, wear shirts that didn't hug her body, and skirts without petticoats because someone in want of a drink wasn't looking for a fancy lady to pour it. He only cared that it was poured.

In spite of her height, in her tavern, she went about barely noticed. And a woman not noticed wasn't likely to bring an unwanted child into the world.

But even as she had that thought, she knew any child to whom she gave birth would be wanted, regardless of which side of the blanket it came in on. She'd never understood ostracizing those born of sin. It certainly wasn't their fault.

Although, to be honest, before Thorne, she hadn't truly understood temptation. If she'd have been able to resist purring while he washed her back, she might have accepted his offer. But she was still quaking from that lurid dream where she'd curled up on his lap and tried to seduce him. Best to get back into some clothes before she found herself traipsing out into the other room and rubbing her body against his as though she were a blasted cat.

Because he'd asked, as she washed up, she noted the bruises on her shin, her thigh, her hip, and elsewhere. Seven total that she could see. A couple of the more tender ones were turning dark and ugly. It had been a while since she'd gotten into a proper scrape. She should have been horrified by her behavior. Instead, she felt quite proud because she was rather certain she'd given as good as she got.

Once she was finished bathing, she climbed out of the tub and dried off. Her head still hurt, a muted throbbing that irritated more than anything. She considered putting on her nightdress and crawling into bed for a few minutes, but her mother would be appalled that she'd wear such a thing when she had company of any sort, much less male. So she decided against wrapping her breasts, and selected a clean shirt and skirt. Leaving her feet bare, she clambered onto the bed.

He must have heard it creaking because he was in the doorway before she'd fully settled in, lying on her side. "You're not going to sleep."

"I'm exhausted. Surely it's near enough to dawn—"

"I've not yet heard the lark."

She released a tired laugh. "You're not going to hear the lark around here. You'll hear wagons, wheelbarrows, horses' hooves, and squeaking wheels. You'll hear life. Let me sleep for just a few minutes."

"I can't. But neither can I read to you as that puts you to sleep. So I'll just have to keep asking you questions." He moved to the edge of the bed and sat.

"Can we dim the lamp?" she asked. "The light makes my head hurt worse."

He extinguished the flame, got up, stirred the fire so it cast a bit more light, but it was far enough away that it didn't hit her eyes directly. When he returned, he stretched out on the bed beside her. "Don't be alarmed. I'm not going to touch you. Just trying to ensure I stay awake as well."

With her back to him, rising up on an elbow, she glanced over at him. Staring at the ceiling with a hand shoved beneath his head, he made her mouth go dry. "At least take off your boots."

He obliged, his action touching a place deep inside her where she'd shoved aside the notion a gentleman would ever place his shoes beneath her bed. He slowly eased back down as though striving not to jar her and shifted his gaze over to her. "So talk to me."

"I don't have much else to say. I've already told you about various liquors."

He grinned. "Ah, yes, I remember that. In spite of the pain and the fog, I wanted to hear what you had to say."

"That's about all I know."

"Tell me about your dreams."

That she dreamed of crawling into his lap and kissing him senseless? Not bloody likely.

"There must be something you dream about doing that you haven't yet done," he added.

She settled back down on the mattress, slipped a hand beneath her cheek, and stared at the dark lamp. Much easier to whisper about dreams when not facing someone directly. "Have you ever been to France?"

"I have. Have you not been?"

"I've never left London."

"You'd no doubt love Paris. From what I understand ladies go there to purchase their ball gowns."

"What use have I for ball gowns? No, I want to visit the various vineyards." She glanced back over her shoulder, but her angle was such that she could see little more than his bare feet. Why did the sight cause her stomach to quiver? "Have you seen them?"

"It never occurred to me they'd be worth my time."

She turned back to the lamp. "I think it would be fascinating to meet the people who give us something that can bring such pleasure. I'd like to pluck a grape from a vine, toss it into my mouth, take off my shoes and walk through the soil that feeds the vines. I'd like to see how the wine is made. And taste it every step along the way."

"I suspect it's rather unpleasant at first."

"Which would make the end result all the more miraculous."

"You like wine."

"Mmm. And whisky." She laughed lightly. "Almost everything I serve."

"I've never known a woman who drinks anything other than wine."

Closing her eyes, she fell into a memory. "When my brothers started drinking, they invited me to join them. I developed a taste for things. I can tell the difference between the good stuff and the rot. You won't find the rot in my place."

The bed shifted and she figured he was rolling over. If she weren't so weary, she might have looked over her shoulder again to see if his feet were stacked upon each other. Instead she welcomed the lethargy.

"Gillie?"

"Hmm?"

"Don't go to sleep."

"I . . . won't."

"Keep talking."

She shook her head as much as she was able without moving it from the pillow. "No other dreams. Just vineyards."

Quiet eased in around them, and she wondered if she should ask him about his dreams. But then he was a duke. He had the money, means, and power to make all of his dreams a reality. What could he possibly wish for that he didn't have? Other than a bride who didn't leave him standing at the altar.

"Gillie?" His voice was low, tender. "Do you know *nothing* at all about your parents?"

He'd asked her before but maybe he doubted the veracity of her answer, thinking she hadn't known him well enough at the time to be honest in answering his impertinent question. They knew each other a bit better now. Perhaps if the room hadn't been quite so dark, or if she couldn't feel the warmth from his body or wasn't aware of the weight of him on the other side of the bed—

If she hadn't been able to smell his tart citrusy fragrance that reminded her of bergamot and lemons. If he hadn't kissed her, if she hadn't taken a blow to the head, she might not have divulged her secret fantasy, one she'd never shared with anyone, not even her brothers.

"When I was younger, a child really, I would imagine that my mother was a princess. She fell in love with someone considered beneath her. I don't know. A palace guard or the village blacksmith perhaps. She was naughty with him, got into a bit of a bother. They wouldn't allow her to marry him, of course, even though he loved her, too. They wouldn't let her keep me because she was so very important and was supposed to make a proper marriage, and I was evidence of her sins. So they left me on a doorstep."

The bed again dipped as his arm came around her, and she found herself spooned within the curve of his body. "You're important, too," he said quietly, near her ear.

She stayed still and quiet, taking pleasure from his nearness, surprised by how natural it seemed to be held by him. She could feel the rise and fall of his chest against her back. So lovely, so calming. Tomorrow night she would miss this, miss him.

She'd always thought it better not to know exactly what one's life lacked. But now she was grateful she wouldn't go to her grave having never been held by a man.

Chapter 16

*H*e awoke with her lovely backside pressed up against his hard cock, his arm around her narrow waist, her hand over his where it rested just below her ribs. Sometime during the night she moved her head from her pillow to the crook of his other arm and it was now as dead as a doornail. He cursed it for being so inconsiderate as to prevent him from feeling even an inch of her.

He hadn't meant to fall asleep, hadn't intended for her to fall asleep, but a stillness had settled between them after she'd told him of her musings when she was a child. She imagined herself to be royalty. She was certainly regal in her bearing. As well as possessing strength, courage, and determination. He hadn't known what to say at that moment and so he'd held her, the words he'd finally muttered inadequate to express how she affected him. There was an innocence to her that belied her rough upbringing. Yet at the same time there was a worldliness to her that indicated she had a far deeper understanding of human nature than he.

To leave her on a doorstep. How could anyone be so cruel? He was well aware the law didn't favor those born out of wedlock. He'd heard and read horror tales regarding how some had been disposed of. She'd beaten the odds and survived. Although he suspected she wouldn't survive much longer if she continued to leap at men.

Her feet were entangled with his, her skirt had hiked up past her knees, and there was that lovely long calf calling out to him to be kissed. He'd like to trail his mouth over it. No, not just it but every inch of her, from the tips of her toes to the top of her head.

Her breathing, a soft hushing that warmed his heart, filtered through the room. He wanted to awaken to the sound again, only with her naked in his arms. He imagined the joy to be had in taking her to the vineyards in France—after a stop in Paris. She might not have use for a ball gown but she certainly deserved one. He thought of buying her gloves and stockings and every bit of feminine undergarment he could think of. He didn't want her wrapping her breasts as though ashamed of them, of being a woman.

But purchasing anything for her was out of the question as was the possibility of again waking up with her in his arms. Even if her mother was a princess, he couldn't offer her marriage. She'd never be accepted by his family, his friends, his peers. For all of her boldness, there was a shyness to her that would no doubt make life in his world unbearable.

Still he found himself studying the slender nape of her neck, unobstructed by long strands of hair. He could see the delicate cords, the gentle slope. In spite of his best intentions, he leaned in and pressed a kiss there. She sighed and his irreverent cock grew all the harder. "Gillie, you need to wake up now, princess."

With a soft moan, she somehow managed to stretch without stretching at all, her body undulating against his in such a provocative manner he very nearly groaned with frustration and aching needs. Slipping his arm out from beneath her head, he rolled over, swinging his legs off the bed and sitting up, clenching the hand that still had feeling in it and welcoming the painful spikes in the other as blood rushed back into it.

"I fell asleep," she mumbled on a yawn and he imagined her stretching again.

"It was near enough to dawn I felt you were safe."

"Why did you call me *princess*?"

He glanced back over his shoulder. Her hair, outside of the bandage that had been wrapped around her head to protect her wound, stuck up at odd spiky angles. He found it adorable. "If your mother was a princess, then so are you."

She slammed her eyes closed. "Don't mock me."

"I'm not." He'd been deeply touched by her story. "I can see you as a princess."

Opening her eyes, she rolled them. "I can't believe I told you that story. My senses must have been truly jumbled."

"I'm glad you did. It never occurred to me how difficult it might be not to know from whence you came."

"It doesn't really matter. Not since I grew older. I have Mum. For all the love she showers on me, she might as well have given birth to me. Shall I make us some porridge?"

She obviously didn't want to discuss it any longer. "Not for me. I should be off." Reaching down, he grabbed his boots, tugged them on. Standing, he rolled down his sleeves and began the process of making himself once again presentable for going out in the world, knotting his neck cloth, slipping on his waistcoat, shrugging on his jacket. He was desperately in need of a shave, but he knew from his earlier time here she didn't have a razor.

"I appreciate that you stayed and looked after me."

"It was my pleasure." He headed out, aware of her hopping off the bed and her bare feet pattering across the floor as she followed him. He opened the front door.

"I suppose we're even now," she said quietly.

He turned back to find her standing near enough to touch, her fingers intertwined in front of her, and he wondered if she'd had to shackle them to keep from reaching for him. He wasn't as gallant as all that. Taking her chin between his thumb and forefinger, he leaned in and kissed her, a short but sweet meeting of the lips.

"Not even close, princess."

With that, he hurried down the stairs and into the mews where he found his coach waiting, his coachman and tiger standing ever alert near the horses.

"Sorry for the delay in my parting, Maxwell," he said to the driver as he neared.

"Not to worry, Your Grace."

"Do hope you didn't spend the night standing out here."

"No, sir. We took turns catching a few winks inside the carriage."

"Still it was inconsiderate of me." He should have sent them home and had them return this morning. On the other hand, he paid them well enough they expected the occasional inconvenience. As he clambered into the vehicle, he told them where he wished to stop before returning to Coventry House.

Not long after, with all his noble bearing on display, he walked into the nearest constabulary building and up to the desk where two men in uniform waited, choosing the one who looked to be the youngest, least experienced, and most easily impressed. "Was a Charlie McFarley brought in here last night?"

The constable nodded. "He was."

"I'd like to have a private word with him."

"Are you his solicitor?"

"No." He withdrew a card from his pocket and extended it. "I'm the Duke of Thornley, cousin to the queen." A very, very distant relation that came about through a series of marriages, not bloodline, but he wasn't opposed to adding weight to his title when warranted.

The man who had been standing straight as a board went even straighter, paled considerably, and nodded with such force it was a wonder his head didn't go flying off. "Certainly, Your Grace, I can arrange for you to have a word with him in the chief inspector's office."

"Not necessary to go to such bother. A quick visit in his cell should suffice. It won't take me but a minute."

"As you wish, sir. If you'll follow me." He grabbed a ring of keys and led the way down one corridor, a set of stairs, and then another corridor, only this one contained a series of iron doors. He opened one at the end.

"I'd like you to stay on this side of the door in the hallway until I knock," Thorne instructed him in a manner that indicated it was not a request but an order.

"Certainly, Your Grace."

He gave an appreciative smile. "Good man."

He walked in and closed the door. Charlie McFarley sat on a rather uncomfortable-looking wooden bench that no doubt also served as the bed. The fellow slowly came to his feet, his fists clenched, his eyes narrowed. His effort to look intimidating lost some of its edge due to his misaligned jaw. "Who ye?" he mumbled.

"The gent you robbed the other night outside the Mermaid and Unicorn."

Rolling his eyes, he attempted a sneer that simply looked ridiculous since his mouth wasn't working properly. "The watch is gone," was torturously muttered, the words barely recognizable.

"I don't care about the watch." With a quick step forward, he plowed his balled fist into the bastard's gut—hard.

With a grunt, gasping for breath, Charlie McFarley dropped to his knees. Thorne crouched, grabbed him by his filthy long hair, and jerked his head back until he could hold the man's gaze. "Last night you bruised Miss Trewlove. If you or any of your cronies ever lay so much as a finger on her again, I shall see you hanged. Have I made myself perfectly clear?"

Charlie McFarley nodded as much as he was able with the vise-like grip Thorne had on him. Thorne tossed him aside like the rubbish he was.

Turning for the door, he needed only two steps to bang on it. It opened and he marched out, feeling a great deal of satisfaction. He couldn't protect Gillie from all the unpleasantness of life, but he intended to do what he could.

SOMETIME LATER HE strode into his residence, and his stomach immediately rumbled. It was early enough that breakfast was still being served, so he headed for the breakfast dining room, having failed to take into account it was late enough that his mother would be there.

"You stink of her," she spat, wrinkling her nose in disgust, rendering her judgment as was her preferred manner for welcoming the day.

"Her?" he asked mildly as he went over to the sideboard and began filling his plate with an assortment of offerings.

"The woman in whose bed you spent the night."

He realized she was correct, as he could smell the faintest hint of Gillie in his clothes. "I daresay, you have bloodhound in your bloodlines. I shall instruct my valet not to launder my clothing then so I may inhale her sweet fragrance whenever I like."

"You're disgusting."

He took his place at the table. "Good morning to you as well, Mother."

"I could always smell the stench of the women with whom your father slept. You're just like him."

That his father had not honored his vows was one of the things that had most disappointed him about his sire, but he saw nothing to be gained in harping on the previous duke's shortcomings, even if those indiscretions had led to the duke's illness and eventual madness. For a time, he'd made all their lives a living hell. "It's been nearly a dozen years since his passing. Surely by now, you should try to move past his transgressions."

"Never." Taking a sip of her tea, she glared at him over the rim of her delicate bone china cup, the slightest tremble visible. "Has there been any luck locating the girl?"

"I assume you're referring to Lavinia. No. However,

I had a recent letter from her indicating she ran off in order to be with someone else." Not her precise words, but he didn't feel a need to share the details. "Therefore, we will not marry."

Her eyes slammed closed, her jaw tightened. She looked to be on the verge of erupting. Had she been a volcano, he had little doubt the earth would be obliterated. Finally she opened her eyes. "Have you spoken with Collinsworth regarding this debacle?"

"I have."

"And what reparations is he prepared to make?"

Wishing he'd had the good sense to have a tray of food delivered to his bedchamber, he arched a brow at her. "Reparations?"

"Yes. The girl broke the betrothal. You are within your rights to sue."

"He's an old friend. I'm not going to sue."

"She has already made a laughingstock of you by leaving you standing at the church. If you don't take some action, the peerage will lose all respect for you."

While he had to admit it had been at once embarrassing and humbling to be left at the altar, it was preferable to taking to wife someone who would be forever longing to be in the arms of another. "I'll survive."

"You really should not have gone with her. I'd heard rumors . . ." She let her voice trail off suggestively.

He wasn't going to take the bait. He'd never been much in favor of gossip, perhaps because so much of it had surrounded him growing up. His father's unfaithfulness was always fodder for the blatherers. "It's over and done. I see little point in dissecting it. Although I suppose I should place an announcement in the *Times*—"

"Absolutely not. Gossip will run rampant as it is."

"Which is the reason an announcement is in order—so we control the facts."

"Will you state you were thrown over? I should think not. It must be carefully worded so it is understood the decision to end things was yours."

He sighed. "Who will believe that when I was the one waiting so patiently at the altar?"

"You announced the girl became ill. Upon further reflection, you decided it would not do at all to marry someone with such a weak constitution who so easily fell sick at the most inopportune moment."

He laughed darkly. "I'm not going to disparage Lavinia. Besides, I doubt there is a woman in all of England who does not fall ill at one point or another."

"Don't announce it. I shall handle getting the news out discreetly. To ensure people understand you are well and truly done with the girl, I shall host a ball as soon as possible so you may select another woman to become your wife. I suggest you go with someone a bit younger, someone who will appreciate the honor you bestow upon her."

He almost asked the butler to bring him some whisky for his coffee. "Mother, I am in no hurry to marry. Lavinia's age coupled with Collinsworth's concerns over it prompted me to ask for her hand earlier in the summer. But there is no reason now to rush into anything."

"There is reason aplenty. We must get this matter behind us, else it will be all that is talked about next Season, in a most unflattering way, with speculation rife regarding why the girl felt a need to run away from you, if she discovered you are like your father.

He has left you a disgusting legacy. You have an obligation to marry and provide an heir before you succumb to his disease."

He sighed heavily. "I'm not going to become ill like Father."

"You live the life of a monk then?"

"I will not discuss this."

She slapped her hand on the table. "The best way to move past this embarrassing episode in your life quickly is to take a wife before year's end. So people are talking about your marriage rather than conjecturing what is wrong with you."

He didn't think it would be as bad as all that, but he would welcome some peace at the table. "The Season is over. I suspect the day after my botched wedding, any families who had remained behind to attend followed the example set by those who had already headed to their country estates and departed the city as quickly as possible."

"They will return to London for my ball, especially as the girls' mothers will be desperate to land their daughters a duke."

"I really think this can wait until next Season."

"You misjudge the damage that chit's disappearance will cause to your reputation and place in Society. I recommend you allow me to select the girl who will make you a proper duchess."

Just what every man wanted: his mother choosing the woman he would bed. With a sigh, he shoved aside his plate and stood. "Seems I wasn't so hungry after all. If you'll excuse me—"

"Do be sure to bathe before joining me for dinner. The wretched smell threatens to make me ill."

"I'll be dining at the club tonight." Heading for the doorway, he signaled to his butler. "Boggins, I'll have a word."

"Certainly, Your Grace."

Once in his office, he walked over to the window and gazed out on the colorful gardens. He'd awoken to sunshine and now dark clouds were moving in. He couldn't help but believe it was the different way each of the women with whom he'd spoken that morning viewed the world. Gillie, who had been raised with nothing, viewed it with hope while his mother, who had always possessed every advantage, took a more dismal view, one that quite honestly made it a chore to be in her presence.

"You're to increase each servant's yearly salary by ten percent," he told Boggins, thinking of Gillie's decision to open her business in Whitechapel because folks needed employment.

"Beginning when, Your Grace?"

He heard a myriad of questions in that one query. "Immediately."

"The staff will be most pleased, sir, by your generosity."

"If they're having to deal with my mother I believe they've earned it."

"She can be quite trying."

He turned around. His butler blushed, shifted from one foot to the other like a school lad caught doing something he ought not. "I meant no disrespect, sir. The duchess—"

"Is more than trying. She's in my world, too, you know."

"Perhaps once she has a grandchild, she'll mellow."

"I'd have a child tomorrow if I thought there were any chance of that."

STANDING WITH HER legs akimbo, her hands on her hips, Gillie surveyed her surroundings. If she didn't lovingly know every nook and cranny, she wouldn't have been able to tell a brawl had taken place the night before. Bless her brothers, her staff, and anyone else who had worked hard to put her establishment back to rights in such short order. "Two tables, twelve chairs."

"Bugger it," Roger muttered.

Looking over her shoulder, she watched as he handed a grinning Finn, leaning against the bar, a fiver. "I told you she'd know exactly what had been broken last night," her brother fairly crowed. "Give her a few more minutes, and she can probably tell you how many mugs were smashed."

"I'm not going to go to that bother," she retorted, having accepted his earlier challenge to identify how much furniture was missing. "Just see that they're replaced."

"Will do," Roger said, before disappearing into the kitchen.

Shifting his stance, Finn knocked his knuckles on the wooden counter twice before meeting and holding her gaze. "Heard you had a fellow staying with you last night. Wouldn't be that duke, would it?"

She sat on a stool. Her head was no longer hurting, but staying awake until nearly dawn had left her drained. "I know you have no love for the nobility, but he's not a bad sort."

"Watch your heart, Gillie. They see us as toys, to be played with for a while, tossed into the rubbish bin when we start to bore them or they spy something shinier or cleaner."

She lifted a shoulder slightly, not completely able to shake off the sorrow. "I was helping him with something and the situation has changed. He has no reason to come around here any longer."

"As though the nobs need a reason to do anything."

Chapter 17

"*I* think Trewlove is Hedley's by-blow."

In the library at White's, enjoying a drink following dinner, Thorne looked discreetly to the side in the direction where Collinsworth's gaze was fastened. On the far side of the room sat the elder duke with his ward's new husband. "I can't deny there's a resemblance."

"Why else would Hedley allow Lady Aslyn to marry a bastard?"

"Perhaps because she loves him." That fact had been obvious during the wedding. The couple had barely been able to tear their gazes from each other.

"Still, to then ensure he was granted membership in the club as though we have no standards here was going a bit far."

"Trewlove might not have the lineage, but he's remarkably wealthy and getting wealthier by the day if rumors are to be believed. He could no doubt purchase the place if he wanted."

"Still, I find it deuced strange the duke seems to be spending more time with the fellow than he does his own son. I've heard he even handed some of his estates over to Trewlove."

"No doubt he fears Kipwick would lose them. The

man has a terrible gambling habit." Thorne returned his attention to sipping his whisky, again finding himself wondering why what had once been so pleasing to his palate was now lacking in flavor. "Sometimes I wonder if we are too quick to judge a man by the circumstances of his birth rather than the strength of his character."

"That sort of talk would give your mother and mine the vapors."

"Indeed." He studied the amber liquid in his glass, wondering why Society found such fault in those born of sin, when they'd had no say in the actions that had led to their conception. If not for some man and woman coming together when they shouldn't have, Gillie would not exist, and without her, he might have died. It made the subject of bastardy rather personal of late.

Out of the corner of his eye, he caught a movement and suddenly the Earls of Eames and Dearwood were standing in front of him. Apparently not everyone had left for the country, but then these were young men and the city no doubt offered far more excitement than their estates. "My lords."

Eames gave a curt nod. "Your Grace." Then a nod to the man sitting beside him. "Collinsworth."

"Eames," Collinsworth said. "Dearwood."

Eames's gaze came back to Thorne. "We were sorry your wedding did not go as planned. Unfortunate that your bride took ill. I hope your sister has recovered, Collinsworth."

"She has," Thorne said, before Collinsworth, who was shifting uncomfortably in his chair, could respond.

"Glad to hear it," Dearwood said. "The wedding will go on then?"

He couldn't quite bring himself to admit the truth of it. "We're still working out the particulars."

"We shall look forward to attending once again when the time comes," Eames said. He bowed slightly. "Do give our best to Lady Lavinia. Your Grace, my lord."

They strode away, an arrogance in their strut that made him want to trip them.

"Impertinent young swells," Collinsworth muttered. "Did you catch the mocking in their tone?"

He had, but rather than responding, he simply sipped his whisky.

"Why did you not tell them the wedding was off?"

"Because it would start a chain of rumors that would change with each telling until eventually it would be reported I'd murdered her or some other silly nonsense. It would be better to announce it in the *Times* so one version is read by all. I'll see to the matter on the morrow."

"Good God, Thorne, I'm sorry for this muck up."

Oddly, he wasn't. Certainly, it would be troublesome to sort everything out and he regretted he'd be unable to carry through on his promise to his father, but he had a greater sense of loss regarding the fact he no longer had an excuse to see Gillie. "I don't suppose you'd sell me the land."

"Unfortunately, one of my more cunning ancestors placed it in a trust detailing that it can be used only as a dowry for a daugh—good God, Hedley and Trewlove are heading in this direction."

Thorne shoved himself to his feet as the two men approached. Collinsworth followed suit. Seeing the two at such close range, he couldn't help but believe the earl had the right of it. Trewlove was Hedley's son.

"Thorne," Hedley said. "I believe you met Mick Trewlove when he married Lady Aslyn."

"Indeed." He held out his hand. Trewlove took it, but it was less a shake and more a squeeze. Thorne returned the favor, asserting himself, communicating he was not one to be intimidated. When they finally released their hold on each other, he introduced the earl, but it was obvious Trewlove's sole interest resided with him.

"I believe you may have made use of my carriage recently," Trewlove said, his blue gaze direct as it held Thorne's.

"Indeed. I was most appreciative of it and your sister's tender care."

Although Trewlove reacted not at all, Thorne wasn't convinced his jaw wasn't on the verge of making an acquaintance with the man's fist. "She is a remarkable woman, your sister."

"She is not as tough as she appears."

"I'm well aware." Based on the muscle flexing in Trewlove's cheek, he was rather certain that his jaw *was* in danger. "I would not take advantage."

"I should hope not. It would not go well for you."

"So your sister informed me."

Trewlove grinned. "She does tend to speak her mind. I'm glad to see you're on the mend."

"Thank you."

With a brisk nod, Trewlove walked off, Hedley at his side.

"What was all that about?" Collinsworth asked.

A warning to stay clear of Gillie. Pity Mick Trewlove didn't realize his sister was worth the risk of encountering the man's fist. Ignoring his friend's question, he said, "You love your wife."

"Undoubtedly."

"How did you know what you felt for her was love?"

The man looked completely baffled. "I just knew. Not falling in love with your mistress, are you? That'd be deuced inconvenient."

"Presently I don't have a mistress, haven't had one since Lavinia and I became betrothed." Which might explain this need he had regarding Gillie. He couldn't deny that he wanted to bed her—desperately. Yet there was more to his desire than just experiencing the physical, than just lust. "If you'll excuse me, I have somewhere else I need to be."

IT WAS UNCANNY, the way she became aware of him when he strode through the door. She watched as he made his way to an empty table in the back where there were more shadows. She allowed the dimness there because she was well aware some of her customers preferred a bit of anonymity. Some were lawbreakers, she had no doubt of that, but their transgressions were petty. Sometimes men and women needed someplace to meet that offered some semblance of privacy.

"Ah, the handsome devil is back," Polly said, her smile far too wide, her eyes too bright. "I'm looking forward to—"

"I'll see to him, Polly," she stated, already pouring the whisky she was certain he'd want, then deciding to pour one for herself as well.

Polly's face fell. "I can see to it."

"Some blokes over there are in need of more drink."

"They're bricklayers, still coated in dust."

"They're honest laborers. And they pay as they drink."

"I reckon Handsome would, too."

"His drink is on the house."

"Got your eye on him, Gillie?"

Ignoring the question, she moved out from behind the bar, wondering why it was that her step had a lightness to it or why it warmed her to the core that his gaze never wandered from her, not even when another one of her serving girls was standing by his table with her hip jutting out provocatively and a good deal of her bosom exposed. She let her girls wear what they wanted because gents tended to slip them extra coins if they enjoyed being served by them—and a bit of flesh always made them enjoy the service more.

Her heart gave a little lurch when he stood as she approached. The gents who frequented this place didn't get to their feet when she neared, as it wasn't a courtesy they bestowed on workers. It astounded her how much it pleased her that he'd extended such politeness toward her. "I have his drink, Lily."

She didn't miss the disappointed look the girl cast her way, had a feeling Lily would have given Thorne her name, directions to her lodgings, and a peek beneath her skirts. She set the tumbler before him. His eyes glistened with humor.

"Are both for me?" he asked.

"No."

"Good." Reaching around he pulled out a chair for her, another polite gesture she wasn't accustomed to receiving. It wasn't a good thing to have him spoiling her like this, treating her as though she were special. She might take it into her head that she was. Still, with a measure of grace, she accepted the courtesy.

When they were settled, he lifted his glass. "To a night without incident."

They both sipped. He closed his eyes, licked his lips. "Why is your whisky so good?"

"It's excellent quality."

"I drink excellent quality elsewhere. No, it has something to do with yours specifically, your presence. You simply make it taste better."

"You're mad."

"Perhaps."

"Shouldn't you be at your club?"

"I was at my club. I was bored. Your brother was there, by the way."

"Mick?" She didn't wait for him to answer. "He always wanted a membership. I suspect he spends a great deal of time there."

"The gent I was with hypothesized that the Duke of Hedley is his father."

She kept her face impassive.

He grinned. "I wouldn't want to play cards with you."

"You'd lose if you did."

"Would I? That may be a challenge I'll have to accept."

She wished she'd offered another challenge, had dared him to kiss her again, to take her hand and lead her away from here into darker shadows, press his mouth to hers and rekindle the fires he'd begun the first time. They hadn't extinguished completely, but remained glowing embers that could again flare up into a consuming conflagration with very little effort.

"How is your head?" he asked.

"A bit sore if I touch it. I strive not to touch it. And how are you faring? After the missive you received yesterday . . . it had to have been a devastating blow and last night I didn't even think to ask how you were holding up." Perhaps because quite selfishly, her first thought had been, "He can't possibly marry her now." As though his being free of her somehow made these unwanted feelings for him swirling around inside her not quite so improper. Not that there could ever be anything proper between her and a duke, but if something improper were to happen it wouldn't be quite so improper.

"Last night our focus was on more important things, and rightfully so."

"Ensuring I didn't sleep. You're avoiding the question."

"To be quite honest, I'm a bit relieved as her reasons for not walking down the aisle were not because of any fault she found with me—other than she could not find it within herself to love me more than she did this other fellow."

"But then you did not love her."

He nodded slowly. "That is true. Land, not love, bound us, and she found it a poor substitute, I suppose, when it came right down to it."

"Do you have any idea who this other bloke is?"

"No. Her letter was short and to the point, although her brother did confess that in her youth she had been friendly with a commoner."

A commoner who quite possibly lived or worked in Whitechapel. That was an interesting tidbit she would store away.

"While I intend to place an announcement in the *Times*, I don't know that she'll have access to the newspaper, and I need to get word to her that things between us are over. That she can return home without fear of being forced to wed me. I've informed her brother to those facts and I need to alert her. But I haven't a clue how to go about it. Her missive came without a hint as to where she might be residing."

She wished it didn't please her so much to know he

was definitely not going through with the marriage. "You could have handbills printed up, alerting her regarding her change of status. Hire Robin and his mates to see them distributed. It's one of the things he does from time to time to earn a bit of coin. He rather enjoys the task."

"Then I shall see it done."

"He'll be pleased. He likes to feel useful." As much as Finn abhorred the aristocracy, she was beginning to think they weren't so awful after all. "I should probably get back behind the bar."

"So soon? It appears your staff has everything well in hand."

"They're good workers." But then she paid wages higher than most and that encouraged them to be.

"So good in fact I daresay they could manage for another day without you. I seem to recall when I was hovering near death—"

"You're exaggerating how badly you were hurt."

The rascal grinned. "I seem to recall you warning me that I was on the brink of expiring. Besides, it felt like it at the time. Anyway, I believe I promised to take you riding and give you a greater appreciation of horseflesh."

"I'm not going to shirk my responsibilities for a day of riding."

"You shirked them when you were caring for me."

"That was different. You were in need."

"I'm in need now."

The way his eyes delved into hers made her feel as though he'd somehow managed to wrap a rope around her chest and was pulling her toward him. She thought he was flirting with her, and she knew naught about flirtation or teasing or how to go about letting a bloke know she would be receptive to a kiss, maybe even a touch of her breast, a squeeze. A strange sensation was occurring between her thighs and she had a strong urge to press up against something firm. "In need of more whisky?" she asked stupidly when some still remained in his glass, when she knew he was referring to other needs, darker needs, naughty needs.

"I need to spend more time with you. My estate is four hours away by coach. I have horses there. One is extremely gentle."

"You want to take me to your estate?"

"You said you've never been outside of London. We'd be killing two birds with one stone."

The thought of leaving what she knew filled her with dread, but then a good part of her life had been doing things that filled her with dread only to be grateful later that she had. But the dread had never been this great. "I can't afford to neglect my business any more than I already have."

"Pity."

He sounded as disappointed as she felt. "Still, I'll think on it."

"While you do that, I'll get muddled. To be honest, based on the past week, I'm surprised I haven't turned to copious drinking sooner."

Men were so unattractive when three sheets in the wind. "The drinks will not be on the house."

"I don't expect them to be."

"Don't you have clubs for this sort of thing?"

"Ah, yes, but people know me there and gossip will abound."

"People know you here."

"Not as many."

She wouldn't be able to keep running over with

drinks. She'd have to let her girls do it. With their fine figures and the jutting out they'd be doing, if he returned to the tavern after tonight, it wouldn't be to see her. She didn't much like the jealousy that swept through her. Still, he wasn't hers, would never be hers, and she'd always prided herself on being a realist. "You should be forewarned I leave gents where they pass out."

He grinned, his eyes sparkling with teasing. "Warning noted."

"I'll bring you another whisky."

"You might as well fill it to the brim."

When she stood, so did he. "You don't have to do that," she told him.

"But I want to."

"If gents stood up every time I neared, they'd be popping up and down all night."

"Then I shall pop up and down all night."

She did wish his response didn't please her so much, but she had a good many more things to keep an eye on than one customer. "I'm going to have one of my girls bring you your drinks."

"As you wish."

It wasn't what she wished, but too much time in his company was likely to make her wish he'd ask other things of her, things that involved going to his estate and doing something other than messing about with horses.

He'd spent many a night in taverns and public houses, drinking the swill, talking with his mates, laughing uproariously about nothing at all, and having a jolly good time so that when waking with a pounding head he could claim the discomfort worth it. But he'd never simply sat in a corner alone, sipping on his whisky, and observing the small details and intricacies of the world that surrounded him, of the woman who fascinated him.

She had to be exhausted, yet her smiles never faltered, she never gave the appearance of impatience. Now and then when someone said something to her, she would laugh, the sound reaching out, circling about, causing others to smile, causing something to stir deep within his chest that lightened his mood more than the whisky. Watching her, he realized she served more than drinks. She served up an attentive ear, a kind word, a soft smile, an occasional laugh. She created an atmosphere of warmth and welcome.

He found himself becoming drunk on her rather than on the spirits she offered.

She'd made a good point: he could have indulged at the club. But he hadn't because he'd needed something more than amber liquid spreading warmth through his chest. He'd needed her.

He wanted her to himself, yet she belonged to all these people. Like him, they came here because of her, because she offered more than a glass of escape. She offered hope that on the morrow, the reasons that had brought them here wouldn't seem so dire.

She'd opened her tavern here because she'd recognized she was needed, but the hell of it was he believed she could have opened her tavern anywhere and met with success, because she offered people a portion of her heart. Without thought, without guile, without expecting anything in return. She was incredibly—

The three empty chairs around his table were scraped across the floor, turned about, and straddled by her brothers, crossing their arms over the backs. It seemed to be a night for the Trewlove men to make their presence known. "Gents," he said calmly.

"Thought you might buy us a pint," Aiden said.

"Gladly, although I'd have not thought she charged you."

Aiden grinned. "She doesn't, but her till can use the coins." He twisted around, held up a hand and three fingers. "Polly, love, three brews."

The lass gave him a smile, the same one she'd flashed at Thorne a few times, that indicated she'd be willing to give him other things as well. Aiden turned back around. "Isn't there a club somewhere in need of your presence?"

"I wanted to ensure Gillie was recovering from the blow she took to the head last night."

"Tell me you didn't take advantage."

"I didn't take advantage."

"Tell me you won't."

He ground his back teeth together. "Nothing will happen between us that she doesn't want to happen."

"She's not to be a duke's plaything," Beast said.

"I hadn't intended to make her one."

Leaning forward, Aiden placed his forearms on the table. "You see, the three of us have mothers who were playthings of the nobility. Finn and I have the same father. He was delivered to Ettie Trewlove's door six weeks after I was. The man had a harem of mistresses. Gillie is not going to become your mistress. We won't let her be hurt in that manner."

Thorne decided, no matter how he responded, they would either not believe him or find fault with his response. There was no love lost here, no trust to be had. "So you're all some nobleman's by-blow. Related to me by any chance?"

"No," Finn stated flatly. "The man who sired Aiden and me was a notorious earl."

"Listen, gents, I appreciate your concern for your sister—"

"I'm not certain you do," Aiden stated flatly, "because if you did you'd be walking out—"

Liquid suddenly rained down over his head, and he jumped to his feet, sputtering and cursing. "What the devil, Gil?"

She stood there, holding two mugs filled with brew in one hand, an empty mug in the other. Thorne had been so focused on her brother he hadn't seen her arrive.

"Polly said you wanted beer," she said.

"To drink, not to bathe in."

"It didn't look to be a friendly conversation."

"He's spending too much time here."

"That's my business, not yours." She gave her other two brothers a hard glare. "You can take your mug, full of beer, and go sit elsewhere or I can pour it over you and you can take your leave."

Thorne rose. "Actually, I was on the verge of offering to buy them a drink."

She narrowed her eyes. "You want their company?"

"I welcome it, yes."

"They're not trying to chase you off?"

"I'm not one to be chased."

She studied him for a full minute before giving a nod. "I suppose you're not." She set a mug in front of each of the two sitting brothers, pulled a towel from the waistband of her skirt and handed it to Aiden. "Dry yourself off, clean up the mess I made, and I'll send Polly over with another beer."

"We're just looking out for you, Gil," Aiden said.

She patted his cheek. "I don't need looking after."

She glanced at Thorne, and he wondered what it might take for her to come over and pat his cheek—or better yet, give him a kiss. That should send her brothers through the roof. Her gaze dropped to his tumbler, still half full. "I don't think you understand the art of getting fuddled. You should have had three of those by now."

He'd been nursing the one, filled to the brim, she'd brought him. "I prefer to savor. But feel free to send another over with your brother's beer."

After she gave a nod and walked away, Thorne retook his seat.

"So why invite us to stay?" Finn asked.

"Because I want you to tell me what Gillie was like growing up."

The brothers exchanged secretive smiles.

"A hellion," Aiden said as he dropped into his chair.

She wasn't quite certain she trusted all the smiles and laughter going on at the table in the rear of her establishment, as she rather suspected she was their main topic of conversation, because every now and then Finn or Beast would glance over at her, looking quite guilty as they did it. They were no doubt telling tales on her.

"Your brothers seem to be getting on with your gent," Roger said.

She was weary of stating that Thorne wasn't her gent so she overlooked that portion of his comment. "I suspect they're sizing him up."

"As any loving brother would. Probably issuing a few dire warnings, too."

They meant well but she was no longer a child in

need of their protection. She glanced over at the clock and saw it was nearing midnight. "Time to close up shop."

"Right-o. Hear, hear, mates! Finish up! Five minutes and out you go!" He began wiping down the counter. She went out into the main part to help her girls start clearing the tables as people departed.

"'Night, Gillie," many called out to her as they headed for the door. This was her favorite part of the night, giving a hug here and there, offering a kind word to someone who might not sleep so well that night. It was also her least favorite as she hauled a few gents to their feet and worked to keep them on a straight path to the door. The worst moments came when someone got all blubbery. It didn't happen often, but it was an embarrassment for both of them, especially when next they saw each other.

As usual, her brothers were the last to wander out.

"He's not such a bad sort," Aiden said as he hugged her tightly.

"He's smooth," Finn said as his arms came around her. "I don't trust him." But then he wouldn't, not under any circumstances. Once he'd trusted the nobility and it had cost him dearly.

Beast was next, his embrace always her favorite because his size allowed him to envelope her in a safe and comforting cocoon. "Take care with your heart."

She wanted to ensure him that she always did, but doubts regarding that particular skill were beginning to haunt her. She was keenly aware she fancied Thorne far more than was wise for a woman who owned a tavern. After seeing her brothers out, she turned, expecting Thorne to be waiting to have a word with her. Instead, following the example set by the men who worked for her, he was lifting chairs onto tables so the serving girls could go through more easily with brooms and mops. He'd set his jacket and waistcoat on the counter, rolled up his sleeves. She could see Polly and Lily fairly slavering at the sight of his magnificent forearms. With a quickness to her step, she crossed over to him. "You don't have to do that."

"If I help, the chore will be done more quickly, which means you can get out of here sooner. You have to be exhausted."

"I'm used to it."

"So tonight you'll have a few extra minutes to yourself."

Had he forgotten himself, his status? She very much doubted it. "A few extra minutes will be welcomed."

It was amazing how much more swiftly everything got done with an extra pair of hands. He didn't balk at hauling kegs or boxing up the empty bottles, but he pitched in, taking on any chore asked of him. When all was done and her staff had made their exits through the front door, she turned to watch as he once again made himself presentable. "Thank you for everything," she said.

"I'm not finished yet. I'll be seeing you safely home."

"I can get my own self home. I do it every night."

"Not tonight."

Seeing no point in arguing with him, she locked the front door. "We'll go out through the back, and check on Robin."

The lad was asleep in his small bed beside the fireplace, the book Thorne had given him tucked up against his chest. Tenderly she brushed her fingers through his hair, then brought the covers up over him. After making certain all the lights were dimmed, and strolling through one more time to reassure herself all was secure, she led Thorne out through the rear exit and locked the door behind them. She wasn't surprised when he took her hand, tucked it within the crook of his elbow, and escorted her down the short flight of steps and toward the taller ones that led to her flat. When they reached the stairs, she turned to face him.

"I'll see you up," he said before she could make any remarks.

"Your thigh—"

"Is well on the mend. I'm disappointed you haven't noticed I have barely any limp at all. Go on with you."

"You're a stubborn duke." Still, up she went, with him following one step behind. When she reached the landing, she once again turned to him, standing only slightly higher than he because he hadn't taken that final step. "I always sit here for a while to absorb the quiet. Would you care to join me?"

The only light came from distant streetlamps, but still she saw his flash of a smile. "I would indeed."

She quickly lowered herself to the landing, her feet supported on a lower step, and waited as he worked his way down until he was sitting beside her, their hips and thighs touching because the stairs were quite narrow. Placing her hands between her knees, squeezing, she closed her eyes, dropped back her head, and inhaled deeply, letting the tension slip away. "My favorite moment of the night," she said on a long sigh.

"Watching you, I would have sworn you loved working in the tavern."

Opening her eyes, she gave a little shrug. "I do. Truly. It's only that there's so much noise—people talking, laughing, glasses hitting the table, or sometimes hitting the floor, orders shouted—some nights I feel as though my soul is being pummeled. A dress shop would have been quieter, but I haven't a talent for creating patterns or doing fine stitchery."

"You did well enough stitching up the holes in my clothing."

"Well enough will not bring a seamstress loyal clientele."

"I suppose not. Your clientele seems quite loyal."

"For some it's a place of refuge from the harshness in their life." She squeezed her knees even tighter, until her hands ached. "I'm surprised Polly didn't offer to take you home with her."

"She did, but I wasn't interested."

Snapping her head around, she couldn't imagine it. Polly was all bouncing energy, ample bosom, and wide hips. She gave a man something solid to hold onto. "Why not?"

His bare hand came up and cradled her chin, his thumb stroking the curve of her cheek all the way down to the corner of her mouth. "Because she doesn't intrigue me. You do."

She'd never had any trouble breathing out here, but suddenly the wisps of fog rolling in threatened to take away all the air. "You might be more fuddled than I thought."

"I'm hardly fuddled at all."

"I'd expected to have to haul you out and to your carriage."

"I'm not one to imbibe to excess—well, except when my bride runs off. Then I seem to lose my ability to think clearly. However, I have ceased to curse my idiocy. Because of it, I became acquainted with you."

As well as some of the more scandalous members

of her family. "What were you and my brothers laughing about?"

"They were telling me about a little girl who used to chase after them, always caught them. She was so fast, people thought she was a lad. You mentioned you wore your brothers' clothing until you were older. Is that the reason you bind your breasts? Because you're not comfortable being seen as a woman?"

"My mum always told me I needed to hide the things men fancied. Otherwise they wouldn't leave me alone."

"You don't have to hide anything about yourself. Not anymore."

"It's a habit now."

"Habits can be broken. You deserve undergarments of silk, satin, and lace."

She furrowed her brow. "You think of my undergarments?"

"I think of you *in* undergarments. I would purchase you some if I didn't think you'd toss them in the rubbish bin."

He made her wish that, at that very moment, she wore something provocative beneath her clothing, something he might take pleasure in removing. She shouldn't want him to divest her of her attire—and yet she did. She licked her lips. He moved his thumb over so it rested against the center of her mouth.

"You did that when you were feeding me broth. Drove me mad to watch that little tongue dart out."

"You ordered me to stop."

"Because I was in danger of embarrassing myself. One thing that makes you so intriguing, Gillie, is that you are so unaware of your ability to drive a man to distraction. I have no other woman in my life to whom

I must remain loyal, which means I am at liberty, if you are willing, to do this."

He moved slowly as though fearful she might bolt, might shove him down the stairs, kick him in his bad leg, react in a way to indicate she didn't want what he was about to do. But she did want it, desperately. She had been thinking about it, dreaming about it, ever since he'd first kissed her, had feared he'd found it unappealing since he had refrained from kissing her again.

But now as his lips touched hers, his mouth settled in, his groan echoed around her, she realized he'd only been acting a gentleman because she'd been injured. And he was acting a gentleman no more.

She parted her lips on a sigh and it was the invitation he needed to take the kiss deeper, to sweep his tongue through her mouth, drag her onto his lap—the ease with which he did astounded her, as she'd obviously misjudged his strength and her willingness to be handled thus—hold her nearer until her breasts were flat against his chest. She wanted to push him down and lie along the entire wondrous length of him. She felt his hard cock pressing against her hip, astonished it had reacted to her nearness. No other man had ever given any indication she was in the least bit desirable. Although to be honest, she'd never wanted to be desired by a man—not until him, not until the duke had ended up in her bed.

She shoved aside all of Finn's warnings. Even knowing she could never be more than a plaything to Thorne, she couldn't help but believe that to have him for a little while would be better than to never have him at all. She didn't want to die an old maid, never having known passion or desire.

He trailed his mouth over her chin and along the length of her throat. "You undo me," he rasped. "Come to my estate and I'll show you stars in the heavens and elsewhere."

His words made no sense to her when he was showing her stars now. "I beg your pardon?"

"You can't see the stars tonight because of the fog. There is seldom fog at my estate. And it is truly quiet there. No occasional clop of a horse, no squeaky wheel, no scurrying vermin."

"I'm not so very brave."

He drew back, and she rather wished she'd kept that truth to herself. "Before I opened my tavern, I was terrified of making a mistake, of letting my family down, of misjudging my ability to manage things. I still worry that my success is a fluke. And the thought of leaving London frightens me as well."

Combing his fingers through the strands at the side of her head, he carefully avoided her injury from the night before. "I wouldn't allow any harm to come to you."

"I know." She wrapped one arm around his neck, while pressing her mouth to the underside of his jaw. Such strength there. How could a man be naught but strength and power anywhere she touched? "But I'm not yet ready to leave London, not even for a few hours."

"Then let's do something in London. Let's take Robin to the zoological gardens, so he can see in person all the animals that fascinate him."

Ah, clever man, to suggest something that if she refused would mean denying pleasure to someone else. Besides, Robin could serve as chaperone so they couldn't get up to any naughtiness. Although she didn't know how effective he might be or if he might be too late. She was incredibly tempted to invite Thorne into her flat, but she knew any invitation would involve more than merely stepping over a threshold. It would involve making their way into her bedchamber and into her bed. "Not tomorrow. I have something I have to do. The day after."

With only his thumb and forefinger, he took hold of her chin and moved her face away from where she'd buried it against his neck, inhaling his marvelous fragrance. "The day after." Then his mouth was back on hers, sealing the promise.

She scraped her hands up into his hair, grateful he wasn't the one with a healing abrasion on his head. It was nice not to have to worry about causing him discomfort, at least there. She rather suspected his leg might be aching by now with her weight still on it. If it were, he gave no indication because he explored the confines of her mouth as though he'd never visited there before, so thoroughly, so intently, inviting her to return the favor. He tasted of the dark, rich whisky he'd nursed for most of the night. She was glad he wasn't three sheets in the wind, that his actions weren't spurred by the liberation that spirits tended to provide. She was grateful if any intoxication was taking place, being with her was providing it because being so near to him, having his mouth working its magic made her light-headed, as though she'd indulged in the finest of liquors.

Warmth sluiced through her, and her body tingled in private places, all the places her mum had warned her men fancied, all the spots she'd carefully guarded. If she could have sealed them off behind iron doors with locks, she would have. Yet even as she had the thought, she knew he possessed the key that would have sprung every door free, even the one to her heart, and that terrified her most of all.

She feared it was already his for the taking.

He drew back, and she nearly followed, nearly latched her mouth back onto his. "I should leave, while I'm still able."

She nodded. "I'll see you the day after tomorrow."

"I shall count the minutes."

She very nearly laughed. The aristocracy could be so charming in the way they spoke. It was little wonder people adored them.

Together, they helped each other to their feet. He walked her the short distance to her flat. Reaching into her pocket, she removed her key, surprised when he took it from her, and unlocked her door.

"Not because I don't think you can do it for yourself," he said, "but because I enjoy doing small things for you. Inside with you. I won't leave until I hear the lock turn."

"Good night, Thorne."

"Sleep well, princess."

She walked over the threshold, closed the door, and leaned against it, tempted beyond reason to invite him in. Her body was thrumming with needs, needs she knew he alone could satisfy. With a trembling hand, she turned the lock. With an aching heart she listened to his footsteps as he left.

Chapter 18

"*C*aw, Gillie, ye got bubbies!" Robin exclaimed as she walked into the kitchen through the backdoor close to the time for them to open.

"You don't say that to a lady, Robin," she stated tartly.

"Where'd they come from?"

Rather than answer, she said, "We're going to the zoological gardens with the duke tomorrow."

"That's where all the animals are."

"That's right. So tonight we'll be taking a bath."

"But it's not Saturday." She always made him bathe every Saturday. It was a condition she'd put in place when she'd agreed to let him sleep inside her tavern. In addition, he had to keep his hands and face clean. Clothes had to be changed every two days. She paid the woman who laundered her clothing to launder his.

"I know, but it's what one does when going out with a duke." She turned to find Hannah smiling at her.

"About time you set those puppies free."

"I was hoping no one would notice." That morning, she'd gone to a shop and purchased some undergarments. The silk and lace with purple ribbons made her feel rather feminine which was an odd thing when she was the only one who knew what all was there. This afternoon she intended to go in search of a new blouse and skirt for tomorrow's outing. Perhaps a bonnet.

"They're going to notice, love. A particular duke especially."

She almost blurted that he'd already seen them. "I'm running behind this morning. We need to get open."

"You might want to check the taproom first."

That statement caused apprehension to rush through her, and it wasn't at all quieted when she walked into the main room and saw all the flowers—a vase of different assorted blooms on every table.

"Aren't they beautiful, Gillie?" Polly asked.

"Looks like a bloody park in here."

"Your gent sent them," Roger said.

She almost reiterated that he wasn't her gent, although she was beginning to feel as though he might be—just a little. He hadn't gone home with Polly. He'd been content to sit with her on the steps and indulge in a couple of kisses. And he'd sent flowers. Enough for every table. He had to have counted them, made a note, remembered how many there were. What a silly thing that was to bring her such pleasure. He'd gone to the trouble to count her tables. "Cheers the place up a bit."

"Suppose it does at that," Roger said.

"We need to get the doors open."

He edged by her, stopped, looked back. "Notice you're not telling me he ain't your gent."

"You're getting a bit bold. I'd be careful if I were you, else you might find yourself let go."

"You deserve someone who does nice things for you."

"They're just flowers." But it was amazing how they made her smile.

And how her smile grew when Thorne walked

through the door later that evening. She poured whisky into a glass for him and reached the table where he'd been heading almost as soon as he did. "I wasn't expecting to see you until tomorrow."

"Why would I deny myself the pleasure of watching you?"

Such sweet words. She wanted to believe them, but her mum had warned her so many times about honeyed words. Yet she couldn't seem to stop herself from believing in Thorne. "Thank you for the flowers. They're all quite lovely."

"I'm glad you enjoyed them." His gaze never wandered from hers, and she wondered if he'd even noticed she wasn't bound up as tight as a drum.

"Robin is excited about tomorrow."

"As am I."

She set his glass on the table. "I need to get back to business."

But before she could make her retreat, he stepped forward and touched his fingers to her cheek. His gaze dipped only a fraction of a second. "I like the new look. I hope you spoiled yourself with silk."

She nodded stupidly.

"You're a beautiful woman, Gillie. I'm not certain you know that, but I intend to prove it to you."

HE LOVED THE way the blush crept over her face whenever he complimented her. As he sat watching her work, he found it difficult to believe she'd gone her entire life without a man appreciating all that she was. Compliments were foreign to her. He suspected no one had ever given her flowers. He wanted to lavish praise, gifts, and kisses on her but suspected too many would make her suspicious.

He hadn't planned to come here tonight, but had arrived at his club and been unable to motivate himself to go inside where all was staid and proper and people spoke in low voices. There was something addictive about this place, about the energy and the excitement, and the absolute joy of being here. Oh, a few blokes were moping about, but for the most part, everyone seemed cheerful.

She brought happiness out in people. He thought she should expand her properties, open another tavern in a different area of London. But if she wasn't there, would it be lacking?

Her brothers weren't here tonight, and to his surprise he found that to be a disappointment. He'd enjoyed his time with them, mostly because they'd been willing to tell tales about her. About the many scrapes she'd gotten into, the many times she'd gotten them out of a troubling situation. A dormouse she'd kept as a pet. She had such a gentle and giving heart he suspected she'd want to release all the animals from their enclosures on the morrow. He was very much looking forward to the outing.

AGAIN, HE STAYED until closing and helped out where he could. She liked that he wasn't the sort who did little more than sit around, waiting to be pampered. Of course, based upon the muscles she'd seen the first night, she'd assumed as much, but still it was somewhat satisfying to know she'd accurately judged him. And if she'd been right about that, perhaps she was correct in her other assessments. He wouldn't take advantage of her, and if their relationship continued, while there might come a time when he would be forced to bruise her heart, he wouldn't break it.

She could go into this situation knowing it would come with a cost, a cost she was willing to pay. She wondered if the woman who had given birth to her had once thought the same, if in the end she'd been left with regrets. So easy to make decisions without knowing precisely what the future held.

This time when he walked her up the steps, she didn't have to ask him if he wanted to sit with her for a while. He merely took her hand, assisted her in sitting, and settled down beside her, hips, thighs, shoulders touching. Perhaps it was because she was so heartened by the flowers or the prospect of tomorrow's outing, but she laid her head against his shoulder. Reaching over, he took her hand, threaded their fingers together, and placed their joined hands on his thigh.

She took a deep breath and released a long, slow sigh of contentment. "I was thinking we should make a greater effort to find your watch."

"Are you searching for an excuse to keep me near, Gillie?" he asked quietly, his voice smooth and hushed, his breath ruffling her hair since his head was so near to hers.

Perhaps she was. He was certain to grow bored with simply sitting on the steps with her, and while he'd suggested an outing with horses and one to the zoological gardens, she wasn't convinced he'd return once the latter was done. She wasn't quite ready to give up her time with him, regardless of how reckless it might be to continue to keep him within easy reach. "I simply know it means a great deal to you and I hate that it was stolen, especially as the incident happened behind my tavern. I feel responsible."

"Only that Charlie fellow and his cronies are responsible, and my solicitor assures me they will spend a good bit of time incarcerated due to their attack upon my person, especially after I speak out at their trial."

"They were unwise to jump a duke."

"Indeed. Especially one who had the good sense to be in an area where he could be rescued by a lovely damsel."

Laughing low, she considered turning into the curve of his shoulder, to hide away from the sentiments she couldn't quite believe were directed at her. "I've never been called that before."

"You should be. Every day."

Not knowing quite how to respond to that, she straightened and stared into the distant street, where the light was dim and the fog would begin rolling in. A comfortable silence wove around them.

"What if you're mistaken? What if a man did find himself falling in love with you?" he asked quietly.

Was he referring to himself? That wasn't possible. It was one thing to believe in unicorns, another entirely to think a man such as he could love her, although she couldn't help but believe that he did fancy her a little. She certainly fancied him. "Why would he be silly enough to do that?"

"Gillie, half the men who come into your tavern are in love with you."

A burst of laughter escaped with the absurdity of his statement. "They love the beer I keep in stock to pour for them."

"They love the manner in which you make them feel special. You do it without even trying, without even being aware you're doing it. It's simply part of your nature. I'm flabbergasted you haven't had an abundance of marriage proposals."

Pressing her hands together, she put them between

her knees, squeezed. "A proposal would be for naught, as I'd not accept it. I'm not giving my tavern to a gent. I've worked too hard and too long to make it what it is. The law would hand it over to my husband as soon as I said, 'I do.'"

"You don't think a man who loves you would take advantage, surely."

"I'm not willing to risk it. Once he had possession of the property, he could sell it and I'd have no say in the matter. I won't be dependent upon a man. My mum was, then her husband died and she had nothing. She took in by-blows for a while. People paid her pittance for that, not enough to keep us alive. She found ways to make do. They weren't always pleasant. So marriage is not for me."

"What of children?"

She'd long ago accepted they'd not grace her life. "I suppose I view the tavern as my child. I'm sorry if I sounded angry regarding the property laws. I don't blame you for them."

"I do have a bit of say. Just not a lot. However, I shall keep what I've learned tonight—and your passion for it—in mind when next Parliament is in session."

"Get the law changed so women can keep their property and they'll be falling at your feet. Although I suspect they do that anyway."

"Hardly."

She nudged her shoulder against his. "You're being modest. I'd wager you've fallen in love a half dozen times at least."

"Not even once."

Shifting her backside, she twisted in order to see him more clearly. Even with only the dimmest of lighting, she could make out his features, perhaps because she had memorized them so thoroughly. "I know you didn't love the woman you were going to marry, but surely in your youth, there was someone."

"No." His voice was low but absent of pity. "To be honest, Gillie, I don't know if I have it within me to love. At some point, I loved my mother. I must have. It is a child's inclination to do so, but she has always been unapproachable and I viewed her from a distance. I was closer to my father, but he was strict and demanding . . . and then he went mad."

She was stunned. He couldn't mean what she thought he did. "You mean insane?"

"Indeed. I wasn't quite ten, but I recall him ranting and raving, terrifying in his madness, until Mother would have the servants lock him in his rooms. I seldom was allowed to visit with him, but when he was on his deathbed, I noticed scars about his wrists, so I suspect there were times they tied him down to prevent him from harming himself or others."

She retook his hand and squeezed. "Oh, Thorne, I'm so sorry."

"It was long ago but between the two of them, I learned love disappoints. And it was drilled into me that I would marry for land, not love. I've liked women, Gillie. I've liked some of them a great deal, but love seems to involve a good deal more than simply liking."

"It requires sacrifice." With another sigh, she placed her head back on his shoulder. "I've never loved anyone either, at least no one beyond family. Now I don't want to love a gent because it would mean sacrificing my tavern."

"Makes us rather perfect for each other, then doesn't it?"

Perfect and yet imperfect. She lifted her head. "You are a danger to my heart."

"No more than you are to mine."

When he took her mouth, she banked her fears, her trepidations, and welcomed him as though it were impossible that they might ever hurt each other. The future ceased to exist, to concern her. All that mattered was the present, this moment, now. The way her body tightened with need, every cell reaching for him because he alone could provide the sustenance needed for continued existence.

It was sinfully sweet, the riotous sensations that bombarded her and swept through her like an over-zealous storm that pelted the earth. Any wise woman would seek shelter, and yet she knew she could find no better refuge than within the circle of his arms.

Cradling her breast, kneading it gently, he emitted a feral growl, one of ownership and possession. The orb she'd always considered such a bother tightened and grew heavy, sending sparks of pleasure throughout her, and she understood at last the value of silk over binding. Binding would have prevented him from squeezing, from testing the pliancy. The silk rubbed over her nipple, not abrading but teasing, causing it to pucker. She'd worn clothing like a shield; now she merely wanted to be liberated and thought he would be extremely skilled at liberating.

Drawing back, he pressed his forehead to hers. "You make me forget myself."

Which seemed a lovely compliment indeed. "The fog is creating a chill. Would you like to come inside?"

Leaning away, he touched his knuckles to her cheek. "If I come inside, Gillie, we're going to do a good deal more than kiss."

She knew that, of course. She needed to reassure him that she did, but the tongue that had been working so well during their kiss suddenly seemed too weary to form another coherent word.

"Let's get you inside," he said. She didn't hear disappointment in his voice, but rather understanding. He knew she had trepidations, had never gone this far with a man.

She wanted what he was offering, and yet she couldn't quite divest herself of all the warnings that had been preached at her over the years, Beast's the loudest of all: *Take care with your heart.* If Thorne came into her apartment, her heart would definitely be at risk.

He stood and pulled her to her feet. "I'm a patient man," he said.

He unlocked her door, opened it, and bussed a quick kiss over her swollen lips before giving her a nudge indoors. She was even slower to turn the lock than she'd been the night before, but turn it she did, eventually.

And later, lay in bed, staring at the shadows dancing over the ceiling, wishing she hadn't.

Chapter 19

"Caw, blimey! Look at his neck, Gillie. It's the longest ever!"

She certainly couldn't argue with Robin's comment regarding the giraffe. He'd made some keen observation about every animal they'd seen thus far, while she'd barely noticed them because her hand was tucked snugly within the crook of Thorne's arm, his other hand resting on it as though he intended to keep it there until the end of time.

He was without his walking stick, his limp negligible. If her eyes didn't fairly devour him every time he made an appearance in her life, she might not have noticed the limp at all, but from the moment she'd turned to find him stretched out on her table in the buff, not the smallest detail about him had gone unobserved. So she knew his hair had been trimmed and a razor recently taken to his face. She was also fairly certain his dark blue jacket and silver brocade waistcoat were recently purchased. The material of both was too bold and bright to have seen the wash even once. His gray neck cloth was knotted in a way that had it flowing into and behind the waistcoat with a single red teardrop pin to hold it in place. His beaver hat was not new, but he looked dapper just the same.

Her clothing from the pale blue blouse to the dark blue skirt and all the silk and lace that resided beneath it was new. She'd spent the afternoon before visiting a dress shop where she had once threatened to geld the former troublesome shop owner if he continued to insist the monthly rent was accompanied by more intimate favors. As Ettie Trewlove had given birth to a daughter out of wedlock due to the manner in which a nefarious landlord collected his rent, her brothers were always keen to put the fear of Trewlove retribution into those who took advantage. After a visit from them, the landlord had decided it was in his best interest to sell the shop to the dressmaker. Hence, the woman had been only too willing to ensure Gillie had something new to wear on her outing. It wasn't fancy, lacking ribbons and bows, but not a single spot on it was frayed or worn. Thorne had seemed to notice, which pleased her.

Then he had handed her a slim box, and inside she'd found the finest pair of kidskin gloves she'd ever seen. She never thought to wear gloves, but of course a lady on an outing with a gentleman needed to ensure her skin never touched his. While she'd considered the gift too personal, she'd not been able to refuse it. Although now she did regret more material separated the heat of his hand from hers.

He'd brought a gift for Robin as well and it had touched her heart more than the gloves: a miniature walking stick that was a duplicate of his, perfectly sized for Robin's height. The lad strutted about with it and used it to point at things. Like the giraffe.

"It has to take forever for the food to get into its belly," he said now.

"I suspect so," Thorne said.

"I would like to have one." He gave Thorne a hopeful look as though he expected him to purchase it.

"Where would it sleep, lad?"

Robin scrunched up his face as though it were a serious question and if he determined the answer he would find himself the owner of a gigantic giraffe.

"These aren't for sale, Robin," Gillie told him. "They're simply to gaze upon, admire, and appreciate."

With a nod, he carried on, making his way to the next enclosure. Each creature they viewed fascinated him, while she was fascinated with the man walking beside her. He exhibited extreme patience dealing with the boy, which resulted in Robin listening intently to instructions and following them: no darting off, no picking of pockets, no trying to frighten the animals. They were to be respected.

"Before your father took ill, did he bring you here?" she asked.

"No. On occasion we would fish in the pond on the estate. He took me hunting once, but pleasant memories of him are few."

"You mentioned that you were fifteen when he passed, which made you a rather young duke."

"Rather. I went a bit wild for a while, angry with him, furious in fact. It didn't help that my mother never had a kind word to say about him." He chuckled darkly. "Theirs was not a love match, but she brought land with her. Every wife of every duke brought land with her. I think the ultimate goal of the dukedom is to own as much of England as possible."

"So now you will seek out another woman with land."

"I suppose I shall. It is the only way to make my

father proud. Strange to seek that approval even after he's gone."

"I think that's natural. I don't even know who my parents are, but I like to imagine that somehow they know I've made a successful go of things."

"I hope they do know, that perhaps they watched from afar. The princess and her guard."

She felt the heat suffuse her face. "I should not have told you about the musings of a silly young girl."

"Not silly, Gillie. I don't think it's uncommon for us to imagine ourselves with different lives when we're young. I sometimes wished my parents were other than they were."

For his sake, she wished they had been. She'd always assumed those of the aristocracy lived without challenges, but it seemed no one was spared some sort of trial. She suspected if she traded places with some noblewoman that she'd find herself wishing she was back in Whitechapel right quick.

"Caw! Blimey! Look! It's a zebra," Robin called out.

They picked up their pace, quickly approaching the enclosure where the lad was hopping from foot to foot, until they could see the brown-and-white striped horse. Although only her head and shoulders were striped. The remainder of her was just brown.

"Actually that's not a zebra," Thorne said quietly. "A zebra has stripes all over it. This is a quagga."

Robin laughed. "That's a funny name."

"It's named after the sound it makes, and this is a very rare creature. Only a few remain in the world. Some speculate that this is the last one the zoological gardens will ever have."

"Why?" Robin asked. She doubted he understood

the term *speculate* but he was quite versed in the term *last*.

"Because so few remain," Thorne said solemnly, "and they're having no luck breeding them. You may be one of the last people to ever see one."

Robin blinked, blinked, blinked. "That's not right." He pressed his mouth into a determined firm line. "When I grow up, I'm goin' to find more of 'em."

"I hope you do, lad."

Robin eased up to the metal bars and stuck his hand through a pair. The quagga approached, nuzzled his hand. Robin petted her.

"He won't find any, will he?" Gillie asked somberly.

"No. I fear it's too late for us to do much of anything for them."

"So they'll go the way of the unicorn?"

He looked over at her. "Yes, I suppose they will."

She felt a profound sadness. "I always thought I was being fanciful believing unicorns had once existed, but it is possible, isn't it?"

"It is indeed."

"If I should ever open another tavern, I believe I shall name it the Quagga, to honor this little lady."

They rode an elephant and a camel. They had a picnic in a nearby park. As they journeyed in the duke's carriage back to Whitechapel, Robin curled against Thorne's side and slept. Gillie found herself wishing she was by his side, instead of sitting opposite him as was proper.

During their outing she'd begun to realize she was falling in love with him, a silly and reckless thing to do, not that her heart seemed to care. She was grateful her days of having fanciful thoughts were behind her, and that she had a more realistic view of the world now. A duke wouldn't marry a commoner from Whitechapel, and while this particular duke wanted land and property, he wanted a good deal more than her small tavern would provide. If anything more happened between them, it wouldn't lead to marriage, although she suspected at some point it would lead to heartache. She wouldn't continue to see him after he married.

When they reached the tavern, rather than going on his merry way, he followed her and Robin in. She had considered not working, taking a little more time to be with him, maybe taking a stroll without their small chaperone in tow, but business was brisk and one of her barmen hadn't shown up for work. His wife had sent word he had a stomach upset. She couldn't leave Roger to manage on his own.

"Tell me what to do," Thorne said, still by her side.

She furrowed her brow at him. "Climb into your carriage and go home."

Tucking his forefinger beneath her chin, looking at her so tenderly—she did wish he wouldn't do that as it sent all sorts of tingling sensations and warmth rioting through her—he said, "No, how do I help? You're short on staff and have a full house and darkness has yet to fall. You'll get even busier then if what I've observed on prior visits is any indication. I can pour a pint."

"You're offering to pitch in?"

"Don't look so shocked. I'm not totally devoid of skills or consider myself above helping when help is needed."

"No, of course you're not." She'd known that, of course. "Yes, I'd welcome your assistance."

It turned out he was not only skilled at pouring a pint

but at carrying on conversations with those who wandered over to the bar—or more precisely he was skilled at listening, expressing sympathy at their troubles.

Somewhere in the back of her mind, she'd hidden away a dream of sharing this place with a gent, but tonight she faced the bittersweet memory. Whenever he passed by her, he laid a hand on the small of her back or her shoulder. Sometimes when she was pouring a drink, she would glance over to see him watching her with a secretive smile as though he took pleasure from her nearness or was considering doing wicked things with her when they closed up for the night. She was certainly thinking about doing wicked things with him.

Perhaps it was because they'd been together most of the day, or the small kindnesses he'd shown to Robin, or the fact he'd stepped up when it was needed, without complaint, but after they'd closed up for the night and he escorted her to the top of the stairs, she didn't lower herself to the landing. Instead she walked straight to the door.

"You're not going to take a moment to absorb the quiet, to relax?" he asked.

Only after unlocking the door and pushing it open, did she turn to face him. "No. Tonight I have something else in mind. Come inside."

"Gillie—"

"I know. I know what will happen. And I want it to. It's my choice and now it's yours. Either go down the stairs or follow me in."

SHE WALKED INTO her apartment and stopped, glancing around, knowing that after tonight nothing in here would ever look the same to her, because everything would carry the memory of this night. The few trinkets, the books, the furniture, they would all bear witness to what was about to transpire. Yet even knowing everything would change, she would change, she couldn't seem to not be glad for the clack of the door closing, the snick of the lock being turned, the click of his footsteps as he neared.

His hands closed over her shoulders, his mouth pressed against her nape. "I like that I don't have to move your hair aside to appreciate the long slope of your neck. It's as graceful as a swan's."

Closing her eyes, she relished the heat of his open mouth again touching her nape, aware dew was collecting, warming her even more. "Not quite as long," she said on a breathy sigh that hardly sounded like her.

"No. Not quite as long." He moved his mouth to the other side of her spine, gave the sensitive skin there some attention. "I want to wash your back, Gillie."

Her eyes sprung open. "Now?"

"Yes. I've dreamed of doing so every night since the one when you turned me away."

"I wasn't turning you away—" She swung around. How to explain?

"I know. You didn't trust me."

"I didn't trust me. When I fell asleep, I had this dream, you see . . ." She let her voice trail off.

"Of me bathing you?"

She shook her head. "Of my leaving the tub and sitting on your lap, naked."

He grinned. "Oh, I very much like that dream. Was I naked as well?"

"No, at least not yet." She was blushing again, she knew it. "I think you might have gotten there if you hadn't woken me up."

"Bad timing then on my part. Perhaps we'll turn your dream into reality." He skimmed his fingers along her cheek. "Let me bathe you, princess."

"It seems a bit decadent."

"Decadent things are all we're going to do tonight."

A shaky shudder escaped as she wound her arms around his neck. "Only if I can bathe you as well. All of you." She hoped her smile was as saucy as it felt. "I didn't wash all of you before."

"You are timid and bold, and I adore both aspects of you."

Her chest grew so tight she thought it might squeeze her heart until it burst. No man had ever adored her. No, he didn't adore *her*. He adored her timidity and her boldness. Then he took her mouth as though to prove his point, and she could not help but believe that he did in fact adore the entirety of her. Otherwise, how could he stir such sweet sensations within her with so little effort?

His arms came around her, pressing her up against the length of his long, lean body. It felt so marvelous, so right as her breasts strained to be even closer, as her legs wanted to spread wide and cradle him so he was nestled against their sweet juncture where an ache had erupted with a force that nearly dropped her to her knees. She needed this man, needed him desperately.

His hands caressed her back, her hips, her bum, and she hated every stitch of clothing she wore that prevented her from feeling his skin against hers.

Breaking off the kiss, breathing heavily, he held her gaze. "Bath?"

She nodded. "Bath."

He dispensed with his coat, waistcoat, and neck cloth, tossing each negligently onto a nearby chair, rolled up his sleeves, and together they worked to prepare the bath. A low fire burned in the hearth and steam rose from the water. A lamp on a table by the bed provided the only other light.

He approached her very slowly, reminding her of the tiger they'd seen that afternoon: long, sleek, predatory. The look he gave her from behind half-lowered lids should not have made her tingle all over, should not have made her want to thrust up her breasts and beg him to suckle them. She imagined all the things he could do with that lovely mouth of his.

He stopped in front of her and skimmed the back of his knuckles over her chin. "Do you want me to tell you everything I'm going to do or just do it?"

"Simply do it, and quickly. I feel as though I'm on the verge of dying here."

He chuckled low, darkly. "Oh, princess, I haven't even begun to make you feel as though you're on the verge of dying."

Lowering his hands, he rubbed his knuckles over her breasts. She'd thought the nipples were already hard, but they hardened further, became tight little balls that seemed to be tethered to her nether regions. She wished she were again wearing trousers and could rub against the seam, for she was in need of some sort of surcease.

"Dear God, you're like kindling, aren't you? The lightest of touches and you burn."

"You're a powerful match."

He laughed. "Not certain I've ever been called that before."

"I don't know how to do this, Thorne. How to be clever and witty and seductive."

"Sweetheart, you seduced me long ago."

HIS WORDS WERE true, not meant to be flirtatious, not intended to woo. Simply to be honest. He wasn't certain precisely when she'd seduced him, but she'd managed to do it without airs or heaping praises on him, without coy looks, or batting eyelashes, or pouting lips. She'd done it with her forthrightness that was more seductive and alluring than all the coquettish flirtations cast his way by others.

She possessed a bit of whimsy with her mermaids and unicorns, but she was also steel and determination, running her business in a manner destined to ensure it met with success. Decisions were based on a goal. Although he suspected tonight's choice had been influenced by the whimsical side of her.

As much as he hated it, he knew there could never be more between them than this. If he were the decent sort he'd walk out. Only no woman had ever looked at him as she did, and he doubted one ever would again. A man was fortunate if once in his life a woman made him feel as though he were a king. She made him feel as though he were so much more.

He had unbuttoned too many bodices to count, but never had his fingers threatened to tremble. He wanted tonight to be perfect for her, to leave her with no regrets. A thousand times he'd imagined her in his bed, in his arms. The material of her blouse parted to reveal cleavage. Tempting cleavage. Then white silk and a purple velvet ribbon, a tiny purple bow.

He helped her get her arms out of the blouse, then tossed it aside. He went to work on the buttons and ribbons of her chemise until it was in a position to join the discarded blouse. Then he simply stared at those lovely, lovely breasts that once upon a time had made the arrival of death seem not quite so daunting.

"Do you remember throwing the mermaid at me?" he asked.

"Yes, of course."

"Coming to the bed all in a fret because you'd hurt me."

"And the blood. Trying to stop the blood so you weren't in danger again of bleeding to death."

"Hovering over me."

"Yes," she rasped. "I remember that very well."

"I desperately wanted to do this." Lowering his head, he pressed a kiss to the underside of her breast.

SHE REMEMBERED THE feel of his warm breath fanning over her skin, but to have his mouth there . . .

And then his hand supporting her breast while he peppered it with tiny, hot kisses and a lap of his tongue, velvety silk, awakening whatever remained of her dormant desires. His attentions were glorious and tender, yet she was also aware of how hard he fought to hold himself back, the tension in his neck and shoulders where she dug her fingers for purchase, to keep herself standing, so she didn't melt into a puddle at his feet.

His mouth journeyed up until it met hers, and the fire burst through her as he once again took possession of lips and tongue, as he claimed what she was so willingly giving. He stroked her bare back, up and down, up and down, before his hands went to work unfastening her skirt. It slid down to the floor, quickly followed by the silk undergarments.

"Sit on the edge of the tub," he ordered, and while her first instinct was to disobey simply because she didn't like being ordered about, her second instinct was to allow him to have his way with her in any manner he so commanded. He was the connoisseur while she was the novice. She would learn all he had to teach and then she'd turn the tables on him.

Hovering on the rim, she clutched the lip of the tub so she didn't fall into it, watching as he swept her clothes aside and went to work removing her shoes, first one, then the other. When they were out of the way, he untied a stocking and slowly, ever so slowly, rolled it down. She didn't know if she'd ever felt anything quite so sensuous. After tossing aside both stockings, his fingers fluttered up and down her calves.

"So fetching," he whispered, lowering his head and pressing a kiss to the side of one calf and then the other. "I look forward to having them wrapped around my waist."

She'd always considered her height an aberration, something that made her less than appealing to men, especially the ones she could literally look down on, but now she understood she would have an advantage with him. They would be locked together thigh to thigh, hip to hip, chest to chest, mouth to mouth. She would require of him no awkward bending or twisting. They were perfect for each other.

Placing his hands on either side of her waist, he supported her, bringing her to her feet. "In you go."

Holding her hand, his fingers snug around hers, he helped her keep her balance as she stepped into the water and sank down within its warm depths. "You should remove your shirt so it doesn't get wet."

"Splendid notion." He freed two buttons and pulled

it over his head. That magnificent chest of his beckoned to her fingers as he crouched before her. She couldn't stop herself from touching him as she hadn't dared when he was injured in her bed: skin to skin.

"I wanted to do this when you were recovering, but it didn't seem right to do so when you were unaware of your surroundings." She loved the feel of his hair tickling her fingers.

"How can a tavern owner be so mindful of propriety?"

"One must limit one's sins." Touching him would have been a tiny sin. What they were doing now was a much larger one. She could only hope that, by avoiding the smaller ones, the larger one would be forgiven.

"Not tonight, princess. Tonight you can sin all you want and I'll hold it secret."

She smiled. "It doesn't feel like a sin." It felt marvelous and right. She who had never been entirely comfortable around men, who had hidden her feminine side from those who might take advantage, felt gloriously womanly.

Taking the soap, he dipped it and his hands into the water, gave her a wink, and scuttled around behind her. Drawing up her legs, she wrapped her arms tightly around them and placed her cheek on her knees. She couldn't stop the low moan from escaping as his large hands landed on her shoulders and slowly caressed. He had no calluses, no abrasions, and yet his palms weren't completely smooth. There was a fine layer of roughness to them that caused luxuriating shivers to cascade through her.

"Would you really have not taken advantage the night I was recovering if I'd given in to this?" she asked somewhat dreamily.

"I'd have tried my damnedest to behave."

"I was fearful I wouldn't have wanted you to. Now I know the truth of it. I'd have begged you to make a wanton of me."

He chuckled low. "I'd have been obligated to oblige, especially as your back is incredibly alluring."

Then why did he take his hands away? Why was he no longer stroking her from neck to lower back? Looking over her shoulder, she saw he was standing, unfastening his trousers. She whipped her head back around. She'd known eventually he would remove them, but didn't want him to see how much she was anticipating it, licking her lips in eagerness.

"Don't be bashful, Gillie. I'm rather certain you've seen me before, since I was naked in your bed."

She nodded. "You're quite the impressive specimen, although I can only compare you to drunkards who forget to properly put themselves away after relieving themselves."

"You have not seen the best of men. I should apologize for every one of them who was ever born."

"You show me the best."

"I certainly intend to try, sweetheart. Move up a bit."

Loving the endearments with which he showered her, she slid forward, heard the water splash slightly, felt it rise, saw his hands gripping the lip, and was keenly aware of him lowering himself until she was cradled between his thighs, her backside nestled against his groin, where the hard length of him nudged against her. The heat that erupted through her was both pleasant and terrifying.

He was stroking her back again, his mouth landing in the curve where shoulder met neck. "You always smell of vanilla, yet you told me you don't cook."

"I like the fragrance so I dab a bit behind my ears each morning."

"Mmm." He nuzzled just below her ear. "Makes you smell good enough to eat."

Laughing, she twisted around and caught sight of his shoulder. The wound was healing, a raw and angry red scar evidence of what he'd endured. Splashing water around them with her movements, she faced him squarely and touched trembling fingers to it. "Oh, Thorne."

"It hardly hurts any longer."

"It shouldn't hurt at all, it shouldn't have happened at all." Leaning in, she pressed a kiss to the puckered flesh.

"Then I'd have not met you." His hand came up, his palm cradling her chin, her jaw while his fingers threaded up into her hair. "And my life would be that much poorer for having not known you."

He brought her mouth down to his. As she adjusted her position to better accommodate him, water sloshed around them. There was barely any room to move, but it didn't seem to matter as they slid along the slick length of each other, passion igniting, desire building. She wanted to run her hands over every inch of him, kiss every scar. Before the night of the attack, he hadn't a single one. She wished she'd seen him unmarred, and yet the scars he'd obtained didn't detract in the least from his magnificence.

And he was magnificent, not only in his looks, but in his actions, running the soap over her body even as he kept his mouth latched to hers, his tongue working its magic to heat her throughout. Even if the water grew chilly, she wouldn't notice, not when she was pressed up against a warm male.

Eventually he had to break off the kiss in order to reach all of her. "It would be an easier chore if I were small."

"I'm glad you're not. I like your height."

"Some of the lads who knew I was a girl—and some of the men now I suspect—would call me Longshanks."

"I can think of nothing finer than being named after a king."

She furrowed her brow. "He was a king?"

"Edward the First. He was known for his height."

"I don't think they meant it as a compliment."

"Still you should take it as one." He held out his hand, the ball of soap resting in his palm. "Your turn."

She took her time, washing him, torturing him with little touches, deliberately skimming her breasts over soapy skin, relishing the sight of him closing his eyes as though in rapture, and hearing his groans. After a while nothing was left to clean and the water had grown too cold for their bodies to keep each other warm. They helped each other clamber out of the tub, and using towels he'd set before the fire, they dried each other off. It was such a natural intimate exchange that she could see herself doing it every night for the remainder of her life.

But it wouldn't be every night. It was merely tonight. Perhaps one or two more, only until he took a wife. It would be devastating to give him over to another, but she had her tavern—which she had neglected rather badly of late—and her family and the people who frequented her establishment. They'd always been enough. They would be again. Simply not tonight.

Tonight her world had narrowed down to Thorne

and only Thorne. Based on the way his gaze slowly perused her, now that all the water droplets were gone and the towel had been tossed aside, she couldn't help but believe his world had narrowed down to her, to only her.

"You are beautiful beyond compare," he said quietly. "And you've done such a splendid job of secreting it all away that I suspect I'm the only chap fortunate enough to have an inkling regarding the treasures you keep hidden."

"I'm beginning to think you spend a great deal of your time with your nose buried in books of poetry."

"You bring out the poet in me." He lifted her into his arms.

"Your injuries," she exclaimed.

"Are almost healed."

She pressed her mouth against the crook of his neck as he carried her toward the bed. "Have I mentioned that you're gorgeous?"

"Scars and all?"

"They give you character."

"They show me to be a fool."

"They show you to be a man determined to survive."

"I hadn't thought I would," he confessed. "Until you came along, and for some ungodly reason, from the start, I didn't want to disappoint you. I desperately wish to not disappoint you tonight."

"I couldn't be disappointed when you're with me." She released a very unladylike snort and buried her face against his neck. "Now I'm the one spouting ridiculous flattery. We'll both be casting up our accounts if we continue along this vein."

He laid her out on the bed as though she were a

gift to be unwrapped, although she was already un-wrapped, so perhaps a gift to be admired. "Spout all you want, princess, and I shall do the same. Neither of us will cast up anything because what we say is for our ears and our ears alone."

Standing there, he trailed one finger—only one when she craved them all—along her shoulder, down her arm, over her hip, along her leg, across her feet, and all the way up the other side until he pressed the tip of that finger against her lip. "You're gorgeous, ev-ery graceful lithe lengthy inch of you."

He left her speechless, but she expected to look down and see herself glowing as though she'd swal-lowed moonbeams. He made her feel like the princess she'd once imagined herself to be.

The bed dipped with his weight as he stretched out beside her, cupped her cheek, and blanketed her mouth with his own. He no longer had to urge her to part her lips; they did so on their own accord, welcom-ing his deepening of the kiss. She rolled up slightly so more of her skin was touching his, skimmed her foot up his calf, then over his knee until her knee was fairly resting on the other side of his hip, her feminine haven cradling his groin, the hard length of his cock grow-ing even longer and harder, granite covered in velvet, pressing into her belly. He growled low and predato-rily, and while she hadn't thought it possible, he took the kiss even deeper, with an urgency that caused stars to erupt behind her closed eyelids.

Little wonder this was considered a sin because if people weren't discouraged from engaging in such behavior they would be doing it all the time. As fre-quently as possible. How was it that married folk, who were allowed, ever got anything else accomplished?

Everywhere their bodies touched created tiny sparks of pleasure that spiraled out to create even larger sparks. She became lost in the sensation of him, the wonder of him, the eagerness with which they touched each other.

Tearing his mouth from hers, he shoved himself down a few inches, plumped up her breast with one hand and offered it to his questing mouth as though it were the finest morsel ever served. As his lips came securely around the turgid nipple, he suckled, and she very nearly came off the bed as pain and pleasure warred for dominance, and pleasure won, sending armies of sensation throughout her. She pressed her honeyed canal against him, tilting up her hips, bowing her back in a way that allowed her to rub her intimate core along the length of his hard shaft.

If the way he jerked was any indication, now he was the one close to coming off the bed.

"You witch," he growled, and she laughed, wondering if such was allowed, but how could it not be when there was so much joy taking place in her bed?

She loved everything he was doing to her, all that she was doing to him. The touching, the caressing, the kissing, the suckling. Here within the shadows with doors locked and windows shuttered, everything felt acceptable. No, it was more than that. Everything felt ordained.

They had created their own little world where sins and regrets didn't exist. Where delicious secrets could be harbored in safety. Where bodies rejoiced with the freedom to explore and be explored.

Bracketing her sides with his large hands, he nibbled at her ribs, leaving little love bites on each one as he journeyed farther down, rolling her onto her back as he reached her stomach and nestled between her legs. His tongue circled her navel, lapped at her skin as he slipped his arms beneath her thighs, his hands coming around to open her wider.

Lifting her back off the bed, curling forward, she reached down and cradled his face between her hands. "Thorne."

He raised his gaze to hers. The desire and yearning she saw mirrored in his dark Guinness-shaded eyes caused liquid fire to pour through her veins and tremors to roll through her. Within the brown depths she saw more than a promise, she saw a vow: he would possess, he would pleasure, he would make her forget her name.

Using his thumbs, he spread the folds as though he were the sun causing petals to unfurl until the small bud hidden away could receive its warmth. Lowering his head, he closed his mouth around her most intimate core and suckled as though she were made of toffee to be slowly savored. Releasing her hold on him, she rested back on her elbows, her spine arched, her eyes closing, her head dropping back, her breaths coming in short shallow gasps. His tongue swirled and taunted. His hands came up to knead her breasts, his thumb and forefinger gently rolling her nipples. Everything was tautening as though he had laced a thousand bits of string through her, threaded them through her nubbin so every time he sucked, they pulled every part of her toward him. Suck and soothe, suck and soothe.

Tremors began undulating through her. Cries escaped through her parted lips. The pleasure was unbearable—

Then it ripped through her, in a maelstrom of glorious colors and magnificent sensations. "Oh my God, Thorne, oh my God."

She heard his dark satisfied chuckle, and it somehow managed to make the sensations even more intense. She felt as though she were falling from the heavens, unafraid because he would catch her.

The bed rocked as he moved up and dropped down beside her. Turning her head to the side, she placed her palm against his cheek. "That was marvelous. But there's more."

Nodding, he skimmed his knuckles along her chin. "But I'm not as recovered as I thought."

She sat up abruptly. "You've hurt yourself."

"No, but I don't think I can support myself as much as I should to ensure you again see stars. And you being beneath me probably wouldn't be good for your healing head either." He patted his stomach. "Straddle me, princess."

"Not until I've tormented you for a bit."

Chapter 20

$\mathcal{T}$orment had never felt so spectacularly wonderful. She was a novice, but also an incredibly sharp woman, which meant she had no trouble at all discerning exactly what to do, although he suspected his moans and groans and occasional "Devil take you" led her in the right direction.

When he went to caress her, she moved his hands over his head and ordered, "No touching."

Torment. Pure torment not to be able to comb his fingers through her short silken strands or graze them along her satiny skin.

She nibbled on his earlobe, swept her tongue over his ear, which had always been incredibly sensitive. She whispered something provocative and naughty.

He furrowed his brow. "Where did you learn that?"

"Drunkards say the naughtiest things sometimes."

"If they said that to your face, I do hope you plowed a fist into them."

"I don't hold drunkards accountable for their words."

He would if he ever heard anyone say something so inappropriate to her, a woman with whom he was now intimate. Incredibly intimate. He could still taste her on his tongue, feel her breasts in his hands, hear her cries of pleasure echoing around him. He'd known she'd be fierce when it came to lovemaking, would pour her entirety into it just as she poured all that she was into every aspect of her life.

Sitting up with her hip against his, gently, tenderly, she leaned over and kissed the puckered scar at his shoulder. "Is it hurting?" she asked.

It ached, but then it always did. He feared it always would. "No."

She rolled her thumb and forefinger around his nipples until they hardened into little balls. "I didn't wash these," she said. "It seemed too intimate. I shall wash them now."

His entire body grew taut as she lapped at the brown discs as though they contained cream and she were a cat intent on sipping every last drop. His growl rumbled from deep within his chest, and he caught sight of her secretive smile. Dear Lord, but she touched him in more ways than he could count, touched parts of him deep inside he hadn't even known existed.

Pushing herself up, she took a leisurely perusal of his body, from his messed hair to his feet, and he wondered where she might go next.

She chose his thigh, to the scar there. Then through half-lowered lids she looked at him very much as he suspected he'd gazed at her when he'd been nestled intimately between her thighs. No, he hadn't looked at her like that at all, not saucily, not wickedly, not so temptingly.

She wrapped her hand around his cock. It jumped. He jumped. Stealthily she inched forward, all the while holding his gaze as though daring him not to look away, holding him captive as effectively as if she'd bound him in irons. She ran her tongue around her lips until they glistened with dewy dampness. He grew so tense his muscles began to ache.

Lowering her head, she kissed the tip of his cock, then lapped at the dew that had gathered there.

"Christ!" He made a move to sit up. Her hand shot up, her fingers splayed against his chest, stopping him. Using little more than her brown-green eyes, she issued her command and pressed him back down. "Gillie—"

"Shh. My turn."

Using her tongue, she stroked the full length of the underside, and he feared he might embarrass himself by spilling his seed then and there. She closed her mouth around him and the heat spread throughout his entire body.

Oh, yes, she was a quick learner, his princess. She tormented him with flicks of her tongue, swirls, long slow strokes. If he hadn't gone ages without a woman he might have been able to last longer. If she weren't the one doing these incredible things to him, if he didn't have a need to possess her so desperately, perhaps he could have lasted longer. But he wanted her fully, completely, absolutely. He needed her as he'd never needed or wanted anything in his entire life.

"Gillie," he repeated, closing his hands around her arms. "Do your damage another way. Straddle me, take me deep within you."

Thank God, she did as he bid, placing her knees on either side of his hips, taking hold of his aching and throbbing cock, and positioning it at her opening. Closing her eyes, she enveloped him. When he encountered her barrier, he grabbed her hips, thrust his own. Her small cry tore at his heart. "I'm sorry."

She shook her head and sank farther down until

she'd taken him to the hilt. "You feel so good. I understand now why people sin."

"This isn't a sin, Gillie. Not when the yearning and desire are so great." He'd almost used the word *love*, but the thought of loving her this deeply, this desperately terrified him and he couldn't give voice to his feelings. All he knew was that no one had ever touched his heart and soul as she did. No one had ever mattered as much as she did. He, who had thought himself incapable of love, was floundering with the knowledge she made him question all he'd ever known about himself.

Cradling her hips between his hands, he guided her as she began to ride him, meeting his thrusts, rocking against him. He watched the wonder spread over her features, could feel the tightening of her muscles around him as their tempo increased into a frenzy, as their gasps and groans filled the air. Clenching him tightly, she cried out her release. As gently, but as quickly as he could, he lifted her off him as his own release tore through him, rocking him to his core as he made a vain attempt to roll to his side and spill his seed into his hand. Instead he made a mess of it.

Pressing her body, against his, she covered his hand with her own. With his free arm, he held her close, wondering if his heart would ever return to a normal speed or if it would always pump with the wild abandon spurred by her nearness.

MAKING LOVE WAS not the tidy thing she'd always thought it to be, and yet as she lounged on the bed, waiting—as he'd instructed—for him to come to her, she couldn't deny there was something incredibly masculine about him standing at the water basin cleaning himself up. "Wouldn't it be easier if we simply took another bath?" she asked.

Chuckling low, he walked over holding a damp washrag. "I haven't the strength to prepare another bath."

Gently, he wiped the area he had earlier licked and the inside of her thighs, tinged with blood. "Did it hurt so terribly?" he asked.

"No."

"There should be less discomfort next time." Pleasure pierced her with the knowledge they would have another coming together. When he was finished, they changed the sheets, then snuggled beneath them, holding each other close.

"How long will you stay?" she asked.

"I'll leave before dawn. We don't want anyone seeing me making my escape." Tucking his knuckles beneath her chin, he held her gaze. "Unless you'd like me to leave sooner, although I'd very much like to sleep with you in my arms."

She nodded, snuggling more solidly into him. She loved the smell of his warm skin. "I'd like that as well."

With his arm around her, he stroked her arm while she lazily drew small circles on his chest.

"Are you having second thoughts?" he asked.

"Second, third, and fourth, but all good thoughts."

"I want you to know I do respect you."

"No, you don't. You whisper in my ear."

He chuckled low. "You have such a lovely ear into which to whisper."

"I never wanted this before, Thorne, before you. Why are you so different, I wonder?"

"Because I'm a duke."

"That has nothing at all to do with it. I don't care

one whit about your title. It's other things. Your kindness to Robin, for instance."

"I was thinking of paying his tuition at a boarding school."

Rising up on an elbow, she looked down at him, studied him. "Why?"

"Because he's a sharp lad. He'd go far."

"He'd only run off. He believes if he stays here, his mother will find him. I think he believes she's a fairy."

"Where would he have gotten that notion, I wonder."

She eased back down and burrowed against him. "Probably from the whimsical tales I wove when he would awaken from a bad dream, tales my mum would tell me when I was a child and sleep would not come."

"Perhaps I'll fund a school nearby. More children would benefit from that, wouldn't they?"

"You're a good man."

"Not so good. I'm six and thirty, and never before gave much thought to those less fortunate than I. I had more pressing matters on my mind: a fast yacht, a fast horse, fast women. Sometime, when you're of a mind, I'll take you to France on my fast yacht and we'll visit all those vineyards."

She couldn't imagine it, doubted they would ever do that, was well aware of her place in his life, what she was to him, and if he were more to her, she suspected she was not the first woman to have reached for and caught something she could never hold forever. He needed a woman who could stand beside him as his duchess. Duchesses did not own taverns. Still, it was a lovely fantasy and she said, "I'll feed you grapes from the vines."

"And I shall lick the juice from your fingers."

She wanted that more than she'd ever wanted anything, but realist that she was, she knew it would never come to pass.

AWAKENING WITH GILLIE in his arms had been one of the more satisfying starts to his day that he'd ever experienced. She was an enthusiastic lover, eager to welcome him into her body—her hot, sweet, tight canal. He'd have luxuriated in her bed all day, but the practical woman had a business to run, so he'd left her while the fog was still thick and the moon still looking down.

By the time he strode into his residence, he was famished and the sun was making an appearance, but rather than risk dealing with his mother, who could already be up, and taking a chance on the ruination of his good mood, he ordered a servant to deliver a tray of food to his chambers.

Once his valet had tidied him up for the day, he enjoyed a leisurely meal in his sitting area, reading the newspaper, imagining how much more satisfying it would be to have Gillie sitting there with him, sipping her tea, reading her own newspaper.

When the knock sounded, he glanced at the clock and realized he'd spent nearly an hour sitting there and visualizing her in this room. Not that he'd ever have her in this chamber while his mother resided here. He could imagine the turmoil that would cause and the misery his mother would deliver to the woman he loved.

That thought nearly had him careening out of the chair. He loved her, loved Gillie. He who had never loved, loved at last. That he was even capable of such intense emotion came as a bit of a revelation. He wanted to throw open all the windows and shout it out to the world—

But he couldn't even tell her, because it would be unfair to her, to him, to them. He could have her here in this bed, in this chamber, but he could not have her as his duchess. He could not ask her to give up the tavern which meant so much to her. He could not take her from all she knew, all the people who would stand beside her and threaten him if he did wrong by her. He couldn't bring her into this world that failed to bring him the barest hint of joy.

Although he had little doubt she could hold her own among the *ton*, at least when it came to socializing. She had an innate grace and confidence that made her any lady's equal. Her speech patterns would mark her as not having been raised among the aristocracy, yet the ease with which she managed to carry on conversations would see her in good stead. She would charm and delight those who would give her a chance, just as she charmed and delighted him at every turn. It was a pity the origins of her birth would prevent those he knew from having the opportunity to spend time in her company.

The knock again resounded, a bit louder and more insistent.

"Enter."

His mother swept in as though pushed by a gale force wind. He shoved himself to his feet as she came to stand before him, her back erect, her hands clasped before her.

"I saw your announcement in the *Times* regarding the end of your betrothal."

He'd placed an advert in yesterday's edition, so proclaiming. It had been short and sweet, indicating a mutual understanding and agreement between all parties involved that a wedding between the Duke of Thornley and Lady Lavinia Kent would not take place. "I wanted to ensure no fingers were pointed or blame was assigned."

"What you have ensured is that the nattering gossips shall have a field day. You must *show* people you are not the wounded party and are quite ready to move on. You have made it more imperative than ever that you select a wife as quickly as possible. Therefore, I have set a date for the ball, two weeks hence. Invitations went out this morning."

He wanted to groan in frustration at her meddling. Instead, he merely said calmly, "Good Lord, the printer must have worked all night."

"I am a duchess. Of course he did, and he was glad to do so."

He couldn't imagine Gillie inconveniencing someone like that.

"I have invited the families with the most eligible girls," she continued. "It will be a small affair, as it has a singular purpose: to ensure you find yourself a bride worthy of your position and in short order."

"I am not yet ready to see to the task."

"Make yourself ready. People are laughing at you, wondering what faults Lady Lavinia found with you to leave you as she did."

"I stated clearly no one was at fault."

"Do you think anyone believes you? What you have done is given fodder to those who would see us fall. Situations such as this are best handled by women, so I am taking the matter in hand. I know we seldom agree but do not fight me on this. You have a duty, an obligation, a responsibility to those who have come before you."

"Already, you have made them all, every eligible lady, seem so appealing," he said caustically, hoping she would catch the sarcasm.

"If you are to have any hope at all of having an heir, you must see to it immediately, as you are developing your father's habits of staying out all night. I am well versed in where that leads."

"I'm old enough, Mother, to live my life without being chastised for it. I believe it's past time for you to move into the dower house."

She jerked her head back as though he'd delivered a blow. "I cannot possibly do that until there is another lady in residence to manage things. Servants will grow lazy without a firm hand. I shall not allow a residence in shambles to be passed on to your new wife. It is a matter of pride."

Pride. Always so much pride in this family.

Although she did have the right of it. He was at an age where he needed to marry and provide an heir. Whether or not he wished to. Crossing his arms over his chest, he gave a curt nod. "I will attend the ball on one condition. You will invite Miss Gillian Trewlove."

"Who is her family?"

"Lady Aslyn married her brother. You should invite them as well, if you have not already."

"Lady Aslyn married a commoner, a by-blow."

"Thus you shall have the distinction of being the first to have them at a ball." He had little doubt his mother knew exactly where to find Lady Aslyn. "You may send Gillie's invitation care of the Mermaid and Unicorn tavern."

She turned up her nose. "A tavern-serving wench?"

"The tavern owner."

"I can't possibly—"

"Then you will have a ball with no Duke of Thornley in attendance." He didn't know why it was suddenly so important for Gillie to be there. Perhaps he wanted to test the waters, to see if she might enjoy swimming in them. But even if she did, she wouldn't give up her tavern for him, nor should she.

"You are going to make a fool of yourself."

"I am going to introduce someone incredibly lovely to my friends and acquaintances. A good many would benefit from knowing her. If you give her half a chance, I daresay you would like her."

"I cannot imagine it, but I will not embarrass this family further by canceling a ball after already canceling a wedding. The invitations you've requested will be placed in the post tomorrow."

"On second thought, give me Miss Trewlove's and I'll deliver it personally."

"I daresay, you will rue the day you brought her into this residence."

"You will treat her kindly, Mother, and you will show her respect or you will find my patience with you to be at an end."

She stormed from the room. He walked to the bureau, pulled open a drawer, and removed a tattered shirt. Returning to his chair, he skimmed his fingers over the tidy and delicate stitching, holding together cloth that had once been shorn by a knife blade going into his shoulder. She'd done more than mend his clothes. She had somehow managed to mend him when he hadn't even realized he was in need of mending.

THE MOMENT HE walked through the door of the Mermaid, she seriously considered closing up shop. Normally she loved every minute of her time inside the tavern, whether she was serving drinks or talking with customers or ordering people about. But now all she desired was time with Thorne. Perhaps she would invite him to join her in the cellar to select a sherry. She couldn't stop herself from smiling at that thought.

Instead of going to a table, he came to her. "I see your man is back tonight."

She knew he was referring to the barman who'd not shown the previous night, but in a giddy part of her mind that she hadn't even known she possessed, she realized he could have been talking about himself as well. Her man. She had a man. She wanted to stand on the counter and shout it to the crowd, but what they shared, what was between them, what had passed between them, was deliciously secret. Reaching into her pocket, she removed a gift for him that had her joyous with anticipation. "Yes. But you're welcome to assist if you like. I need someone to keep track of the time."

Taking his hand, she pressed the cool gold against his palm and closed his fingers over it. Slowly he unfurled them and stared at the timepiece. The awe and wonder on his face caused her chest to tighten and her eyes to sting. Gradually, as though journeying through a maze of memories, he brought his gaze back to hers. "You found it."

Her smile so big she feared her jaw might come unhinged, she nodded. "Petey stopped by this afternoon and told me he'd been hearing talk of a fancy timepiece. He had an idea where we might find it. So off we went."

"I thought never to see it again." He opened the cover, looked at the face where the hands marked the passage of time. The proper time as she'd set it earlier and carefully wound it. Tenderly he cradled her face, stroked his thumb over her cheek. "I don't know how to repay you or Petey for this."

"Oh, Thorne, when will you learn that the joy you feel at making someone else happy is payment enough. Although Petey will be getting free meals and beer anytime he wants."

"I'm fairly certain whatever fence you got this from did not simply hand it over. I've no doubt you paid a pretty penny for it."

"Pittance." A day's earnings, but money well spent to see how very touched he was to once again have the timepiece in his possession.

"At the very least, allow me to pay recompense for that."

"It's a gift, Thorne. Accept it as that."

He nodded. "I'm so touched, Gillie. I shall no doubt think of you more often than I do my father when I look at it."

For a time perhaps, but eventually memories of her would fade, and he would again associate it with his father because those ties were stronger, had lasted longer, encompassed generations. She squeezed the hand that still held the watch. "I'm just so pleased you have it back."

"I'd kiss you soundly this very minute if it wouldn't cause scandal," he said.

"You can do it after we close."

Something warm and tempting flashed in his eyes. "In the meantime I wouldn't mind working back there with you where it's a trifle small and I'd have excuses for touching you whenever we have to edge our way past each other."

So he did much as he'd done the night before, pouring drinks and talking. She wondered what these good people would think to know they were being waited on by a duke. While Finn had heard his position, it had never been declared for all to hear and she never addressed him as "Your Grace." Perhaps because she'd never ceased to see him as simply a man, even though she knew deep down he was so much more and could never be hers completely.

In a way, he belonged to England, sat in the House of Lords, tended to the Queen's business, created and altered laws, saw to the good of the country. Mick had wanted his father's acknowledgment because he'd yearned for the exaltation that came with being related to nobility, but she had never desired that for herself, other than the fantasy she'd had as a child. The upper echelons were beyond reach for most, for the simple folk, the commoner. It didn't mean they couldn't achieve worthy positions—it simply meant they had to work harder for them because nothing was given to them.

Although having gotten to know Thorne, she realized nothing came without a price. For all his social standing, he wasn't nearly as free as she. He was playing at being a bartender, but it wasn't something he could do forever, no matter how much he might enjoy it. Just as she was playing at being his lover. She couldn't be it forever, no matter how much she might enjoy it.

He would marry and she would not. He was responsible for providing an heir. She would not marry a man she did not love, and she suspected that in her lifetime there would be only one. This one. This one she could not have.

Through Finn she had learned they were not for the nobility, not for the long term. But she could make the most of the short term.

So when the tavern was closed up tightly for the night and they reached the top of the stairs, she didn't stop to sit and absorb the quiet. There would be an abundance of other nights for that, nights when she would sit there alone and think of him and what had been—and she wanted minutes and minutes and minutes of memories she could flip through, without having to revisit one too often because she had an abundance of others hoarded away.

Instead she led him into her apartment, into her bedchamber, into her bed. With remarkable speed they divested each other of their clothing before tumbling onto the sheets. With his body half covering hers, he clamped a hand along the side of her face and captured her mouth with a fervor that might have frightened her if she weren't as eager to seize his. She loved the hunger that welled up between them, the attempt to satiate that hinted any quenching would be short-lived. Always, she would again want his mouth on hers, always she would crave the taste and feel of him. Always.

Which made their coming together bittersweet.

"This might have been the longest day of my life," he rasped as he trailed his mouth along her throat. "Waiting to have a moment alone with you."

"I wasn't certain if I'd see you tonight."

"An act of Parliament wouldn't have kept me away."

But a wife would, although she didn't say that, wasn't going to think about that. She knew of at least five women who had taken men to their bed without benefit of marriage. This very moment she was lost in sin and yet she couldn't seem to care. The sensations rippled through her as his hot mouth and nimble fingers had their way with her, kissing here, nibbling there, stroking here, pinching there, while hers responded in kind, tormenting him—based upon his moans and groans that were music to her ears.

Then he shifted her so she was beneath him and he was above her, his hips wedged between her thighs. "Wrap your legs around me," he ordered.

"I didn't think you had the strength to support yourself."

"I've another day of healing behind me. I'm going to risk it."

Lifting her hips, she wound her legs tightly around his waist, more than ready when he plunged into her. She loved the way he stretched and filled her, the weight of him over her. Cradling her head between his hands, he dipped down and took her mouth while she skimmed her fingers down his back and gripped his buttocks.

Moaning low, he began rocking against her, carrying her to dizzying heights of pleasure and torment. Every bone and muscle wanted to curl in on itself; every bone and muscle wanted to explode in release. Nothing had ever felt so good, and she knew the next time she would think the same thing. No matter how often she'd thought of what had transpired last night, the memory of it wasn't as good as the reality.

As the world exploded around her, as she flew apart and came back together, she knew memories would not be enough to sustain her, but they would be all she had and she would cherish and hoard them. She became aware of his frantic pumping, his harsh breathing, his stifling moans—

Then he pushed himself free of her, burying his face between her breasts as he shook with spasms, spilling his seed in his hand in an effort to protect her from anyone ever learning of her sins.

Chapter 21

*H*e'd never known as much contentment as he did with her nestled within his arms. She was warmth and goodness, and in spite of her growing up on the streets, she possessed an innocence that made him want to protect her, even knowing she was fully capable of protecting herself.

"I might be becoming addicted to you," she said quietly, and he chuckled.

"No more so than I am to you."

She trailed her finger over his chest. "I'm always amazed when you offer to help out, whether it's assisting with customers or tidying up."

"I've never been one for lazing about."

"You must have your own affairs to see to."

"Most of those I can handle during the day."

Shifting until one of her legs was positioned between both of his, her lovely thigh pressed up against his cock, she lifted herself up and gazed down on him. "What sort of things does a duke have to do?"

"I have four estates so I must read reports from the stewards of each, approve repairs and maintenance, make decisions regarding how to increase the income generated by each. Meet with my solicitors regarding various situations that arise. Meet with bankers regarding investments. A lot of meetings."

"And you must marry."

A prospect that should have brought him joy rather than despair. "Yes. And I need to have an heir."

"That's a nice thing about being a commoner. We don't have to marry; we don't have to provide children. Your sort always seems to be on show."

"I suppose we are. One of our duties is to ensure fodder for the gossips and the gossip rags. Without us, they would cease to exist."

"I wouldn't like being the focus of everything."

"Is that the reason you stay behind the bar?"

She nodded. "I love owning the tavern, but I'd rather do it quietly. Mick is different about his hotel. It's important to him that people see him as much as they see what he has accomplished. Perhaps it's simply because he's a man and feels he must come across as a conqueror."

"You're a much more subtle conqueror. People could underestimate you."

"Which I can use to my advantage sometimes. Charlie certainly didn't think I would jump him."

"But he knew you weren't to be trifled with. It's the reason he ran off."

"When will you run off, I wonder."

He combed his fingers through her hair. "I won't run off, Gillie."

"But there will come a night when it will be our last night. When it comes, please tell me."

He knew they would be the most difficult words he'd ever utter, but he cared for her too much, respected her too much to bed her while bedding a wife. "It won't come for a while yet."

If he didn't need an heir, didn't need a wife who understood the intricacies of Society, it might have never come. But it would, it would have to because he had responsibilities, because he'd made promises. Yet he would delay it as long as possible. "My mother is hosting a ball in two weeks. I'd like for you to come."

Scoffing, she flopped over onto her back. "No bloody way."

He rolled over until he was positioned as she had been, with his leg between hers, his thigh pressed up against the sweet haven he was going to visit once more before leaving. "The Season is over. There won't be many people in attendance. Your brother Mick is to be invited, so I won't be the only person you know."

"Why would you want me there?"

"Because I want to introduce you to my mother, to people I know. You're a fascinating woman, Gillie, and they will be intrigued."

"You want to display me like an animal at the zoological gardens."

"No." He was appalled by the very idea, but how to make her understand? "You're a successful businesswoman. Born to the streets, yet you've risen above them. You deserve to be recognized for your accomplishments, to move about in circles where you can influence people who have the means to address social injustice."

"They're a bunch of nobs."

"You're judging them harshly, when they won't do the same of you."

"Of course they will. They've been doing it my whole life."

"Then prove them wrong. Your speech proves you're educated, even if that education didn't take place in private schools. You're graceful and strong. To be admired." He trailed his mouth along her throat. "Besides, I want to waltz with you. I don't want you to be a secret."

"But I am, and what we are doing here can't be shared."

Kissing the sensitive spot below her ear, he heard her soft sigh. "We're not going to tell people what we're doing here but I know your world now, Gillie, and it's not at all what I thought it would be. You're asking me about my world. I'm requesting you simply step into it for a night, share it with me. You might find it to your liking."

If she did, perhaps he would no longer have to contemplate ever giving her up.

THE FOLLOWING AFTERNOON as Gillie strode into the Trewlove Hotel and marched up the stairs, flight after flight, to the top floor where her brother had his offices and his residence, she knew it wouldn't make any difference at all if she found Thorne's world to her liking, but she had to admit to being curious about it— not so much his world, as learning more about him. What did his residence look like? How did he treat his servants? And then there was the prospect of meeting his mother, his friends, which made her at once want to jump out of her skin while also having her curiosity racing forward with glee. What were they like, the people with whom he surrounded himself? She was anxious to meet them because one's friends were often a reflection of oneself. And all she knew about him was narrow, were his interactions in her small section of London. His life was much broader than that, wider, encompassed a good deal she couldn't even imagine.

She'd been a fool to accept the invitation, to tell

him she'd come. He'd used nefarious means, asking her over and over until, during a moment of weakness when she'd been unable to remember her name, she'd agreed to attend. Before leaving her that morning, he had pulled the gilded invitation from his jacket pocket and handed it to her. She'd run her fingers over the embossed script, striving not to be intimidated by it.

She had a vague notion regarding how to go about preparing herself to attend her first ball. It might have been more concrete had she attended Mick's wedding, but at the time she'd expected to feel rather out of place at the elaborate affair, pretending to be something she wasn't. But now she had a strong urge to prove to herself, if to no one else, she was worthy of entry into the highest of social circles—without putting on false airs or acting in a manner that wasn't true to herself. She had learned a good deal from the tavern owners for whom she'd first worked. Mrs. Smythson had insisted she join her for tea every afternoon and had taught her comportment. "The world is uncommonly unfair to women," she'd once told Gillie, "but that will not change until women make it so. You do the cause no great service by hiding what you are. Embrace it and show the world you are a force to be reckoned with."

The couple had no children, and Gillie often thought her presence in their lives filled a hole in their hearts. Mrs. Smythson had taken her shopping for her first frock. Gillie had never cared for the frilly, preferring the practicality of simple skirts and shirts. Nor did she have the patience for or the desire to spend time putting her hair up into elaborate coiffures, so she kept it short and tidy. Changing the manner in which one had lived for so long necessitated compromises, and in the end she was happy with Gillian Trewlove.

So while she was nervous about attending the ball, she believed that when it came down to it, she could hold her own. Still, a bit more polish wasn't out of order. She'd caught the attention of a duke when she'd once thought she'd never catch the attention of any man. Perhaps she could do right by him in a larger world, perhaps there was a small part of her that thought maybe she had the wrong of it: that for them there would never be a final night.

Such a silly thought. Still it was there as, with merely a passing glance, she walked by the glass door with *Trewlove* etched in it proclaiming the rooms beyond as belonging to her brother—as though they could belong to anyone else—and continued on to a set of polished wooden doors that led into his flat. She'd visited on a couple of occasions, intrigued by the notion he required so much grandeur while she yearned for none at all. But then Mick had always known his father was a duke, had resented that his sire refused to acknowledge him, and had felt he had something to prove and that involved mimicking the world of the aristocracy as much as possible. He'd accomplished that with great success and shared all that he'd learned with her. But he viewed everything through a masculine eye, while she was in need of a feminine one.

She knocked. Waited not even a heartbeat before a footman opened the door.

"Miss Trewlove."

Whenever anyone addressed her as such, she felt a great need to look around in order to determine to whom they were speaking. She'd never been comfortable with the formality, even from servants or employees. She was a fool to seriously consider attending the ball where there would be naught but formality. "Is Lady Aslyn about?"

After ushering her in, he said, "If you'll be so kind as to wait here, I shall inquire."

Which made no sense. Either she was or she wasn't. Shouldn't he know? Still, she stood in the entryway while he headed off. A few minutes later, her brother's wife rounded a corner, smiling brightly, her blue eyes glittering with joy and her arms outstretched. "Gillie! How wonderful that you've come to call."

She towered over the woman, so she had to bend down considerably in order to return the hug Aslyn offered. "I hope I'm not disturbing you."

"Never." Aslyn stepped out of her embrace. "Did you let Mick know you were here?"

"No, actually, it's you with whom I wish to speak."

She appeared both delighted and confused, no doubt because Gillie had not gone out of her way before to spend time with the Earl of Eames's daughter. She'd assumed they'd have nothing in common, and while she liked her well enough, she didn't think she'd be interested in discussing the process of fermentation. "Wonderful. Join me in the parlor and I'll send for tea."

She followed Aslyn—who alerted a nearby footman they were in need of refreshments—into a front room and dropped into a chair while her hostess seemed to float down into hers, adjusting the positioning of the wide skirt of her green-striped frock with its numerous flounces and taffeta bows, aspects which would prove a hindrance when hauling casks up from the cellar. Her blond hair was swept up off her neck, curling tendrils framing her face. Gillie didn't want to consider how much effort the woman would put into going out of the residence when she put so much effort into her appearance for remaining in it.

"How have you been?" Aslyn asked, and Gillie heard the true interest in her tone.

"I've been busy with the tavern and all. Mick doesn't come as often since he got married."

A light blush crept over her sister-by-marriage's face. "We've been a bit busy as well."

A few nights ago she might not have guessed what they were busy doing, but she certainly had a fairly good idea now. She decided she might as well get down to her reason for being here. "Are you familiar with the Duke of Thornley?"

Aslyn blinked with apparent surprise. "Yes, I've known him for some time."

"I met him recently, on his wedding day, actually—or what was supposed to have been his wedding day."

"Oh my goodness. Is he the man Mick saw leaving your residence? He told me about him, thought he was a beggar."

Gillie explained all that had happened.

"Oh my stars. I hadn't heard anything about that." She shook her head. "Well, I heard Lady Lavinia had taken ill, and then I saw the announcement that the betrothal was off. But the truth of it, what actually transpired—I daresay I don't blame them for keeping everything so very hushed."

"He thought it best, and it's not something a man boasts about, is it?"

"You have the right of it there. Men can be far too prideful."

She knew her brother Mick fell into that category. Actually, on second thought, all her brothers did. "As a result of all that happened, I've been spending a bit of time in his company." She cleared her throat. She wasn't going to go into the specifics of that time. "He's invited me to a ball his mother is hosting."

Aslyn smiled. "Indeed. How lovely. Mick and I received an invitation to the Duchess of Thornley's ball not more than an hour ago."

She couldn't help but be impressed. Thorne worked rather quickly when he wanted something. "Needless to say, I've never attended a ball, most certainly not one involving nobility. I thought perhaps if you could walk me through my paces, tell me what all is expected, what all happens, then I could ensure I know everything before arriving. I'm a firm believer in being prepared."

Aslyn's smile grew. "Well, you'll want a ball gown, of course."

"I was going to visit with my seamstress this afternoon."

"Two weeks is not much time to stitch one up. Perhaps you should consider using my dressmaker. She has ample experience in ball gowns."

"I'll not take coins from Beth's pockets."

"Perhaps we could have them work on it together. A few more hands should make short work of it."

"Yes, all right. I do want it to be a little less plain than what I normally wear."

"We shall ensure it is beautiful."

She couldn't imagine it, but then that was the reason she'd come here. "What else do I need to know?"

"I assume Thorne will want to waltz with you."

"He mentioned doing so, yes. I thought to ask Mick to teach me the proper way to do it, so I don't embarrass myself." Her brother had learned long ago from his widowed lover.

"You're not going to embarrass yourself. Do you know how to curtsy?"

"I've never had a need to."

"You'll need to curtsy to his mother."

"Why?"

"Because she is a duchess, it is her ball, and she is his mother. And it is what one does."

Gillie suspected a good part of the next two weeks was going to be spent learning to do things simply because they were what one did.

"I think we should invite Fancy to join us in educating you," Aslyn said. "As her time at the finishing school is only recently passed, she should have much to contribute, probably things I wouldn't even think about teaching you, since everything is rather second nature to me now."

"I have only a few hours available each afternoon. I still have my tavern to see to."

"We shall make it work."

Chapter 22

𝒯he days passed far too quickly, and Gillie soon found herself staring at the gorgeous ball gown spread out across her bed, the deep purple silk and satin, glistening in the lamplight, the delicate embroidery in the bodice that must have taken hours to stitch. Over the past two weeks, she'd had numerous fittings, had seen it coming together as several seamstresses worked on it, yet still she was in awe by all the details of it and the knowledge that very soon it would grace her body. It had been delivered only that afternoon, and she'd hardly been able to take her eyes from it, imagining how it would catch the lighting as Thorne waltzed her around the ballroom.

She did want to waltz with him—badly. He came to her every night, but it never seemed to be enough. She always wanted one more night, one more memory. Tonight's would be one unlike any they had ever shared.

She stood a few feet away from the bed where an assortment of silk and lacy undergarments also waited for her. Aslyn had provided her with a list of the order in which the items went on, but as she perused it, it seemed impossible to complete the task in the time remaining before Mick arrived with his coach to escort her to the affair. She'd already bathed, was wearing nothing but her night wrap, but dear Lord, she should have begun dressing at dawn. Why did women have to wear so much? It was like putting on armor, which she supposed proper ladies did to ensure they didn't engage in improper behavior. A gentleman couldn't get through all of that very quickly in order to reach the heavenly parts. Although if he did manage to reach them, she supposed his determination was to be applauded.

She rather liked that Thorne didn't have to work so very hard to get her out of her clothes. They'd certainly not be engaged in any naughtiness this evening. She shouldn't have been disappointed, and yet she was. On the other hand, perhaps he'd embrace the challenge of proving her misconceptions wrong. She could always hope.

The loud knock on her door caused her to jump. She had no time for visitors. It came again with a more urgent pounding of fists. With a sigh, she headed for it. No doubt trouble was brewing belowstairs. She'd have to change into her work clothes, go handle the matter—and once down there, something else would need her attention and before she knew it, the ball would be over and she'd have missed it. Perhaps it was for the best.

While she felt prepared for the evening, the real test would come when she arrived. She knew all the proper forms of address, to whom she should curtsy, to whom she should not. She knew the acceptable topics of conversation—boring though they were. She understood her opinions might be too radical for some. Over the years, she had learned to blend in even within her own tavern. She could blend in tonight.

Opening the door, she gaped at her smiling sister-by-marriage. "Bloody hell, is it already time?" How long had she been staring at the clothing on her bed?

"Not yet. We thought you could use some assistance," Aslyn said, as she edged her way past Gillie, followed by Fancy and two other ladies—servants based on their dress—carrying an assortment of boxes.

"What are you doing here?" she asked her sister.

Fancy smiled. "I wanted to help."

"You're not putting flowers in my hair. I've told you before I'm not a bloody garden." Fancy had promised to adorn her hair with flowers for Mick's wedding. One of the reasons she hadn't gone was her fear of looking ridiculous.

"We have something better." She went to the table where the servants had set the boxes, opened one, reached inside, and pulled out what looked to be a ball of hair—a red mahogany. She smiled brightly. "It's a hairpiece. Aslyn assured me women wear them all the time. We had a devil of a challenge finding the right shade, but I think we managed. And we brought some lovely pearl combs with which to secure it."

"I like my hair as it is."

"Yes, but . . ."

It was fine for a tavern but not for an aristocrat's ball. And she did so want not to embarrass Thorne. "I suppose the gown would look nicer if my hair were longer."

"Nan can work magic with hair," Aslyn said, her own blond tresses gathered up into a soft sweep with curls dangling provocatively here and there.

Gillie assumed Nan was the maid who was busily bobbing her head. "Yes, all right. Let's see how it goes."

It went horribly. Her strands were tugged and pulled until she was surprised they remained attached to her scalp. But she couldn't deny when the additional hair and combs were in place that it was difficult to tell she was a woman who wore her hair in a style more suited to men. Her face was framed in delicate curls that invited a gent to toy with them.

"Oh, don't you look lovely?" Fancy asked on a sigh.

"The weight feels odd. I'm not used to my head being so heavy."

"You'll grow accustomed to it," Aslyn assured her. "Once the gown is in place, you'll be all balanced out."

Another series of tugs and pulls occurred as layer upon layer of undergarments, including a corset—a torturous device that had to have been invented by a man who despised women—was slipped down, up, over and around her. She could barely breathe and her bosom was in danger of escaping its confines. But when the gown was finally in place and she stood before the mirror, she reluctantly admitted that perhaps it had all been worth it. Although she'd never before had so much skin exposed.

"Oh, Gillie," Fancy whispered. "He's not going to be able to take his eyes off you."

"I doubt he'll even recognize me, will probably think I didn't come." She was finding it more difficult to breathe and it didn't have anything to do with the blasted corset. "I'm going to make a fool of myself— and him in the process."

"No, you're not," Aslyn stated emphatically. "Besides, Mick and I will be right there with you, and if you find you're uncomfortable, we'll leave. But you should at least make an entrance."

An entrance. "Yes, I'll thank his mother for the invitation, have a dance with him, and then leave. That should be sufficient for the night."

"It won't be too terribly well-attended, because most families are already in the country, so it should be a fairly relaxed atmosphere for you to make your debut," Aslyn said.

"My debut? I won't be attending any other balls after this one."

Aslyn and Fancy exchanged glances.

"I won't," Gillie insisted. She was going tonight because he'd asked and she didn't want to disappoint him.

Although she very nearly tripped going down the stairs, even though she'd hiked up her skirt. She was wondering if there was any fabric left in England. It seemed the seamstress had used every bolt she could get her hands on for this skirt. She wanted to hate it, every inch of it, but the truth was that it made her feel like a princess, made all those long-ago dreams and yearnings rise to the surface. She was happy where she was, content with her life, and didn't want to wish for anything else.

But when Mick, standing beside one of two waiting coaches—the second she assumed designated to return the maids and Fancy to their respective residences—grinned with appreciation, she couldn't help but be glad she would have this night. Perhaps every woman should have one evening of fantasy.

"You look beautiful, Gillie," he said. "I do hope you'll save a dance for me."

She scoffed. "As though anyone else is going to ask me to dance."

"I have a feeling you're going to be very surprised."

She very much doubted it. She turned to Fancy. "I wish you were coming."

Her sister smiled. "I'm planning to make quite the splash next Season. I'll be all of ten and eight and Mick has promised me a proper coming out. Meanwhile, take note of everything you see and tell me all about it on the morrow."

Careful not to mess her hair—it was truly irritating to have to think about things like that—she gave Fancy a gentle hug before turning back to Mick, giving him her hand, and welcoming the support as he helped her into the coach. He assisted his wife, who took her place beside Gillie, then climbed in and sat opposite them.

"Are you nervous, Mick?" she asked as the coach took off. "Will it be difficult for you tonight?"

"I've not yet been completely embraced by the nobility, but I have a wife with a good deal of standing among the nobs, so I don't think I'll receive too many cuts."

"People know you've been accepted by the Duke of Hedley," Aslyn said. "They won't want to offend him."

"He won't be there tonight," Mick reminded her.

Gillie knew the duke and his duchess never made the social rounds.

"No, but his ward will be, and I shall report anyone who is unkind." Aslyn squeezed Gillie's hand. "To either of you."

While she was reassured by the words, she was also quite anxious. There would be far too many people in attendance she didn't know. She would have to pay close attention during introductions to ensure she addressed them properly. But all that mattered was the one person she did know. She hoped he'd be pleased with all the effort to which she'd gone to make herself appear acceptable to those who mattered to him.

SHE SHOULD NOT have been surprised to discover his residence was multiple times the size of her little tavern—and that was just what she could see as the coach slowly traveled up the drive, a queue of other carriages making their way around the circle, people alighting and heading inside. Inhaling a deep breath, she reminded herself they were no better than she.

"He certainly seems to have a fine house."

"It's only brick and wood," Aslyn said.

"A lot of brick and a lot of wood. Whatever will I talk to these people about?"

"Mostly the weather," Aslyn told her.

Gillie laughed. "How business is good when the day is warm but even better when the cold winds blow because those without are looking for shelter?"

"Something like that. Just rely on our mock conversations if you find yourself floundering. You handled those quite nicely."

Aslyn had tutored her on a gamut of topics, forcing her to discuss matters over which she had no interest as though she was enthralled by the subjects, practicing hour after hour.

The coach finally came to a stop in front of the wide steps—a huge reclining lion on each end—that led up to two open doors, a footman standing at attention on either side. Another footman stepped forward and opened the carriage door. Aslyn slipped her hand into his gloved one and allowed him to hand her down. Gillie followed her example, expected she'd be doing so for a good bit of the night. Mick alighted.

"Shall we?" he asked.

Now that she was actually here, she was rather anxious to catch a glimpse of Thorne's world. She followed her brother and his wife up the steps and into the entranceway. Once over the threshold, she came to an abrupt stop at the cavernous room and the black marble staircases that swept up and around on either side. Portraits, so many portraits, lined the walls that he had to be able to trace his ancestry back to Adam and Eve. She couldn't fathom it—to know what the person who came before you looked like and the one before him and the one before him. To know the features of the person they'd married, the shade of their hair. To see your deep brown eyes, the shape of your nose, your strong jaw in so many others. She'd never had that, had never missed it, and yet now she couldn't help but believe what a wonderful bit of history it would be to possess all that knowledge.

"Gillie?" Mick asked gently, snapping her from her reverie.

"Sorry. It's just so much to take in." Besides all the portraits, there were statues and vases, some empty, some overflowing with flowers. There were tables and chairs and—good Lord, was that a knight?

They wandered into a parlor where there were so many sofas, chairs, and small tables it was a wonder anyone could move through it. A maid took her wrap, along with Aslyn's and her brother's hat, before directing them toward a door at the far end of the enormous room. There were fewer portraits here but a good many paintings of the countryside. Quaint and harmonious. She could imagine finding some peace in this room.

Leaving through the doorway, they entered a wide corridor and followed the length of it until another servant pointed them toward some stairs. "You'd need a map to live here," she muttered as they began the ascent.

"You learn your way around very quickly," Aslyn said.

"Did you grow up in a house like this?" Gillie asked.

"Very similar."

"It's grand but also seems a bit of a waste." She couldn't imagine all the years and all the coins it had taken to fill these rooms with *things*. Much better to fill them with people, which she supposed was why they put on balls and dinners and other fancy affairs.

As they neared the top of the stairs, she heard music, lovely music, gentle and slow, coming through the open doorway where people took turns to move through it. She would dance at least once to music like that. Perhaps she could find a music box to play the tune for her whenever she wanted to remember this night.

Then they crossed over the threshold. A tall fellow dressed in red livery asked their names and when he turned away from them, his voice boomed out, "Lady Aslyn and Mr. Mick Trewlove. Miss Gillian Trewlove."

She began the descent into an enormous room of mirrors, flowers, chandeliers, balconies—

And him.

Thorne was waiting at the bottom of the stairs, his forearm resting on the newel post, his smile for her and her alone. She knew it as clearly as she knew she needed breath in order to live—even though at the moment it was a bit difficult to come by. He was gorgeous, simply gorgeous, in a black swallow-tailed coat, white brocade waistcoat, white shirt, and black cravat. And there was a golden chain dangling from a button to a small pocket where she had no doubt his watch was nestled, back with him, exactly where it belonged. All the hours of preparation with dress fittings and waltzing lessons were suddenly worth it, just for a few minutes of gazing on him in all his glory.

Then he was reaching out for her, his white-gloved

hand extended toward her. Without thought or purpose, she placed her gloved hand in his, hating that any cloth at all separated them. His fingers closed around hers with such surety that every doubt she possessed about being here melted away.

"Miss Trewlove," he said quietly, lifting her hand to his mouth, pressing a hot lingering kiss there. "I'm so pleased you could join us."

"I'm pleased as well."

He grinned. "Liar."

"No, really." She glanced around. "It's all so magnificent." Her gaze came back to him. "You're magnificent."

His eyes glowed with pleasure, but she didn't think it had anything to do with her compliment but had more to do with her presence. How was it that he could make her tingle all over with little more than his nearness?

Releasing her hand, he shifted his gaze to the couple. "Lady Aslyn."

"Thorne. I believe you've met Mick."

"Indeed. It seems marriage agrees with you both."

"I find it much to my liking," Aslyn said, clearly comfortable with the duke. "I'm sorry your own nuptials didn't go as planned."

"I'm not." Taking Gillie's hand again, he tucked it into the crook of his arm. "Come. My mother is looking forward to seeing you again, Aslyn, and meeting two new members to your family."

If the woman standing not too far away as rigidly as possible was his mother, then Gillie doubted the duchess looked forward to anything in her life. She stood there as though she were the model for the carving of a bust for the prow of a ship, a figurehead that would no doubt send the most dastardly pirates sailing in the opposite direction. Thorne folded his fingers over Gillie's where they still rested in the crook of his elbow, offering her reassurance, which she didn't need. She'd dealt with those stern disapproving looks her entire life, and knew the best way to deal with them was to offer the mere hint of a smile, as though she harbored a delicious secret the other would die to know.

The duchess eyed her critically, somewhat suspiciously, before turning her attention elsewhere. "Lady Aslyn."

"Your Grace," Aslyn said sweetly, with a deep and graceful curtsy. "It's a pleasure to see you looking so well."

"It's kind of you to say so." She clutched her fingers in front of her. "This must be your husband."

"Yes. Allow me to introduce Mick Trewlove."

She angled her nose haughtily as though she smelled something unsavory. "Mr. Trewlove."

He bowed his head slightly. "It's a pleasure, Your Grace." He didn't reach for her hand, no doubt because he wasn't certain she could unknot those tightly coiled fingers.

"Mother, I'd like to introduce Miss Gillian Trewlove," Thorne stated formally.

It seemed to take years for the woman to finally turn her head back to Gillie. "Miss Trewlove."

For all of the welcome in her tone the duchess might have just been introduced to horse dung.

"I've been looking forward to meeting you, Your Grace," Gillie said as politely as possible when she dearly wanted to smack the woman for not extending that plump little hand to her brother.

With a sniff, the duchess pursed her lips. "I realize

you are no doubt unfamiliar with such regal affairs, but you are to curtsy before me."

"Mother—"

Gillie heard the displeasure in his voice, the warning, and squeezed his arm where she still held it before he could continue. She'd never needed anyone to stand up for her, didn't need it now. She'd practiced for hours to master the proper amount of dipping, lowering of her eyes, humbling expression. The queen of England wouldn't have found fault with her effort were she to see it.

"I don't bow," Gillie said quietly, gently, but with enough steel in her voice to mark it as an unarguable matter.

The Duchess of Thornley merely blinked as though she'd quite suddenly lost her bearings. "I beg your pardon?"

"I don't bow before someone without knowing if they are worthy of such an honor. Lady Aslyn knows you and felt you worthy of receiving her curtsy. Perhaps when we are better acquainted, I shall feel the same."

"I am a duchess."

"I'm a tavern owner. I suspect we're both accustomed to ordering people about."

"Why, you impertinent little—"

"Mother, I would watch your tongue if I were you," Thorne said sharply, but quietly so that no one nearby would hear. "Do remember I control your allowance."

With a deep breath, no doubt needed for calming, she glared at her son. "And you remember your duty."

"Always. Now if you'll excuse us, I intend to have a waltz with Miss Trewlove."

"And every marriageable lady here."

As though Gillie didn't fall into that category, which of course, she didn't. She wasn't going to hand everything she'd worked so hard to attain over to a man—and English law, which had never done her or her siblings any favors, would make her as little more than chattel, giving the single property she owned over to her husband. She wasn't going to allow a man to determine her *allowance* or anything else about her. She wanted a relationship of equal terms, which meant one that existed outside the bonds of marriage. Perhaps the woman who had given birth to her had felt the same, perhaps she'd been strong minded, strong willed and willing to face whatever consequences befell her. Gillie couldn't help but wonder what her portrait might have looked like.

Thorne led her to the edge of the polished dance floor where couples circled about with abandon. "I'm sorry," she said quietly. "I simply couldn't give her the satisfaction of a curtsy, not when she was looking down her nose at Mick like that."

"I'm glad you didn't."

She jerked her head around to find him looking at her, a tenderness in his eyes. Lifting a gloved hand, he lightly touched his fingertips to her cheek. "She was abominable. Had I known her good breeding was to be left in her bedchamber, I'd have not exposed you to her. But you handled her admirably."

"I didn't find it much different than handling a drunkard. Never give any quarter."

His laughter rang out around them. People nearby turned their attention to them; even some of the dancing couples cast a look their way. "She would be appalled to be compared to someone well into his cups."

Gillie shrugged her shoulders. "All sorts come into a tavern. Some bring their troubles, some their joys. Some their obstinacy. I learned fairly quickly I could never back down from whatever they brought with them. Your mum isn't a happy woman."

"She is happiest when she is unhappy."

"What a sad way to live."

"I quite agree. What have you done with your hair?"

She did wish he'd taken his abrupt change in conversation in another direction. Rolling her eyes, she confessed, "It's a false piece. Fancy's idea. I feel like it's going to fall off at any moment and the hounds will rush in, thinking it's a fox."

"No hounds here. At my estate, however, we have an abundance. I'm hoping you'll change your mind and join me there sometime."

"Is it as posh as all this?"

"Posher." The music grew silent. He offered his arm. "Ready for our waltz?"

"More than ready." Placing her hand on his, she could hardly believe she was actually going to dance with him. She fought to ignore the stares, the whispers. There just seemed to be so many of them, people wondering who she was, why she was with him. "Why did you invite me?" she asked as they reached the very center of the dance floor.

"Too many reasons to count," he said as the strains for the song began and he took her into his arms, sweeping her over the polished wood.

She thought if she hadn't practiced endlessly with Mick as her partner that she still would have been able to waltz with Thorne, without stepping on his feet or making a misstep. It was as though every aspect of her body was in tune with his, as though she could have followed him to the ends of the earth without tripping once.

"You're not quite comfortable here," he said solemnly.

"It's not you," she assured him. "It's the gown. So much exposed skin."

"Are you cold?"

"No, but people are staring and they can see so much of me . . . I'm not used to it."

"They are no doubt staring because they've never seen such beauty. However . . ." He came to an abrupt halt, released her, and shrugged out of his jacket.

"What are you doing?" she asked, stunned as he began working her arm into one of the sleeves.

"I don't care about your hair, Gillie. Whether it's short or long, it matters not to me." He draped the jacket around her and eased her other arm into place. Tugging the lapels, he held her gaze. "I don't care what you wear. You could be dressed in a shroud for all the difference it would make to me. You're not comfortable with so much skin on display? Then we won't let it be on display." He slipped one hand beneath the jacket, positioned it on her back, took her other hand, and led her back into the waltz.

"People are staring even more now," she told him.

"I couldn't care less. Are you more comfortable being covered?"

She hated admitting to a weakness. "Yes."

"There you are then. I am more comfortable as well. And since we missed a few steps this round, we shall have to take a turn about the floor during the next dance as well."

She did wish he hadn't been so thoughtful, hadn't

noticed her discomfort and then taken matters in hand to make her feel more at ease. His actions did strange things to her heart, made it squeeze so tightly it caused a prickling in her eyes. "Thank you."

"My pleasure, princess. Seeing to you is always my pleasure."

Chapter 23

$\mathcal{H}$e suspected that on the far side of the ballroom someone was handing his mother her smelling salts. That he might have looked ridiculous dancing with a woman who was wearing an evening jacket mattered not at all. The only thing that mattered was Gillie.

He'd been a selfish bastard to prod her into coming, yet he'd wanted to dance with her, and the thought of an evening without her in it was so deuced disagreeable. When had it happened that it was pure torment to go so much as a day without seeing her?

And he wanted to show her off, introduce her around. If she were any other lady, people would see him talking with her at balls, dinners, and recitals. They would see him promenading her through the park or taking her on a carriage ride. But everything with her was new, exciting, and so very different from anything he'd had before.

"I do like the gown, however," he felt compelled to tell her. "The color suits you."

"I had to put on a thousand undergarments to make everything fit and fall properly. Being a lady is a lot of work."

"I appreciate you went to the effort."

"I appreciate you covered it up."

"But in my mind I can still see every glorious inch. The gown is quite provocative. Makes me want to trail my mouth where cloth meets skin."

Her cheeks turned a soft pink that hinted at a blush. "Shouldn't gents have to show their skin as well?"

He raised his eyebrows. "That would be interesting, wouldn't it? Although I don't think we look quite so enticing when bits of us are showing."

She glanced around. Fewer people were paying them attention, and he hoped by the time they finished their second dance, she might be comfortable enough to hand back over his jacket. While he didn't care what she wore, he couldn't deny that he very much did appreciate the way the gown molded to her torso, the way it displayed her bare shoulders and neck.

"If I lived in a house such as this one, I think I would forever worry about knocking things over and breaking them," she said.

"You grow accustomed to where things are. I could probably walk through the residence in my sleep without bumping into anything."

"I saw armor in the front hallway."

He nodded. "It belonged to the first duke. Of course, he wasn't a duke until he wore that armor and fought for a king—quite spectacularly if legend is to be believed."

"You know all your ancestors," she said in awe.

"Not the ones before him, which I've always found to be a shame. I suspect they were the most interesting of the lot."

"And your mum's family? You know it as well?"

He'd never referred to his mother as Mum, which he viewed as a warmer, more intimate address. He found it interesting that Gillie didn't hesitate to use the term, but then, based on the little bit he knew about the woman who had raised her, he suspected she was a good deal more demonstrative with her affections. "Back generations. Her father was an earl. Her brother now holds the title."

"Is he here?"

"No." Thorne wasn't about to marry one of his cousins, so his uncle hadn't bothered to leave the country for the ball his mother had insisted upon hosting in the off-Season. "I suspect he's well ensconced in grouse hunting by now."

The music drifted into silence. He wished he could claim a third dance, but people would really be staring at her then, and speculation about her would begin making the rounds. He was rather certain it was already, but he had no desire to taint her reputation, and giving her too much attention would certainly accomplish that. "It is with a great deal of regret that I must see to my other guests," he said. "I'll escort you to your brother."

"You'll want your jacket. It wouldn't be proper to greet them without it."

"I can jaunt upstairs and fetch another."

She smiled, such a sweet endearing smile that he wished he could order everyone to leave so he could spend time only in her company. "I can fetch my wrap if I start to get those chills again."

He assisted her with removing his jacket, then shrugged into it. She straightened his lapels, such an intimate, personal act, one that made him wish she could do it every morning of his life.

"You're such a handsome devil," she said.

"Know that if the ladies are looking at you, they are doing so with envy as none wear a gown as well as you do. If the gents are looking at you, know they are doing so with longing. Be certain they don't hold you too close while waltzing or I may have to challenge them to a duel to protect your honor."

"I can see to my own honor, thank you."

"I've no doubt of that, but it doesn't mean you should have to." Offering his arm, he walked her over to the edge of the dance floor, where her brother waited. Mick Trewlove was an intimidating fellow. Even if Thorne hadn't spotted him, he'd have felt his gaze burrowing into him. When they reached him, Thorne took Gillie's hand and pressed a kiss to her knuckles, reluctant to leave her. "I'd like to claim the last dance."

Nodding, she wrote his name on her dance card. With that, he turned on his heel to see to his duty.

It was with a bit of regret that Gillie watched him walk away. Based upon the number of dances listed on her card, it would be a while before she spoke with him again.

"You seem quite comfortable with him. Is he courting you?" Mick asked.

"Don't be daft." During all the hours he'd instructed her in waltzing, he'd kept his opinions to himself, hadn't interrogated her to determine why she would be invited to a duchess's ball. "Although he was the man who got into your carriage—"

"I'd deduced that much, thank you very much. Have you been seeing him since?"

"It's complicated."

"I won't stand for him taking advantage."

"I won't stand for that myself. Where the deuce is your wife?"

He chuckled low, knowing full well she was seeking to change the subject. "Visiting with those she knows. We're supposed to search for her now that your dance is done."

Only they didn't have to search for her because not even a half minute later they spied her coming in their direction, a gentleman walking beside her. Gillie was aware of her brother stiffening, no doubt with jealousy because another man was in close proximity to his wife. "It won't do any of us any favors if you plant your fist in his face," she told him.

"The thought never crossed my mind."

"Liar." She smiled as they approached, and the gentleman—the top of his head didn't even come to her shoulder—blushed.

When near enough, Aslyn immediately placed her hand on Mick's arm, no doubt also aware of the tension radiating through him. "Lord Mitford was in want of an introduction." Elegantly, she turned to the man beside her. "My lord, allow me the honor of introducing my husband, Mick Trewlove, and his sister, Miss Gillian Trewlove. The Earl of Mitford."

"My pleasure," the earl said. "I have always found our affairs far too restricted and am always intrigued when I meet someone not born into our ranks. I am familiar with your success, Mr. Trewlove. Well done, I say."

"Thank you, my lord," Mick said, although he didn't sound particularly grateful by the praise. "My sister is a success in her own right."

"Indeed." He turned to her. The smile that wreathed his face made his otherwise bland features more interesting. She took an immediate liking to him. "How might you have achieved your success, Miss Trewlove?"

"By hard work."

He laughed. "I daresay I stepped into it with my thoughtless question. In what endeavor, might I ask?"

"I own a tavern."

"How intriguing. I don't suppose you'd be kind enough to honor me with the next dance."

"I'd be delighted."

"Splendid. Shall we?" He began to offer his arm, stopped, looked at Mick. "If that is agreeable to your brother."

"Gillie doesn't need my permission," Mick said. "She does as she pleases."

"How intriguing. Quite independent, are you, Miss Trewlove?"

"I tend to be, yes."

He offered his arm once more, not hesitating this time. "You must tell me all about your tavern during our dance."

The next tune began, and she found herself circling the dance floor with him. He wasn't quite as accomplished as Thorne, but then she had to admit she was probably biased. He asked her a series of questions and responded to each of her answers with, "How intriguing" before asking the next. Until at last she asked, "Do you attend many balls, my lord?"

"Have I stepped upon your toes so many times that my social graces are being called into question?" There was a twinkling in his eyes.

"No, my lord, but you do seem a bit nervous."

"You are quite right. Much to my family's disappointment, I'd rather be off reading a book, but my sister wished to attend tonight and as my mother was feeling poorly, it was left to me to escort her. She has high hopes of catching the eye of the Duke of Thornley and ultimately becoming his duchess."

Gillie's stomach hit the floor and she somehow managed not to trip over it. "I suppose many of the ladies here tonight are hoping for that."

"Indeed. However, after observing the manner in which the duke gazed upon you while you danced with him, I sincerely hope she fails in her efforts. She'd not be at all happy married to a man who loved someone else."

She shook her head. "You're mistaken there. The duke and I are merely friends."

"The advantage to being a wallflower, even a gentleman wallflower, Miss Trewlove, is that one becomes a keen observer. May I introduce you to my sister? I think she might benefit from knowing you."

When their dance ended, he did indeed introduce her to his sister, Lady Caroline, and two of her friends, Ladies Georgiana and Josephine.

"Miss Trewlove is a woman of business," he told them. "An independent sort."

"How intriguing," Lady Caroline said, while her friends nodded. "Are you a dressmaker, then?"

"No, I own a tavern."

The ladies' eyes widened. "Scandalous," Lady Georgiana finally uttered. "Utterly scandalous."

"Yet intriguing," Lady Caroline said, and Gillie was beginning to suspect the lady and her brother led boring lives since they found everything "intriguing." "I daresay, Mitford, we shall see Miss Trewlove safely delivered to her chaperone if you wish to go on."

"I don't wish to be rude," he said.

"I'm actually of an age where I don't need a chaperone. I can see to myself, my lord. Thank you for the dance."

"My pleasure, Miss Trewlove." And he walked away.

"Conversation is such a chore for him," Lady Caroline said. "I am impressed, Miss Trewlove, that you managed to put him at such ease he didn't stutter. Now, he'll go search out a corner where he can read whatever small book he has tucked away into a pocket."

"I found your brother a delight, Lady Caroline. He cares for you immensely."

"And I for him. So how is it that you know Thornley?" the lady asked.

Mrs. Smythson had taught Gillie that one did not ask personal questions, and Lady Caroline's seemed rather personal. The ladies in this group were more girls than women, so perhaps they hadn't learned all the proper niceties yet. If anything, they were only a tad older than Fancy's seventeen years. She had a difficult time envisioning Thorne with any of them, but then that was no doubt spurred by jealousy. These girls were marriageable; she was not. "Our paths crossed one evening near my tavern."

"Tell us more about your tavern," Lady Georgiana demanded. "However did you come to own it?"

"Well, I purchased it."

"Why?" Lady Josephine asked.

"Because I'm a bit stubborn and find working for others to be disagreeable." While the Smythsons had been fair to her, she'd longed to be in complete charge of things.

"But the wrong sort of people go to taverns," Lady Caroline said.

Angling her head in surprise, Gillie held the woman's gaze. "Laborers, merchants, seamen. I suspect a good many of the gentlemen here stop by a tavern now and then. Do you not find the Duke of Thornley upstanding?"

"Don't be ridiculous. Of course we do."

"He has visited my tavern. As has my brother. He owns a hotel and a good many buildings and other businesses."

"He's as rich as Croesus from what I understand," Lady Georgiana said. "Are you wealthy as well, Miss Trewlove?"

The two other ladies gasped. "Georgie!"

The lady slapped her hand over her mouth. "My apologies, Miss Trewlove. I forget myself. You have no airs about you which makes you rather easy to talk to."

"I'm not offended, Lady Georgiana. I've been asked worse."

"Still, I was rude beyond measure. Lovely weather we're having of late."

Gillie smiled conspiratorially. "Do you really enjoy talking about weather?"

"I abhor it. I'd rather discuss you. You must have incredible freedom."

"I can do whatever I like, but mostly I work, because I like that people come to my tavern at the end of the day to relax. I'll pour them a pint and they'll tell me their troubles, and mine then become insignificant."

"My troubles always seem so great, perhaps I should open a tavern," Lady Josephine said.

"Don't be a silly goose, Josie," Lady Caroline said. "Marriage is in your future, my girl."

As if on cue, three gentlemen approached. Lady Caroline introduced Gillie to a marquess, an earl, and a viscount. Then the gents escorted the ladies onto the dance floor. Gillie turned to find Aslyn standing nearby.

"I was keeping watch in case I needed to step in, but that seemed to go well," her sister-by-marriage said.

"I'm a curiosity."

Aslyn smiled. "As am I. The daughter of an earl who married a commoner. People speak to me as though they're not quite sure who I am any longer."

"I'm sorry you had to come on my account."

"On your account and Mick's. As much as he claims otherwise, he still has a desire to be accepted by the nobility. Attending affairs such as this one will eventually lead to that acceptance." She wound her arm through Gillie's. "So let's mingle, shall we, and speed that acceptance along."

Aslyn introduced her to several other girls, and while each name was preceded by the word *Lady*, Gillie couldn't quite view them as anything other than lasses. They were so deuced young.

Had she ever in her life appeared so innocent, so fresh faced? She wasn't comfortable when she was the topic of conversation, even though, like Lord Mitford's sister and her friends, they seemed intrigued by her independence, but she was always grateful when the conversation drifted onto other matters. Inevitably they tittered about how handsome Lord F was or how funny Lord G could be or how witty Lord K was. While she had nothing of consequence to contribute to those conversations, she knew madness would take hold if her evenings were spent doing little more than discussing the attributes of gentlemen.

But then these ladies were searching for a husband, and perhaps that was the way one went about it. What she did know was that the individual attributes these lasses practically swooned over in one gentleman here and another there, all came together in Thorne. That he had their attention and the yearnings of their young hearts. That if he were to ask any one of them for her hand in marriage, she wouldn't hesitate to accept.

That whatever time with Thorne remained to her would be short-lived.

"I'M PLEASED TO find you're still here," Thorne said quietly as they strolled along the garden path where the occasional burning torch provided a modicum of light.

He'd invited her for a turn about the gardens, and since her next few dances were free, she'd gladly accepted. Three other gentlemen had approached Aslyn for an introduction to her and had then proceeded to ask Gillie for a dance. While she enjoyed circling the floor, no one else brought her the pleasure Thorne did. So she was glad she was available to stroll through the garden with him. It was torment to watch him waltzing with one woman after another, even as she understood he was expected to do so.

As soon as they'd gotten outside, he'd draped his jacket over her shoulders, and she welcomed his warmth seeping through her skin. Perhaps there was an advantage to having so much exposed after all. "Talking with nobs isn't as taxing as I thought it would be, especially when I can turn the conversation from weather to liquor. Even the ladies seem to be intrigued by the notion of my freedom to do as I please."

"I daresay you'll have them all traipsing off to run businesses if we're not careful."

"Would that be such an awful thing?"

"A lord's wife has a good deal of responsibility:

overseeing the management of various households, depending on how many properties her husband holds, making morning calls, which might seem trivial, but they create alliances through which their husbands benefit. They wield a great deal of power over Society, which is not to be discounted. They are also engaged in charitable works. Who would do all that if they were occupied with business?"

Occupied with business as she was. "It does seem overwhelming, but I think you underestimate how much they could oversee."

"Perhaps. But then they are also to produce an heir and a spare."

"I understand why you need a son, but a child should be wanted for more than that." She didn't think he had been. And a wife should be wanted for more than land and her womb.

"You seem to have caught the attention of a few gents. I noticed I'm not the only one with whom you've waltzed."

"Nor am I the only one with whom you have."

"True. It's obligation on my part."

"To pass the time on mine until the final waltz of the night arrives," she said provocatively.

His grin flashed in the darkness. "Why, Miss Trewlove, I do believe you've mastered the art of flirtation."

"I merely speak what's on my mind."

"I like that about you, Gillie. I always have."

They walked along in silence for several minutes, and she could almost envision doing this every night instead of sitting on her steps.

"You should see these gardens in the daylight," he said. "They're quite colorful."

"They smell lovely."

"Over here, they smell even better."

He led her off the path, through a maze of hedgerows where no torches danced with flames to show them the way. She imagined as a young boy, he'd made his way through them many a time, pretending to be an explorer or perhaps to simply escape from the rigid demands of his parents.

"Was your father as standoffish as your mother?" she asked.

"You are kind with your words. She is hard and brittle. I remember my father being strict and stern, but I don't recall him ever being intentionally unkind. But after he took ill, he was never quite himself."

"That can't have been easy."

"But we carry on, don't we?"

They did have that in common. They reached a dead end. Moonlight glittered faintly along the top of a tall brick wall. Suddenly she found her back against it, his jacket shielding her skin from any abrasions as his mouth landed on hers with surety and purpose. She wound her arms tightly around his neck, loving the press of his body against hers, knowing she would never get enough of this even as she understood a time would come when she wouldn't have his nearness, when he would be pressed up against someone who knew how to properly serve tea and select correct utensils for eating.

But not tonight. Tonight he was hers as much as it was possible for him to belong to her, for her to belong to him. He lived in a world of refinement and polish, not quite as foreign as she'd imagined it. Still she felt like a mermaid following a unicorn into the woods, all the while knowing that at some point, she would have to return to the sea.

He dragged his mouth along the column of her throat, and she dropped her head back to give him easier access.

"Dear God, I've wanted to get you alone ever since you descended those stairs," he growled, low and feral, his chest reverberating against hers, causing her nipples to pucker in spite of all the ridiculous layers of material separating their skin.

"I've wanted you to get me alone," she confessed, taking satisfaction in his dark chuckle that sent his heated breath skimming along her bared collarbone. This style of frock was becoming more appealing by the minute. As he trailed his mouth over the exposed swells of her breasts, she was actually regretting that the neckline wasn't lower.

"I would take us from here this very minute if it wouldn't be the height of rudeness," he said, nibbling along the side of her neck until he nipped at her earlobe.

In his position, he had to consider things like that, had to always be conscious of his reputation, his standing among his peers. He couldn't simply run away or escape. He couldn't dance every dance with her, couldn't spend time with only her. Duty, responsibility, expectations guided him—as they should. She was impressed with his discipline, that he didn't do what he wanted, but did what was required, what was necessary. He put his own wants and desires aside.

A time would come when he would put her aside as well. She understood that, accepted it. No matter how much it saddened and devastated her, she would hold her head high when the moment came.

He began gathering up her skirts and petticoats, bunching them at her waist, even as his mouth continued to play havoc with her skin. His hand slid down to her knee and wrapped around it. He lifted her leg and anchored it around his hip, his back. She was grateful for her height, for the ease with which she could stand there, holding him near with her calf and foot.

His fingers danced over the outer portion of her thigh, up and down, up and down, until he moved to the tender and sensitive inner edge, his fingers no longer frolicking but slowing to a meander until they reached the haven that was already moist and aching for him. "You're so wet," he rasped.

Moving her hand down, she rubbed the swollen length of him. "You're so hard."

"Aching with need, actually, need that will go unsatisfied until later. But you, princess, you need not wait."

He stroked, slowly, determinedly, applying pressure to the small, swollen bud with his thumb, even as he slid two fingers inside her. A tiny cry escaped, and he took possession of her mouth with an urgency, capturing her moan, her whimper, her sob as the pleasure became too much, as the sensations rioted until she shattered in his arms. She clung to him as the spasms rocked through her, wave after wave, with the night breeze wafting over her skin and moonlight washing over her, over him. She thought he'd never looked more beautiful standing there so pleased and happy as though in giving to her, he'd given to himself.

He pressed his forehead to hers. "My mother, blast her, offered chambers to some of our guests who didn't want to reopen their London residences for only a few days. I won't be able to leave until they are all abed, but I will come to you as soon as I am able. Wait for me, but don't remove this gown. I want to take it off you."

How easily those words aroused her all over again. She was a wanton of the first order, and she didn't care.

AFTER THEY'D RETURNED to the ballroom, she'd danced with Mick, who she suspected, based on the way he studied her, knew exactly what they'd been up to in the garden. Although she wouldn't have been surprised to learn he and his wife had been in another part, up to the exact same thing. It didn't escape her notice that Mick touched his wife whenever she was in reach—her hand, her shoulder, the small of her back. Before, it had amused her to see her brother so smitten, but now that she was suffering through the same condition, she didn't find it at all humorous.

Once their dance was finished, and it became obvious he wanted to take a turn about the floor with Aslyn, she assured them that she was at ease in her surroundings and had received enough introductions they didn't need to hover around her. She could handle herself. She hadn't needed to tell them twice. It brought her a great deal of joy to watch her brother gliding over the floor, his wife in his arms, his gaze never leaving hers, to know he was well and truly in love and loved.

Not wanting them to find her there, mooning about, when they were done, she decided to go in search of Lady Caroline, as she'd enjoyed visiting with her, or maybe even Lord Mitford, to determine if he was truly sitting in a corner somewhere reading a book and to thank him for his earlier kindness. When a footman offered her a tray with coupes of champagne, she didn't hesitate to take one. While enjoying a sip, she glanced around and spotted a small shadowy alcove, palms standing guard on either side of it, their leaves partially hiding the entry, a perfect place for a timid lord to seek a momentary escape.

The greenery had just brushed against her arm when she heard a feminine whisper, ". . . deuced odd, I tell you. The way he looks at her. I've no doubt she's the reason Lady Lavinia cried off."

Gillie stopped in her tracks, was about to reverse course when another lady, her voice somewhat raspy, said, "She's a tavern owner. She can never be more than his mistress."

"I rather liked her," a third voice chimed in.

"If he asks for my hand, I'll let him know straight-away I'll not put up with him being involved with an-other woman." The first voice.

"Lady Lavinia no doubt gave him the same ultima-tum." The third. "And you see what that got her. No wedding whatsoever."

"But she was ill. That's the reason there was no wedding. Thornley announced it. I've called upon her twice and been informed she is indisposed. I fear she's deathly ill, and he feared she'd be unable to con-ceive," the raspy-voiced one said.

"No." The first voice. "Something odd is afoot with this Miss Trewlove. No other woman garnered his attention upon her arrival. But for Miss Trewlove, he walked right up to the stairs and waited for her to de-scend. Kissed her hand. Mark my words, ladies. The Duke of Thornley will not be taking a wife anytime soon."

Not wishing to be spotted eavesdropping, Gil-lie turned on her heel and began walking away. She couldn't identify who those voices belonged to, but also had no desire to know. Aslyn had warned her gossip abounded, and she'd come here knowing full well a good bit of it might revolve around her, but she hadn't much liked hearing what they'd said about Thorne. None of them were deserving of him.

In need of more fresh air to clear her thoughts, she stepped out onto the terrace with its bricked wall and steps—with lounging stone lions on either side of them—that led down into the gardens. Walking along the lighted path through the rhododendrons and roses was probably not the thing for a woman alone to do, so she meandered over to a corner of the terrace, leaned against the waist-high wall, and sipped the excellent champagne, wishing she could take a peek at the cask in order to determine its origin and vintage. Perhaps Thorne would give her a tour of his wine cellar before she left. She imagined he had an excellent array of the finest vintages that would put her own small stores to shame.

"A lady risks her reputation by slipping out of the ballroom alone."

Gillie twirled around to face the duchess. "I was growing quite warm."

"I daresay wearing a gentleman's jacket will do that to a woman."

She wasn't going to point out she no longer wore the jacket, because the duchess wasn't blind. She lifted her glass. "You wouldn't happen to know the origin of this fine champagne, would you?"

"Most certainly not. That is the butler's job."

The litany "Remain pleasant" raced through her head. "You must give him my compliments then as he did an outstanding job selecting this evening's offerings."

"He will not marry you, you know."

"The butler? Oh, what a pity as he has such excellent taste in champagne."

"My son," the prow-shaped woman said so tartly Gillie was surprised lemons didn't fall from her mouth.

"I'm well aware of that, Duchess."

"He will tire of you in short order. He is like his father in that regard, with an insatiable appetite to bed all manner of women, which is the reason my husband took the pox so young. When our two children died, he was already infested—I had barred him from my bed, so we couldn't replace what we had lost."

"Even if you had other children, they'd not have replaced what you lost. People cannot be replaced."

"You dare to correct me?"

"You are in need of correcting."

"You impertinent—"

"Yes, I am quite impertinent. I don't consider it a fault."

"Those with whom my son associates will. He is going to marry one of these girls."

Although she was well aware of that, the blow of the words spoken aloud was effectively delivered to her gut, her heart, her head, but she refused to show any reaction. In addition to being quite impertinent, she knew a thing or two about being stoic.

"That is the reason they are here," the duchess carried on. "So he may choose one to wed before the year is out. His tendency to bed any lady who spreads her legs will see him following the path of his father into lunacy. He needs to provide an heir before the pox befalls him."

"I suspect he is more discerning than you might think."

"Oh, I very much doubt it. I smell the stink of you on him when he returns home in the mornings." She took a step forward. "You will never be more to him than a mistress. You are a commoner. He is a duke. Your place will always be in the shadows, not at his side."

"Yet, I have been at his side several times this evening."

"Because you are a curiosity."

"If you'll be so kind as to excuse me . . ." She edged past her.

"I am not yet done with you."

Gillie turned back. "But I am done with you. I have a knack for judging people right off. A fellow can come into my tavern without a penny to his name and ask for a pint. I look him over and if I determine when he has the means he'll pay me for that pint, I pour him one. If I determine he won't, I show him the door. Unfortunately, Your Grace, I'd be forever showing you the door."

"You impudent—"

"You think you're better than me because they placed you in a bassinet when you were born instead of on a doorstep. It simply means you had a cozier bed. Now, if you'll excuse me, it's nearly time for the final dance of the evening where I will joyously find myself wrapped in your son's arms." She hadn't danced with him since their first two waltzes and needed time to compose herself before seeing him again. He was too observant by half, and she didn't want him knowing that his mother had unsettled her.

Hearing the woman sputtering as she walked away, she did hope the duchess didn't have an apoplectic fit. How in God's name had Thorne turned out to have any decency about him at all?

She considered actually strolling into the gardens, but she wasn't going to give the duchess the satisfaction of witnessing her doing something even more scandalous, so she returned to the ballroom. But all the din bombarded her. She needed someplace where she could absorb some quiet, or lacking that, since she doubted very much the orchestra was going to cease its playing, she required a few moments in solitude. Surely in this grand residence was one room where she could gather herself.

She was heading for the stairs when a gentleman, who looked to be Thorne's age, stepped in front of her. His blond hair was perfectly styled. She could find no fault with his features but was left with the impression he considered himself more handsome than he was.

His blue eyes slowly wandered over her as though he were snipping away at the stitching of her gown to see what resided beneath. "I daresay, Thorne has excellent taste when it comes to his mistresses."

"I'm not his mistress."

He smiled, a hideous smile, one she wanted to slap right off his face. "His paramour, then. A tavern keeper. That puts him in the lead I think."

She furrowed her brow. "I beg your pardon?"

"In our youth we started a game: sleeping with a variety of women. An actress, an opera singer, a shop girl. You get the gist. You're the first tavern keeper."

She did, but refused to believe she was on a list. "I'm a tavern *owner*. And as you and I have not been properly introduced—"

"The Earl of Dearwood, Miss Trewlove. Your next lover."

A burst of laughter broke free from deep within her. "You're daft. I promise you'll never be my lover."

"When he is again betrothed, he'll release you. He's never been one for balancing two women at once. Then you shall become mine."

"I'll never become yours. Now if you'll excuse—"

She made to walk by him.

He wrapped his fingers around her left upper arm. She stilled. "Unhand me, sir."

"Take a turn about the garden with me. When we are done, you may decide to spend the full of tonight with me rather than with him."

Couples were waltzing over the dance floor. People were standing nearby but it was late into the night, and she suspected they'd indulged in the champagne to such an extent they were no longer paying attention to the details of their surroundings, so they weren't noticing the inappropriate way he held her arm. Or perhaps it was the pleasant expression that never left his face, the way he could look as though he wasn't saying ugly things to her. He'd never speak to the daughter of an earl or a duke in such a manner. But then she was neither, and he knew it. Her name told him that much, and he thought little of her because she owned a tavern. "I'll warn you, sir, once more. Unhand me. Or I shall be forced to punch you."

He chuckled low, darkly. "You are a feisty wench. I see why Thorne is so taken with you. I can't wait to experience your fire when you spread your—"

Her balled fist struck quick and hard, an uppercut to his chin that sent his head flying back and him reeling, arms windmilling, into the dancers before he landed prone on the floor with a thud. Women screamed, couples scattered. The orchestra went quiet. People stared at her, stared at Dearwood.

Suddenly Thorne burst through the gathered crowd,

placed a gentle hand on her shoulder, his eyes scouring her as though he was searching her for injury. "What happened?"

"I asked her to dance," Dearwood announced loudly, holding his jaw, trying to shove himself to his feet, but seemingly unable to get his legs beneath him. Two gentlemen helped him up. "I merely asked her to dance."

Thorne didn't look at the man who claimed to be a longtime friend. He merely held her gaze. "Gillie?"

She knew, with every part of her being, he was asking her to confirm or deny Dearwood's words, and that he would believe her over whatever nonsense the earl blurted, but she couldn't tell him the truth, the ugly sentiments the man had uttered. She couldn't admit to him or the gathered crowd that someone thought so lowly of her, would think her worthy of such debasement. She heard mumblings and mutterings from those standing around her, and the truth to which she finally gave voice was probably not the truth he wanted to have confirmed. "I shouldn't have come. I don't belong here."

WITHIN THOSE FEW words spoken, Thorne heard a myriad of others: *I don't belong with you. You don't belong with me. Our worlds can't be mixed.*

He had little doubt Dearwood was lying, but what proof did he have for calling the man out? And the fact she wouldn't tell him alerted him that the blasted earl had done something more than ask her for a dance, something she feared would bring judgment upon her, not the man who deserved it.

"What the devil is going on here?" his mother asked, sweeping into the circle.

"A misunderstanding, I think," Thorne said. He turned to Dearwood. "I suggest you leave immediately, so you can have a physician examine that jaw."

Dearwood, to his credit, merely nodded and began walking away.

"I warned you about inviting—"

"Mother." She snapped her mouth closed. "I believe our ball has come to an end. Miss Trewlove, allow me to see to your hand."

She angled her chin. "It's quite all right, Your Grace. I'm accustomed to jabbing drunkards."

A few gasps filled the air.

"I believe it's time we took our leave," Mick Trewlove said, coming to stand beside his sister.

"I'll escort you to your carriage," Thorne said.

"Please don't," she said, and his heart squeezed painfully.

"Gillie, I'm not going to have you walk out of here alone as though you've done something unforgiveable. I've known Dearwood a good many years, and I know you'd have not struck him if he didn't deserve it. Allow me to escort you out."

She nodded, and he offered his arm. Thankfully she placed her hand in the crook of his elbow. He waited until they were out of the ballroom, with Mick Trewlove and Lady Aslyn leading the way, before asking, "Did he really ask you to dance?"

"He did."

"I suspect that wasn't all."

"Thorne."

He pulled her to the side, near the armor that had once protected an ancestor, and he wished to God he could protect her as effectively. "In a few minutes those who are not staying the night will be walking past here to get to their carriages. What did he say?"

She licked her lips; a small pleat appeared between her eyebrows. "He told me about a contest you and he engaged in, to see who could bed the greatest variety of women. He was quite impressed you'd added a tavern owner to your list."

He slammed his eyes closed, cursed beneath his breath. When he opened his eyes, he pressed a kiss to that delicate crease before holding her gaze. "Gillie, that was more than a dozen years ago, when I was young and ill advised. You can't possibly believe what's happened between us is because of a stupid game from my youth, surely."

She shook her head. "No. But he called me out for being your mistress, informed me you would toss me over and then I would become his. People know what's between us."

"They're speculating, guessing. It's what they do, damn them all to hell. I'm so sorry, princess."

"I'm not a princess, Thorne."

"You are to me. I need to finish up here, and then I'll come to you."

He was grateful she nodded, that she wasn't entirely done with him. After he saw her safely into her brother's carriage, he headed back into the residence. People were wandering into the entryway. "I say! I have an announcement you won't want to miss. Everyone make your way back to the ballroom, please."

Expecting something titillating, perhaps even his disclosing which lady had caught his fancy, no one hesitated to return to the grand salon. Standing at the top of the stairway, he looked out over the eager crowd.

Only his mother appeared worried. For good reason, he supposed, since he continually disappointed her.

He cleared his throat. "A few weeks ago, on the evening of the day I was to marry actually, I made a visit to Whitechapel and was attacked by some ruffians. Miss Trewlove stepped in and saved my life—literally. She did it all while knowing nothing at all about me. Not my rank or my position. Fully cognizant of how gossip travels among us, I'm rather certain even those of you who were not introduced to her are aware she owns a tavern, the Mermaid and Unicorn. Since that night, on occasion I have visited and always been made to feel welcome. As a way of thanking her for her kindness, I invited her to my mother's ball, knowing hers are always splendid and beyond compare, and rather enjoyable. To those of you who made Miss Trewlove feel welcome, thank you. To those of you who did not, you missed the opportunity to meet a rather exceptional woman and your lives are poorer because of that."

Turning on his heel, he began walking from a room that was so quiet he would have heard a plume from his mother's adorned hair fall if it had come loose.

Chapter 24

Sitting in her front room, awaiting Thorne's arrival, Gillie was hit with the realization that her last dance with Thorne was actually the final one for eternity. At the time, she'd thought they would have one more, would end the night circling the ballroom together. So now she concentrated on striving to absorb each moment of what had been their final waltz until it was a part of her, until it could never be forgotten, hoping it would carry her through the days and months and years ahead.

The way his eyes seemed to adore her, the shade she would see every time she poured a pint of Guinness. The manner in which the lights from the chandeliers glistened over his silky dark hair. The faintest of shadows that had hinted the stubble would soon begin to assert itself, allowing that no razor would ever hold it at bay for long.

His hands securely holding her, his long legs brushing up against her skirts, the way he swept her over the dance floor with such ease there might as well have been no one else upon it.

She recalled inhaling his tart fragrance, taking pleasure from his secretive smile, granted only to her, granted always only to her. He would dance with others at other balls. Some day, very soon, he would waltz with his wife. And she wondered if, when he did so, he would think of her.

Shifting on her sofa, she was torn between wishing she would haunt him and hoping she didn't. She wanted to be unselfish, wanted his wife to be first among women in his eyes, but she couldn't quite let go of the hope that he would, from time to time, think of her. They had shared something precious and rare, but she knew deep in her heart the time had come to end it. With her dressed in her fancy clothes and the lovely strains produced by the orchestra still lingering in her mind. She had followed the unicorn into his world, but it was time now to return to hers, without him.

When the knock sounded on her door, she rose calmly to her feet. She'd removed the false hairpiece earlier, because she'd wanted to welcome him into her abode as herself. It had been a silly thing to wear it. There had never been any artifice between them. She wanted his fingers tangled only in her own tresses, not in some that might have once belonged to another woman or, heaven forbid, some domesticated animal. She'd yet to remove her gown and all its underlying layers, and when she opened the door, she was grateful to see he'd come straight to her without changing from his evening attire.

One step over the threshold, one slam of the door, a toss aside of his hat, and he had her in his arms, his mouth carrying her away on a current of passion and desire—too soon, too fast, before she'd told him the truth she'd come to understand.

Pressing her hand to his chest, she pushed him back until she could gaze into his eyes, and there she saw he had come to the same conclusion as she.

"No," he said quietly.

"I wanted you to tell me when it was our last night to be together." She brushed the dark locks from his brow. "So I will give you the same courtesy. When you leave at dawn, you will not return."

"What happened with Dearwood, whatever my dragon of a mother might have said—"

She pressed her fingers to his lips. "They have nothing to do with us, with this. It was the girls more than anything. One of them is your future, and I will not share you. Or perhaps it was all the portraits. One day one of them will be of your son, *must* be of *your* son. Before tonight I don't think I truly understood the legacy for which you are responsible. You have to see to it, and you have to see to it without me."

He closed his eyes. "Gillie—"

"I will not be your mistress and I cannot be your wife. Let me go, Thorne, let me go on my terms. Give me that."

He opened his eyes. "I would give you the world if I could."

She smiled as sweetly as she was able. "Give me tonight, every minute of every hour. And it will be enough."

Without another word, he lifted her into his arms and carried her into her bedchamber.

It had taken her hours to put on the varying layers of clothing. It took him only minutes to remove them, took her less time than that to remove his. Then they fell on her bed as they had so many times before, a tangle of limbs, feet stroking calves, gliding sinuously up, thighs holding close, hands exploring, arms wrapping, capturing, embracing. All the while their mouths taunting and tasting, their tongues lapping and licking, their teeth nipping and biting.

He marked her with love bites in places no one would ever see: a shoulder, the swell of a breast, a hip, the inside of a thigh. She returned the favor, nuzzling his neck, leaving a mark that branded him as hers, but only temporarily, only for a few days. It would fade away, and she could only hope the memory of her wouldn't.

Because, like a miser, she would hoard the remembrances of every moment spent with him. The way he had fought to reach the top of her stairs when surrendering to death's knell would have been easier. The way his heated breath had first brushed over her breasts. The way he looked at her through his spectacles, the way he watched her without them. Their walks through Whitechapel when she could see he was viewing it for the first time as it truly was, when he was noticing how it differed from the other areas of London he visited. His gentleness with Robin. His kindness with her patrons.

What it had felt like to waltz within the circle of his arms. The absolute joy and sense of fulfillment that overcame her each time he joined his body to hers. And all the smaller moments that rested in between the larger ones.

She knew they would all come upon her at the oddest times, whether she wanted them to or not. He was part of her now, even when he wasn't with her. She would hear him, feel him, taste him, smell him. She would see him in rumpled sheets and whisky poured and bath water steaming. When she sat on the landing outside her door to absorb the quiet, the shadow of his presence would be there with her.

He journeyed the length of her body, from the top of her head to the tips of her toes, and she'd never been more grateful for her height, for every inch that made the sojourn one that happened without haste, that went on seemingly forever. When he started back up, kissing her calves, the backs of her knees, the inside of her thighs, he took a detour to the heavenly haven she would only ever share with him.

His mouth, his gloriously wicked mouth, worked his incredible magic, as she dug her fingers into his shoulders, wound her legs around his waist, gazed down on him as he lifted his eyes to hers, daring her not to look away, but to hold his gaze while he plundered.

Her breaths came in short shallow puffs, and his eyes darkened, letting her know how very much he enjoyed watching her come undone. *Feel my rapidly pounding heart,* she wanted to whisper, *the scalding heat coursing through me, the nerve endings that seem to be shooting forth bursts of fireworks, small and large, all colors.*

But even without giving voice to all the astonishing sensations traveling through her, she suspected he knew because he became more diligent in his efforts, applying pressure with his tongue, closing his lips tightly around her, sucking, soothing, swirling.

Watching, always watching. Witness to her nipples growing even more taut, to the fine layer of dew gathering between her breasts. Hearing, always hearing. The whimpers and moans that escaped unheeded through her parted lips. Feeling, always feeling. The trembling of her thighs as the pressure mounted. Tasting her, inhaling her fragrance. All of her sensations were wildly alive, and in his dark eyes, she could see he relished and shared in them as well.

He knew the torment she experienced because he did all in his power to increase it, to ensure when the release finally came—

She was screaming his name, bucking, her back arching, but always her gaze was locked with his.

Shooting upward, he plunged deep and sure, before her spasms could subside, while she was still lost in the throes of a cataclysm that was so intense, she might never recover. She wrapped her legs tightly around his hips, holding on as he pistoned into her, over and over, while he rained kisses over her breasts, her throat, her face.

And then he left her, and she clutched him tightly as shudders rocked him, and he spilled his seed in his hand. The temptation to urge him to stay inside her had never been stronger, but she understood the wisdom of his actions. With his head on her belly and one arm wound securely around her, he held her near while his tremors mingled with hers, eventually subsiding into oblivion.

SHE HADN'T MEANT to fall asleep, hadn't wanted to miss a single minute of the time left to them. She knew a burst of panic when she realized he wasn't in the bed, feared he'd left without a final goodbye, but then she saw him standing at her window, the curtain pulled back on one side allowing the moonlight to filter in and lovingly caress one half of his lovely backside. She did love the length and strength visible in his corded muscles, the way they all came together so beautifully to form such perfection. She loved even more how satisfying it felt to her hands to run them over all the abundant ropes of sinew.

His gaze was focused on some far-off object she couldn't see, and she wondered if it were even visible to him or if he were seeing instead possibilities and impossibilities. "Thorne?"

"I was just thinking that I never had the opportunity to teach you to appreciate good horseflesh."

Slipping out of bed, she padded quietly across the floor, pressed her chest to his back, and wrapped her arms around him. "We always knew we would never have more than this."

Within her embrace, he turned and cupped her face between his hands. "But I want more. With you."

"It was always to be temporary, Thorne."

"When it matters the most, you're always so damned practical."

Lifting her hands, she brushed her fingers over his hair. "Make love to me again."

And he did, again and again. With her on top, him from behind, spooned around each other, then finally once more face-to-face, with her beneath him, relishing everything about him.

She could have sworn she did indeed hear a lark trilling outside her window that morning as they both dressed, he in his ballroom finery and she in her plain shirt and skirt. Last night she'd been a princess, but she was once again a tavern owner as she walked him to the door. "I'm not going to follow you down."

He merely nodded and cupped her cheek with one hand. "You are a remarkable woman, Gillie Trewlove. I am a better man for having known you."

"Find a bride who will not leave you standing at the altar."

Leaning forward, he pressed a kiss to her forehead. "Goodbye, Gillie."

Then he walked out of her flat, out of her life. And she, who had no memory of ever crying, curled up into a ball on her sofa and wept.

Chapter 25

$\mathcal{F}$rom the outside, the small house in the rookeries of London's east end gave the appearance of abandonment, dilapidated and worn, but inside it provided a wealth of warmth and love. Even as a girl, after scrubbing steps all day, Gillie had looked forward to returning here, where her mum's arms would come tightly around her and the aromas of cinnamon and vanilla would waft about her, where a freshly brewed cup of tea was always waiting for her.

"You've not been to see me in a while," her mum said now, releasing her hold on Gillie and stepping back. "I suppose it has something to do with those worry lines between your brows. You never was any good at hiding your troubles from me. Let me prepare you a cuppa and then we'll have a nice little chat."

Only it wasn't going to be a nice little chat, no matter how much her mum wanted it to be. A cup of tea wasn't going to help. Neither was all the liquor in her stores at the tavern. "I've done something really stupid, Mum. I went and fell in love. And now his babe is growing inside me."

In spite of the precautions they'd taken or tried to take. Perhaps he hadn't left quickly enough, perhaps some of his seed had spilled inside her before he'd withdrawn completely. It had been nearly a month since she'd seen him; two since she'd first welcomed him into her bed. Her breasts had become tender, but she'd thought it was just because they were no longer bound, and the freedom she'd given them didn't offer enough support. Then she'd looked at her calendar and realized she'd not had a menses since she'd first been intimate with Thorne. She'd always hated being cursed each month, so she hadn't missed the inconvenience of having to deal with it, not until she comprehended what its absence portended.

Sympathy washed over the dear woman's face. "Ah, you silly girl."

"I'm sorry, Mum, I'm so sorry." Tears welled in her eyes, clogged her throat. "I know it's shameful and you'll never want to see me again—"

Her mum's arms came around her once more. "Oh, pet, now you're being an even sillier girl. You come over here and sit down."

Her mum guided her to a chair by the fireplace, and even though no fire burned, Gillie suddenly felt warmer. The woman she'd loved for as long as she could remember knelt in front her, gave her a handkerchief, and took the hand that wasn't busily wiping away the irritating avalanche of tears. "You're not the first to lose her head over a fella and do things she wished she hadn't."

She sniffed, an incredibly unladylike noise. "That's the thing, Mum. I don't wish I hadn't. I'm glad I did. As I said, I love him. So much. I always knew we couldn't have forever, but it was enough to have for now. Until we couldn't have that anymore either."

"He won't do right by you, then?"

Shaking her head, she wiped away the last remnants

of her tears. Putting everything into words, saying it aloud was making it easier. "He's a bloody duke. He's to marry some lord's daughter, someone who knows all the fancy ways of being a lady. I told him I wouldn't step out with him any longer. But I'm going to keep it, Mum. The babe."

"Gillie—"

"I know it'll mark me. I know people will probably stop coming to my tavern, but I've been saving my money, so maybe I'll sell my place and move to a little cottage in the country. I don't know. I just know I can't give it up. It's all I'll have of him, but it'll be enough."

Her mum squeezed her hand. "Then we'll make that be enough, won't we?"

"You don't have to stand by me, Mum."

Brushing Gillie's hair back from her face, her mum offered a tender smile. "Where else would I stand, love? You're my daughter. I've raised six children who came to me because of a bit of naughtiness. I'm not going to turn my back on a little one who belongs to one of my precious children."

"Thanks, Mum."

She patted her hand. "Now don't you be fretting. Everything will work out."

SHE WAS ACCUSTOMED to doing for herself, so it was with a bit of resentment she accepted the recent limitations of her body and decided hauling kegs would be tempting fate to take the precious babe from her. Although the suspicious perusal Roger gave her when she asked him to bring up a box of assorted whisky bottles tempted her to plant her fist in the center of his face.

"You've never needed my help before."

"I don't need it now. It's just that you're brawny and it's silly for me not to take advantage of that, especially considering how well I pay you."

"Not like you to put on airs."

"Not like you to question my orders."

He narrowed his eyes. "You've been different of late. I can't quite put my finger on it. It's like your monthly is lasting forever."

She sighed heavily. "Get the damn bottles."

With a negligent shrug, he headed out of the room to do her bidding.

"You should probably tell him," Finn said, leaning against the counter. Her brother had arrived a few minutes earlier, removed his cap, and been studying it as though he'd forgotten its purpose.

"He'll figure it out soon enough and then he'll probably quit."

"I doubt that. I think you underestimate how much you're loved, Gillie."

"Until there's scandal."

"Maybe, maybe not. Can I have a word?"

She moved up to the counter. "Of course."

He jerked his head to the side. "Over there."

She followed him to a table in the very back corner of the tavern. They hadn't yet brought back the shutters on the windows, so they were deep into the shadows. Finn pulled out a chair for her, waited until she sat before taking the place opposite her. She wasn't accustomed to her brother being quite so accommodating. Not that he was ever rude but all her brothers understood she could fend for herself, preferred it.

He took the seat opposite her, clasped his hands on the table, and met her gaze head-on. "I love you like a sister. I'll never love you more than that. I don't have it in me to do so, but if you'll marry me, I'll do right by you and this babe."

"Finn—"

"It'd be a marriage in name only. I'd never expect you to honor your wifely duties." She'd never seen her brother blush before. The deep red blotching his skin was a sight to behold. "As I said, I think of you as a sister."

"I know you do, Finn," she said quietly. "I think we'd both be miserable if we tied the knot. But I do appreciate your willingness. Besides, someday you're likely to meet someone who'd make you regret already having a wife."

"My heart's locked up tight, Gil. The offer will remain should you change your mind."

Laying her hand over his tense ones, she rubbed them, trying to get him to relax, knowing he was battling memories. "Still love her so desperately, do you?"

His response was simply to look beyond her as though gazing into the past.

"What was her Christian name?" she asked.

His gaze, hard as a diamond, cold as ice, came back to her. "I've not spoken it in eight years. I'm not going to do so now."

Pressing her forearms to the table, she leaned forward. "You called her Vivi, but what was her real name?"

"Christ." He shoved back his chair.

"I think she's here."

He froze, stared at her. "What do you mean *here*?"

"In Whitechapel."

"Why would she be here?"

"I don't know but—" She reached into her pocket, brought out the miniature Thorne had given her, and placed it on the table. She'd debated with herself a thousand times whether she should tell Finn what she suspected, whether it was to his benefit to bring up the past or to leave it buried. "I thought she looked familiar, but I'd only seen her once and that was years ago. She's somewhat older in this painting."

Slowly he sank back into the chair. He didn't touch the portrait but neither did he take his eyes from it. "Where did you get this?"

"From Thorne. I was trying to help him find her. She left him standing at the altar."

Leaning back in the chair, he crossed his arms over his chest. "I'm not surprised. She has a habit of breaking her promises." He studied her for a long moment, shook his head. "I hope you didn't give the scapegrace your heart, Gillie."

"Tell me the pain lessens over time."

His expression was one of sadness and sorrow. "Wish I could, but I won't choose now to start lying to you."

Not exactly what she'd wanted to hear, but a little over a month after saying goodbye, it was what she'd begun to suspect.

THAT NIGHT BUSINESS was booming at the Mermaid, and she wondered how long before it might begin to dwindle. As long as her bosom jutted out past her stomach, perhaps none would be the wiser concerning her condition. And if she stayed behind the bar, few would be likely to get a good enough look at her to detect that she was increasing. As her stomach was beginning to round, she was rather certain she'd gotten with child the first night she and Thorne had come together.

"Hello, Gillie," Aiden said as he slapped a hand on the bar. "I'll have a pint of dark stout, the darker the better."

She poured his drink and set it on the counter. "Enjoy."

He took a long, slow swallow, then wiped his mouth with the back of his hand. "Have you got a minute?"

"For you, anytime."

"Good. Let's go over there." He led the way to a vacant table with other vacant tables around it, held out a chair for her—

"I haven't lost the ability to see to myself," she muttered as she sat.

"Didn't think you had. I was just being polite." He set his glass on the table, grabbed a chair, swung it around, and straddled it. "I've been doing some thinking of late."

"Glad to hear you've taken up a pastime."

"Very funny, Gillie, very funny. That's what I've always fancied about you, your humor."

"You're too easy to tease, Aiden."

"That I am. I also have an extremely successful business that I'll be expanding soon. You have a good business here—"

"I have an excellent business here. It sees me in good stead."

"But imagine if we were to combine our assets. We'd be quite the couple to be reckoned with."

She stared at him. "And how exactly would we combine our assets?"

"Through marriage."

"You're asking me to marry you?"

"I'm *suggesting* you marry me. You're not really my sister." He leaned toward her, an earnestness in his eyes. "Look, Gil, life is going to get really hard for you. I know a gaming hell owner isn't ideal husband material, but it beats the alternative. You know you're going to get ostracized."

"I know."

"People are likely to start drinking elsewhere."

"I know. I'll probably end up selling the place."

He grimaced. "But you've worked so hard. You've poured your soul into the Mermaid."

She placed her hands over her belly. "But now there's something—someone—else I want to pour my soul into."

For a moment, his eyes dipped to the shelter she'd created before meeting her gaze. "We'd have fun, Gil. I could show you a good time, better than that fancy duke showed you."

She very much doubted that. Still she grinned at him. "Drink up, Aiden. Free drinks are all you're going to get from me."

"Bugger it, then. I won't touch you, but I will give you marriage and respectability—"

"I love you, Aiden, but after a time I think we'd each be plotting how to kill the other with the least amount of bother." She shoved back her chair and stood. "But thank you for the *suggestion*. It means the world to me."

"Will you send a girl over with a couple of more pints? I'm going to need to drown my sorrows at you turning me down."

"Such rubbish," she muttered with a smile before heading back to the bar. Still it made her feel special that Aiden and Finn were willing to saddle themselves with her. But if she couldn't marry for the sort of passionate love that could exist between a man and a woman, she didn't want to marry at all. She thought about Thorne and the atmosphere in which he'd grown up, with nary a whisper of love. How could one learn to love if one had never been loved?

She got to the bar to find Beast waiting for her. His

hands were clasped around a tankard so tightly his knuckles were turning white. "Gillie, I wondered if I might have a word."

Cradling his jaw with one hand, she smiled tenderly at him. "No, Beast, I won't marry you."

Relief washed over his features as he slowly released a breath he might have been holding since he walked in. "I wouldn't be bad as a husband."

"You'd be wonderful, but I think we both deserve to marry for love."

"Not in my future, Gil. Even if I'd been born on the right side of the blanket, I'd have still not been wanted, still would have been brought to Mum's door. There's no denying that."

She shook her head. "People are idiots. No matter what this babe looks like—"

"You're with child?" Roger asked.

With a low growl, she swung around and glared at him. "Keep the news to yourself."

"Why didn't you bloody well say? You shouldn't be standing." Reaching over the counter, he grabbed a stool, hefted it up and over, and set it down. "Sit."

She didn't usually take orders, but her legs were beginning to ache, so she settled down on the stool. It would be nice to sit in between pouring drinks.

"Was it that toff? If your brothers and I were to have a word with him—"

"No," she stated sharply. "I'm on my own in this."

He grinned sadly. "No, you're not, Gil."

"He's right there," Beast and Aiden said at the same time and she wondered when Aiden had wandered over.

"It'll all work out," Aiden told her.

"That's what Mum said."

"She usually knows."

"But you need to tell him, Gil," Beast said. "It's not fair to him not to know."

She nodded. "I know. I will tell him. After the babe is born, after he's married." After she'd sold the tavern and moved to a cottage in the country. After she could prove she expected nothing from him.

WHILE THE RAIN pattered the panes, Thorne sat at the desk in his library and looked over the offers he'd received in writing from a dozen fathers. During the six weeks since the ball, viscounts, earls, marquesses, and dukes had met with him or written to him in order to discuss the possibility of his marrying one of their daughters. Every daughter came with a parcel of land—some large, some small—because everyone knew the Dukes of Thornley coveted land. Fathers had even brought their daughters who had yet to have their coming out, so he could get a preview of next year's offerings, in the hopes he might make a preemptive proposal and save them the bother of a Season.

It was a dismally depressing way to select a wife. He certainly wouldn't use this method for his daughter, should he ever have one. The gent was going to have to woo her, spoil her, love her, and prove he would treat her with the utmost care. And if his daughter wanted to marry an untitled gent, by God, he'd make that happen as well.

As for himself, he had a duty to honor and a vow to keep.

All the women he was considering were poised, graceful, and beautiful. Each was a lady fit for a duke, and yet each seemed wrong.

He reminded himself that he came from a long line of dukes who did not marry for love. These ladies brought with them property that would expand his holdings, the holdings he would pass down to the next duke, his son. Each brought a pure bloodline their children would inherit. Each brought good breeding that would make him proud as they hosted affairs, visited with royalty, made their mark on Great Britain.

Each was rather dainty. Would any of them have the gumption to haul him upstairs if wounded, to harangue him into fighting to survive? Would any look into the faces of the poor and offer them help? Would any crouch before them and offer them kindness?

His entire life he'd been instructed, tutored, and educated on the sort of woman he would marry, the echelon of Society from which she would be heralded. There were the sort of women men wed and the sort they bedded. Regardless of how a man might feel about them, they were relegated to a certain role in his life.

He reached for the nearby tumbler and took a sip of his whisky, remembering when he had savored the flavor in a small tavern where life moved about him with smiles and laughter—both of which were now remarkably absent. They'd never existed in this house. There had never been any evidence of love or caring. There had been naught but accusations, anger, and arguments.

He was now spared his mother's constant finding fault with him because he had moved her into the dower house. He'd thought he'd welcome the peace brought by her absence. Instead he found he missed her for some unfathomable reason. Perhaps because it was too damned quiet now, so quiet he heard the ticking of the clock on the mantel, the crackle of the fire, the occasional rumble of the thunder, and the *tap-tap-tap* on glass.

Removing his watch from his waistcoat pocket, he rubbed his thumb over the engraving. A dozen times—no, two dozen, three—he'd nearly gone to the Mermaid, nearly gone to her. But she didn't want his world of balls and dinners and musicales. She had no interest in fancy gowns and glittering jewelry and beribboned hats. He often thought of her in the purple ball gown, but more often he envisioned her in her simple shirts and petticoat-less skirts, the way she strode with purpose and determination through her tavern, through life. A practical woman who opened her heart to friend and stranger alike, with a streak of whimsy to her, who created fairy tales about her origins and believed in mythical creatures and recognized how great a loss it was when another was on the verge of being extinguished.

Tap-tap-tap.

He'd heard about a zoo in Europe that was striving to breed a pair of quaggas, and he'd sent them funds to assist in their efforts because he'd thought it would please her to learn that the beast would carry on, would not die away. That there would be no last time of gazing on one. Because last times were hard, even when one knew it was the last time.

Not a day went by that he didn't want to gaze on her again, to converse with her, to watch her moving about with purpose but still managing to find the time to place a comforting hand there and offering a kind word elsewhere. To watch her putting tokens in grubby hands and receiving smiles in return. She created smiles, basked in them. He didn't think he'd smiled once since he left her, knew he'd not laughed.

"Make me proud," his father had said. The Dukes of Thornley stood above all others because they increased their legacy and holdings by marrying women for land. What rotten bargainers they were, the lot of them.

Tap-tap-tap. Tap-tap-tap.

He glanced over at the glass door. Lightning flashed, outlining the wraith who stood there. Good God! Tucking the timepiece away, he leapt to his feet, rushed over, and jerked open the door. "Lavinia?"

The boom of thunder, another flash of lightning. Taking her arm, he dragged her inside and shut out the rain. "Lavinia." He'd given up hope of ever seeing her again, in spite of the handbills he'd paid Robin to spread about.

Unbuttoning her pelisse, she removed it. "Apologies but I'm dripping on your carpet."

He took it from her and tossed it onto a nearby chair. He didn't care about the dampness or the wet. "Get by the fire. Shall I send for tea?"

She offered him a small smile, and he wondered if she'd always appeared so sad and he'd merely overlooked it. "A bit of brandy, if you please."

As he poured, she wandered over to the fireplace, lowered herself into a chair, and rubbed her arms. The frock she wore was plain and frayed, and he would have wagered it came from a mission. He hated the thought of her scrounging among others' discards, but couldn't help but be impressed that Gillie had the right of it. But then of course she had. She understood people far better than he ever would. She understood motivation, fear, and longing.

He handed the snifter to her, watched as she brought it up, inhaled the aroma, and took a small sip. "Why didn't you come in through the front door?" he asked, as he sat in the chair opposite hers.

"I wanted to be certain my brother wasn't about to haul me home. I got your missive."

Missive? "Ah, the handbill."

"Yes. Clever of you."

"It wasn't my idea—and it was weeks ago, so I thought it had been fruitless."

"I spent a lot of time debating whether or not to come. Then I decided you were kind in your efforts and I wanted to reassure you, in person, that I am well. My letters were the coward's way. You deserved to be told everything in person."

He settled back in the chair, placed his elbow on its arm and his chin in his palm. "In your letter, you mentioned you were in love with someone. Have you married him?"

She shook her head. "Oh no. But he takes up all of my heart and there would have been none to give to you. Also . . ." Her voice trailed off as her attention went to the fire.

He waited in silence, not prodding, not prying. Gillie had taught him that sometimes mere presence was enough and patience was kindness.

She took another sip of brandy, licked her lips. His body did not tighten, nothing called to him to take possession of that mouth. Since leaving Gillie, in spite of all the ladies paraded before him, he'd been as chaste as a monk. He'd begun to think she'd cast some spell over him, and never again would the sight of a woman arouse him.

"There are sins in my past, Thorne." Somber and solemn, she looked at him. "They are not to be forgiven."

He wanted to ask what they were but he wasn't certain he had any right to know.

"I could not bring myself to stand in that church

before you and God and pretend purity. And I couldn't marry you knowing I couldn't give you the love you deserved from a wife. What would have been between us would have been awkward and cold, through no fault of your own. Guilt would have made me a wretched wife, and you are worthy of so much better. My mother gave no credence to my mounting concerns and doubts. I assumed, perhaps unfairly, that Collinsworth would side with her, so I did not confide in him. Instead, at the first opportunity presented to me, I ran. I do not expect you to forgive me—"

"I do forgive you," he said quietly.

Tears welled in her eyes. "Thank you for that."

"How are you managing?"

"Quite well actually."

"Collinsworth has hired men to search for you."

Another sad smile. "I doubt they will ever think to look where I am."

"Will you not tell me?"

She shook her head, sighed. "So now you will marry another?"

He chuckled low, darkly. "Indeed. As a matter of fact, I've been looking over the candidates. Perhaps you'd like to help me choose your replacement."

"Choose someone with whom you cannot live without, for if you do not, you will discover that you cannot live at all."

Chapter 26

She was relatively confident the door had been opened a hundred times that day, that night, so she wasn't certain why she was drawn to the present opening of it, what had prompted her to glance over when she hadn't before. Perhaps it was because she'd always been able to sense the force of him when he strode in. He stopped just inside the doorway, removed his hat, and studied her as she stood behind the bar, holding his gaze, not looking away.

He was devilishly handsome in a dark blue jacket, gray waistcoat, and pristine white shirt and cravat with the tiniest pin holding it in place. It was just so damned good to see him. She'd missed him so much. But she had to give nothing away, nothing at all. She'd not burden him with things that couldn't be changed.

Finally, he strode across the room until he was standing in front of her. "Hello, princess."

"Thorne." Why did her breath choose that moment to leave her? "You look well."

"Looks can be deceiving. I'm actually quite miserable. Lavinia came to see me. I think she is even more miserable than I."

"So will the two of you become betrothed again?"

"No. I decided I didn't quite like the legacy my ancestors had left to me of not marrying for love."

Without taking her gaze from him, she reached for the stool, drew it against her backside and sat because it wouldn't do if her knees suddenly turned to jam. His Guinness eyes revealed so much, too much, everything he'd ever felt for her, everything he ever would.

"I love you, Gillie. I was daft enough not to know that's what I felt for you because I've never loved or known love before you. I think of you every minute of every hour—convinced it's only lust and desire. But I'm not always thinking about kissing you or touching you. I see things I want to share with you: a rare blossom, a phrase in a book I'm reading, an article in the newspaper. I hear things—the song of a bird, a lecture, an interesting bit of conversation—and I want you there experiencing them with me. I have had a dozen ladies brought before me and watched as they walk, so straight, so proper, that I can almost see the invisible book balancing on their heads. So calm, so reserved, so deuced boring. Almost absent of life. And I thought I can't, I can't marry any of them, not when I yearn to be with another, not when the only joy I've ever known isn't standing beside me. Slowly, little by little, you captured my heart, made it yours. It will never belong to anyone else. Marry me, Gillie."

She would not be marrying only a man, she would be marrying a duke, someone with responsibilities to England. She had caught a glimpse of his life, of the history that had led to his being who he was. It was overwhelming and so much grander than her small piece of London. She would overhear ladies discussing her and men would make advances toward her. Slowly, she shook her head.

"I know you worry about your tavern, losing it to your husband, but we can place it in a trust before we marry so it remains yours."

Once that had been her worry, but no more. She trusted him with her tavern. "It's not that. It's that I don't fancy your world."

"Then we'll live in yours. We'll find a small residence somewhere nearby. You won't have to live at Coventry House."

"You are a duke. You belong there. You have responsibilities—"

"I can still see to them. I won't give up my responsibilities or my duties, but my life can be here with you, if you'll have me." Placing his hands on the counter, he vaulted over it until he was standing beside her. In her surprise, she shoved back the stool until she was again standing. "Gillie, I—"

His gaze lowered to the slight roundness in her belly. It wasn't much but he was familiar with every inch of her, and she knew he could tell her body had changed. Slowly he lifted his gaze to hers, and she could see the hurt and disappointment reflected in his dark eyes. "Why didn't you tell me?"

"Because your life was elsewhere and at some point you were destined to marry another."

"Ah, Gillie."

"I'm keeping it. I'm selling the tavern because once people know, they'll shun me." And that would be by the end of the night because people were standing around listening. "But I have money saved—"

"You're not selling the tavern." He cradled her cheek. "Do you love me?"

Why did this man so often make her eyes sting? "With all my heart."

"Then marry me." He pressed his forehead to hers. "You told me how scared you were before you opened the tavern and I know you're scared now, scared you'll fail, but, Gillie, I swear to you that I would not ask you to become my duchess if I did not think you'd be the finest one England has ever known."

"I still don't know which fork to use."

Leaning back, he smiled tenderly. "Sweetheart, you'll be a duchess. You can use any damned one you want and people will love you for being eccentric. Marry me."

How could she not? He was correct. What did utensils matter when she would have him? "Yes. Yes. Yes!"

He lifted her up and swung her around within the narrow confines of the bar, and then amid a round of cheers, he kissed her thoroughly.

NO ONE SEEMED surprised when she handed the reins to the tavern to her head barman and followed Thorne out into the night. He wanted to take her someplace special, someplace elegant and worthy of her, but he also wanted her comfortable and at ease, so he escorted her into her flat. Once there, with the door closed, he dropped to his knees and pressed a kiss to her belly. "I'm so sorry, Gillie. I thought I was being ever so cautious."

Even though he knew abstinence was the only method that guaranteed the outcome he'd been seeking, he'd been too weak to abstain because he'd wanted her so desperately.

She buried her fingers into his hair. "I was incredibly happy when I realized I was carrying your child, Thorne."

He lifted his gaze to hers. "Your life would have been remarkably hard."

"But also wonderfully joyous. Your babe, inside me, then in my arms. I want this child." She lowered her fingers, held his face between her hands. "I want you."

"No more than I want you. God, Gillie, I have missed you." He pushed himself to his feet and took her mouth with all the longing that had haunted him for six weeks now, with all the fervor that had simmered whenever he thought of her, whenever he was tempted to go to her, whenever he forced himself to stay where he was.

How had he ever thought he could live without the taste of her, the fragrance of her, the sound of her sighs, the feel of her in his arms?

Drawing away from the kiss, she gave him a sultry smile before reaching down, taking his hand, and leading him into her bedchamber. Stopping beside the bed, she faced him and very slowly began unbuttoning her shirt.

He wanted to help her and yet he sensed that for tonight, it was important she set the pace, determine the direction. This brave, strong woman who would have endured being ostracized in order to bring his child into the world, to have kept it at her side, to have given it a home. When her clothes were a pile on the floor, he could have sworn a blush swept up over her from her toes to her hairline.

"My body has changed somewhat."

Her breasts were larger, her belly slightly more round.

"Yet all that I love about you remains the same," he said.

"Oh, Thorne."

She was in his arms before he took his next breath,

as though she might have doubted his earlier declaration, as though she feared his offer was not genuine. He loved this woman, every aspect of her, and he would spend the remainder of his life proving that to her. For all her boldness, there was still a part of her that believed she deserved being left on a doorstep; buried deep within her was a little girl who wanted to believe she was a princess.

He intended to treat her as though she were a queen.

He was aware of her working to remove his clothes. Then her hands were moving across his chest, over his shoulders.

"All that I love about you remains the same," she said.

"My upper torso?"

"Everything. Your inner strength, your determination, your kindness. The way you blush at bawdy entertainments."

"I did not blush."

She gave him a secretive smile, just before she nipped his chin. "You blushed. You were so sweet afterward, explaining that what we'd seen was not the way it was between a man and a woman."

"Sweet? I shall show you sweet."

AND HE DID. Laying her out on the bed, kissing and caressing every inch of her—even though there were now a few more inches of her here and there. Soon there would be quite a few more.

"When will we wed?" she asked.

"Before the month is out, to stave off the gossips when my heir arrives early."

"Can we marry here in Whitechapel, with only friends and family about?" Someplace where she would be comfortable, where they would be surrounded only by those who loved them, who wouldn't gossip about them.

He rose up over her. "We shall marry wherever and however you want. Then we are going away for a month."

"Thorne, I have a business to manage. I thought you understood—"

"Vineyards."

She blinked at him. "Pardon?"

"I'm going to take you to vineyards, pluck grapes off vines, and feed them to you."

She laughed. "I can find new wines for my tavern."

He nuzzled her neck. "It would be good for business."

Once again she laughed, until he took her mouth and she was no longer thinking about vineyards or wines or business. She was thinking only of him, this gorgeous wonderful man who caused her heart to sing.

When he entered her, she wrapped her legs tightly around his hips. "Don't leave me this time."

And while she saw in his gaze that he understood she was telling him that she wanted him to pour his seed into her, he said, "I'll never leave you again."

They moved in tandem, hips thrusting, until pleasure overcame them both, until they both cried out.

As they held each other close, lost in the aftermath of incredible pleasure, she realized she'd been wrong. She'd never been a mermaid and he'd never been a unicorn. They always had simply been two people destined for love.

Chapter 27

"*H*ey, Gil, there's some posh lady out here looking for you," Roger said from the doorway leading into the kitchen. "She was knocking on the door—well, she wasn't, a footman was—quite insistently, so I opened it even though we're not yet ready to serve. She ordered me to fetch you."

Posh lady? Certainly not Aslyn. Could it be the woman Thorne had been searching for? No. When she stepped into the taproom, she saw much to her astonishment, the prow of a ship, the Duchess of Thornley, standing there. It seemed she was going to begin her morning with an unwelcome battle. "Your Grace."

"Miss Trewlove. I am in need of a word."

Gillie had a fairly good idea of what that word might entail—canceling her marriage to Thorne, which she absolutely was not going to do. But she would let the termagant have her rant and then send her on her way. She walked to a nearby table and pulled out a chair. "Would you care to sit?"

The duchess glanced around. "Everything appears clean."

"It is clean."

"Your tavern is rather nicer than I expected."

Gillie was fairly certain the comment was meant as

an insult, but she knew the tact she would adopt with this woman. "I shall take that as a compliment."

"As it was meant." The duchess lowered herself into the chair.

Gillie took one opposite her and waited, girding herself against whatever ugliness the dragon was going to toss her way.

"My son informs me that you are to wed. That the ceremony will be a small affair, with merely family and the very closest of friends to attend, and is to take place in a tiny church located in this area of London, and that simply will not do."

"It's what we want."

The duchess released a long sigh. "My dear girl, you are marrying a duke, and as his wife, you will discover there is a great deal in life that you *want*, that you may not have. It must be at St. George's. It must be a grand affair to which every member of the *ton* is invited. You must demonstrate to the world that you will make him a worthy duchess."

"Your Grace—"

"I know what you are thinking, my dear. That I am a meddling old woman and do not know of what I speak. But you must understand that a duke's power comes from his duchess. Do you think I invite ladies over for tea simply because I enjoy tea? No, it is so we can determine what it is our husbands should think and can then go home and tell them what they should think. We are the ones who pay attention to the smallest of details. We are the ones who influence their opinion when it comes to acts of Parliament. Oh, yes, men hold the reins, but we are the ones who slip lumps of sugar to the horses and ensure they go in the direction the men indicate. You cannot hide away here."

"I'm not hiding away. It's my business." Although if she were honest with herself, perhaps she was, just a tad.

"Why do you think Lady Aslyn married your brother at St. George's? Because it was the first step in seeing him accepted by the nobility. Is he totally accepted? Of course not. Do you have any idea what a boon it was to his reputation to have received an invitation to my ball? You can wield the same power, but you must assert it from the beginning. Yes, I know you are going to continue to manage your tavern and to labor here, and that nothing I say will sway you from your course, but you must marry at St. George's and you must live at Coventry House. Every duchess before you has ensured her duke is viewed as powerful and influential. If you truly love my son, you must see him not diminished in the eyes of his peers and you must not punch lords in ballrooms."

Gillie did wish she hadn't brought up that embarrassing episode. "I wasn't planning to make it a habit."

"I've no doubt Dearwood deserved it. I've never much cared for the man. In his youth, he was not a good influence over Antony. I wished countless times he'd find other company and told him so. Of course, the more I insisted, the more attached he became to Dearwood."

She'd never heard anyone refer to Thorne by his first name, but there was something profound and deep within the word when the duchess said it. "You love him."

"Dearwood? Good God, no. Don't be absurd."

"Your son."

The duchess angled her chin haughtily. "Naturally. I realize I have a rather acerbic manner, but I was taught from an early age that one does not show one's feelings. It doesn't mean they're not there."

Gillie could see that now. They were all trying to protect themselves from hurt, and in so doing they'd walled themselves up. Perhaps she would become a duchess who could teach them not to be so cold. She couldn't imagine inviting ladies over for tea but a bit of sherry might be in order.

"So will it be St. George's?" the duchess asked.

Gillie took a deep breath. In for a penny, in for a pound. "If Thorne is in agreement."

"Very good. And we shall have the most exquisite gown made—"

"Your Grace, I don't know what all Thorne has told you, but we're in a bit of a rush."

"My girl, I am a duchess. We shall have a hundred seamstresses at work. It will be done in the blink of an eye. And then—my word, what is that?"

Gillie looked over her shoulder to where the duchess was peering. Robin was crouched beneath a table. She'd been so focused on the duchess that she hadn't seen him slip out of the kitchen and into the taproom. "Robin, what are you doing?"

"I wanted to see the posh lady." He crept out from his hiding place and slowly approached until he was standing before Thorne's mother. "Are you a fairy?"

No doubt to him, with the sparkling jewelry draped around her neck and wrists, her elaborate dress of velvet and satin, her enormous beribboned hat, she did appear to be a rather magical being.

"Don't be absurd," the duchess snapped.

Gillie was on the verge of chastising her, but before she could Robin said, "When I grow up, I'm goin' to be an explorer and find another quagga."

"Oh, dear boy, by the time you are old enough to go off exploring, there will be no more quaggas at all. You must not waste your time searching for one. You must face reality and ensure no other creature goes the way of him." She leaned forward earnestly. "You must become a member of Parliament where you can express your opinions, make people listen to you."

"What's Parliament?"

"Oh, my goodness." She looked at Gillie. "Is he an orphan?"

"He is."

"Why is he not in a home for wayward children?"

"He likes living here."

"That will not do at all. I shall have to take him in hand."

"I beg your pardon?"

"With your additional duties, you won't have time to see to him. I shall see to him."

"I gots to protect this place," Robin piped up.

"And are you paid for this duty?" the duchess asked.

"A shilling a week."

"I shall pay you two shillings a week as I reside in a house much larger than this. You can live there and protect it."

Shaking his head, Robin backed up a step. "I don't want to leave. Me mum will look for me here."

The duchess appeared sad. "You are too young to be one of my husband's by-blows as I've no doubt he had many, but not so old that you couldn't be the son of one of his offspring. Think about it, young Robin, and when you are ready for grander things, you let me know."

With a nod, he dashed off.

"You wouldn't take him in, surely," Gillie said.

The duchess stood and tugged at her gloves, avoiding Gillie's gaze. "I have recently come to believe I might acquire a soft spot for orphans. And my residence is so terribly, terribly quiet."

Gillie couldn't help but think that it might be possible she and the duchess would indeed become allies—if not friends—in the end.

HE'D STOOD HERE before, and it had been much different then. He'd stared at his father's timepiece that had been placed in his hand with his father's dying breath, and he'd watched the minutes ticking by, thinking of all the things he could have been doing that day, wishing his bride would arrive so they could get the burdensome exchange of vows over with. Now he had no desire to monitor the slow movement of the hand on a watch or to do anything that would distract his attention away from the opening into the church because he wanted to see his bride as soon as she appeared, wanted to be the first to lay eyes on her, as he stood with Collinsworth beside him, signaling to all of England that his friend approved this match and that whatever had transpired that caused his sister not to show was water under the bridge, had not lessened the strength of their friendship.

Before he'd felt nothing at all, just another chore to be done in a long list of duties that he was to accomplish before he died.

Now he felt everything: excitement, potential, anticipation. He no longer thought about dying. Instead he thought only about living, living each day with Gillie. With her smiles, and her laughter, and sex. Most decidedly sex. He would love her until she couldn't stand to be loved any longer.

And then he would love her some more.

Suddenly everyone rose to their feet and she was there, strolling up the aisle, on the arm of her brother, Mick Trewlove, her sister leading the way, her other brothers following behind. He could see them all at the edges of his vision, but she was at the center of it. Had his father truly lived his entire life without this, without knowing what it was to feel complete and whole when a woman smiled at him with all the love she felt reflected in her eyes?

She wore a light beige gown of silk and lace. White was for virgins, she'd told him, and even though he was rather sure that a good many women who weren't virginal wore white on their wedding day, he didn't argue with her. Whatever she wanted to wear was fine with him. Orange blossoms held her veil in place.

Fancy took her place near the altar. As Gillie neared he was incredibly glad she had changed her mind about where the marriage would take place, that he had this day to let everyone see how much he adored her.

Unexpectedly she stopped at the front pew where his mother stood, studied the woman who had given birth to him, then before all of the *ton*, she dipped into the most graceful, elegant curtsy he'd ever seen. If he weren't wearing his spectacles so he could clearly see all the details of Gillie's face as they exchanged vows, and if what he viewed in the distance wasn't a bit blurred as a result, he thought he might have detected a fine sheen of tears in his mother's eyes as she gave Gillie a curt nod.

Gillie rose and, with her brothers in tow, took the last few steps toward him.

"Who gives this bride?" the reverend asked in a thunderous voice that echoed up to the rafters.

"We do," her brothers announced in unison. One by one they each gave her a kiss on the cheek before taking their place beside their mum on the first pew, until only Mick was left. He placed her hand on Thorne's arm and gave him a look that promised retribution if he disappointed her. If he disappointed her, he'd *ask* for their fists to be directed his way.

"No false hair today?" he asked her.

She shook her head. "I come to you as I am."

"I'd have it no other way."

Then as one they turned to face their future together.

FOLLOWING THE WEDDING, they'd held a reception that had gone into the late afternoon. Then Thorne had bundled her into a coach and brought her to Thornley Castle. Her trousseau and an abundance of clothing the duchess had insisted were necessary had been delivered earlier in the day. On the morrow, she and Thorne were heading to the vineyards of France and then Italy.

Upon their arrival at his estate, he had taken her on a leisurely tour of the manor. Room upon room upon room.

"I shall forever be getting lost," she told him now.

Chuckling, he drew her near, kissed her. "Simply find a bell pull, tug on it, and a servant will come lead you to safety."

"It's impressive, Thorne. I've never seen anything like it."

"I have something else to show you. I've been saving it for last." Taking her hand, he led her along corridors and finally down a narrow set of stairs. At the bottom was a small alcove. At the end of it was a door. He lifted a lantern, the flame inside flickering, off a hook on the wall, and held it aloft. "I instructed the butler to leave this room unlocked for tonight."

He shoved open the door, took her hand, and escorted her into an enormous room with a long table in its center, and cask upon cask upon cask lined up on shelves along three of the walls.

Releasing her hold on him, she pressed a hand to her tightening chest and raced to one of the oaken barrels. "Oh, my God. So many." She trailed her fingers over one after another, recognizing some of the names etched in the wood, knowing they were a vintage far superior and more expensive than anything she'd ever carry in her small tavern.

She swung around and faced him. "If you'd offered to show me this fine collection instead of your horses, I'd have come when you invited me."

After setting the lantern on a hook, he strode over to her, bracketed his hands on either side of her waist, and smiled. "I didn't want you to fall in love with me for my wine."

She wound her arms around his neck. "Never." Giving him an impish smile, she added, "But it certainly does increase your appeal."

Lifting her up, he set her on the table, wedged himself between her legs. "I've been wondering something all day. Why did you curtsy to my mother at the church?"

She skimmed her hands up into his hair, smiled softly. "Because I decided she was worthy of my curtsy, because she does love you, and because she gave me you."

"Ah, Gillie, you can so easily drop me to my knees."

Although it was a bit of a challenge, she managed to get her legs wrapped around him, held him tightly. "I'd rather have you standing. Take me here, take me now. Make me your wife."

"Princess, in my heart, I think I did that the first time I ever laid eyes on you. I have never felt for any woman what I have felt for you from the beginning."

He lowered his mouth and poured all that he was into the kiss, into her. He was the finest of wines, the richest of flavors, the most intoxicating of men. And he was hers.

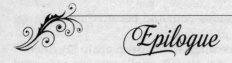

Epilogue

Thornley Castle
1872

*T*horne had wanted his first child to be born at his ancestral estate, and Gillie had accommodated his wish. She didn't have it within her to deny him anything he desired. So now she sat in a massive bed in an elaborately decorated room, in a fresh nightdress, her husband fully clothed, except for his jacket and boots, sitting beside her with his arm around her, her head tucked into the hollow of his shoulder as they both gazed down on the babe she had spent the better part of the night bringing into the world.

The child had arrived with the last song of the nightingale, the first trill of the lark.

"Trust you to not even be able to properly bring a child into the world," the dowager duchess said with a sniff, standing near the foot of the bed. "Your husband is a duke. Your first order of business is to give him an heir."

"I find no fault with my daughter, Mother," Thorne said patiently, and Gillie heard in his voice the love he already harbored for their child, her tiny hand wrapped snugly around the finger he had offered to her.

"With that shock of red hair, she will have to constantly wear a hat lest she be burdened with freckles," his mother said.

"She will have an assortment of hats," Gillie assured her. "And frocks and trousers."

"Trousers?" The duchess sounded truly horrified.

Gillie, wicked girl that she was, did so enjoy the moments when she appalled the duchess with her observations and comments. In the months since her marriage, the two of them had come to an under-standing—neither was going to change for the other and so they had accepted, not quite grudgingly, that harmony between them was better than rancor. "She will be chasing after her brothers or they will be chasing after her."

"You are not so young that you can delay overly long seeing to your duty."

"You need not worry, Duchess, as I am most eager to welcome my husband back into my bed."

"And you—" The duchess pointed at her son. "You are not to look elsewhere while your wife is indisposed. She is deserving of your loyalty."

He pressed a kiss to her temple. "She is deserving of everything."

"Still, I do wish you would give up that deplorable tavern."

In the end, Gillie had moved into Coventry House because she wanted their children to know of their ancestors, and she had fallen in love with the resi-dence. Each morning, she would ride in a coach to the tavern, but was actually spending fewer hours there as she was discovering being a duchess brought with it many duties she truly enjoyed, mostly charitable works and visiting with tenants, ensuring servants were happy. Often Thorne took Robin on outings.

They'd discussed making the lad part of their family, but Robin was convinced his mother would someday come for him.

"Gillie enjoys her tavern, Mother, and as long as she does, we will keep it."

"Actually I was thinking of opening another," she said.

"Dear Lord. Then you must hire a nanny."

She stroked her daughter's cheek. "I was raised without a nanny and I turned out all right."

"More than all right," the duchess admitted. "But that is not the point."

Gillie suspected they'd be arguing the point for a good while to come, but then she and the dowager duchess often argued, usually good-naturedly. "Would you like to hold your granddaughter?"

The duchess pulled back her shoulders. "I thought you would continue to torment me and never offer."

Ever so carefully, she took the babe. "Hello, precious child. I shall teach you what your mother will not: how to be a proper lady."

And Gillie's mum would teach her how to be a survivor. Thorne had sent word to her family shortly after their daughter made her entry into the world, and they were expecting everyone to arrive before nightfall to welcome the newest member into the family.

The duchess moved off to a rocking chair in the sitting area, and Gillie could hear her cooing to the babe.

"What shall we name her?" she asked Thorne.

"Victoria, Charlotte, Alexandria. Something fitting for a princess." Skimming his finger along her cheek, he turned her face toward his until their eyes met. "She will know the best of both worlds, yours and mine."

"Unfortunately, she will probably know the worst as well."

"With you as her mother, she will learn to be a dreamer and realist. But she will always know who her parents are and that she is loved."

"I have to confess, Thorne, that until I held her, it had never occurred to me that the woman who gave birth to me had loved me. How could she have given me away if she had? But now I know she could not have held me without loving me, at least a bit. I'll never know why she left me on Ettie Trewlove's doorstep, but I have to believe she did it because she truly believed it was best for me."

"I'm sorry she'll never know the remarkable woman you are. Or how very much I love you."

He lowered his mouth to hers, kissing her tenderly. And she could not help but think that it was a grand thing indeed to be loved by this duke.

Coming next

Finn's story

They call her Finn's Folly, an earl's daughter who captured his heart, only to betray him. But now their paths have crossed again. Can the sins of the past be forgiven in order for them to have another chance at love?

The Scoundrel in Her Bed

Coming February 2019!

IMP 0811